THE THREE GRACES

THE THREE GRACES

AMANDA CRAIG

abacus
books

ABACUS

First published in Great Britain in 2023 by Abacus

1 3 5 7 9 10 8 6 4 2

A CIP catalogue record for this book
is available from the British Library.

Hardback ISBN: 978-1-4087-1468-3
Trade paperback ISBN: 978-1-4087-1469-0

Typeset in Goudy by M Rules
Printed and bound in Great Britain by
Clays Ltd, Elcograf S.p.A.

Papers used by Abacus are from well-managed forests
and other responsible sources.

Abacus
An imprint of
Little, Brown Book Group
Carmelite House
50 Victoria Embankment
London EC4Y 0DZ

An Hachette UK Company
www.hachette.co.uk

www.littlebrown.co.uk

For Kate Saunders,
Kathy Lette and Jane Thynne

Author's Note

Some Italian sentences and words are not translated, either because they have become familiar to English readers, or because their meaning should be clear from the subsequent text.

The style of the word 'black' varies according to who is speaking and thinking.

Contents

Preface

In most novels it is taken for granted that people over fifty are as set in their ways as elderly apple trees, and as permanently shaped and scarred by the years they have weathered. The literary convention is that nothing major can happen to them except through subtraction. They may be struck by lightning or pruned by the hand of man; they may grow weak or hollow; their sparse fruit may become misshapen, spotted or sourly crabbed. They may endure these changes nobly or meanly. But they cannot, even under the best of conditions, put out new growth or burst into lush and unexpected bloom ... But the self, whatever its age, is subject to the usual laws of optics. However peripheral we may be to the lives of others, each of us is always a central point round which the entire world whirls in radiating perspective. And this world, Vinnie thinks, is not English literature. It is full of people over fifty who will be around and in fairly good shape for the next quarter-century: plenty of time for adventure and change, even for heroism and transformation.

Alison Lurie, *Foreign Affairs*

Tho' much is taken, much abides; and tho'
We are not now that strength which in old days
Moved earth and heaven, that which we are, we are;
One equal temper of heroic hearts,
Made weak by time and fate, but strong in will
To strive, to seek, to find, and not to yield.

ALFRED, LORD TENNYSON,
'Ulysses'

Prologue

A Blow of Air

The night Enzo Rossi shot a man, he had left his bedroom window open.

It was not at all usual for him to do this, for he was fearful of catching a *colpo di aria*: that is, a blow of air. But it was spring, and this month the nightingales had arrived in Italy.

At first, he could not think what had woken him. In the abandoned olive groves and wooded mountains, few sounds apart from the rush of the river in the valley ever disturbed human beings. He lay still in bed, listening and staring up at the blackened beams of his bedroom just visible against the whitewashed ceiling. What was wrong? The house he rented was over seven hundred years old, and often creaked to itself with changes of temperature, but being almost at the end of a rough, stony track it was rarely visited. Once, it had been part of a small, scattered hamlet filled with interconnected families; now it was the last house on the hillside still lived in by a local person, the others all being owned by foreigners. He was alone.

At this recollection, Enzo groaned. The loss of his wife had come as a relief because of their bitter quarrels; but the loss of his daughter was like a wound that kept breaking open and causing fresh pain. When she vanished with her mother, Fede had been eight years old, the age that was the most enchanting of all ... though he had believed the same when she was seven, six, five, and back to when she first emerged into the world, blinking like a little owl with a tuft of dark hair on her head. He had never known a love for any other person like that he felt, irrevocably, for his daughter: it had been like being hit in the heart by a bullet. Yet she was lost to him. His wife had taken their child away to live in her own country, knowing that this was the surest way to break his spirit.

Ever since, despite ringing his wife's mobile, her parents' home and writing text after text, Enzo had heard not one word. He didn't know whether they were dead or alive, though he suspected that they were somewhere in America and wanted nothing more to do with him. Had she met another man? Had he really been such a bad husband and father? Anguish and distrust poisoned his blood, making his stomach throb like a second heart. Every night he drank himself into oblivion to forget this pain, and every morning he woke cursing his life and his wife, and all foreigners.

It was not only Fede that had been taken from him. Living alone in the house his family had always rented, he was being burgled repeatedly. Despite closing shutters and bolts as well as locking doors, there was a continual assault by thieves – not Italians but 'gypsies', Albanians and what were called, indiscriminately, Africans. In the beginning, when it was just a few bits of food and things that even a poor man can afford to lose, he had shrugged his shoulders because he felt sorry for those less fortunate than himself. But then it had become much worse.

Everyone who lived in the countryside was being preyed upon by these migrants, or vagrants, who were little better than Mafiosi. There were gangs of foreign thugs that came up to people trying to run small hotels or restaurants, demanding money, and others who robbed homes, even those of people like himself who had little or nothing. It didn't matter whether the houses were lived in or not, they would force their way in and take whatever they could. His TV, his laptop and several knives had been lost in this way, and, worst of all, his peace. Caught between fear and anger, he slept with a gun under his bed.

Mostly, he did not sleep at all.

He listened to the song of the tiny bird nearby. Sometimes it flooded out in a long and lyrical melody, then tripped, clicked, whistled and switched. Its powerful voice moved from the piercingly sweet to the painfully percussive, a musical machine gun that drilled into his skull before easing his headache with its modulations. It was dementing in its unpredictability: yet as long as he heard it, he felt as if his sufferings had a voice.

The nightingale paused, and in the silence, there was that slight noise again. He listened intently. Could it be an animal? The hills were plagued by wild boar, snuffling and rootling and fouling the ground. They had thick, hairy hides that were as tough as armour, and tusks and hooves sharper than many blades. They were afraid of nothing, even poisonous snakes. Enzo and his friends hunted boar in season, and it was solely due to their efforts that there were not many more destroying what remained of the vineyards.

He should frighten it away. Neither he nor his elderly neighbours wanted intruders around. They were all retired, or in search of peace. That was the point of living out in the countryside.

The sound of stealthy motion came again. His heart began to thunder so loudly that for a few moments he could hear nothing more. Then his pulse steadied. Someone was trying to open the door downstairs. Enzo groped for the gun under his bed and sat up.

In the rage that replaced his fear, his thoughts became marvellously concentrated. A few weeks ago, his hunting dog Violetta had been poisoned, presumably to prevent her alerting him to intruders. He had found her in the yard below, foaming at the mouth after eating a piece of meat he hadn't given her, and although the vet did his best the poor bitch died in agony.

'What kind of person does that to an innocent animal? *Stronzi!* If they ever try it again, I swear I'll shoot them dead,' Enzo said to anyone who would listen. There were plenty who did, for Italy, with its long, elegant boot sticking tiptoe like a nervous person's foot into the ocean, was perilously close to North Africa and Eastern Europe, twin sources of trouble. What had once been an advantage to conquest and trade was now a hazard to prosperity and stability. Fifteen centuries ago, the Roman Empire had been destroyed by the plague that crossed the Mediterranean; now, it was people. The recent pandemic was proof of that. His country had always been the first victim of any bad thing, and was the first place that war, famine and disease arrived in Europe.

Those living in and around Santorno were far away from the sea-landings in the south, but they felt their effects. A population that was largely homogenous in appearance, religion, diet and customs became increasingly anxious, then angry, when they saw so many people who were very different from themselves in their streets. There were those who went out of their way to show compassion, but there were others who asked, with increasing insistence, why should these be our burden?

Italy had plenty of problems of its own, they could all agree on that. Successive corrupt and incompetent governments had not helped it, and neither did the extreme reluctance of many citizens to pay taxes to Rome. Italy as a nation had existed for barely a hundred years, one region still could not understand the accent of another and after centuries of wars and invasions its local populations were suspicious not just of neighbouring countries but of other towns just a few kilometres away. Nothing, however, was as alarming as the migrants, whose numbers, hundreds of thousands each year, were seen as a visible manifestation of all that was wrong in the world. Crime had soared: not the familiar Italian kinds such as the bribery of officials or using the black market, but robbery, drugs and assault. All these, Enzo was now certain, were the fault of foreigners.

Si, si, si, si, si, the nightingale agreed.

Enzo was a Tuscan, and if he looked down on the Milanese ('almost Germans') and the Romans ('practically Africans') and absolutely despised the Umbrians ('uncivilised'), the fact was that his people were in danger from the criminal elements now at large. He and certain citizens would meet on Sundays, in private, to practise shooting.

'The migrants will kill us in our beds, my friends, and you know what the worst part is?' Enzo's buddies agreed. 'If Italians lay one finger on them as intruders, *we* are the ones who end up in prison! Nobody else will help us. We must be prepared.'

Enzo thought of himself as a good person. He went once a year to Mass, and he did many kind things for his friends and neighbours, for there was nothing he could not turn his hand to. Having been married to an American, he spoke excellent

English and could drive, cook, do minor building work, clean swimming pools, prune vines and pick up people from Perugia airport. In the past, he had worked at every kind of job, from selling second-hand Fiat cars to searching for old houses in the countryside for a real estate agency. He had never betrayed a comrade, hurt a woman or hit a child. He was enterprising, adaptable, brave, kind and as honest as anyone could be in these difficult times, but at forty he felt his life was becoming a tangle of miseries, and the lack of sleep had driven him close to insanity.

Now, hearing the thief attempting to break in, his hands barely shook as he lifted the gun he kept under his bed and locked its barrel into place. It was not his hunting rifle or his shotgun, both were kept locked away in a secure place, but a pistol with a solid chestnut handle and a short steel stock, a design that had not altered for over a hundred years. He had inherited it from his father, who had been given it by his own father during the time when a weapon was all that stood between Tuscany and Fascism.

The feel of the wood and steel in Enzo's hands steadied his breathing. It was beautifully balanced, with a curved steel trigger that almost begged to be pulled. The nightingale, trilling urgently said, *Si, si, si, si, si, si!*

Stealthily, he opened the casement and leant out. There! A figure, hardly more than a shadow against shadows, was below. He could see the ominous puff of dark hair, and hear the intruder's harsh breathing. Enzo lifted the pistol to his windowsill and released the safety-catch. Then, just as the figure looked up, he fired.

1

The Dogs of Santorno

The three women who met for coffee in Via Nazionale every Saturday morning were united by age, exile, the love of dogs and their disinclination to discuss their infirmities.

'Enough of the organ grinding!' Marta declared if anyone complained of arthritic joints, failing eyesight, dizziness or debility. Between them, they had four breasts, five eyes and three hip replacements. These were the price of living long lives, as were one divorce, one widowhood and one husband with dementia. Age had not diminished them: quite the opposite. They had become more concentrated versions of themselves, just as a pot of soup does the longer it is simmered.

'One must not look back,' was Ruth's philosophy. 'To look back is to regret what can't be changed.'

'Dogs are happy because they live in the present, and so must we,' agreed Diana.

'*Evviva!*' said Marta. 'Let us live and love, for tomorrow we die.'

7

Framed by the window of the Bar Degli Artisti, the three friends sat at an outside table in the sunlight, watching the world pass by. It was a warm day, as warm as an English summer, and they were discussing their anxieties about a dog they had passed, locked in a hot car outside the city walls, which might soon be in difficulties. A waiter was keeping an eye on them in case they wished to add to their weekly order of coffee and pastries. Had they been in any other country, they would have been ignored: they were each, after all, over eighty. But in Italy a woman of any age will be noticed, especially if she has style, and a canine companion.

Diana Evenlode had a Labrador, as good-hearted as she was stupid. It was not her dog, she would explain, only her husband no longer went shooting and Diana couldn't bear to put a Lab down before its time. Besides, Bella was superior to a burglar alarm, and she would eat almost anything. Diana's tweeds were so thickly matted with dog hair that sometimes people wondered where one ended and the other began. Being the sort of person who always feels cold, even on a warm day, she wore two cashmere polo necks, pockmarked by moth holes, under a quilted olive gilet, and a toque of real leopard-skin. It was the kind of clothing that only small girls and elderly women could possibly carry off, and Diana, as a former Deb of the Year, always did. She balanced her galoshes on Bella, lying beneath the café table in just the right position to act as a foot warmer.

Marta Koning had a little white terrier, the focus of her life and the bane of everyone else's. Of course, she loved her daughter Lottie and her grandchildren Xan, Stella and Rosie; but she adored her dog, though he did not deserve it. Every yap, lick or glance from his eyes was taken as proof of his devotion. Marta always matched Otto's collars to her spectacles, and as both had white hair these were usually noticed.

'If you do not want to be knocked over by a passing car when you are over eighty, you must wear bright things,' Marta would say. She was a great one for proclamations of this sort, and her friends loved her despite it, partly because she was the eldest of the three and partly because she had the self-assurance that comes with being a renowned concert pianist.

Always chic in the German fashion, Marta was punctilious about having a manicure, a pedicure and the regular attentions of a hairdresser. Today, in honour of the imminent arrival of her grandson, she wore a violet jumper, a green jacket, a black fedora hat, an emerald silk foulard and bottle-green slacks. Her spectacles were bright green with tiny violet rhinestones, and on the lapel of her jacket she wore a large silver brooch shaped like a peacock feather. Diana, observing this, blinked. Marta gave a faint smile; she couldn't care less if a member of the English aristocracy disapproved of her appearance, because she disapproved of their existence.

As it happened, Marta and Diana were related by marriage. This was nothing remarkable, for the Evenlodes were connected to any number of people; a hundred and fifty years ago, they had made a habit of having very large families, most of whose members survived to have large numbers of children themselves. These tended to be healthy, unimaginative people who could be relied upon to lead troops into hopeless battles, farm unproductive land, and head failing banks in whatever corner of the world they happened to find themselves. Marta's late husband Edward was one of the few Evenlodes to have had the bad taste to exhibit artistic leanings, which perhaps accounted for his marriage to a pianist from Berlin.

Diana was of the generation of Britons who regarded all Germans as enemies, and she and her sister-in-law held each other at arm's length for a number of years before becoming neighbours in Italy. They had not, in truth, appreciated each other in the past. Diana was always polite, but every now and again she would unconsciously refer to Germans as 'Huns', at which point Marta, whose father had been interned by the Nazis as a Communist, would raise an eyebrow. Had they not been fellow foreigners in a provincial town, it was unlikely that they would have become friends. Yet late in life each discovered that despite their differences in nationality, lifestyle and politics they could both like and admire each other. What they had in common was not just happenstance, but a steely sense of morality and generosity that had evolved into a reluctant warmth.

'Marta is not exactly my cup of tea,' Diana confessed to Ruth, 'but despite her ego, she is a very decent sort'; whereas Marta said to Ruth, 'She has views that bring me out in humps, yet her heart is in the right place.'

To both, Ruth said, 'It's more important to see the good in people than to focus on small differences.'

Many find this to be the case, especially when living abroad. Propinquity forces intimacy, and theirs was even stronger because two years ago, the world had ground to a halt. Weddings and funerals, offices, aeroplanes, bookshops, festivals, concerts, businesses, cinemas, churches, schools, theatres, restaurants and cafés were all suddenly closed in the face of a deadly disease. Italy, grievously afflicted in the beginning, had been especially strict. Living near each other, Ruth, Marta and Diana shared the services of Enzo, whom they paid to collect medicines and food at a time when even country roads were blocked by soldiers checking documents. Defiantly, they still walked to each other's homes, played games of online Scrabble, shared books, recipes and become even more attached both to their dogs and to each other.

'I am really quite worried about the poor creature in the car,' Marta said to Diana.

'What breed is it?'

'A shih-tzu.'

'Such an unfortunate name.'

'But not its fault,' Ruth reminded them.

'The Italians don't understand dogs are *not* fashion accessories,' said Diana, with a covert glance at Marta's spectacles. She thought, and Marta knew she thought, them ridiculous.

'I know we are lucky to have our darlings,' said Ruth. 'Besides, dogs are like babies: if you love one, you love them all.'

Seated on Ruth's lap, as if on a throne, was Dash. She did not object to this; after all, what warm-blooded creature would enjoy putting their bottom on cold medieval cobbles? A black-and-white Cavalier King Charles Spaniel, Dash combined the best characteristics of both canine and feline, being an energetic companion and a strokable comforter. He was exquisitely beautiful, and when denied anything would assume an expression of such Christ-like suffering that most hearts melted. Consequently, his waistline left something to be desired. Ruth claimed that her dog had big bones.

'No, honey, not mine!' she said as his snub nose approached her plate. A pink tongue appeared, the pastry disappeared, and Ruth said, '*Bad* boy.'

Bella snorted and Otto gave a jealous growl from beneath the table. But it is one thing to have a dog as small and soft as a velvet purse, and another to have a dirty, snappish terrier or a large, arthritic Labrador. Dash lifted his face to Ruth's to exchange a smile of mutual adoration.

'You are putty under that dog's paw,' said Diana, and Ruth answered guiltily, 'I know.'

For the three friends, their dogs compensated, somewhat,

for not having been able to embrace the youth that consoled their own failing bodies. Now, however, their grandchildren were returning after a prolonged winter, like migrating birds on the warm winds of spring. Not only this: Ruth was hosting a wedding.

'So romantic!' said Marta, and Diana added, 'They are the most beautiful couple.'

Both women smiled at her, for Ruth was impossible not to like. She was the expatriate who had lived longest in Santorno, having retired there in the early 1990s.

'I want an adventure before dementia,' was how she put it, and as her home and friendliness were both delightful, she never lacked for company.

Marta had been a neighbour in Hampstead, teaching Ruth's youngest son Daniel at the Royal College of Music. Their relationship had been kept up via emails and long calls over decades of separation, so much so that Ruth often stayed with Marta when in London, and Marta and her daughter Lottie had holidayed with Ruth every summer in Italy. Many years later, Marta, too, sold up in London and followed her friend. Her flat was not in the Tuscan countryside, however, but just outside the city walls.

'I do not need half a hillside, like Ruth. I am a little old lady, and all I need is my piano.'

People always laughed when she said this, for anyone less like a little old lady than Marta would be hard to imagine. She was a musician first and a human being second. Having just one spare room to offer guests meant that she saw her daughter and grandchildren far less often than she would have liked, but she was happy in her new home.

'It suits me perfectly,' she told everyone, especially Lottie, who rang several times a week from England to check on her mother. 'Nothing is going to happen to me, except death, and that happens to everyone.'

Xan was coming to stay for a whole fortnight. Marta had not seen her grandson, except on Zoom, for two whole years; and a year in old age feels as long as it does in infancy. Her joy at this was slightly tempered by the knowledge that he would probably be spending almost all his time at Ruth's home rather than her own.

'How are the wedding preparations coming along?' she asked Ruth, who grimaced slightly.

Oliver Viner was marrying Tania Noble in Santorno, and ever since he announced this, his grandmother's tranquil existence had been thrown into turmoil.

'Are you *sure* you don't want to get married at your parents' place? It would be so much easier for your family and friends,' she suggested; but Olly answered with his robust laugh, 'Do you know, Granny, it takes almost as long to drive from London to Devon as it does to fly to Perugia? Besides, the weather is so much better in Italy, and people are longing to go abroad again.'

This was true. After two years of fear, loss and misery, everyone who could afford it was on the move and life was getting back to normal. To travel, to spend, to enjoy was an imperative filling the young like helium gas.

'Just how many people are you expecting?' Ruth asked.

'Oh, not many.'

'How many is that?'

'About ninety.'

Ruth could not help gasping a little.

'But darling Olly, where am I to put everyone? La Rosa can't sleep more than twenty, even with airbeds.'

'Don't worry, most will stay at an *agriturismo*. Or a hotel.'

'Won't that cost them a fortune?'

'They can afford it.'

Ruth had only the vaguest idea of what her grandson's friends did for a living, but they seemed to have surprising amounts of disposable income, despite being members of the generation that she kept being told were doomed thanks to Boomers like herself owning all the housing that they could not afford to buy. Ruth had her NHS pension, and a nest egg, but she did not *feel* rich. Her American medical degree had been paid for with blood and toil, and her British qualifications also. The Belsize Park boarding house that she bought with her husband on a council mortgage in no way resembled the white-stuccoed palace it had become; it was cheap in the 1960s because it was falling down, and stuffed with sitting tenants, paying a pittance for their rooms in an area generally considered to be unfashionable and sordid. Over the ensuing decades, Ruth reclaimed it floor by floor, and felt she had worked and saved hard for every bit of her luck in the London property market. Her children's children, however, seemed to think that she and her peers should atone for the ease with which they had become homeowners.

'But we lived on rice and beans! And you have things we never dreamt of owning at your age, like TV sets and fridge-freezers,' Ruth pointed out.

'Yes, only we have nowhere to put them in,' they answered.

Being kind-hearted, she did her best to make amends. After selling up in London, she had given each of her three sons a deposit in order for them to buy places of their own, and to her nine grandchildren there was a small, tax-free sum every year for which they were duly grateful. She knew that she, like all her peers, were members of the luckiest generation in history, and she tried not to take this for granted. However, hosting a wedding was a big ask. Olly had no idea of all the bother involved, but that was part of the optimism and enthusiasm that helped him bounce through life.

The first born in any family is often given more than their fair share of confidence, and Olly was not just the eldest of five siblings, but the first grandchild. Ruth adored him immoderately, perhaps because she had never had much time to enjoy her own sons. A beautiful little boy, he grew up to be clever, handsome and charming, and by the time he was thirty, he made a fortune. Josh and Anne Viner lived in a remote rural area where people lived in chilly old homes, drove mud-splashed old cars and distrusted all enterprises that required new clothes; their son's rebellion was to work in the City, live in a penthouse flat on the South Bank, and spend whatever he liked. He met his bride the correct modern way, through a dating app for graduates.

'She's a nice North London girl, half-American, and her mother is Jewish,' he told Ruth, who was relieved. After nine months together, he brought her out to Italy between lockdowns, and, when Ruth told him that he shouldn't let this one get away, proposed.

Since then, Ruth had been in a frenzy. She was used to hosting guests of her sons', and she loved entertaining friends, but a big wedding like this felt like climbing a mountain. Increasingly, the thought that she was approaching the end of her life intruded, though she made a conscious effort to ignore it. Both Marta and Diana were concerned at her growing fatigue. They all felt more frail than before and ignored it too, because there was nothing to be done but, as Diana put it, keep buggering on.

'At least ask for professional caterers,' Diana advised. 'In my day, the bride's family paid for *everything*.'

Ruth wondered about this, as well. Had the world really changed so much? Tania's father was a partner in Cain, Innocent, a major American law firm. Surely, he should be writing out a large cheque to cover his daughter's wedding? (*Did* people still write cheques?)

'You really should not be shouldering this burden, my dear,' Marta added, fanning herself. 'My goodness, what a hot day it is!'

'I expect it will rain next week,' Ruth said. She kept trying to feel cheerful about it all, for what could be more charming than two people who loved each other getting married from her home? Especially if one of them was her own grandchild.

As they sat there, one of the beggars that ventured into the town approached them, smiling. He put out a hand.

'Good morning, ladies. I am coming from Africa. Please, could you help me, please?'

Marta and Ruth shook their heads automatically and looked away, but Diana felt in her purse.

'There you go,' she said, putting a euro in his palm.

The man gave a formal little bow. 'I give you a blessing, lady.'

'Thank you,' said Diana, dismissing him.

As soon as the beggar wandered on, the waiter frowned at her.

'Contessa, you should not give those people your money. It only encourages them.'

'I thought I could do with a blessing,' Diana answered, and Ruth said, 'Darn, so could I. I'm having conniptions about this wedding.'

To Ruth's generation, a wedding was a gentle ceremony, perhaps with some protest songs and a little hash, but it soon became clear that something more elaborate was expected for Olly and Tania. There were going to be smart young people and a ceremony at Santorno's Town Hall, and, worse, the whole event was going to be watched online by millions of people she'd never met. The thought made her shudder.

Olly told her, 'It will look fantastic, don't worry. You see, Tania is a vlogger.'

'She works in forestry?'

'No,' Olly shouted with laughter. 'She's one of the top influencers in Britain.'

Ruth guessed this must mean something to do with social media. All kinds of jobs that hadn't existed ten years ago now seemed to dominate the economy. Olly himself worked in something called hedge funds, another mystery profession involving money rather than farming. But the days when people did straightforward professions like medicine, law, publishing or accountancy had vanished. Everything involved the Cloud, as if people were being swept up like mortals in Greek myth, and carried away by the gods. When she tried to ask what these jobs meant, he would smile at her kindly and say, 'You wouldn't understand, Granny.'

It made Ruth grimace, because she remembered uttering these exact same words to her parents, back in the day. When she confided in Marta, her friend said, 'They think they know everything. We've lived half a century more than they have, but heaven forbid we might actually have *learned* anything!'

What did reassure her somewhat was that she and Marta knew the bride's mother, Polly Noble, in the casual way that many families of privileged professional people often do, because they had both lived in the same area of the capital. North London, to those like the Viners, is not so much a location as a state of mind: gently pink, moderately affluent and sufficiently international to embrace Europe, Asia and Africa while regarding both the South and West of the capital with suspicion bordering on hostility.

Almost everyone whom Ruth knew was drawn from this environment, and she occasionally felt guilty about this, for there were many millions of people who, she was aware, did *not* share her tastes, politics, beliefs or her good luck. What they had instead was their families, like Diana, or their communities, like Giusi Guardi. Giusi (whom they all thought of as Juicy, but was actually called Giuseppina) was the only daughter of a *contadino* whose family had for generations past actually lived in Ruth's own house, as tenant farmers of the Felice estate and its grand Palazzo. She was a pretty, lively young woman who in addition to running the family's business would deliver meals to those who paid her. Juicy was a wonderful cook; Ruth needed her help.

'Are you *sure* you can manage?' Marta repeated.

'Sure,' Ruth said. 'Nowhere is lovelier in spring than Italy.'

'Except England,' said Diana, under her breath.

Will I ever see a bluebell or a foxglove again? she thought. Italy had wildflowers too, as abundant as those in a Renaissance painting, but it was only when you were deprived of your native flora that you realised just how unique it was. Diana missed her homeland with a silent ferocity that was indistinguishable from the broken sleep that also plagued her.

'I was wondering,' Ruth said, 'how dreamy it might be to have great big vases full of cow parsley for the wedding.'

'Don't you mean Queen Anne's Lace?' Diana asked.

Ruth and Marta exchanged glances. It was typical, they thought, that Diana should be snobbish *even about weeds*. But it was also so funny that they each began to laugh, until Ruth collected her manners and said, 'What is the difference?'

'Queen Anne's Lace has a darker centre. Said to be caused

by a single drop of royal blood,' Diana answered promptly. She did not understand what she'd said to amuse them, but foreigners were peculiar. 'Also, it has more backbone for floristry. Cow parsley flops.'

Ruth smiled at her, because Diana never flopped. She always sat up straight, and she never complained, though they knew she could well have done so. However bad their lives sometimes felt, Diana's always made them count their blessings: this, too, was another reason why they liked her.

Diana added, 'If you need an extra pair of hands, just say the word. It's the only thing besides touch-typing and ballroom dancing that I was taught to do.'

'I would love that,' Ruth answered, truthfully.

Walking back from the town towards the countryside, the three women stopped by a car. It was still parked in the sun, and as they passed, they heard a faint, high whimper.

Their own dogs stopped, and whined back. From inside the car, a small furry face popped up.

Marta asked, 'How long has that poor doggie been there?'

'Since this morning.'

'There's no opening for air.'

'Disgraceful. Italians have *no* feelings for animals.'

The three women bent over, peering into the car.

'No water either. Dogs die in hot cars.'

'What should we do?'

'The authorities won't take any notice,' Ruth said. 'I tried with that wretched dog of Enzo's that was always chained up and howling.'

'I told him off about that, too.'

'Shall I try Enzo? Maybe he knows who to call.'

'He's fetching my grandson from the airport,' Marta answered.

'And Tania,' said Ruth. 'Oh dear. What can we do?'

The little dog in the hot car whined again, and the three women exchanged glances.

'Cruelty to animals is as bad as cruelty to children,' Marta said decisively. 'We must do something to rescue him, even if it means breaking the law.'

'Strangely, I don't give a shit about that these days, do you?' Ruth said.

'No.'

'No.'

Diana clenched her left hand into a fist and slowly, painfully, scraped a circle in the glass of the driver's window with the stone on her ring before saying, casually, 'Anyone got a rock?'

2

A More Interesting Existence

At the back of the little plane, Xan was remembering that Ryanair forced you to choose between financial prudence and physical inconvenience. He was over six foot tall, which meant he was jammed into his seat like a human corkscrew. He turned his attention once again to Ian McEwan's *Nutshell*, and thought how much worse it might be to be fully aware, like Hamlet, but in the womb.

There was almost no pain that did not become more bearable with a good book. He didn't care whether it was about aliens in space or adultery in nineteenth-century Europe, literature was his drug of choice. Xan could read in almost any situation. He would read when feverish, broken-hearted, hungover, depressed, ecstatic and with pneumatic drills shaking the walls next door. The exception, annoyingly, was travel. Planes weren't quite as bad as cars, but the unique combination of nausea and claustrophobia brought on by flying meant that reading was almost impossible.

Ryanair was also part of a longer-term problem facing his family because without its cheap direct flights to Perugia, it was doubtful that his grandmother would have emigrated to Italy in her old age. It had made living abroad seem almost like commuting.

'Santorno is only a hop away,' Marta had reassured them. 'You can visit me for the weekend. Many flights are just thirty pounds, less than a train ticket to Exeter.'

'But Mutti, what if you get ill?' Xan's mother asked. 'What if you have a fall and nobody finds you?'

She replied, 'If I fall, I fall, Lottie. At least I will be in Italy, which is the closest I will ever be to paradise.'

Six years later, she seemed happy, and they all tried to be happy for her. Why shouldn't a person move to another country, just because they were elderly? She had sold her terraced Georgian house in Church Row for millions, bought herself a serviced flat in Hampstead to use when she felt like staying in London, and had another in Santorno. Xan admired his Oma's spirit, alternatively known as bloody-mindedness.

'To be honest, I have had enough of Britain, and I am upside-downing,' she had said. She took Brexit as an indication that a foreigner like herself was no longer welcome, even though she had lived in London for most of her life.

'You can come out and visit me whenever you please,' she informed them.

Xan's family tried, but their visits were like seeing Marta age in stop motion. At the end of her seventies, she had been upright, vigorous, formidable. Now, her spine was beginning to bend, her thick white hair had thinned and each time he visited she had shrunk another centimetre.

It is the unique and monstrous cruelty of being mortal that everything that makes life worth living gets stripped away from you, piece by piece, Xan thought, and that you know it. Would it be less horrible if you could remain just as you were at twenty, and then keel over? His vitality, surging daily, made him feel invincible, and fearless. At the same time, he was painfully conscious that he lived in a continual atmosphere of suspicion and distrust.

In the past three years he had been stopped nine times by the police, and strip-searched once, an experience that still made his blood boil when he thought about it. To have a total stranger undress you, without consent, feel your private parts and treat you like a criminal suspect for no reason other than skin colour came as a shock. It had never happened to him when he was living with his mother and grandmother in the privileged purlieus of liberal Hampstead; now that he was spending more time with his father's family in South London, it was a different matter.

'What did you expect?' his stepsister Zuhrah asked. 'Around here, you're like everyone else.'

It was not entirely true, because his father and stepmother were, respectively, a molecular physicist and a medical researcher at Imperial. The Okigbos and their two children lived in a comfortable semi-detached suburban home of the sort that filled his white relations with horror, but which they were extremely proud of. He loved both sides of his family, but his awakening to what it meant to be mixed-race was not without its shocks and discomforts.

Xan was the result of Lottie's one-night stand with a stranger at a party in her early twenties. She'd been too drunk to even find out his name, and it had taken some effort on Xan's part to trace Julius years later. He had never been bothered by this in a school environment where what mattered was whether you were smart, gifted or had rich parents. The one time another pupil said something racist to him, the boy had been hauled up before the Head, and given such a telling-off that he left soon after. Xan hadn't forgotten it, but mostly because everyone else was so upset on his behalf. To be accused of racism, in this world, was literally the worst thing anyone could imagine. It took his becoming a student at UCL for the truth to dawn.

'When I walk through my hall of residence people assume I must be there to sell drugs,' he told Lottie.

'So prove them wrong. Just be confident.'

But Xan felt neither white enough nor Black enough. He wasn't dark like his father, but his colouring, his hair, his features were not European. These days, there was an extra aggravation because white people assumed that, thanks to positive discrimination, he must be having an easier time. Yet even though he graduated with a First, he had found it no easier to get a job than anyone else. Xan was still renting the cramped and dirty ex-council flat off Kentish Town Road that he'd found as a student. He earned a living working as a tutor for kids who would never have to become a Deliveroo slave if they failed their exams. Far from graduation being the start of a bigger life, it felt as if his horizons were shrinking. There was little comfort in knowing that nearly every-one his age was stuck in a prolonged adolescence with no end in sight.

'We're Generation Rent,' his best friends said. 'We just have to suck it up until our grannies die.'

But Xan, who loved his Oma, didn't want to think of that. He knew that Marta, despite her air of insouciance, feared death. He'd nursed her a few years ago when she'd broken her leg. For all her toughness – a toughness both of the spirit and of one who had lived through the Fall of Berlin as a child – she feared losing her independence almost as much as she feared losing her life.

The plane tilted, and Xan clamped the earphones closer to his head, as if by keeping his eyes closed and his ears filled with Nina Simone, he could shut out reality.

I wish I knew how
It would feel to be free

Leaning out from his seat, he spotted Tania Noble ahead. Great, Xan thought. Bridezilla herself. Marta had told him he'd be sharing a lift from Perugia airport with a couple of other wedding guests who were arriving early. Of all the people to find himself in a taxi with, this was the person he would least have chosen.

Xan glared down the aisle. A few years ago, they had been part of the same friendship group, because Tania had gone out with his best friend, Bron, all through the sixth form. When she dumped him, Bron underwent a sort of nervous breakdown. Xan couldn't forgive her for that, and he'd been in two minds about whether or not to come out to the wedding.

'Why should I spend time with a bunch of spoilt white people during my precious holiday?'

'Look at it this way, you can kill two birds with one stone,' his stepfather told him. 'You can see the old monster and have a livelier holiday than usual because there'll be plenty of people your own age to hang out with.'

'It'll probably suck.'

Yet a big house party could be fun, and he'd never been to a wedding before. There might even be some pretty girls . . .

The little plane landed bumpily, opened its doors, and the warm air of Umbria rushed in. Xan was struck by the way the colours of the Perugia airport were exactly those of the red and green robed angels on either side of Piero della Francesca's *Madonna del Parto*. Was it a coincidence? Or was it because the colours of the national flag were also red and green? In Italy, you never knew.

The queue for Britons took a while to move forward, but Xan held his shiny new maroon passport with a grim pride and stayed with the Italians. It was thanks to his German grandmother that he could get this and work in the EU if he wished. He'd brought his old British one too, just in case, though its soft-faced sixteen-year-old version of himself now looked barely recognisable, and would soon need renewing. He felt obscurely relieved that his passport was scarcely glanced at by immigration officials.

'*Salve*, Xan,' said Enzo. He was waiting for them on the other side of Customs, and Xan grinned.

He liked Enzo, whom he'd met on previous trips to see his grandmother, though he had severe reservations about his politics. Marta called him her Figaro, which was a bit patronising except that he looked exactly the way Xan had always imagined the Barber of Seville to look – smart, energetic and just a touch roguish, as full of opinions as he was of gossip. It was his proud boast that he never drank water ('I despise water'), beginning each day with a small glass of red wine, which continued until he went to bed; such was his liveliness that some wondered whether he might not be permanently tipsy. His handsome face beamed with geniality, and he had the quality of *sprezzatura* that makes certain Italian men irresistible company. From driving Marta about to smoothing the bureaucratic nightmare of her move, from regularly picking up her family when they flew over to see her to light gardening and shopping, Enzo had quickly become a trusted friend. He rendered small services in return for cash (which he never asked for), and his dignity was almost as great as that of the elderly people he helped.

Enzo looked past him and beamed.

'You know the *bellissima* Tania – and Polly?'

'Yes,' Xan said shortly. He watched with bemusement as Enzo seized Tania's hand and brought it towards his lips, then turned with no less enthusiasm to that of her middle-aged mother. She, at least, did not recoil, but blushed and smiled.

'Hello, Enzo! Xan, good to see you again,' said Polly. 'You're coming to the wedding, aren't you?'

Xan agreed that he was, adding pointedly, 'Olly's family are friends of ours in Devon.'

'So you are a friend on both sides, then,' Polly responded with a warm smile. 'Look, Tania, even the countryside is bridal! All those blossoming acacia trees!'

He expected Tania would queen it in the front, but after all her suitcases had been piled into the boot of Enzo's car, she climbed into the back with him. Polly began a conversation with Enzo, who did his usual terrifying thing of driving very fast along the motorway. Xan stared out of the window, letting Tania's chatter wash over him.

' . . . and you know, like, I know that even if I *do* get a spot on my wedding day, I can put some ice and salicylic acid on it, though if I avoid anything that's, like, chocolate or dairy I shouldn't get one . . . '

How could anybody be this idiotic? Tania was supposed to be bright, but to hear her you would never guess it. Of course, Xan had the opposite problem. His way of showing a girl he was interested in her was to engage in a vigorous debate, until she either ran away or agreed to sleep with him. It wasn't a notably successful technique, as he was discovering in the sexual desert of his twenties, because girls his age were already thinking about finding some older guy to buy a flat with.

Tania was not the sort of girl Xan liked, but she was exquisitely beautiful. He could tell that Enzo, too, was aware of this; presumably, it was partly her presence that was distracting him to drive so badly.

'Cretino! Look where you're going!' he shouted at another car.

They passed Lake Trasimeno, its waters eternally that shade between green and blue that is somehow more lovely than either. Xan remembered it from previous visits, but it was always a shock to find it at the other end of the motorway tunnel between Umbria and Tuscany.

'Where are you staying?' Tania asked him. Her voice was soft and gentle, but he found her annoying, as just another airheaded girl.

'With my grandmother.'

'Oh. In the countryside?'

'No. Santorno.'

'La Rosa is so pretty. I'm really looking forward to seeing it in the spring.'

'Everywhere here is,' said Xan. 'All sunshine and wisteria.'

'I *love* that film,' said Tania, clasping her hands together. '*Enchanted April*, I mean.'

'The book is better,' Xan said automatically.

Tuscany always seemed to send people into an idiotic swoon, he thought, which they ascribed to Renaissance paintings and Edwardian literature, but really it was because of films in which everyone was English and middle class and, naturally, white.

Xan was tired, and irritated. Half of him wanted to join Extinction Rebellion, and the other half longed to get on the biggest, dirtiest aeroplane he could and see the world before it burnt to a cinder.

He envied his parents' generation, but he envied his grandmother's even more. They had lived through a time when it was perfectly clear what evil was, and it made choices much simpler.

One of Xan's earliest memories was hearing Marta sing 'The Red Flag'.

> *The people's flag is deepest red,*
> *It shrouded oft our martyred dead*
> *And ere their limbs grew stiff and cold,*
> *Their hearts' blood dyed its every fold.*

Music, rather than politics, was her true religion, however. She believed in God, or rather, she believed in Bach; 'Which is the same thing, in my view,' she would say. But Xan's world, the world of the twenty-first century, was not so clear-cut.

In the past, he'd despised his stepfather for writing for newspapers across the political spectrum (Quentin was proud of being able to manage, as he put it, 'the bile and smuggery of the Left and the guile and thuggery of the Right') because surely an adult should *know* that one was morally superior to the other.

Yet now that Xan himself was in the world of work, he discovered that although plenty of left-wing people talked the talk, they did not walk the walk. Friends of his stepfather, who wrote for publications that he wouldn't touch with a pair of tongs, turned out to be the ones who actually tried to help him get a job, whereas the nice, liberal ones couldn't be bothered to lift a finger, saying they were against nepotism. It was excruciating, because Xan wanted everyone to be on the right side. The only problem being, he was not entirely sure what this was.

Enzo, on the other hand, was very sure.

'The thing is, Polly, if I don't take some of my money under the table, the taxes leave me with nothing. In effect, we are paying almost eighty per cent in Italy. Without the black market, nobody can survive.'

'But Enzo, it's very important to pay taxes. What do you think pays for your hospitals, or this road we're driving along?'

Enzo snorted. 'Not the Umbrians! Those people ...'

And he was off on one of his other rants about how base and coarse the Umbrians were, unlike the glorious Tuscans. Xan caught Tania's eye, and stifled a laugh. He had seen fire-breaks up in the mountains between Tuscany and Umbria that stopped to the millimetre on the regional border, as if fires had any respect for man-made lines ... It wasn't only a regional matter, between Umbria and Tuscany, and it was called *campanilismo*. If you weren't born within the sound of your parish church bells, you were a foreigner in a community. Marta gave a piano recital every May in Santorno, to a local and an international audience, but the fliers for it had been rejected in neighbouring towns, even nearby ones like Cortona and Città di Castello, because only the Santornese would turn out for it.

'Sometimes it seems as though Garibaldi never existed,' she told him.

Enzo did seem to be particularly tense today, however. He had big bags under his eyes, and his hands were shaking. As they turned off the motorway to begin the ascent into Santorno, he spotted a couple of women in tight miniskirts and low-cut tops waiting in a lay-by.

'*Porca miseria!*' he exclaimed. 'Whores. Disgraceful!'

'How do you know?' Xan said at once, bristling, because the women were Black.

'How would you like *puttane* on *your* doorstep? People like that import crime and drugs.'

Xan considered retorting that every migration brought people both good and bad – the Italians had, after all, brought the Mafia with them to America – but he was both wary and weary.

'Excuse me,' Enzo said. He must have seen Xan's glowering expression in the rear-view mirror, because he took both hands off the steering wheel to make a placatory gesture. The car, travelling at 90 kilometres an hour, swerved, and was righted again by his knees. 'I know you are not like these people, Xan. You British do not understand how it is for us.'

'Yes,' said Xan, 'only my father came from Nigeria and my grandmother from Germany.'

All of a sudden, Enzo's courtly good humour evaporated, and he took both hands off the wheel again to beep his horn furiously.

'*Stronzo! Cretino! Mi rompi gli coglioni!*'

Everyone else in the car gasped, and Tania let out a small scream. The lorry gave an answering blast.

'Do not be afraid, *signore*,' said Enzo, while the car shot past a lorry, veering perilously close to the concrete barrier on the motorway. 'I am an expert driver, and can guide the car perfectly.'

'Please – please don't,' said Polly faintly.

Xan said, 'What's wrong with that crazy driver?'

'That is my enemy, Stefano, he is a *mascalzone*.'

'A cream cheese?'

'That's mascarpone. He means a scoundrel,' said Tania. Xan remembered that she had read French and Italian at Bristol.

She probably knew what the rude words Enzo had just shouted meant, too.

Polly said sharply, 'Enzo, we would appreciate it if you keep both hands on the wheel.'

'But of course,' said Enzo. 'In any case, Stefano has lost the race. *Cretino!*'

He blasted his horn again, and behind them, the lorry responded with an even louder blast.

Xan shook his head. Batshit. Mind you, he thought, his grandmother and her two friends were all mad, too. He didn't like to admit it, but sometimes he was just a little bit afraid of what they might do.

3

A *Living Doll*

Tania jerked awake. She had been half-dozing for the duration of the flight, something that was easily done because she'd been up before dawn to get to Stansted in time.

Actually, she'd have left it until a little bit later because the drive from her mother's home in Camden Town to the airport only took fifty-five minutes max before dawn. But Polly insisted on leaving at 4.30 because they had luggage to check in, which included Tania's wedding dress. Or rather, two wedding dresses because she had one full-length gown for the official service, and another one for the party after, each loaned by world-famous designers. It was fashionable to hire rather than buy wedding dresses, which was cool and #eco-friendly, but Tania and her followers knew that she hadn't yet decided whether these were actually the ones. Plus shoes, make-up and pretty much everything else was free too, because this was the thing, everyone wanted the publicity.

Tania sighed, and closed her eyes for a moment. People

thought vlogging must be easy, but being an influencer meant never being off duty. Even getting on to the plane she had to have a selfie taken with two followers, though from their acrylic nails you'd never know it. Tania didn't want anyone to feel bad about themselves, but the truth was almost everyone did feel just that because they hadn't lucked out in the genetic lottery.

'I'd give anything to look like you,' one had gasped.

'Thank you,' she answered. If only you knew, she thought.

Ever since Tania turned eleven, life had been horrible. Stick-thin and tall for her age, she could not go into Topshop without being pounced on by a scout from a modelling agency. As far as she and other girls could see, she wasn't even pretty. She had almost no breasts, big shoulders and her front teeth were too close together, but somehow the camera made her look good. Eventually, aged fourteen, she was signed, and discovered why models look bored. It was all about doing nothing except during the instant when she had to jump in the air, or bend backwards, or stare into the camera lens while photographers issued a stream of instructions. She soon learned the language of fashion, how to walk, wear make-up and talk about little but clothes and appearances. She was to show no emotion, unless instructed, but that was fine because as far as everyone else could see, Tania was a living doll.

There was another person inside this shell. That Tania had written poetry, loved nature and was as sensitive as she was obsessive. Her first boyfriend Bron had known some of that side of her. He was gentle, clever, and very serious: anyone who knew him knew he was going to be a surgeon. They'd grown up together, and were best friends before going out. When she'd ended it, because they were going to different universities, he'd been horrible to her.

34

'You're so completely frivolous,' he'd said. 'I don't know what I ever saw in you.'

Beauty distorts perceptions, like a powerful lens that can turn the rays of the sun to flame, but it is not the fault of the lens. Tania was hurt, but never showed it. After all, she had not asked to be a genetic freak. She longed to be loved for herself, but her personality meant this was not going to come easily, if at all. What she presented was a perfect blank.

'Queen Tania,' her brother Robbie called her, and it was true, there was something regal in her manner. She would smile gently, but rarely laughed or cried or hardly ever looked people in the eye, except to stare them down. Boys who pursued her without success claimed she was boring, and those who succeeded said she was frigid.

'Everybody is shy,' her mother told her. 'Everybody has to make an effort to put other people first.'

'I *am* trying, Mum.'

'Yes, you are, darling. So please, put down your mobile.'

She was addicted to her iPhone – who wasn't? – but had really not intended for any of this social media stuff to happen. When she'd dressed up in a pink unicorn costume and videoed herself scampering about her street during the first lockdown, it had been out of pure boredom. But somehow, those few seconds, uploaded onto her TikTok account, had gleaned her over a hundred thousand likes. When she posted more, about her home-made beauty tips, these grew to a million. Suddenly, she was an influencer.

Being an influencer had pretty much taken over her life these days. She didn't do one of those silly little dances or songs that other social media aspirants posted, she refused to wear a bikini and she didn't talk about her traumas. Yet everything that 'Tanyaa' ate, wore, recommended or put on her body was followed with avidity. She was thought charming, funny, pure, gracious and delightful simply because of the way she looked. Over three million followers now seemed fascinated by her life. As a result, she had an agent, a media platform, and more free stuff than she knew what to do with. What, really, was the difference from modelling other than keeping most of the money she earned?

Nothing about her life was real until it was posted on social media. The strangest thing was that it left her very little time in which to actually live.

Polly was horrified.

'Don't you understand that you're invading your own privacy? Don't you understand that it only seems to be free because what you're selling is yourself?'

But Tania couldn't see this. What was the point of living and dying in privacy, aka obscurity, if you could have #fame? Deep down, she knew that she was afraid of real life – life without filters, as she thought of it – but who was to say that this was the only way to live? If Tania, or Tanyaa, could float above all that was gross and cruel and vile, why shouldn't she? People kept going on about how important it was to #BeKind but really, in her experience, who *was*? And who cared if people thought they knew stuff about her (they didn't, actually, she'd lied about her birthday and quite a few other things, duh!)? She wasn't doing anything tacky: quite the opposite. Everything in her life was #lovely, #pretty, #fresh and #kind. Especially now she was marrying Olly.

Tanyaa's wedding was a big event in the world of Insta, TikTok and YouTube vloggers, and it felt quite important to Tania herself. Everyone had been so fed up with baking sourdough, so it was no surprise that total strangers were in love with the romance of it all. They logged on every day just to find out what new images and videos were posted, and she was able to keep her followers updated three times a day. Getting engaged had doubled, trebled, quadrupled her viewings, especially because she never showed Olly's face, just a few details like the back of his head, or his hands, keeping him slightly mysterious. She was the main event, and he was her chief follower. Her wedding would look both aspirational and affordable, romantic and fresh, and if *this* was frivolous, then how come she was also raising a million for charity, too?

Olly thought it was a laugh.

'You really don't mind?'

'What's not to like? We'll have a great party, people will give us loads of cool stuff and then we'll be married.'

Everybody wanted to hang out with her, but Tanyaa kept her distance. When, occasionally, she encountered some of the girls who had made her miserable at school, she felt especially #blessed. She didn't say anything, she just looked at them.

Her little brother called it 'The Medusa Stare'. He was the only person who laughed at her now.

'But you are coming to Italy for my wedding, aren't you?'

'I wouldn't dare miss it,' Robbie replied.

Where Olly was genial and easy-going, Tania took life very seriously, far too much so for someone who was not doing what Polly considered to be a serious job. Still, as Tania herself pointed out, 'You're a human rights lawyer. Nothing I can do will impress you.'

Tania was defiant about marrying so young. Polly herself had only been a couple of years older when she'd married Tania's dad (now divorced), and Tania's much-married American grandmother Betty had been just twenty-one, the first-time round. Pretty women married early if they were smart, that was what Betty always said; but Polly asked, 'Don't you think it might be wise to wait a little longer?'

'Olly is over thirty, Mum, and I'm investing in my youth,' Tania said. She was afraid of losing what she thought of as her only asset, and had once told her mother, in a moment of rare frankness, 'I know nobody would find me interesting if I didn't look as I do.'

'Of course they would. But ultimately, having an inner life is what counts.'

'I have loads of hobbies,' Tania replied.

Olly radiated confidence of the kind that is bestowed on the Oxbridge graduate – the belief that you were one of God's elect simply because a couple of weary academics in a medieval college had decided to pick you, rather than another applicant with the same examination grades. But from this, all else flowed.

'I love making money,' he once told Tania. 'People think there's something shameful about capitalism, but they wouldn't prefer to live in North Korea, would they? I believe in living my best life.'

'So do I,' said Tania.

The landscape beneath the little plane tilted alarmingly as it flew over Lake Trasimeno, in preparation for landing. Out of these waters, Botticelli had painted his Venus emerging on a scallop shell, completely naked but for her knee-length hair. Tania looked so like his image that some men went completely mad. Even this morning, with her face hidden behind dark glasses and her hair inside a baseball cap, male fellow passengers were giving her the imploring gazes of a dog confronted by a sausage. One stopped by her seat and said, 'Ciao, bella. English? American?'

Tania ignored him steadfastly, though when he moved on,

she muttered to her mother, 'What is it about guys that they think they can hit on me all the time?'

Polly said, 'It's not the worst problem to have.'

'You think? Right now, I'm so stressed that it feels as if I have snakes under my scalp.'

Tania scratched under her cap with a finger, then stopped by an effort of will.

'Well, I don't think you'd have millions of followers if you weren't pretty. I do hope you will go back to a real job.'

'I can't, Mum.'

Tania had tried, she really had, and had got a job with an online marketing company on graduation, but the catcalls, propositions, texts and so on were disgusting, even before she got into an office. Being able to stay at home and earn a living just by talking to her mobile phone was, by comparison, a breeze.

Nobody could work out where her looks had come from, though her dad was still handsome, and her grandmother Betty had been a famous beauty. She was exquisitely proportioned, her eyes, her lips, her nose, her hips like a mathematical calibration of female perfection, but what made her exceptional was her hair. It sprang from her scalp in torrents that were sometimes copper, sometimes blonde and sometimes almost pure gold. People would ask whether it was real, touch it, or even (surreptitiously) attempt to snip a few strands when she sat in front of them. It fell to the top of her thighs, and it had never been cut.

'If you have such an amazing colour, it seems a shame not to have as much of it as possible,' Polly had told her, and Tania's grandmother Betty agreed. What they never noticed was how sad she looked beneath it.

Polly believed that she didn't care what her children did, as long as they were happy. It did not occur to her that happiness, unlike examination results, is without definitions or boundaries, and that her fond maternal wish put a terrible burden on them. Robbie had escaped to university in California, but apart from her three years in Bristol, Tania had seldom left home. Were anyone to ask her about her future, she would have said, 'I suppose you live for a few years, and then you die.'

Olly seemed boundlessly optimistic, however. Nevertheless, he was tired of swiping on dating apps. He wanted a life with a wife, and Tania ticked all the boxes. The powerful engine of his certainties chugged ahead through the waves, and she was able to bob along gracefully in his slipstream. Polly thought him quite marvellous, and to her he said the one thing that she wanted to hear above all.

'I want to spend the rest of my life keeping Tania safe.'

Tania wanted to be kept safe, too. There was something in her past that she had told nobody, and she intended to keep it that way.

4

Qui Siamo in Italia

It was Ruth who first discovered the charms of Santorno back in the 1990s, and she was, in her way, the leading light in the expat community. She would never have put it like that, of course. Her manners were absolutely perfect in their blend of West Coast warmth and East Coast discretion. She was continually in awe of how old everything in Italy was, but also enjoyed good plumbing and the internet. Perhaps the most American thing about her was her scrupulous attention to money; but then Ruth, as the daughter of two Hollywood scriptwriters forced to flee McCarthyism, had grown up counting her blessings.

If there is such a thing as a generic Tuscan hill town, Santorno was it. Smaller than Cortona or Montepulciano, but larger than Volterra or San Gimignano, it had the harmonious mixture of Etruscan, medieval, Renaissance and Baroque architecture that are typical of the region. Its buildings were painted in shades of ochre, cream, pistachio or pink, its towers were castellated, and it seemed to have changed very little in over two thousand years. Remote both from the ugliness of developers and the conveniences of modernity, its main street became a heaving open-air restaurant in summer, but returned to the quiet dignity of a provincial centre in winter. Its real business took place in the new town below, but tourists and expatriates rarely ventured past its railway station; and, when they did so, mentally held their noses.

Ruth found her new home by chance, as a newly divorced woman on a walking holiday. Staying at a *pensione*, she wandered out of town and found herself walking along a winding mountain road punctuated by tall cypress trees. Another diversion brought her to the ruins of a large stone farmhouse surrounded by half-overgrown olive groves, vineyards and soft new grass. There were many such abandoned dwellings then, and Ruth had no hesitation in exploring. On the ground floor there were empty stables and chicken coops. An external flight of stairs from the courtyard led to three large rooms without any corridor. Its floors, pitted with dirt and bird droppings, were tiled with terracotta, its roughly plastered walls bulged with damp and its windows rattled with her footsteps.

'A death trap,' said Ruth's eldest son, when he came to inspect it.

'I know, Tom. Only, *look!*'

Every window framed a landscape worthy of a Renaissance painting. The hills, half furred by wild woods, swelled into enamelled skies, and the grass below was strewn with primroses, periwinkles, violets, iris, poppies, cornflowers and orchids.

'You can imagine Botticelli nymphs and gods dancing here,' Ruth said dreamily.

Other countries beside Italy have warm weather, sublime

42

skies, mountainous peaks, verdant woods and olive groves yet do not, somehow, suggest they belong to a world elsewhere. At any rate, Ruth experienced a surge of passion that changed the course of her life. All love affairs are an imaginative experience, and this is as true of property as it is of people.

If I lived here, she thought, I could be happy again.

Although her career as a consultant psychotherapist had brought many satisfactions, Ruth was conscious of sorrows. She could not save those who did not wish to be saved. The failure of her marriage ('I asked Sam to choose between me and the bottle, and he chose the bottle' was how she put it) had been even more bitter, though the relationship had given her three sons whom she adored. For over twenty years, she had toiled for the mentally unwell in the windowless rooms of the Royal Free Hospital, talking to people in the grip of clinical depression or worse and pouring out every drop of wisdom and medical learning she could dredge up. In middle age, she felt she had earned the right to do something for herself.

'Why the heck *not?*' she said, aloud.

The semi-ruin was for sale. She put in the asking price demanded by the estate agent (this being, naturally, double what was asked of locals, but to a Londoner astoundingly cheap) and set about making the place habitable.

In the beginning, Ruth and her sons had come out to La Rosa for holidays that were anything but relaxing. ('An adventure!') There was no running water, so to fill a cistern they had to use a hand pump from a well that sometimes ran dry in summer. They experienced Christmases in a single room warmed by fires whose heat vanished instantly up the chimney. The house was home to rats and bats, scorpions and lizards. The hectares that came with the house were half submerged in a tangle of thorns, and vipers trickled down the crumbling walls like water. It was desperately uncomfortable and ravishingly beautiful, two qualities that, in Italy, often go together.

But eventually, with toil and money and hope and imagination, ruin retreated; the biggest pestilence became hunters. Ruth's *Divieto Di Caccia* signs were punctured by lead shot. It was the only time she ever hated Italians.

'This is my property, and a refuge for nature!' she would shout at men who paid not the slightest notice. They knew that Italian law gave them the right to trespass wherever they wished from September until March, provided they carried a gun. Only when Enzo came out, with his own rifle, and informed his compatriots (usually those arrogant Milanese, he informed Ruth) that he alone had permission to shoot there was she left in peace. He stuck to wild boar and rabbits, so both were satisfied with this arrangement. They became friends.

Having made her house habitable, Ruth could not help interfering in the land that was now hers. Before long she had collected a succession of old horses, stray cats and flocks of wild birds. Locals called her 'Root', being unable to pronounce the 'h' in her name, and she liked that, too.

'I have returned to my roots,' she told family and friends, and although they smiled at the way she called Italy 'Idaly', as if it were a home to the subconscious, everyone was happy for her.

Thirty years on, the Belsize Park house was long sold and the Tuscan property market had crashed. However, La Rosa now had big couches with loose linen covers, a swimming pool, and a courtyard where family, friends and guests could meet up for meals under the pergola. Her most intelligent purchase was a dozen good-quality single mattresses that could be zipped together in pairs to make super-king beds, ensuring that couples could enjoy nights as well as days. It was not, by any stretch, a villa of the kind featured in glossy magazines, being what is politely described as rustic, but it was the perfect place in which to swim on a hot summer day, make fires in a cold winter night or just drink a glass of good wine.

She did a few rentals of her converted outhouses on Airbnb, while keeping open house for family and friends. Her only regret was that with every year fewer of the latter remained alive. All the more reason, she told herself, to encourage the next generation to have children in turn.

At present, she was fussing over bedding. Before Olly's announcement, she had, in fact, been looking forward to a smaller and more private celebration of her own eight-ieth birthday, repeatedly postponed in the pandemic. Characteristically, she had switched her plans into the wedding instead. The spring belonged to the young, after all, and in any case, she was not sure that living into her eighties should be celebrated. Certainly her best friend in Italy, Beatrix, had recently decided to exercise her rights as a Dutchwoman to quit early. Remembering this, Ruth winced. Beatrix, too, was having a party in ten days' time, but it was to say goodbye to family and friends before being euthanised.

Still, Ruth reminded herself, I am doing just fine. Her parents had died so long ago that she could barely remem-ber them, until she looked in the mirror and saw their faces looking back at her, healthier and happier than they had ever been.

How astonished they would have been, those brave old Jews, to see where she had wound up! Having fled rural Poland for New York, they had been almost fanatically urban. Ruth had been their shining star, the cleverest child who had gone

45

all the way – first to Harvard, then to London. Yet after all that, the apple never falls far from the tree, and her love of farming would have been familiar to her ancestors in their shtetls. That this had come about not in America but in Italy would have puzzled her relations even more. Luckily, she had help with her projects.

In the olive grove below the garden, a deafening mechanical whine rose up. Raff was wielding the strimmer, his rope-coloured hair and pleasant face concealed by an orange helmet that made him look like one of the Playmobil knights that her grandchildren once liked to play with.

The twenty hectares of abandoned olive groves and vineyards that came with La Rosa had always been a headache. In the beginning, there had been dying branches raised to the sky out of waves of brambles, like the hands of drowning people. It had taken a decade before she felt able to tackle these, and the sheer volume of work was beyond one middle-aged psychotherapist who had led a sedentary life.

'Everyone likes the idea of owning land until they realise that even the smallest bit of it involves incessant labour,' was how Diana put it. 'That's why the world is abandoning farming. And then you get ramblers, thinking that the countryside is a kind of Disney park.'

However, La Rosa's unpolluted, unimproved hectares turned out to be a cornucopia. Ruth, who had begun her project barely able to tell the difference between a blackbird and a crow, discovered a place that was vivid with life and interest. Hoopoes, green woodpeckers, eagles and small owls were just a few of its marvels; often, on walks, she would come across a tortoise the size of a dinner plate walking gingerly up a slope, or a porcupine shaking its armoury of long, bi-coloured quills. What was more remarkable still was that all this wildlife could coexist with farming, provided it was the kind that did not involve tractors, pesticides and fertilisers.

'Just think, if we could only work with nature instead of against her, we could save the planet,' she said. This became her creed, and although she did not go quite so far as to embroider cushions with commandments to tread lightly on the earth, it was sometimes a close thing.

What helped her were the WWOOFers, or volunteers from World Wide Organisation of Organic Farms. In return for nothing more than their board and lodging, idealistic people were prepared to toil away for up to six hours a day just to promote the good life. Every year, up to half a dozen heroes, some with degrees in agriculture but most without, came to help her prune and pick olives, tend vines, look after her animals and encourage native flora and fauna.

'But what if one of them turns out to be, I don't know, a nutter?' asked a son. 'You're all on your own out here. Italy isn't safe. All kinds of people wander about.'

'I hope I could spot those, after thirty years working in mental health,' she said. 'Besides, I've learned to be very selective about the kind of workers I accept.'

It was no use, for instance, taking anyone who just wanted to have a free holiday in Italy, as had been the case with one man who had spent a fortnight eating his head off and smoking dope. Nor was it necessarily a good thing to get someone who had a Ph.D. in biodynamics, who would criticise how she ran things. What she needed were people who were both hardworking and nice to be around: the kind of people who, when they arrived at La Rosa said, not 'What's the Wi-Fi passcode?' but 'This is paradise'.

'But my dear, what if they turn out to be fearful bores?'

Diana asked. 'If you employ someone, you can at least sack them.'

'Not always,' Marta said. 'Employers owe employees minimum terms and consideration.'

'I've learned that if I ever think that they *might* work out, it's always awful,' Ruth told her friends. 'It's the ones whose faces are full of joy when they arrive who are the best, even if they've never held a spade or cooked a meal in their life.'

Marta nodded. 'Yes. You need to look for enthusiasm and a good heart, just as you do in a husband.'

'I think manners and common sense might matter more,' said Diana.

So far, Ruth had hosted scores of WWOOFers from all over the world, ranging from a Spanish university student who was recovering from an abortion to an Australian who criticised her organic credentials and left after three days. In between these were dozens of successes, ranging from German engineers who wanted a working holiday to teenagers who appeared, like so many of the young, to have missed out on learning any practical skills because their parents were so frantically busy that it was surprising that they had ever found any time to procreate.

'You know,' Ruth said to her friends at the kaffeeklatsch. 'I think I may have done more to help people with my little farm than I ever did with drugs and therapy.'

'If you were in a fairy tale by the Brothers Grimm, I'm not sure whether you would be a good witch or a bad one.'

'Oh, a good one, Marta, I hope,' Ruth answered. As a Jungian, she took fairy tales seriously as a source of profound psychological wisdom.

'Nobody ever sees themselves as wicked, do they?' Diana mused. 'Everyone thinks they are heroic, even when they're not.'

'True; but I do at least *try* to do good. I think that if you have good intentions, it must count, don't you?'

Yet Ruth had hesitated over Raff, even after the usual Skype interview. He was English, and the English did not always perform manual labour well, being prone to their weird class anxiety. Furthermore, his CV was patchy – not that this was unusual in the new generation, with the gig economy and a tendency to quit careers even in their mid-twenties. She had the feeling that he was not quite what he appeared to be: after all, an intelligent, reliable young graduate with no visible tattoos does not spend seven years doing nothing more than drift.

He'd arrived the previous autumn, pitching up in his battered blue VW camper van, a stocky young man, pale and clearly troubled, though he had loved La Rosa instantly. He slept in the studio cottage, and at first, she could hear him shouting out at night from bad dreams. Yet he buckled down right away, and there was nothing he could not turn his hand to, from digging ditches to mending things to raising chickens. Unflagging, level-headed, competent and good-natured, Raff shared her passion for ecology. He watered the plants in her vegetable patch with the stinking but nutritious brew of rotting comfrey that they responded to, and forked over the compost bin without being asked. He was the one who had climbed up the big oak tree in winter, and cut off the annoying branch that was blotting out the view, while leaving the brown owls nesting there undisturbed. He had dug a big new water reserve above the house, and diverted the rainwater running down the hill to use in time of drought, greatly to the delight of frogs, toads and wild birds. He was especially good with animals, whether it was picking a grass seed out of Dash's paw, or splinting the leg of a sparrow.

The garden had never looked better, because he'd sowed hundreds of white flowers in preparation for the wedding celebrations. They were now coming into bloom, and Ruth recognised snapdragons, cosmos and night-scented stock, as well as fancier perennials like delphiniums and regale lilies.

'Where did you learn to do this?' she asked, impressed.

Raff shrugged and said, 'YouTube.'

Most people couldn't wait to pour out their hearts to her, but Raff was so reserved that it was hard to know whether he had one. Ruth gathered he was the son of a single mother and had grown up in the country. She was not good enough at English accents to know whether he was middle class or not, but he had nice manners, competence, humour and initiative: in short, he was good company as long as you didn't probe. Was he an ex-convict? A former psychiatric patient? An introvert? It was hard to tell, and what mattered more was that she liked him.

'But then, you like everyone,' Marta reminded her. 'Even myself, and I am hard to like.'

'No you aren't,' Ruth said. 'You're wrapped up in music, which is wonderful but a little different to most of us.'

Such was Ruth's retirement. She had plenty of good friends around Santorno, but Marta's emigration from London had been especially gratifying. Enjoying excellent health, Ruth did all she could, from having her teeth whitened to getting her eyebrows tattooed, to ignore the minor tragedies of Anno Domini. She had never been pretty, but her strong face surrounded by its mass of curly, dyed hair, was so often creased in sympathy or laughter as to make her agelessly agreeable. With so much good fortune she could have no complaints: that was, until Olly's wedding came along.

In the past few months, Ruth had found her tranquillity under siege. April, which she usually looked forward to ardently, had been made miserable by all the planning headaches, and by May she was having so many heart palpitations that she wondered whether she needed medication. What was it that made her so uneasy about the wedding? Was it just the understanding that her privacy and peace were going to be disturbed by up to a hundred strangers, and viewed by millions online? She'd looked at Tania's vlog, briefly, and found it mildly amusing, but then the marketing departments of all kinds of manufacturers and designers began sending unwanted freebies to her address, and she was constantly having to field enormous cardboard boxes delivered to her home by exasperated drivers for DPD who churned up her road and found their satnavs did not work in rural Italy.

'It's a bit like the Sorcerer's Apprentice,' she confided to Diana and Marta. 'Great at first, but you can't turn it off.'

Every day, deliveries of chocolates, wedding favours, cosmetics or shoes arrived. Ruth was shocked and angered by the sheer wastefulness of it all. She recoiled from excess, and her grandson's life, and future wife, seemed mired in materialism. Was it that which made her restive and anxious?

'How can anyone begin to need all this *stuff*?' she demanded.

'I've had to get my cleaner to come in every other day to sort out the deliveries because the other residents in my building complained,' Olly told her apologetically. 'Sorry, Granny. It'll stop soon.'

'But what will she *do* with it? I can't keep it.'

'Don't worry. She sells it on eBay, you know. Or gives it to charity.'

'Just as long as it's all gone when you leave, I don't care. The storeroom is bulging, and Raff can't find his tools.'

'I doubt he could find his own arse,' said Olly. 'Honestly, Granny, having hippies hanging around is not a good idea.'

'Raff isn't a hippy,' Ruth said. 'Believe me. I was at Woodstock, and I know.'

To calm herself, Ruth pottered over to say hello to the horse. He gave her palm a whiskery nuzzle, then crunched the Polo she gave him. Immediately, Ruth felt cheered. How delightful everything was! Lavender shrubs shimmered with black-and-white swallowtail butterflies and the moths that looked like tiny humming-birds. The iris were open, their violet and blue heraldry pushing out of both flowerbeds and the tops of stone walls. All around, the terraced groves pulsed with bright pink rock roses, yellow marigolds and scarlet poppies. The sharp vernal odour of newly cut grass and clover was better than any one of the perfumes couriered to Olly's bride. Such a strange way to make a living! But Tania was going to be staying with her for a full ten days before the actual wedding, and she was looking forward to getting to know her better. She struck Ruth as a little lost, but Olly was clearly smitten and that was what mattered.

Behind her, she could hear Juicy chatting to Raff. Ruth wondered whether they were sleeping together, because she could see he was attractive, and a girl as pretty as the Guardi daughter could hardly want for admirers. They must be about the same age, not that she could judge any more. Everyone under fifty merged into youth, and everyone young was beautiful. (Actually, everyone was beautiful, if you saw them with love, but that was another matter.)

'Lunch!' she called, and rang the school bell she kept to summon guests.

Ruth was pooped today because she had been woken at dawn by Dash. At two, he was in the full glory of his own youth, barking at something outside, and she had been forced to let him out. When he bounced back in again, he was panting, reeking, and looking disgustingly smug. Wild cat, she guessed, or a fox.

'Stop that!' Ruth said. 'It has as much right to be here as you do.'

Dash leapt back on to her bed and fell instantly asleep.

Perhaps one of the reasons why I love dogs, she thought, is that I can tell them off without hurting their feelings. Ruth had a favourite heroine: Trollope's Madame Max, the supremely intelligent, witty and well-behaved widow who has been described as the greatest gentleman in Victorian literature. Madame Max always knew exactly what the right thing was to do or say in a tricky situation, and although it was no longer possible to write letters to people pointing out the errors of their ways, Ruth liked to think that she, too, could guide her family and friends on to better paths. What was the point of living a long life if those you cared about couldn't benefit from it? She was proud that she'd encouraged Olly to propose to Tania when they'd come to stay the previous September.

'You don't have for ever, just because you're a guy, Olly dear,' she said. 'A girl like Tania won't stick around if you don't marry her.'

'But what if she won't have me?'

Ruth looked at her grandson in astonishment.

'Why wouldn't she? You've got everything a girl could want! Why not ask her, right here? It's the most romantic place in the world.'

Olly had done as she suggested – he'd even bought Tania's engagement ring from the jeweller in Santorno, an act which won him a devoted local following – and Tania accepted him. Of course she had. Ruth was absolutely delighted. Maybe, she thought, I'll even see some great-grandchildren before I kick the bucket. She'd once believed that grandchildren would be enough, but increasingly, she hankered after the next generation, too. Was it knowing that the rest of her parents' families had died in the Holocaust? Or was it just that she herself loved life as a gift? Once again, she thought of her friend Beatrix. How I shall miss her, she thought.

She sat down to eat her sandwich under the pergola. At least, she thought she had left it there, but there was just an empty plate. That wicked Dash! Unless she had forgotten actually to make the sandwich, and only thought she had done so? Ruth paused. Any lapse in memory at her age caused a little lurch of fear.

But no: here were the crumbs on the plate. Could Raff have thought her lunch was intended for him?

'Oh well, it's not as if I can't make another,' she muttered. Dash, the rascal, was nowhere to be seen. Like all spaniels, he chose to hang around the prettiest woman in the neighbourhood.

Ruth could hear Juicy singing as she worked.

So darlin, darlin,
Tan by me
O, O, O tan by me . . .

Ruth smiled. Juicy was one of those people she enjoyed having around, much as she did a bowl of shapely fruit. She herself had abandoned the struggle to keep her figure long ago. 'Giving up pasta doesn't make your life last longer, it just makes it feel as if it does,' was her motto, but Juicy somehow managed to have both a healthy appetite and the slender, long-legged figure that made Italian women the envy of the world.

54

Her table was, perhaps, another reason why her eldest grandson had chosen to have his wedding at La Rosa. However, Ruth's cuisine was the kind that derives from recipe books and a good income; Juicy's was a matter of tradition, humility and inspiration. A grating of nutmeg in her tiramisu, a drop of basil oil in her ravioli, the addition of fennel leaves to a saddle of wild boar – all these and many more made her a local legend.

'How did you learn to cook like this?' Ruth had asked. 'Did you go on a course?'

'No!' Juicy replied. 'My mother taught me, and her mother before her.'

Ruth loved Italians, who struck her as similar to Jews in their warmth, their veneration of the family (especially mothers), their enterprise, their inventiveness and their humorous melancholy. That this feeling was not shared by everybody was always a source of some surprise to her.

'*Qui siamo in Italia*' (here, we are in Italy) was a phrase uttered by many expatriates to account for various irritants. It was true that there were a regrettable number of these. Even under their best prime minister in decades, the natural genius of this people had perpetual employment in outwitting the bureaucracy and corruption that tried to beggar and depress them. However, nobody is perfect and Ruth never regretted her decision to retire to Tuscany.

'I am a rootless cosmopolitan, and Italy is the best country in the world for that,' she said.

Expats had an agreeable life, even if most around Santorno did not have swimming pools. There were cheap trattorias, and every turn in the road gave on to glorious views.

'As long as I have air conditioning for the summers, I do not care,' Marta said.

Marta, too, was a *Dottoressa*, having taught at the Royal College of Music, and with a couple of Deutsche Grammophon recordings to her name she was considered a distinguished addition to local life. It should not have irked Ruth and Marta that Diana was clearly regarded as their social superior, but it did.

'It is ridiculous to have waiters run out with a cushion for one at a café, but frightfully nice,' Diana would say complacently at almost every kaffeeklatsch.

Ruth and Marta, whose bottoms and backs also ached for support, did their best not to feel somewhat put out by this mark of privilege. Each felt that they had earned their titles, whereas what, really, had Diana *done* apart from marry a viscount's son? Marta was especially annoyed, and her husband had actually been Perry Evenlode's younger brother.

'Toffs are philistines who think of nothing but farming and shooting things.'

In every friendship between more than two people, there is often one who binds the rest together out of irritation. Diana Evenlode was that glue. Though fond of her, Ruth and Marta enjoyed complaining to each other about her.

'Everyone is a monster when you get to know them, but some people are more monstrous than others,' was how Ruth put it. Diana was a practising Christian who had, they felt, a distinct lack of humility; she made it plain that she believed the English were superior to all other nations, and she was an unabashed snob. ('Though,' Marta would add, 'everyone is snobbish about *something*. In my own case, Wagner.') Diana refused to meet the oligarch who now owned Palazzo Felice, because she had known the old contessa and did not wish to see what barbarities he had inflicted on an historic building.

'I am sure it will all be gold toilet seats. That man is a crook,' she said indignantly. 'How the British Government, let alone a Conservative one, could have seen fit to give him an OBE is a scandal.'

'Yes, but he has done so much for the Arts,' said Marta.

'Do you think that washes his crimes away?'

'We don't know for sure that he killed people, do we?' Ruth asked.

'Believe me,' Diana said, 'at the heart of every great fortune is a great crime.'

As the wife of an Evenlode, Ruth thought, she ought to know. Just how complicit Diana herself had been in the actions of her husband in Zimbabwe was never entirely clear. She was (in her prickly way) kind and honourable: though Ruth always offered to pay for their coffees and slightly stale *cornetti* at the kaffeeklatsch, Diana was adamant about not taking charity. She accepted Ruth's frequent invitations to lunch at La Rosa, while saying that she didn't believe in returning 'cutlet for cutlet', but never arrived empty-handed even if her own gifts were always home-made, like blackberry jam or useless bits of needlework that Ruth never knew what to do with. Living on the cusp between poverty and parsimony, Diana was a great one for re-gifting presents they themselves had given her, beautifully re-wrapped in brown paper and satin ribbon. (Some years, the same box of Floris soaps shuttled between the three of them for months, on the tacit understanding that it was never opened.)

However, Ruth never forgot that when she had been ill and alone with the virus, Diana had been the one person to visit her every day, even though this was strictly forbidden during the first pandemic. She walked up the hillside to bring a thermos of hot soup and fresh-baked bread.

'I don't want you to come down with it too,' Ruth wheezed.

'Pish!' Diana said. 'People go on about it being a tragedy to die in your eighties, when it's just natural.'

Diana also refused to put Perry into a Home when his dementia accelerated. Because of this, Ruth and Marta felt a little guilty criticising her. They blamed Perry for her faults, as women do when someone they like has married someone who is disliked.

'Whenever I see her, I am reminded why it is so much better to be husband-free,' Ruth said, and Marta, though she loved and missed her own dear Edward every day, could not but agree.

It was not that all men were as appalling as Lord Evenlode. They had both, in the course of their long lives, encountered some who were not remotely like him. Yet good men are as rare as hens' teeth, 'whereas among women', Marta observed, 'virtues are unremarkable, because everyone takes us for granted'.

Being old friends for the better part of fifty years, Ruth and Marta were extremely frank in conversation; Diana was more reticent. She never discussed sex, but then she would say something unexpected like, 'Have you read that book on the gut? *Life-changing*, especially if one puts Debrett's Peerage under one's feet when on the loo.'

Money was something else. Both Ruth and Marta were retired on excellent pensions and the proceeds of their homes in North London, but Diana told them that she and her husband now lived on the State Pension. The former owners of Fol Castle in Cornwall, they had passed it on to their son to avoid inheritance tax.

'How can a family that owns a castle *possibly* be poor?' Ruth asked.

'I believe that it belongs to his family, in trust.'

'You'd think they could at least have sold a spare cottage or something.'

'But it is often all or nothing, with an estate. I do not understand it myself, but she probably has no say in it anyway. She's proud, but not mean. She can't really afford the money she gives to those beggars, but she still gives it.'

'I wonder why her relations do not take better care of her and Perry,' Ruth said.

Marta grimaced. 'The only things the Evenlodes care about, besides land, are dogs and horses.'

Diana's sorrow was not for herself, but for her son.

'If only Andrew would find himself some nice gel,' she would say. 'He did marry once, back in the 1990s, but it didn't work out.'

Privately, Ruth thought that Andrew Evenlode, now pushing sixty, was one of those Englishmen who was so far into the closet that he was practically in Narnia. On the rare occasions when she met him, he had always struck her as one of the most charming of men, and the loneliest.

But not everyone is as lucky as I am, she reminded herself. Her failed marriage had been more than compensated for by her wonderful three sons and nine grandchildren, especially Olly.

Although no grandparent should have a favourite, Olly had been the apple of Ruth's eye from the moment he was born. He would spend the greatest amount of time with her, especially during the summer holidays, because with four other children and two careers, his parents were frantically busy.

'I've always felt this to be my real home,' Olly told her. He shared her passion for Tuscany.

'Devon is lovely, but just too damp,' he said.

In her heart, Ruth hoped to pass on La Rosa to him. None

of her other grandchildren seemed interested in organic farming, and Olly, despite his stellar career, was keen, at least on the wine-making side. He even spoke fluent Italian. How this could come about when both he and Tania lived in London was hard to imagine, but she still hoped.

With a slight effort, she snapped the damp pillowcases, one of them nibbled by mice, free of creases. The next chore was to put up the rainbow-striped double hammock in the grove. There were two olive trees that were just right, being on the edge of a terrace with a particularly good view. She imagined Olly and Tania lying in each other's arms, gazing up at the stars . . . She had enjoyed a few romantic evenings in it herself, not so long ago.

Ruth paused. Juicy had appeared in the grove with something in her hand.

'Root, look.'

She held it up. It was an old cotton T-shirt, and part of it was stained with dark reddish-brown splotches that at first Ruth mistook for rust. She looked more closely, and realised why Juicy was upset.

'Blood?'

'*Si*. It looks fresh.'

'Do you think somebody had an accident?'

'I don' know. Look, there's . . . a hole.'

The hole was a small dark ring, like a charred halo, and it was surrounded by a thick encrustation. More blood. Turning the shirt over, Ruth saw a second hole in the sleeve.

Ruth and Juicy exchanged glances, the same thought in both their minds. Such holes could only have been made by a bullet.

'I think you'd better show me where you found this.'

5

La Docciola

Every day, Diana Evenlode wondered how much longer she could continue without putting a pillow over her husband's face, and suffocating him while he slept.

A few hundred metres down the lane from Ruth, La Docciola was perched beneath a sheer rock face. In summer, this provided some welcome shade. In winter, sheets of water cascaded off a ledge into the narrow gully behind the cottage, and in particularly bad weather this would seep through the stone wall and flood the kitchen floor.

Naturally, the Evenlodes had been unaware of this detail when they bought it one spring. The poetry of living in a Tuscan cottage carried them away. But life must, as Diana observed some time later, be lived in prose, and when they discovered that in winter their new home was even colder and damper than the one they'd left behind in Cornwall, another bitter quarrel erupted.

'You know what *la docciola* means? The awful shower. The clue was in the name, you fool,' Perry Evenlode told her.

'"Into each life a little rain must fall."'

'This isn't a little rain, it's a bloody torrent You'll have to get it fixed.'

'With what? You know we don't have a bean.'

'You'll have to sell some of your jewellery, then.'

'You know perfectly well that I have only one piece of any value left, and that will be my pension when you're gone.'

'You grasping old bitch.'

'If I'd given you everything, I'd be left destitute. We both would.'

When they moved to Italy, Perry had been still hale, handsome, energetic and astonishing at eighty-five. A couple of inches shorter than the man she had met at seventeen – the ex-officer, colonial farmer and a future MP whose mistresses, it was said, would if laid end to end stretch from Britain to the furthest reaches of the Empire (how tired Diana became of that old joke) – but still *there*. He'd been able to walk down the Via Nazionale on her arm, wearing the same corduroy trousers and tweed jacket he had worn sixty years ago, his eyes unclouded and his hair abundant. He had never had a day's illness and didn't understand why anyone was ever unwell.

'Women's problems!' he would say of her own hip replacement, hysterectomy and mastectomy. 'Brace up, stop whining.'

It wasn't until she found him trying to boil one of his wellington boots that she realised how advanced his dementia had become. Diana now used a hoist to get him up in the morning, and apart from the day-care centre run by nuns, did everything for him.

Diana was a strong countrywoman, used to jobs like mucking out as well as looking after a house with over fifty rooms and a garden with five hundred leathery rhododendrons. Even in her eighties, she remained tougher than many people half her age. Yet courage has its limits, and Diana was fast approaching hers.

Every morning except Sunday, she would manoeuvre her husband into the car before folding his wheelchair and lifting it into the boot of her white Fiat 500 to deposit him at the convent next to Santorno's *ospedale*, where people who were frail or living with dementia received exceptionally good, cheap day care from nuns. The whole thing had to be repeated again in reverse in the afternoon. It was exhausting, yet somehow, thanks to her hip and knee replacements, she was able to do it as long as Perry didn't lash out. She fed him in the early evening, changed him and put him to bed in the sitting-room divan, wearing a nappy under his pyjamas and lying on top of an incontinence sheet. He went out like a light, until 4 a.m., when the real battles began. Her bedroom was directly overhead, with only a row of terracotta tiles between them, and though she locked him in, he would get up and start wandering about, shouting confusedly. She then had to stagger down the narrow, slippery flight of steps to try to get him to go back to bed. It was like dealing with a baby, only one that was the same height as herself, and, even now, much stronger.

'Goodbye, darling,' Diana told him, as always, depositing her husband in the day-care centre.

'I never loved you, you withered cunt.'

'I'll see you later,' she said calmly. She never knew how much the nuns, who were mostly from Romania, understood.

'I don't need you, I need mercy!'

It was hell, utter hell, and what was worse was that everybody, including perfect strangers, knew about it.

A couple of years ago, she had made the mistake of letting Ben Gorgle into her home. The American journalist looked like a toad in a black beret, but could turn on the charm in buckets. Diana never read his kind of stuff, but she knew he had been quite successful as the inventor of something called the 'dirty axle' school of writing. (This seemed to involve trailer parks, whatever they were.) She invited him to tea, and he told her some amusing stories about famous people, having, like all journalists, a collection of deliciously scandalous stories that he would pay as his entry into almost any social circle worth knowing. Even though Diana hardly recognised most of the celebrity names, she was flattered by his assumption that she did.

'I think I met him when Perry was in the House,' she said vaguely.

In among many extravagant lies, Gorgle claimed that he was writing a piece for a glossy magazine about the upper classes living in post-Brexit Europe.

'So I would very much like,' he said, gazing at her through his round tortoiseshell spectacles, 'to interview you, Viscountess, as the leading light of the expatriate community.'

Flattered, Diana agreed. She never read any magazines apart from *Country Life* (on whose cover, long ago, she had featured), *The Oldie* and the *Spectator*, but she had a vague idea that it might amuse her remaining social circle. The American magazine mentioned was famous and glamorous. What could be the harm in it?

Even when Gorgle asked permission to photograph the pictures of herself and Perry, which had been taken on the family farm, she suspected nothing. She had spoken graciously, if nostalgically, about their time in 1960s Rhodesia, and of how Italy reminded her of Southern Africa. Of course, Perry had voted against Independence, and yes, his own father had held strong views about the native people, but times were different then. Only when various surviving friends and relations contacted her after publication did she realise the error of her decision.

The article was picked up by the British press, the Italian press and much shared on the internet. Complete strangers unleashed their anger and contempt on her as a racist, and Italians took immense umbrage at being in any way compared to Africans. The most humiliating thing was that her mention of reduced circumstances sounded self-pitying.

'Mummy, why didn't you *tell* us you needed money?' asked her daughter Etta. She was the only one who had married respectably (baronet, stockbroker).

'Darling, we're fine. Really. You know how journalists make things up.'

Perry had not been a great catch when she met him. He was the second son, the one who had to oversee the family tobacco farm in Rhodesia. His elder brother was the heir. Enormously jolly and profligate, Toby would roar around in his sports car with another model beside him hoping to become the next viscountess. His only aim in life was to have fun, while Perry slaved away in Rhodesia.

'Hideous,' he would say, looking up at Fol's granite machicolations. 'High Victorian pretentious bollocks.'

Diana silently agreed with this. Her own family home, Lode, was the Great Good Place, and all the time she was growing up she had been conscious that every bite she ate belonged to her brother.

'*Why?*' she demanded.

'Primogeniture.'

'But I'm older than he is!'

'Our brothers, sons, fathers, brothers are the ones who count,' her mother told her. 'Not us.'

She was the granddaughter of an earl with a title far more ancient and a line more respectable than that of the Evenlodes. Diana had been born just before the war began, and Diana's brother just after that, so they lived at Lode. They never knew their father, a pilot killed in the Battle of Britain, or the uncle who was the heir before him.

What neither Perry nor Diana foresaw was that both their brothers would die without issue. Toby Evenlode dropped dead of a heart attack aged forty-five ('He ate one Quality Street chocolate too many,' she told her own children), and Diana's brother perished in a crash in Kenya. The Fol estate then came to Perry, and Lode to her son Andrew. So it was Lode, an exquisite Jacobean house in the Cotswolds, that had to be sold. It broke Diana's heart, for although she loved her family, she loved her home as much.

Marta, she knew, could not understand this.

'When I was a child, Berlin was largely destroyed,' she said. 'What matters is people.'

'Buildings long outlast people,' Diana answered.

Diana tried her very best with Fol, brashing the rhododendron and under-planting it with bulbs and ferns. It had got Fol into the Yellow Book's National Garden Scheme, but she had never loved it.

'Fifty-two rooms, and the only one warm enough to live in is the kitchen,' Diana would sigh.

'Why do you want to be warm?' Perry retorted. 'If you want to be warm, put on another jumper and chop some wood.'

Diana had a tiny inheritance of her own, and with it she bought La Docciola for just thirty thousand euros, ten years earlier, when her friend Claudia Felice knew she was dying.

'I want you to have something of mine, and the Russian who will buy the palazzo has no interest in it,' Claudia said.

'What about selling it to a local family?'

'My dear Diana, nobody wants to live on these hills anymore.'

It was hardly surprising, really. There were just two rooms on each floor, though a bathroom had been built out of breeze blocks at the back of the hillside. The cooker ran on gas cylinders, although the cottage had running water and electricity; the thick external cables dated from the 1970s. There was no central heating, just a wood-burner in the living room, whose metal chimney ascended through Diana's bedroom, raising the temperature from arctic to merely freezing. She tried to grow English cottage-garden flowers, as well as vegetables, in a climate that veered between -3 and +32 degrees. She washed herself and Perry, shivering, with a sponge and bowl of hot water boiled on the stove.

It was a lifestyle that would have been familiar to most countrywomen in previous centuries, and it was still preferable to the ugly blight of modern housing creeping across the plains below, with its wincing bright lights, sprawling supermarkets and factory outlets.

'How *can* they want to live in those horrible modern places?' Ruth would lament; but Marta, always more shrewd, said, 'Because they are warm and easy to clean.'

The labours it took to make La Docciola at all habitable only Diana knew. She turned her hand to everything from repointing (just like icing a cake) to basic plumbing. She was immensely practical, but then she had no training to be anything else. Her grandfather taught her to ride, she had received a smattering of French lessons from a Belgian refugee in the village, and her mother had taught her to read, write and be a good plain cook. Otherwise, she was expected to find a husband as soon as possible. Her brother was sent to Harrow, but there was no money for her schooling.

'Education is wasted on girls,' her grandfather said, and as the books in his library had not been added to since the turn of the century, there was nothing to tell her any different.

All Diana owned were her looks, and it was because of these that she was given a Season in London, though her grandfather had to sell a picture to pay for it. She was just seventeen, her profile regular and her figure elegant. As was usual in that time, her dresses were sewn by her mother, and she made them look far more expensive than they were, even though these gowns were like gym kit: designed to last only a few weeks but to withstand vigorous exercise (and pawing) in the evening.

By day, she had been enrolled in a typing course so that – should she fail – she would have something by which to earn her living. But she had not failed.

Perry was twelve years older than herself, an ex-Army officer, handsome, blond and glamorous. He was in search of an heiress, but found himself drawn instead to a young woman who seemed to stand out from the rest 'like a swan among geese', as he put it. They met three times before he proposed.

Fear, pain, anxiety, uncertainty, jealousy or passion were what small boys of their class were sent away to school to suppress from the age of seven, and the same (but without an education) was expected of girls. Diana fell in love.

'He won't be faithful,' her mother warned, 'but you will find him perfectly all right if you become friends.'

Had Diana understood that the year of her coming out was the one small space of potential freedom she had between leaving her grandfather's house and entering her husband's, would she have picked up her ball gown, like Cinderella, and run? The idea never crossed her mind. Not many years after her wedding, she saw pictures of young women dancing in miniskirts and the kind of make-up that six years earlier would have been unthinkable even on stage. She was one of the last proper debutantes in her generation, she had executed the right steps in the prescribed dance, she had been Deb of the Year and she was married before she turned eighteen.

'Just think, Mummy, you could have been part of the Swinging Sixties,' her daughters liked to tease, but Diana had only the haziest idea about sex, except that it was necessary in order to have babies. It was a bit of a shock, at first, but she adored Perry and quickly became pregnant with the first of three daughters.

In the first years of marriage, they were out in Rhodesia, surrounded by tobacco, miles from civilisation. She had her husband, she had her children, she had a lovely colonial house – surely that was enough? Within the little circle of her family, she could be natural, and she closed her eyes to the rest. She was very busy running her domestic life, and in her few hours of leisure returned to reading authors who knew her world and its walled garden of privilege and privation, ignorance and worldliness. Even though the legs of her bed stood in saucers of water to prevent ants from crawling up them, and the acacia trees rang with the doleful cries of the go-away bird, she did not miss the company of other people. She was used to being alone, and preferred not to go into Bulawayo or the country club that Perry frequented.

There had, in fact, been one friend before Ruth and Marta, and it was because of Claudia Felice that Diana came to Santorno first, in 1957. They met while the Evenlodes were on honeymoon on the Amalfi Coast and found themselves in the same hotel as the widowed contessa. She was too old to be of interest to Perry, but the two women struck up a friendship. Wandering together through the streets of Capri, meeting for drinks and swims in tiny rocky coves where every pebble shone like a semi-precious jewel, they all got on so well that the relationship was continued after the Evenlodes returned to Africa.

Claudia was a great and serious reader. Gently, she suggested the Englishwoman try to expand her horizons beyond a mixture of Jane Austen, Trollope and Georgette Heyer, reassuring her that she could try Tolstoy, Flaubert, Proust, Dante and George Eliot without fear of being thought too brainy. ('In any case, who is to know?') She was from a noted Ligurian family, as intellectual as it was noble, and she had lost both her husband and her only child in the war. They kept up a correspondence, and visited each other after the Evenlodes returned to England. When Diana finally gave birth to the longed-for heir, she asked Claudia to be his godmother.

'But she's a Left-footer!' Perry objected.

'Catholicism isn't catching, you know, and at least Andrew will never want for a berth in Italy.'

Thinking of her son, Diana sighed.

'What Italians get right is that the love of a mother for a son is much more intense than that for a daughter,' she said to Ruth and Marta on one of their kaffeeklatsch mornings.

'But how can you say that?' Ruth asked. 'A daughter is flesh of your flesh and bone of your bone. Much as I love my sons, I always longed for a girl. You never lose a daughter.'

'That's the point. The love you feel as a mother for a daughter is for something familiar, because you know what a girl is. I always felt that giving birth to my girls was completely natural, but having a son was *extraordinary*.'

'I would never have wished my Lottie to be a son,' said

Marta, with some indignation. 'I could not be prouder of her, or happier to have a daughter.'

They did not understand; how could they? Primogeniture did not rule their existence as it did hers. Besides, Andrew was exceptional. With him, she had experienced for the first and only time of her life, the bliss of passionate love returned.

'When I grow up, I want to marry you, Mummy,' he told her. He lay in her arms, gazing into her eyes with complete adoration, just as she gazed into his.

'But I'm afraid I'm married to Daddy, darling.'

'Maybe he'll die.'

Perry did not die; on the contrary. He saw which way the wind was blowing in Rhodesia, managed to sell up and get back to England before the War of Independence kicked off; their neighbours had not been so lucky. Murdered, raped, their home and lands reduced to rubble by the angry and envious. Was it wrong to deplore this? It was such a relief to get out, she sometimes thought that this was why she had finally conceived a son and heir. Once Perry won his seat, they effectively lived separate lives, and it never crossed her mind to ask for a divorce. All she cared about were the children, especially Andrew, her perfect little boy.

'I love you, I love you,' her son would whisper every night, and she would say it back, like two mirrors reflecting each other to infinity.

'Come *on*!' she said to Bella. The Labrador was fossicking about in the side of an olive grove, occasionally uttering a deep bark. It was the kind of behaviour she displayed as a gun dog, when on the trail of a wounded animal. There must be blood somewhere. 'No, not that way!'

Bella, nose to the ground, was bent on going along the path that led up the hill to Ruth's. Diana hesitated, steadying herself with her rubber-tipped stick. Every so often, the whole world seemed to lose its moorings and float up and down, but walking together for at least an hour every day is part of the sacred bond between dog and human. Despite being greedy, stupid and lazy, Bella was probably the only living creature who gave her unquestioning devotion – though Diana knew she put Perry first.

He did not return the dog's feelings.

'All that bitch does is eat and crap,' he said. 'Useless animal. You should have her put down.'

'I'd sooner take you to the knacker's yard.'

'Eh?'

'I said, I'd find that very hard.'

Bella was still tracking something, because every now and again she would give a deep, gruff bark, and turn to look imploringly at Diana with her dull, peat-brown eyes.

'What is it, silly?' she asked.

There must be some wounded animal on the hillside. If she found it alive, she could at least put it out of its misery – or ask Enzo to bring his gun. Thank goodness for Enzo! Diana particularly appreciated his help because he never asked her for any money, though of course she did pay him a little, as a matter of honour. His family could trace their lineage back to the Etruscans; she could not help but be impressed by this. The only person who didn't use him, it seemed, was the oligarch who had bought the palazzo – but then he had imported his own staff, by all accounts.

'All shaved heads and hearing aids, like gangsters,' Marta told them. 'Such a pity because Enzo could certainly do with a patron.'

'I think he's his landlord, isn't he?'

'Yes. The contessa sold almost all the houses on the hillside, but Enzo's still belongs to the Felice estate. I expect that's why the road to your home and his is so dreadful.'

In winter, the lane became the bed of a stream, interspersed with huge, smooth boulders that surfaced out of the stony topsoil like the backs of whales. It really was sinking into wilderness, and Enzo claimed that there were now wolves back in the hills, as well as the ghastly wild boar. She sometimes came across tortoises that had tumbled down a wall and found themselves upside-down, waving their little scaly legs in the air unless she bent down and turned them right way up. She would be just as helpless as they if she fell over, and it was as though thinking about this made it more likely because, in the next instant, Diana's foot slipped and she found herself collapsing inexorably and excruciatingly, into a ditch.

6

What You Do Isn't the Same as What You Are

Enzo deposited Xan outside Marta's flat in Santorno, or as close to it as he could get. All traffic that came up had to turn around the War Memorial just before the town walls, for the old town was closed to cars and buses, and so the loudest sound now was the tumbril drumbeat of wheeled suitcases being dragged by tourists. In summer, thousands walked past Marta's building to get to the Via Nazionale and the Piazza della Repubblica.

Marta was unfazed. She would go out early in the morning, and otherwise lived for music.

'I do not think about what I can't change,' she said. 'That is the secret of happiness, you know. To live in the present and never look back, like Orpheus.'

Xan could hear the sound of her playing coming through the French windows of her flat below the parterre. It had a high stone wall, and just one entrance, which she liked because it made her feel secure.

'*Sempre la musica!*' her new neighbours would mutter occasionally, and Marta made sure that she kept her windows shut when playing Beethoven or Rachmaninov.

'People want to ban Russian music because of Putin,' she said. 'What fools! There are no limits to music. It is the universal language.'

'I thought that was sex.'

'Don't be ridiculous, my darling.'

Today it was nothing more dramatic than Bach's 'Well-Tempered Clavier'. Xan's grandmother's hands were slowly succumbing to arthritis, her joints swelling like the confined roots of trees from a pavement, but she still played superbly. He waited until she reached the end of the movement, then rang the bell.

After a pause, Marta's voice said loudly over the intercom, '*Si?*'

'Oma, it's me,' Xan said, suppressing a flicker of irritation. She couldn't really be expecting another guest, though perhaps it was wise at her age to be cautious. He hoped she had remembered to get in some proper food for his lunch. He was ravenous, whereas she often forgot to eat anything. It was one of many things that his mother had instructed him to report back on.

Marta buzzed open the door and Xan looked down a short flight of steps to see her beaming, with Otto yapping from between her legs.

Xan dropped his rucksack on the top step, and came down to give his grandmother a big hug, very gently because these days she felt as light as a leaf. He could feel her revelling in his strength; a deep affection and sympathy between them persisted, despite many months of separation and not many emails or calls.

'How is my favourite grandson?'

'I'm your only grandson, aren't I?'

'As far as I know.'

They both laughed because even the most regular-seeming families could turn out to have unexpected additions. Xan had been thrilled to discover a huge array of cousins and aunties on his Nigerian side.

'Is there lunch?'

'Yes, my darling. Juicy made us a chicken casserole.'

Xan was touched, as large young men usually are when they know their hunger is likely to be sated.

'This is always so nice,' he said, looking round.

Even in a different country, and a completely different setting, Marta's flat felt very familiar. Instead of the high ceilings and tall sash windows he had grown up with in Hampstead, there were big chestnut beams overhead, and small, deeply recessed windows. Yet there were her Afghan rugs, her bits of Biedermeier, and the Fazioli grand piano that he remembered from the drawing room in Church Row. Really, the latter was the only thing she cared about. She kept its twin in the Hampstead flat to which she now never returned.

Sometimes, Xan thought that his problems stemmed from being the only person in his family without a vocation. It was a real affliction, even if it was one shared by much of the world. He had his First ('Just like everyone else,' his stepfather said; adding, 'In my day, those actually meant something') and spoke German, he had passed grade exams in piano, he could drive and teach English as a Foreign Language, but he had absolutely no idea what to do with the rest of his life.

'Why don't you retrain as a doctor?' his father asked.

'I'm no good at maths.'

'How can you not do maths?' Julius was genuinely astonished.

'I don't know. I just can't. It's like not being able to sing.'

At least Marta never nagged him.

'What you *do* isn't the same as what you *are*,' she said. 'Your path will become clear. It may just take you a little time to find it.'

He looked through the window at Marta's tiny garden, flooded with greenish light. The sun was so much stronger than in London that everything grew in an almost tropical abundance. She was bored by gardening, as she was by cooking, but must have been paying someone to tend the wisteria and the climbing roses, because they looked rather neater than usual. Of course, he thought, she had the money to do so.

'It still feels exactly like you, Oma,' he said. 'Maybe it's your paintings.'

'Yes, I wouldn't part with those. They are partly what brought me here, after all.'

For over twenty years, Marta had collected an artist called Kenward who had grown in value and reputation. Nobody seemed to know anything about him, but he clearly had some connection to Santorno, because one featured a view of the town, though he mostly excelled at still lives. It was hard for Xan (or anyone else) to explain what made them remarkable, but ordinary domestic things like flowers, vegetables, paperbacks, a jar of Marmite and old wooden chairs, depicted in a flicker of minutely Impressionistic colours, seemed charged by an inner light and beauty.

'They are lovely,' Xan said, looking at one again. 'So intimate and tender. Though they are also very cleverly structured.'

'Yes,' she said. 'Of course, it's the kind of thing that is completely out of fashion. Nobody likes scrupulous observation, do they? But I don't care, and in a hundred years' time people will still love them. I wonder what his connection to Santorno is.'

Xan and his grandmother chatted away. Marta made a point of speaking German to him, and he was glad of it now because he was thinking of emigrating to Berlin, like many of his peers. London had become unaffordable to those interested in the Arts. They swapped stories of the past year, and despite having shrunk another centimetre or three she seemed her old self, though on her second journey to the sink, she stopped and grimaced.

'Are you all right, Oma?'

'Just back pain,' she muttered.

'Have you seen the doctor?'

'Yes. Don't nag me!'

Marta had always been an active, healthy person but no matter how much turmeric and aspirin and olive oil a person took to stave off decrepitude, the human body could only last so long. She was looking not just old but worn out. Xan felt a pang of anxiety. She had been fine when she moved out here six years ago, but he now saw that there is a great deal of difference even between your seventies and your eighties.

'What are your plans? I lead a very quiet life,' she was saying. 'Though I am giving my annual recital in the piazza next week. Ivanov is sponsoring it again.'

'Who?'

'The oligarch who bought Palazzo Felice. I must have told you about him? Goodness knows what he'll do now everywhere is clamping down on Russian money, but there seems to be enough. I suppose musicians are cheap. Especially compared to a football club.'

Xan yawned. He was sleepy from having had to get up at 5 a.m. to catch the plane and longed to crash out. But if he did so, there would be acres of time that night to fill, and his Oma went to bed at 7 p.m. He could wander round Santorno by himself, but where was the fun in that?

'I'd like to see inside the palazzo.'

'Maybe I can get you invited. I play for him once a week. It's well worth seeing, if you get past his security.'

'Why does he need that?'

'Because he's afraid of Putin.'

'I thought you said he's an oligarch?'

'Don't you know that that awful man murders everyone, his own former cronies especially? Ivanov spent seven years in prison. He got out, but he lives in a state of continual fear – or paranoia – and he lives apart from his wife and family in London. They're all under a cloud, even those who are known opponents of the war with Ukraine. Vasily's yacht has been confiscated, but so far, the Italians haven't tried to take away the palazzo. Maybe the music festival helps.'

'Are you really up to performing, Oma?'

'I am falling to pieces, but slowly.'

'I'm sorry.'

'Thank you, my darling. I have my brain, my hearing, my piano and my doggie. Those are all that matter.'

But she was tired, and when Xan, restive after spending the whole day indoors, offered to take Otto out for a walk along the parterre that evening, Marta accepted with evident relief.

The little terrier was only too eager to go, scampering up the steps, yapping. It was annoying, but at least Xan was out, with the swifts wheeling and screaming. Xan bolted down a sandwich as he walked. He breathed more easily, relieved.

The parterre that ran from Santorno to the countryside was about a kilometre long, flat and gravelled and planted with pollarded horse chestnuts, limes and cypress trees. Ideal for babies in buggies, courting couples and those who wished to enjoy the constitutional benefits of the evening *passeggiata*, it was closed to traffic except at its furthest end when a road that looped around the town joined it. Behind this, the rest of the hill rose, encircled by the high stone walls, treetops and the half-hidden tower of the Palazzo Felice.

'Come on, Otto,' said Xan.

Freed, the terrier became a different animal, inquisitive, bold, independent. Backwards and forwards he ran, scampering off to investigate under bushes with a wagging tail. It must be a dreary life for a dog here, Xan thought, but it was unthinkable for Marta to be without a companion. Xan had grown up with Otto's predecessor, Heidi, a very different personality and one he'd been fond of. Otto's solid white shape trotted along parallel to his own progress, and the dog was obviously enjoying his evening walk.

'Otto!' called Xan. 'Not too far!' The dog turned and gave him an unmistakable grin.

Ahead, the fuzzy darkness of the countryside began, punctured by a few lights up and down the hillsides. If he continued walking for some twenty minutes, he'd come to La Rosa, just as Ruth Viner had done all those years ago. There would be people his own age there, and something more than the somnolence of senescence. It was a tempting thought, even if he had no wish to spend any more time with Tania than was strictly necessary.

Now the parterre stopped and became a road, so the occasional car came past. One began crawling along beside him. His sisters sometimes teased him about being 'pretty', and maybe this driver thought he was too, because he leant out of the window and whistled.

'*Ciao, baby!*'

Xan gave him a glare and said, in his deepest voice, 'Vafanculo!'

The car ground its gears and accelerated up the road to the mountains.

'Idiots,' he muttered. At least he knew the Italian for 'fuck off'. Obviously, they must have thought he was streetwalking, because why else would a Black person be out at night?

Otto was reluctant to turn back, and Marta had given him her spare key. She'd be snoring her head off by now; it would make no difference to her whether he returned now for an evening of cable TV or stayed up carousing until past midnight. After all, this was supposed to be a holiday for him, not just duty. He whistled to put the dog on the leash again, and half-turned, calling, 'Otto!'

Suddenly, he was conscious of someone having crept up on him very close, too close.

His forearm was seized with a powerful grip and a man said, harshly, in English, 'Got you.'

7

The Bloodstained Shirt

'Anything?'

'No.'

'They've got to be somewhere.'

The two women examined the T-shirt again. The holes, with their charred entry and bloodstains, impressed both Ruth and Juicy unpleasantly.

'*Dio*,' said Juicy. 'What can we do?'

Ruth remembered her sessions working as a junior doctor in A&E, over half a century ago.

'I think it is a bullet hole, but it's passed through the fabric on both sides, look, so probably went right through whoever it was. That might be why there's so much bleeding.'

'Is that a good thing?'

'Yes, in a way. It means whoever they are is less likely to be dead. Though there's infection, and shrapnel. Any wound like this is bad.'

They looked in the woodshed, the pizza oven, the

still-ruined outhouse that housed a mound of compost, and in the pergola where her children and grandchildren played ping-pong, but there was nobody.

'How very strange,' she remarked. 'A real mystery! I hope that whoever it is has found help.'

'Is something missing from the washing line? Maybe they took something else to wear.'

'I can't remember what I hung up,' Ruth said. 'Some old clothes, I think, but then most of my clothes are old.'

A part of her was now wondering whether it had been Dash who had stolen her sandwich, or whether a human being had taken it. When Ruth first arrived, crime had been so alien that nobody even locked their doors. Now, shutters were reinforced with steel, and wrought-iron grilles barred the ground-floor windows. It made little difference whether a house was lived in for just a few weeks a year or all the time. Houses were ransacked and emptied of every stick of furniture. One friend, an Englishman on the other side of town, even put a false wall into the downstairs living room, to make a walk-in cupboard where his Bose CD player and his big flat-screen TV were carefully concealed whenever he went away.

'You should do it too, Ruth,' he'd advised. 'You never know, with all the Albanians about.'

'I'm sure not all crooks are Albanians,' she said, with asperity. 'Aren't they the country that takes more refugees, despite their poverty, than most others? I'm sure they don't deserve their reputation.'

She had nothing but compassion for the folk trying to escape tyranny for a better life. Hadn't her own ancestors done exactly this when fleeing the pogroms? Though they should not steal, of course. She would happily donate clothes, and food, and gave money every year to organisations that tried to help them, though it was a drop in the ocean. The local dog charity here had more donations than the one for people. She waved to Raff to come over.

'I think someone may be hanging about,' she said softly.

'What kind of a someone?'

'A gypsy, perhaps, or a migrant. We think they might be injured. I'm a bit worried because of Tania and her mother arriving at any moment.'

'I'll help you look.'

'Don't frighten them, if you find them. We've looked everywhere.

'There's still my gaff,' Raff said. 'I left it unlocked because I've been cleaning it out.'

Ruth watched him ascend to where his camper van was parked, discreetly, in an out-of-sight grove further up the hill. He'd moved out of the studio cottage to make way for the wedding guests, and was sleeping there again. She'd heard him playing his guitar the night before, singing softly.

Alas, my love, you do me wrong
To cast me off discourteously;
When I have loved you, oh so long,
Delighting in your company.
Greensleeves was my delight,
Greensleeves my heart of gold
Greensleeves was my heart of joy
And who but my lady Greensleeves?

He had a nice voice, and played well, but what was astonishing was that, ever since the nightingales had arrived, they had begun to join in. At first, she thought that it must be a coincidence, but their improvisation was perfectly timed, weaving in and around the melodies Raff sang. Ruth listened, open-mouthed.

'Wow,' she said when he stopped. 'I've heard of nightingales following human musicians, but I never expected to hear it. You should sing when the others arrive.'

Before long, Raff returned.

'Find anybody?'

'Nothing. I'll look down the hillside as well. I've got some brambles left to strim.'

He put his orange helmet back on and lowered its mesh visor.

There was no point worrying. She certainly wasn't going to tell her sons, or her guests. Everything was dangerous, and these days there were so many ominous new developments that people had more to worry about than a wedding. She'd hoped the party would be a celebration after two years of misery, but now it seemed it might be more like a last hurrah before the whole world slid into catastrophe.

She waved away a large, black bee that droned past her face. Birds chirped in every tree, and she heard the cuckoo announce its arrival for the hundredth time. She couldn't help liking the roguish cheek of the parasite. But she did *not* feel the same way about the wretched Ben Gorgle.

These days, he seemed to be everywhere. His 'Letter from Italy' for the *New Yorker* was replete with triumphant moans about Britain as a place so corrupt, costly, overtaxed, cold and overcrowded that he had no regrets about leaving it, except that Italy was too corrupt, costly, overtaxed, hot and under-populated to endure, either. If only he would move back to the States! But he was far too busy sucking the sap out of expat society here. Ruth had been very prepared to welcome him as a fellow-American, until she'd read what he'd written in another magazine about Diana and Perry.

That awful article! Ruth was pretty sure that Gorgle would never have picked on the Evenlodes had they had money. It was like shooting fish in a barrel to go after a pair of elderly, impoverished English aristocrats, and even if his account of Perry's family's behaviour in colonial Zimbabwe was pretty shocking, it was all a long time ago, and one of them had dementia.

'I am just so sorry,' said Ruth guiltily, because she had introduced Gorgle to the Evenlodes.

Diana said, 'That's the trouble with bounders. They prey on the unwary. I do worry about the way you trust your Woofters.'

'WWOOFers,' said Ruth. 'Don't. What is life without trust?'

'A great deal less tiresome, I should think,' Diana said; but Ruth thought, no wonder you have so few friends.

The article had continued to generate scandal and ill-feeling for many months. It required the experience of living through the pandemic together to make people shrug their shoulders and move on. All, that is, except Diana.

'My mother always said that one should only appear three times in a newspaper: when hatched, matched or dispatched. I wish I'd remembered that before speaking to the wretch.'

'I miss the days when being a journalist required rat-like cunning,' Marta remarked. 'These days, the only qualification seems to be the total absence of shame.'

'Isn't your daughter Lottie married to one?'

'That is how I know,' Marta said. 'Still: at least he isn't prime minister.'

Ruth came back to the present as a car door slammed, and she heard Dash's joyful bark. A moment later, her guests arrived.

'Welcome, my dears,' Ruth said. Her spaniel switched his attentions without hesitation from Juicy to Tania, rolling over invitingly to have his tummy tickled by the most beautiful woman present. 'Dash, behave!'

'Wow. It's like being in an Instagram filter,' Tania said. 'What's the Wi-Fi code?'

As before, Ruth was momentarily struck dumb by the young woman who was to be her grandson's bride. It was as if one of the goddesses she had imagined when she first saw La Rosa had stepped out of a painting to stand before her. Tania was quite used to having this effect on people; in fact, she never noticed it.

'Wonderful!' said Polly. 'What a glorious place.'

Ruth said, 'You are most welcome, both of you.'

She showed them to Polly's bedroom in the main house, then to the little studio cottage to one side of the courtyard, where Tania would reside until her wedding night.

'I thought this would make a romantic bridal bower,' she said archly, then cursed herself because, after all, Tania and Olly had been living together over the past year, and she was suffering, uncharacteristically, from nerves. However, the studio cottage (formerly a pigsty) was covered in climbing roses, and had the most privacy as well as delightful views down the valley. Ruth had even bought a new king-sized mattress for its galleried sleeping area, and picked flowers for a vase on its dressing table ... It was difficult to know whether Tania liked or disliked her efforts, because she looked at it all without expression. Then she went up to a painting that was slightly crooked, and straightened it on the wall.

Maybe she's just tired, Ruth thought, as they went out again on to the courtyard. She said, 'It'll be just us for a few days, until the rest of the family arrive.'

As she spoke, her gaze travelled down the hillside, and she saw Raff, helmetless, moving up the road towards the house with unusual slowness. As more of him became visible, she saw why. He was carrying Diana in his arms.

'Raff, what's happened?'

He stopped and stood very still, looking up at the group above him. The afternoon light caught his hair. The cuckoo called in the silence, and then he said, 'I found Lady Evenlode on the road.'

'Fainted,' Diana said in her clear, loud voice. 'I've buggered my ankle.'

Raff set Diana down on a chair.

'May I check to see if it's a sprain or a break?'

She nodded, and he began, very carefully, to feel. Then he said, 'I think it's a sprain. The swelling is quite slight. You need to elevate it, and wear a compression stocking with ice.'

'But maybe, just to be sure, get it X-rayed?' Ruth suggested. 'I'm sure you're right, Raff, but at our age, it's easy to break bones.'

'Quite,' said Diana. 'You're not an expert, are you? Ruth is a doctor.'

Raff stood up at once.

'Of course. Excuse me.'

He turned, and went inside. Ruth, who had flinched at Diana's tone, asked Juicy to make tea and bring painkillers.

'You poor dear,' she said, examining the ankle in turn. 'It must be sore, but I think Raff is right, it's a sprain not a break. Why not rest a while? If it starts to swell alarmingly, Enzo or I can drive you to the hospital right away.'

Diana agreed, and closed her eyes.

If only she weren't so rude to people she considers beneath her, Ruth thought. It always made her furious, because surely you should be more, not less, polite to those without money or power. But her neighbour was lonely, unhappy and disappointed in life, and Ruth's private grumbles gave out because she knew that Diana was dealing with her husband's dementia all alone in her cottage. How would she get Perry into the car and out of it with a sprained ankle? She would need help, and that meant asking Enzo or (if he'd agree) Raff. Yes, Raff was probably better. It was a pain because Ruth had a million chores that needed doing at La Rosa, but people who needed help must take priority.

How long could Diana continue to look after her husband in this way? She was gallant, but caring for someone with dementia was a sentence that could continue for years, and the Evenlodes hadn't the means to fund private care because they'd handed their home over to Andrew. It was the opposite to Marta, fretting over her investments instead of giving away most of her money to her daughter and grandchildren, just in case they had a personality change and stopped caring for her if she became too frail to live alone. Ruth called this 'the Lear fear'. It was a kind of mania that ate away at family affections, because millennials like her grandchildren could look forward to nothing but student debt and a lifetime of renting. She herself had given away as much as she could, keeping enough to cover nursing costs, if she required these. Even if there were chores that wanted doing, nobody needed more than two hundred thousand pounds, at least not in Britain. The trouble was, no adult knew when they were going to die. Not unless they were like Beatrix, who was exercising her right to be euthanised in Amsterdam.

Oh my poor friend, Ruth thought. Are you the wisest of us, or the most foolish? The thought of death was always there in her thoughts, and those of her friends, but she was determined not to let it cast a pall on her life, however long or short that might be.

Lying down for her siesta and staring up at the beams overhead, Ruth marshalled her spirits. Beatrix had made her choice. She still had a dozen beds to prepare for the wedding, and the missing owner of a bloodstained shirt to find.

8

Tea At the Palazzo

Tap tap tap.

Marta was having the same nightmare. It had been a feature of her life for as long as she could remember, though it was only since she turned eighty that it had become an almost nightly presence.

Tap tap tap.

In the darkest hours of night, she would lie there, heart racing, while her limbs turned to stone. She was walled up, hardly able to breathe, but on the other side of her tomb something dreadful was happening. An almost soundless anguish was seeping through the wall, overlaid by grunts and scuffles. The sounds accelerated, and so did the feeling of despair, until at last there came a cry, like a knife going into her heart.

At this point, Marta always woke up in such terror that it took a few moments to understand that she had been dreaming about the past, and the soldiers and her mother were gone.

Rest in peace, Mutti, she thought, staggering up to relieve

her bladder. The Fall of Berlin, when she was six years old, was largely obliterated from her memory, but it returned to her in nightmares: not the bombings, or the hunger, but what the Soviets did to women, girls and even young boys. It was an atrocity that most people never spoke of. Her mother had tried to say that she, too, was a Communist. A generation of women had been traumatised, and many who survived had not been able to have babies. Even now, the German population was in decline, which was the real reason why Angela Merkel had accepted so many fleeing Syrians. All her life, Marta had sworn to hate Russians, yet as a result of coming to Italy she had, somehow, become quite friendly with one.

Nobody was quite sure what to make of Ivanov. On the one hand, he was one of the hated oligarchs. In Tuscany, you could hardly throw a brick without hitting such people, though they mostly congregated around Lucca or Portofino and Italians (unlike British people) were much more relaxed about immense wealth. Yet now, because of what Putin was doing in Ukraine, their assets had been frozen, and everybody felt this was a righteous step towards punishing corruption, bullying, murder and lies. Ivanov himself, having left Russia to live in exile, was not in the same category as some, though he was rumoured to have some sort of criminal past back in the 1990s. Was that criminal according to Putin, however, or criminal according to international law?

Marta did not care about politics. To play for an appreciative and informed listener is all (besides payment) that a musician requires, and she was splendidly remunerated as the star turn of Santorno's Maggio Musicale and for giving Ivanov private recitals every week. Her visits had continued even during lockdown, when nobody was supposed to leave home: somehow, despite the roadblocks and paper-checking, the police turned a blind eye to her expeditions to the palazzo. She actually felt sorry for him. Ivanov was not just a lonely man, but one starved of company and culture.

'All the streaming services, books and amusements that money can buy do not compensate for not hearing live music,' he said.

Today, Xan would accompany her there. It is good for a young person to meet the rich, even if the rich are rarely interesting to the young or vice versa, and Marta thought it might do her grandson good to be exposed to a variety of people, because she worried about his drifting through life. It would be entertaining to see what he made of Ivanov ... Against her better judgement, she had become interested in him, but contacts with billionaires come at a price, and she worried that she might somehow be corrupted by his wealth. Though there was also something else. Although she was conscious that, since her visits to the palazzo had become common knowledge the Santornese treated her with more deference, she had recently had the feeling that she was being watched.

How this came about, she wasn't sure, but she often had a strange, crawling sensation even when she was in her bedroom. Her mobile phone also seemed to cut out, or be strangely echoey.

Marta knew she should pay attention to her instincts. Human beings are rarely wrong about this sense, and as a former Communist, her own mother had been bugged in West Berlin. She had no idea how it was done now, or why she was being spied on, but she was sure it was something to do with Ivanov. Had her connection to him come to the attention of the FSB? Or perhaps, the Italian security services?

Or it could be the start of dementia. That was always the other possibility, which every elderly person feared. An instant's forgetfulness, hesitation or repetition of an anecdote could herald the start of mental decline. Marta could not face the route that Beatrix had chosen, but she had a stash of powerful opiates to take if she thought that she was losing her mind, and was brave enough. Though how many other people did she know who had done this, then forgotten they even had them until it was too late?

Otto was a great comfort. He always barked if someone was coming to her front door. His furry, stocky body was like that of a teddy bear. When she returned to bed, he would snuggle into the crook of her arm, near the place where her left breast had been excavated, and she would sigh and fall back into unconsciousness.

'You look so like your Vati,' her mother's voice murmured in her memory. 'He had fair hair and blue eyes too. They couldn't believe that he wouldn't join the Party.'

Her mother was a doctor, not allowed to practise in Nazi Germany, which meant that most of her work was abortions. These clients would come to their home, in the middle of the night, and be led downstairs to the cellar where their unwanted baby could be hooked out into a bucket whose contents would then be emptied directly into the sewer. Marta remembered the cellar vividly. It was where she, and everyone else in her block, had hidden when the Russians came.

It was one of the things that she liked about her new home: it was up in the light and air. The old building that her flat was carved out of did have a kind of basement, being built on a hillside, but the entrance to this from the street below was locked and padlocked, and she never used it.

Xan couldn't understand this. Marta's serviced flat in Hampstead, which she now rarely used, had three bedrooms, so why not the place that she actually lived in?

'You mean you *also* own the floor below? Why don't you convert that and make more bedrooms, so we can all stay?'

'It would cost too much, just for a week's visit, and it'd always be dark and damp. Much better for you to use Ruth's or stay one at a time.'

The *piano nobile* was always the place to be. The first floor had light and air and security. Other than birdsong and the clangour of church bells, there was no disturbance, though sometimes the whine of Vespa scooters and the smells of cooking food found their way upwards from the street that led out of town.

Soon the clatter of daily life would begin, with the steel shutters of shops being rolled up in the Via Nazionale. She sighed, and patted around the bed for Otto. But her fingers met her duvet, not fur. More awake, now, she felt with her other hand. Nothing.

She remembered, now. Xan had taken Otto out for a walk the evening before. Had they not come back?

Marta opened the door to the spare bedroom very quietly. It took a moment for her eyes to adjust to the gloom, but then she made out two slight mounds, the form of her sleeping grandson and Otto. The dog lifted his head briefly and looked at her through half-open eyes, then slumped back down.

Well! Marta thought. She was glad because she knew that Xan didn't really like Otto, something that always causes a devoted dog-owner pain. It was strange: you could accept that not everyone liked your child, but it hurt if people disliked your dog, because a dog held a piece of your soul. Her greatest fear was that she would become too ill to look after him, and then Otto would starve to death unless her daughter came out to rescue him. Nobody else could be trusted, so Lottie always made sure that his pet passport was kept up to date, just in case.

Marta dressed, made herself a pot of strong black coffee, swallowed a painkiller and a few other medications then took Otto out for a brief, excruciating walk. When she returned, her grandson was up.

'Good night?'

Xan paused in the act of shovelling an enormous forkful of fried egg slathered in ketchup into his mouth.

'Actually . . . it was weird.'

'How so?'

'I walked to the end of the parterre. This big guy grabbed me. It was quite scary. He seemed to think he knew me, and that I should come with him in his car.'

'How unpleasant,' Marta said.

'I was, like, pretty freaked out, you know?'

'Did he do anything to you?'

'No. As soon as I spoke to him, he let go. I don't know if he thought I was a prostitute, or something, but he kept asking me what I'd done to his friend. I told him I didn't know his friend, that I'd just arrived from London and was staying with my grandmother, and eventually he believed me.'

Marta said, 'I wonder who he was? Not Italian, I take it?'

Xan shook his head, and all the burnished mass of his hair quivered. 'More like Eastern European. He spoke English to me.'

'I wonder whether this has anything to do with Ivanov.' Marta selected a banana, peeled and cut it into quarters, thoughtfully.

Xan looked up. 'Is he a thug too?'

'One never knows what a Russian has done. Whatever else he is, he loves classical music.'

'Really? The few rich people I've ever met have all been knobs. There was this boy at my school who was given a

Maserati for his seventeenth birthday. He smashed it up in a week, and you know what? He was given another, the next week.' Xan paused. 'Actually, we felt sorry for him. He never saw his parents, just the housekeeper.'

Marta said, 'The rich, like the poor, are always with us. Today is when I go to the palazzo for tea. You are invited too.'

'Great!'

They exchanged grins; she was relieved to see that her grandson was not going to reject an invitation on principle. Marta disapproved of wealth, intensely, but made an exception for those who, like the Medici, spent it on culture.

'I'd better get dressed, then.'

'Oh, are those pyjamas?'

'It's called sleepwear.'

She shook her head, and sat down at the piano while he shaved and changed. There was never a day of her life when she didn't play, or rather, work.

In Berlin, she had been a young star, winning a prestigious international prize for young pianists that led to her equally prestigious recording contract. It had seemed quite natural to her to get these accolades, and she had taken it in her stride. Her bombed and battered city had risen from its ashes, and so did she. But then she met Edward Evenlode.

The Englishman had been the oddest man she'd ever seen – tall and thin, with a long sad face that rarely smiled. He told her that he sang *lieder*, which was absurd because surely no Englishman could do this? But when he began to sing Schubert, powerfully, richly, with a sublime intelligence and feeling, nothing in her life could be the same again.

During the years of her marriage, and for many decades after, Marta put the solo performances to one side. She had little choice, really, because even before she left Germany she suddenly and comprehensively lost the confidence of the prodigy. It seemed like the price of love, for though she had had plenty of affairs, once she met Edward it took longer and longer to reach that serenity in which nothing matters but the music. She was excruciatingly aware of herself in a way she had never been before, and eventually stopped being able to perform as a soloist.

Yet when she accompanied her husband, those fears vanished. He was so solid, so reassuring, so marvellously *English*.

'Come on, sweetheart,' he'd say. 'You can do it. You can, you know.'

She could, as long as he stood between her and the audience. He sang, she played for him, and that was all that mattered apart from being together. His was the greater talent, and he could make those ravishing sounds while, he told her, thinking about quite different things. It welled up out of him as naturally and effortlessly as if he were a bird. She, however, had to concentrate ferociously. Nothing was given to her any more, it was all discipline and will.

He brought her to England, and introduced her to his family, who of course disapproved. Slowly, she understood that it was not just because she was from a country that had been at war with theirs, but because they were aristocrats and she was bourgeois. Edward ignored them; he and Marta lived in the world of musicians, the only people who mattered, and their happiness was completed by the arrival of their daughter. Then, when Lottie was eight, he dropped dead of a heart attack.

Marta survived because she had to. Bereavement became like the pain in her back, something she always felt but managed to over-ride.

'I'm ready,' Xan said.

Marta returned to her body, wincing. She gave them both a quick lunch. As so often, it was burnt because she'd wandered off at the crucial moment.

'I'm sorry,' she said. 'I just hate cooking.'

'But don't you find it a creative pleasure?'

'No.'

She felt quite indignant at this idea that cookery was creative. It was like when people said, 'You must love playing the piano.' Playing consumed her, she had no choice whether to love it or hate it (though the music itself was another matter). Only amateurs could enjoy what was, to her, sheer, unremitting work.

'So what is he like, this oligarch?'

Xan was driving; she knew it was nice for him as he could not keep a car in London. Otto thrust his head between them. He loved expeditions.

'You will see,' Marta said, gasping a little as Xan overtook a three-wheeled van. 'I'll be interested to know what you make of him.'

'Why is he in Tuscany?'

'I don't know. Maybe he prefers it? He's very reclusive, and yet also frank. Putin's war is a disaster for him. He told me he's down to his last million. Or maybe billion. I forget which.'

Xan laughed sarcastically. 'What a nice problem to have.'

'You understand, for the super-rich a million is very little.'

'Only they don't need all that, do they? Nobody does.'

'No. But almost everyone you know, including yourself, has more than they need.'

'Except,' said Xan fiercely, 'the rich have so *much* more.'

'Oh, life is not so rosy for Ivanov, either. How would you like to live surrounded by armed bodyguards?'

'Not a lot.'

'Effectively, he's a prisoner here.'

'Better than most jails.'

'Yes. All the same, a prison is still a prison.'

'Do you like him, Oma?'

Marta said, 'My darling, he loves music.'

For her, the love of classical music was such that anyone who shared her passion was someone she was prepared to like. Those who pirated pop online didn't even bother with it: that was how niche and endangered it was. Every year, when she had been in London and going to recitals, she saw how the only people who still treasured this sublime art seemed to be the old, and dying, and this was an almost unbearable thing because when the audience for classical music was gone, the essence of the human spirit would be no more.

'So, what did he do to make Putin angry with him?'

'Who knows? I think oligarchs are almost all living in fear these days, even his generals. He sees their money as his. Vasily barely escaped.'

'How did he do that?'

Marta smiled. 'If you are rich enough to have a private plane, I believe travel is not so difficult. He may be a murderer and a crook, but he is not a philistine. Though Ivanov does annoy me with his curated life. To the rich, everything must be perfect, you know, and perfection is the enemy of the good.'

'Why so?'

'Because perfection can only belong to God.'

'You should tell that to Tania.'

They were now above Santorno, and the road was abominably bad, causing the car to bump and buck as it went over ruts and boulders. Marta gritted her teeth as, despite Xan's care, she was jolted about. Then the car went through an ornate gate set in a high stone wall, guarded by caryatids, and the road suddenly became smooth. All the small irritants of the normal world fell away. There were no more tin signs, no bits of plastic caught in verges, just the unalloyed beauty of Italy. Beyond a long avenue of cypress, blossoming orchards spread their branches over a flock of geese and some very white sheep wandered among wildflowers. Hoopoes and doves fluttered, and from one tree the tail of a peacock cascaded like a bolt of shot silk.

'It looks like a painting of paradise,' Xan remarked.

'Yes, but instead of being watched by God, we have been observed by dozens of security cameras. You must stop at the next gate.'

'What if I don't?'

'You will be shot dead.'

'Good to know.'

Two men in black stood on either side of a steel gate, and although it took a moment to realise that the slants of darkness strapped to their torsos were sub-machine guns, they exuded menace.

Xan said, 'Do you think they shave their heads every day? Or do they have so much testosterone that it all falls out?'

'Quiet, my darling. They don't like jokes.'

Marta put down her window.

'Miss Koning?'

'Yes. And my grandson, Alexander Bredin.'

The guard scrutinised a tablet in front of him. She had been asked to send Ivanov's secretary a photograph of Xan's passport, and sent his British ID, being suddenly nervous about the newer one because Russians could still be odd about Germans.

'You are expected. Go straight ahead.'

Marta nodded, and they continued on. As they drew up

inside a courtyard surrounded on three sides by a loggia, the gravel crunched under their wheels.

'The sound of money,' she remarked. 'So like applause.'

'You aren't afraid of rich people, are you?'

'No. You cannot be an artist and afraid.'

'Why not?'

'Art must be stronger than fear or love.'

Xan looked around. 'Golly,' he said.

The palazzo seemed almost to float above the plains. Nothing could be seen of the ugly modern sprawl at the base of Santorno; even the roads were hidden by thick woods and olive groves. Apart from the car, everything looked as if it had been transported from the fifteenth century. A fountain cascaded out of the urn of a marble giant crouched in a cave hewn from the hillside behind them, and formal beds were punctuated by huge terracotta pots containing lemon trees heavy with fruit and flowers. They walked forwards on to a wide grassy terrace. Some way below, Xan spotted a swimming pool, not the usual garish turquoise but a deep emerald green. It was the kind of garden that made you realise that everything that you had ever seen before was vulgar.

'I was expecting bling,' he said.

A slim, clean-shaven man approached them. He was immaculately dressed and, as ever, wore kid gloves.

'Maestra.' Ivanov put his hand over his heart and bowed.

To Xan, Ivanov said, in a slightly glottal accent, 'Welcome, Alexander.'

Marta was pleased to see that her grandson took this in his stride.

'Thank you for inviting me. Your view is amazing.'

'This was a former fortress, built by a Medici. They always chose good positions, ones that could be defended, and this one is by one of the architects who designed the Ducal Palace at Urbino. Though mine is superior, I believe. Would you like tea before or after your grandmother's recital?'

He eyed Otto, who was cocking his leg against a large stone urn.

'I will put my dog in the car,' Marta said reluctantly. Every time she visited, she brought Otto, and every time there was a silent battle of wills as to whether he would be allowed to stay with her.

The homes of the very rich are not so different from the rest, she thought, only with more flowers, heat, paintings, upholstery and, above all, space. A wall is still a wall, a door is still a door, yet there was not a light switch here that was discordant. The level of detail at the palazzo always astounded her. Everything was flawless, harmonious, luxurious, in keeping with the Renaissance era yet unblemished by age. Curtains of woven silk cascaded to the floor in colours that would have graced a ball gown; Ivanov told her that he had these made by Fortuny. The chairs were upholstered in vellum. The cabinetry and ironwork must have employed entire villages of craftsmen, and looked as though they had been there for centuries rather than brought in just a few years ago. The hardback books piled everywhere were clearly read, and the marble fireplaces carved with centaurs and cherubs had fires burning with just the right amount of warmth for a spring afternoon. In among various exquisite paintings, she could see the jewel of Ivanov's collection.

This was a painting by Artemisia Gentileschi, and was as startling as it was striking. It had been in the palazzo originally, in the days of the old contessa, and it now hung, restored to splendour, in the entrance hall.

'You like it?'

'Very dramatic,' said Xan, with a touch of insouciance that made Marta proud of him. 'Is it Judith and Holofernes? She looks as if she is about to stab him on that crimson bed.'

'Cupid and Psyche. In the myth, she is about to kill him but instead, falls in love.'

Ivanov peeled off his gloves as he walked, and dropped them on the marble floor where a servant was already on hands and knees, cleaning away their faint footprints. New gloves were instantly produced by another servant on a silver tray, and he put these on without breaking his stride.

'A precaution,' he said, seeing Xan's stare. 'You have heard, perhaps, of the Skripals?'

'Do you think someone is going to get through all your security to put Novichok on your door-knob?' Marta asked.

Ivanov said, 'Anything is possible. Putin fears poison too. Why do you think he sees visitors at one end of a very long table?'

'Fear of infection?'

'There are rumours that he has cancer, but I believe these to be wishful thinking.'

He took Xan on a tour. To hear him describe the struggles involved in restoring the palazzo, in the teeth of the Belle Arti and many natural obstacles, you would think he had done it by himself; but he was justifiably proud of what he and his architect had achieved. They went all the way up to the top of the tower, where a steel contraption was mounted on the platform.

'What's that?' Xan asked.

'Anti-aircraft gun,' Ivanov said.

'You think you could be *bombed* here?'

'Anything is possible.'

Marta exchanged glances with Xan. It was so peaceful,

so remote and well guarded, it was hard to see anyone getting through.

Ivanov led them to a smaller room, where a blaze on a wrought-iron basket grate was sending out a scent of apples. It was a surprisingly cheerful and intimate space, though Xan murmured to Marta, 'Is every chair supposed to look like a throne?'

As soon as they sat down, two servants in long white aprons appeared bearing silver trays with silver teapots, and mounds of assorted sandwiches, pastries and finger cakes.

'Eat,' Ivanov said, seeing Xan's eyes light up. 'I am sure you are hungry. I was always hungry at your age. English breakfast or Earl Grey? Or perhaps vodka?'

Marta never ate before a recital, so she and Ivanov chatted, mostly about music, while her grandson tried not to shovel this feast into his mouth too fast. Ivanov's Russian Blue came and jumped fluidly on to Xan's lap, and began kneading his legs with its claws. He tensed.

'Do you not like my cat?'

'I'm allergic, sorry.'

Ivanov said, 'How sad for you not to be able to enjoy these beautiful creatures.'

'Oh, I enjoy looking at them.'

Ivanov clicked his tongue, and the cat jumped off Xan and on to his lap. The Russian peeled off his gloves to run his hands luxuriously through the smoky fur. The cat's eyes, ringed with emerald, half-closed. Ivanov smiled as it purred. His face looked completely different for a moment: younger and more human.

Marta said, 'My grandson had a strange experience last night, at the edge of the parterre. Tell him, Xan.'

Haltingly, Xan recounted the assault on him during his walk. 'They sounded, kind of, Eastern European?'

'It was not one of my men,' Ivanov said at once. 'But I will call my head of security.'

He pressed a button on his mobile, and one of the bullet-headed guards appeared in seconds. They spoke briefly in Russian, then the guard said to them in English, 'Perhaps they are Albanians. We know there are some in this neighbourhood.'

Marta said to him, 'I thought you might like to know. Just in case, they are, well ... '

Ivanov grimaced. 'The kind of people I must guard against are ... how can I put it? Not ones that you would be likely to see.'

An expression crossed his face that made him look almost careworn.

Marta asked, 'Would you like me to play for you?'

'Please do.'

His piano was far more ornate than her own, but with an exceptional purity and clarity of tone that made it a delight to play. She lost awareness of everything but Bach, and Couperin, and Chopin, those complex melodious patterns and deep emotion she adored and spent her life interpreting. Ivanov was an excellent listener, and their tastes were very similar. Her friends described his little music festival as 'art-wash', as if art could ever wash away blood. Yet art generally feeds off horror and suffering, much as a rose feeds off excrement, she thought. Perhaps the people who had once owned this palazzo had been the same: monsters who nevertheless loved beauty.

Most monsters that Marta had ever encountered, especially wealthy ones, cared nothing for art, unless it had a huge price tag attached, and could be shown off in a home. Whatever he had done, Ivanov was a rare being.

'I wish you had made more recordings, Maestra,' he said when she ended. 'Now, please, eat.'

She allowed herself a single macaron from the glass epergne piled high with small pastries, a pale green pistachio whose colour and delicacy made her particularly happy.

'These are excellent. Where do you get them?' Xan asked; and their host answered, in mild surprise, 'My chef makes them.'

Of course. Once more, Ivanov pressed a button, and his chef appeared. She was a small, round Slavic woman who looked anxious until Ivanov passed on Xan's compliments, at which she smiled and bobbed a curtsey.

Xan was eying the macarons again, and Marta looked at him sternly: given half a chance, she knew he would eat them all. Ivanov caught her expression.

'I will get my housekeeper to put these in a box.'

Afterwards they went out for a brief stroll. The nightingales, never silent for long, were intensifying their melodies as the sun began to set. Chuck, chuck, chuck, wizz, wizz, she thought. They were crazy little birds.

'So beautiful,' Xan said. 'How many variations do they have?'

'Who knows?' Marta said. 'I think, over thirty. Some people find them *gemütlich*. Myself, they remind me of sentimental music.'

'I've never heard a nightingale before, though I love them because of Keats.'

'Our greatest poet, Pushkin, also wrote a poem about the nightingale,' Ivanov told him. 'Have you read him? No? You should, even if his genius can never be conveyed in English. He was mixed-race, like yourself.'

Marta could see her grandson bristle at this.

'Really?'

107

Ivanov said, 'He was proud of his ancestry. His great-grandfather was kidnapped as a child in Africa. An ancestor of Tolstoy's rescued him from slavery, and presented him to Peter the Great. They became friends.'

Xan said, disbelievingly, 'It sounds like a fairy tale.'

'In Russia, at least, such stories are true. How else would a man like myself come to all this?'

'Er, oil wells?'

Ivanov bared his teeth.

'Let me show you my garden.'

The flowerbeds were perfumed with the scent of chocolate, because they were mulched with cocoa shells, this being apparently the best (and most costly) compost in the world. It was certainly preferable to animal manure, Marta reflected. She was increasingly irked by Ivanov's supercilious air, as if he had nothing to do with the thug currently bombing and murdering thousands of people with the misfortune to be his neighbours. Yet the palazzo gardens, famous even in the days of the old contessa, were coming into their full glory and it was surely better for Russian millions to be spent on this rather than weapons. The two men wandered down an avenue of topiary figures, first created four hundred years before, then a succession of Baroque stone fountains and pools. Marta sat on a bench, having released Otto into the grounds to have a little walk. Even if Ivanov disliked dogs, it was cruel to keep hers from a little freedom. She felt tired, her trim body, kept supple for so long with Pilates, aching profoundly.

If I were in London, I'd see a consultant, she thought; but the idea of battling through Milan and then explaining her symptoms in her minimal Italian was a difficulty too many. Better to sit quietly, and rest.

All at once there was a hideous howling sound, and two

small animals streaked past. One was Ivanov's cat, no longer languid but fuzzy with fright; the other, Otto. Thundering along on his stubby little legs, the white dog did not come close to catching his prey, but the cat shot up a tree. It remained there, hissing curses, while Otto barked.

'Otto! Otto!' Marta shouted. *'Hör sofort damit auf!* Stop that at once!'

Mortified, she hobbled over to put him on the leash, but he danced away indignantly. Couldn't she see that a mortal enemy was at large?

'So sorry,' Marta said to the oligarch.

'Put him back in your car, immediately.'

Ivanov was furious. Marta had the apprehension that, were he a fraction less self-controlled, he would have killed her dog and possibly herself on the spot. One of his bodyguards materialised, picked up Otto by the scruff of his neck and hurled him into Marta's Mini.

'That dog is an idiot,' Xan said disloyally; though really, Marta knew, the idiot was herself. What had possessed her? She knew perfectly well: there was only so much she could take of inordinate wealth before something in her wanted to explode.

'Do not bring that animal here again,' said Ivanov.

Marta said, 'I have apologised. We will go.'

His housekeeper hurried out with a white cardboard box, ornately ribboned, containing the little cakes left over from their tea. Normally, this gesture touched her but she felt humiliated, as if she were a pauper. Wordlessly, she handed the box to Xan.

They left at speed, Otto standing on his hind legs on the back seat, and continuing to bark defiantly.

Xan said. 'Are you all right, Oma?'

'Yes, thank you,' Marta said grimly. She was driving, her back forgotten in her rage. 'Your unkind words about my dog were noted.'

'You did bring him deliberately, didn't you?'

'That thug thinks that, because he spends an infinitesimal fraction of the wealth he stole from the Russian people on music, he can buy *me*. Well, he cannot.'

Bump, bump, bump down the awful road. When they got on to tarmac Xan said, 'If you don't mind, I might get out and walk for a bit. I haven't visited Ruth yet.'

'Fine. Take the cakes to her,' said Marta; adding pointedly, 'You've had quite enough.'

9

The Lost Guest

Xan strode down the track that led to La Rosa. Marta's anger didn't upset him. He was used to her prickliness, and had enjoyed tea at the palazzo; it was a world away from his normal life in the ex-council flat that he rented with a couple of friends.

'Fuck them,' he said to himself. 'They're all old.'

As if summoned by his thoughts, Xan glimpsed Enzo's Fiat far below on the winding road up from the valley. To avoid a chance encounter, he headed for a ruin to one side of the road.

There were still many of these abandoned houses, half submerged in brambles. Despite the perennial fantasy of living under the Tuscan sun, few foreigners wanted the fag of rebuilding, and he could understand why. This cottage was roofless and half blackened, presumably after a fire, and a budding fig tree sprawled over part of it. Xan could see the tiny swellings that would become figs. He had a dim memory of picking some, when he and his family had stayed at Ruth's in late summer three years earlier.

Now, though, it was only spring, and the air was cooling. Xan was just beginning to be glad of his hoodie, when he heard a sneeze.

He paused. If it was Tania, he didn't want to be seen.

The ruin smelt of acrid fig leaves and sharp human sweat.

'Hello?' Xan said, hesitating. There was a sudden movement, and he looked down to see a figure in the shadows. 'Are you OK?'

He saw a young man who was, to his immense surprise and delight, Black. He was wearing a Harvard sweatshirt, jeans and trainers, and had a small backpack at his feet.

'Are you English? American?'

'I speak English,' said the stranger hesitantly.

'Are you one of the guests at La Rosa? I'm Xan,' Xan said.

'My name is Blessing.'

Xan sat down on a ruined wall and grinned. Somewhere nearby, a bird chirped and whistled, and a robin answered it. Another started up down the hillside. It sounded so much like a conversation that Xan laughed, and so, suddenly, did Blessing.

'I'm from London, but my dad's Nigerian. You?'

'Zimbabwe.'

Xan said, 'Cool. I'm on my way to Ruth's. Have you met her yet?'

'No,' Blessing said. 'I am a little confused.'

'I'm not surprised.' Xan saw that the lost guest was looking exhausted, and somewhat grubby. 'La Rosa isn't the easiest place to find. I'm going there too, so I'll take you up to the house. You must be one of the first wedding guests to arrive.'

'OK.'

Further up the hill he heard the sound of a hand-bell, which was what Ruth rang when summoning guests to the table.

'Come on! Ruth isn't strict about anything apart from being punctual for meals.'

Blessing answered hesitantly, 'If you are sure?'

Xan said, 'Yes, of course.'

'I have no gift for her,' Blessing said. 'My luggage is also . . . lost.'

'Tell you what,' said Xan, on impulse, 'why don't you give her this box of pastries? She doesn't know I was bringing it for her, and old ladies like that kind of thing.'

'I should like that,' said Blessing.

Xan was charmed by the formality of his English. He wondered whether Blessing's gentle manner was a Zimbabwean thing, just as his father's confidence was supposedly a typical Nigerian thing. Every race had stereotypes, of course, and he disliked these, even if they were sometimes amusing when individuals like Enzo apparently conformed to them.

They came into the courtyard of La Rosa. Its lights shone warmly on to beds filled with tall white flowers. It looked amazingly smart, Xan thought, compared to the laid-back scruffiness on previous visits.

'Xan, dear,' said Ruth, emerging with a distracted air. 'Just pick me some 'erbs, would you? Oregano and mint, I think. Oh, hello, have you just arrived? Do you need help with your luggage?'

Xan said, 'Blessing's luggage was lost.'

Ruth grimaced. 'Darn, I hope you can get it back from the airline.'

'But he brought you these.'

Blessing handed over the box that had come from the palazzo. Ruth put on her spectacles, undid its ribbons, and her face lit up.

'Macarons! My, what a treat. Thank you, Blessing. Now,

what do you need? We can lend you anything; my grandsons are always leaving clothes behind, and I know we've a new toothbrush too. So, you must have been at Harvard with Olly? He's been awful about letting me know who is coming but it's first come, first served here and there's only Tania and her mom, so far. I can put you in the stable block, over here; we've turned it into a dormitory for all the cousins. There's a shower, and towels.'

Almost inaudibly, Blessing thanked her.

'See you in a few minutes,' Xan said, as Ruth went off to find some spare clothes. She was a dear, he thought, and turned into the house feeling cheerful. Clearly, his holiday wasn't going to be quite as dull as anticipated.

In the kitchen, Juicy was assembling supper. It smelt wonderful, but then everything that she cooked did. He glanced at her bum admiringly. Unlike Tania, she looked as if she actually enjoyed sex.

'Ciao, Xan,' she said.

'Ciao,' he replied, blushing slightly. She must be almost thirty, but still.

Xan helped to lay the long wooden table in the cavernous kitchen. When its fat pillar candles were lit, and big ceramic bowls of pappardelle and salad carried over, it all looked so festive that he felt a momentary pang of guilt about leaving Marta alone.

Staying at Ruth's, he texted. *Come too?* She probably wouldn't even check her mobile, old people never did.

Tania, already seated, raised a hand when they entered.

'Have you come far?' she asked Blessing in her queenly manner. Xan snorted as Blessing just said, 'Yes.'

Other guests were not quite as welcome, or welcoming. He saw Diana, sitting bolt upright at the table. She did not acknowledge Xan and Blessing's arrival, whether because she was half-blind, or racist, he couldn't tell, but it was pretty rude considering she was his great-aunt. Maybe she simply didn't recognise him? After all, they'd last met about ten years ago, when he was in his early teens. Her husband sat in his wheel-chair in a corner, and Xan, who had last seen him as fit and healthy, was quite shocked. Admittedly, he was in his nineties, but it looked as if he'd had a stroke. Ruth's latest helper, who quickly introduced himself as Raff, was crouched down to Perry's level, feeding him.

'That's it, slow and steady,' Raff said, squatting beside the wheelchair. 'How about if I make this into a sandwich, sir?'

The old man made a gobbling noise. Raff folded some scrambled egg and peas into a small parcel, guiding Perry's spoon towards his mouth. The action was repeated, patiently and gently, again and again until all the food that had been barely touched was eaten. At this point, Lord Evenlode farted loudly.

Everyone pretended not to notice, until Tania said, 'Pew!'

How dreadful to be at the end of your life, Xan thought, and to be a nuisance or an embarrassment. Or perhaps his great-uncle never cared what other people thought about him. He'd seen him when invited to family gatherings at Fol Castle in Cornwall. They had never been pleasant, and Perry had called him a piccaninny. Xan hadn't known what this meant, but when he realised it was a racist word for a child, he felt sick with rage, humiliation and shock. Lottie had refused to visit them again, when he told her.

Now, as so often when with white people, he felt himself splitting into two. Half of these people he knew and liked, and the other half he knew and disliked. He scrutinised them all. Ruth was wearing those dangly earrings that made her look a bit silly, and loose denim-coloured garments that seemed simple but probably cost more than Xan's monthly rent. Polly was a classic middle-aged lawyer on holiday in a striped shirt-dress and discreet jewellery. His great-aunt looked as if she'd just pulled on whatever clothes came to hand in a hurricane, but also (annoyingly) rather elegant. Raff was in a sludgy jumper and combat trousers combination. Worst of all was Tania, as perfect as if she had stepped out of a fashion magazine in a long floral dress and cardigan that were unmistakably boho designer. Only Blessing was normal, in his jeans and sweatshirt.

Poor guy! Nobody apart from Xan talked to him much. Xan made the effort because he had gone to too many dinners where nobody ever talked to him, either, as if his Blackness made him invisible or contagious. Was it because, as his mother claimed, people were unable to process the unfamiliar? But why *should* it be? There were so many white people, in Europe, and so few like him. How would they feel, transported to Lagos, where they would be in a minority?

Or am I becoming bitter and unjust? Xan wondered. His father had told him that this was what everyone had to guard against.

'No country is perfect, Xan. But this is your country, as it is mine and our family's. Britain has moved a long way away from how it was when I was your age.'

Xan's stepsister rolled her eyes at this.

'Enough of the first-generation immigrant gratitude, Dad,' she said.

He noticed that Blessing, though clearly hungry, was eating slowly and carefully.

'Is the food OK for you?' Ruth asked Blessing.

'Yes.'

Tania said, in a tone of wonder, 'Why don't the plates match?'

116

She was staring at the crockery on the table.

Ruth replied cheerfully, 'I guess we're just not a household that goes in for matching dinnerware.'

No, of course not, Xan thought: you're above all that stuff. There was the assumption here that everyone lived at a certain level – university, foreign travel, cars, Netflix – and if he were to tell them that he was vegetarian because he couldn't afford meat rather than as the result of a moral choice, it would cause embarrassment.

The pappardelle kept them busy for a while. Juicy was horrified that they were having salad with it.

'But Root, this is not what Italians do,' she said.

'Why not?'

'Pasta is *pasta*, not a main course.'

All the company laughed.

'Traditions are made to be broken,' Ruth said. 'Just think, Juicy, when Marco Polo brought back noodles from China, how many Italians had the genius to turn them into fettucine, rigatoni, ravioli, tortellini, fusilli, pappardelle and spaghetti. Whereas the Chinese have gone on just eating noodles, because they have no freedom to innovate. I think pasta should be allowed to be eaten with salad, don't you?'

Polly said mildly, 'I think that theory has been discredited, actually.'

A jug of red Santornese was passed round, made from La Rosa's own vineyards; as Ruth said proudly, the whole supper had come from within a thousand feet of where they were sitting, 'including the wild boar salami'.

'Really?' Diana asked.

'Yes. Enzo's wonderful at turning boar into sausages and things. I think, if he didn't live so close, my vineyards wouldn't stand a chance. He's a good shot.'

Xan noticed that Blessing had gone very still.

'I saw him in his car when we were walking back here,' Xan said. 'Does Enzo live on this hillside?'

'Indeed he does, past that appalling road below La Docciola,' Ruth replied. 'I don't know how you have the nerve to drive it twice a day, Diana.'

Diana shrugged. 'It's always worse after the rains,' she said. 'At least we're not down by the mill. That really is impassable except on foot.'

'Such a shame it's abandoned again.'

'It won't be for long,' Juicy said. 'There are always indigents looking for a place to stay.'

'Half the buildings in Santorno are empty, too,' Xan said.

'Well, you know,' Juicy said, 'Italy has the lowest birth rate in Europe.'

'But I thought Italians loved babies.'

'We do,' said Juicy. 'But the problems for us are the same as for all women. Not enough money, or jobs. And also, not enough good men to go round.'

'There are always good men,' said Polly. 'Just as there are good women. But they often don't find each other, do they?'

'So, how did you like Harvard?' Ruth asked, gesturing to Blessing's sweatshirt.

'OK,' said Blessing, looking down at his plate. His voice was hardly above a whisper.

'Just OK? I had a *ball*.'

Xan said to Ruth, 'It's not that fun being a student these days.'

'Olly enjoyed grad school, but I know it's become very big and quite corporate,' Ruth said. She persisted, determinedly, and asked whether this was Blessing's first time in Italy.

'Yes,' he said simply.

'Do you live in London, Blessing?'

'No,' Blessing answered, in his quiet voice. 'I am from Harare.'

'Harare?' said Diana, perking up. 'We lived in Rhodesia for a few years. Had a splendid time. Didn't you, Perry?'

A dim light kindled in Lord Evenlode's eyes. 'Rather,' he said.

'All ruined now,' Diana said. 'The same story everywhere. Corruption and violence, but somehow, it's preferable to the Empire. People are starving in what used to be the bread basket of Africa.'

A wave of embarrassment passed over the rest of the party. And yet, Xan thought, if there was one former colonial country that probably *was* a bread basket turned basket case, it was Zimbabwe.

Tania said to Blessing, with unexpected tact, 'I'm sorry about your luggage getting lost. I've got a ton of hair products, all free stuff. Would you like to come and see?'

She scraped back her chair, and Blessing stood up to follow her.

'Er . . . ' Xan said, not knowing whether to join them. Tanya looked over her shoulder.

'Don't worry,' she said. 'Blessing is my guest too.'

10

At The Bar Degli Artisti

It was not yet Saturday, but the three friends had decided to meet midweek.

'Getting away from home is a holiday, right now,' said Ruth. 'I'm exhausted.'

'I'm not surprised,' Diana told her. 'You have taken on a lot, my dear.'

Marta said, 'I thought you're used to hostessing.'

'I am,' said Ruth, 'but not like this. And it's so darned *expensive*.'

The three friends exchanged glances. Money was something that they all worried about, especially now. Everything had doubled in price, especially gas, and many thought that, by the end of the year, it would quadruple. It was not just a question of putting on another jumper to stay alive when in your eighties, and Diana was already fretting about firewood to keep the room in which Perry slept heated through another freezing Tuscan winter. His chilblains, and hers, took months to heal.

'Even pasta has gone up fifty per cent,' Ruth said.

Marta sipped at her cappuccino, then dabbed carefully at her upper lip to remove the foam moustache clinging to her moustache. 'Has the bride's family not paid off?'

'I think you mean paid up,' Diana said.

'Well, she has given me something,' Ruth answered, though in truth Tania's mother seemed to be under the illusion that three thousand euros would cover her costs. 'I've tried reaching out to Tania, but maybe she expects everything to be free because of her influencing. And my home is so *noisy*.'

A handful of Ruth's grandchildren had also arrived, but the only young person she found bearable was, to be honest, Blessing, and of course Raff. The rest were adorable, and yet, sadly, badly brought up. They never even unloaded the dishwasher, just created mess and complained about internet connectivity. In her heart, however, she knew that this wasn't the real reason why she felt so anxious.

'Do you need more help?' Diana asked. There were few things she enjoyed talking about as much as staff. Ruth had been annoyed by this until she worked out that, for Diana, a life with any kind of domestic help was a kind of fantasy.

'I don't know. The help I have seems to have gone off the boil, recently,' her friend answered. 'Even Raff never seems to be around when I need him.'

Diana sighed. 'Maybe that's my fault.'

'How so?'

'After my fall, I asked him if he'd mind helping me with Perry in the mornings and evenings. You know, putting him into the car and to bed.' She looked uncharacteristically anxious.

Ruth said, 'Of course he's free to do whatever he wants in between the farm work.'

'It's just that Perry *is* rather difficult. When he's in a mood,

121

he makes himself completely rigid and heavy, like a toddler, and getting him in and out of the Fiat is a battle.'

'It must be,' Ruth said. 'I thought you didn't like him? Raff, I mean.'

'Your Woofter? (Such a silly name, what does it stand for? No, don't tell me, I'll forget.) I think he's a good egg.'

'He is.'

'Even Perry seems to like him.'

'He's the best helper I've had so far,' said Ruth. 'If only he weren't leaving!'

'Oh no!' Diana exclaimed. 'What a *bore*.'

Ruth and Marta exchanged glances, because both suspected that some of Diana's dismay might be because Raff would never accept payment for his services.

'And now Juicy has told me that she can't continue either.'

'Why?'

'Her business is taking up more and more of her time. She's quite the local entrepreneur these days. Exports to Britain and Germany.'

Ruth sighed. Once upon a time, Juicy had been her cleaner. How could she have foretold that the sweet little *contadina* would grow into such a successful businesswoman?

Marta said, 'Do you ever wonder what will happen to your property when you become too old to look after it?'

'I've asked my sons, but they're not interested,' Ruth answered. 'None of my grandchildren would appreciate this life, apart from Olly, and *his* job . . . '

'I thought professionals can work anywhere in the world, thanks to the internet,' Marta remarked.

'I don't pretend to understand what they can and can't do remotely. But it isn't that simple,' Ruth said. 'No, what worries me is this wedding.'

122

'You mean, the marriage?'

'Whether,' Ruth said slowly, 'I was wrong to encourage Olly and Tania to marry. I am not sure they are really suited.' There! She had said it. She looked down into her cappuccino unhappily. 'They seem so different, somehow.'

'My dear, there's nothing anyone can do about that,' Marta croaked.

Diana nodded; over a quarter of a century ago, she had perceived that the only girl her son and heir briefly married was hopeless. It ended without children, but the relief of this was outweighed by sorrow as Andrew showed no sign of wishing to repeat the experience.

'What is wrong with the bride?' Marta asked.

Ruth said, 'I don't know. She's very beautiful, of course, and successful, and yet . . . Somehow, I thought Olly would at least want a sense of humour.'

Diana said, 'She might find it hard to show her feelings. I know I did.'

'But you were just eighteen,' Marta reminded her.

'Seventeen,' said Diana. 'Tania is what, twenty-five?'

Ruth nodded. 'The age at which the human brain is supposed to be fully mature.'

'Marriage is an enormous risk,' Marta said. 'Like putting your hand in a bag of snakes, and hoping to pull out an eel. That's what my son-in-law says.'

'Well, it's mostly drudgery, isn't it?' said Diana. 'Especially in somewhere like Fol.'

'I thought you loved Fol?'

'I loved my childhood home, Lode. The most perfect small house in England, Pevsner called it. Fol is like something on a biscuit tin.'

Once again, her friends wondered how anyone who had

owned a castle in Cornwall could be genuinely poor. Was it an affectation? Marta always claimed that the aristocracy, like the Queen, had perfected parsimony as a kind of art and always had funds tucked away, but Ruth was certain that Diana's poverty was real. Even so, their friend's eyes always became misty when she mentioned Lode.

The aristocracy really does care more about inheritance than anything, Ruth thought, but she patted Diana's hand. 'I know, home is so important, isn't it? And yes, Marta, I do worry about what will happen to La Rosa. I've put my heart's blood into it. Oh dear, look who's coming.'

Someone was walking down the Via Nazionale with his shopping on one arm and a woman on the other.

'*Achtung!* It's Gorgle and his latest,' said Marta out of the corner of her mouth. 'Unless she's his daughter. No, don't catch her eye – she's probably an artist.'

The three friends dreaded artists, who were always holding *vernissages* at which other expatriates were expected to buy their work, usually out of sheer embarrassment.

Marta's warning came too late.

'Ruth, Marta, Lady Evenlode, *che meraviglia!*' said Gorgle. 'You look younger every month. And there's little Dashy, *carissimo mio!*'

The spaniel was wagging his plumy tail. The three women arranged their wrinkles into expressions of polite reserve.

'So cute,' said his admirer, fanning himself. '*Dio, quanto sono caldo oggi!*"

Ruth snorted, for unlike the others her Italian was good enough to know that he'd just announced he was sexy today, and Gorgle was sporting baggy checked shorts and a Gap T-shirt which revealed every bulge, topped by a black beret set at a rakish angle. Always larding his conversation with Italian, his flattery in public was underscored by his spite in private. She knew perfectly well that he had described her to mutual friends as 'a fat Jewish shrink', and hauled her dog back on to her lap.

'Oh, such a little fur-baby,' said Gorgle's companion in a cooing voice. She was introduced as Sheryl, or possibly Cheryl, a 'singer-songwriter-actress'. Beneath the table, something growled.

'Behave, Otto!' said Marta.

'A little bird told me that your grandson is getting married to Tanyaa,' Gorgle remarked, oblivious. 'Sheryl is a fan. A great fan.'

Sheryl put her hands together piously. 'She's *so* much classier than Kim Kardashian.'

'Well, that wouldn't be hard,' said Ruth.

'Who?' Diana asked, bewildered.

'It'll be, like, the wedding of the year!'

'Even the Santornese are captivated,' Gorgle added.

It was obvious that they were angling for an invitation.

'It's just a small family event,' said Marta.

Diana fixed Gorgle with an eye like a marble of blue ice, adding, 'You'll be able to see it when she walks up this street to the Town Hall, like everyone else.'

Gorgle said blandly, 'Maybe I'll write a piece about it.'

Ruth gave the journalist a withering look. 'Is that what you call it? In my day, it was called mud-slinging.'

He cleared his throat. 'Well, we must be getting on with our *passeggiata*. I need to go to the supermarket to ask for some *prosciutto senza preservativi* before they run out. A *presto*, dear ladies.'

'Asshole,' muttered Ruth, as the couple continued towards the main square. 'I wonder whether he knows he's asking for ham without condoms?'

'You can bet he's saying *far* worse about us,' said Marta. They settled back in their chairs, greatly cheered by the energy of dislike.

'Those teeth! Why do Americans look identical when they smile?'

Ruth said mildly, 'Not all of us do, you know. Or only those who can afford dentistry, which is less than half the population. Anyway,' she added, 'even if Gorgle is a nuisance, he's kind to dogs.'

'Only because house-sitting, rather than writing, is his real job,' said Marta. 'And dogs don't know any better.'

The blue and gold clock in the main square began to strike midday, and then all the other bells joined in.

'If you could be young again, would you?' Diana asked.

Marta said, 'Certainly not! Though I would love to have the strength and health I once had.'

'It's such a bore, isn't it? Just when you have worked life out, you have to leave it.'

'On the contrary, death is what gives our existence distinction, and definition,' Marta said. 'Like the black background to still lives.'

'When I was a gel,' said Diana, 'I thought life was a picnic. I didn't realise that I was the sandwich.'

'Do you think it's like that for young women now?' Ruth asked. 'I mean, it's got to be better if someone like Tania is able to make a living as an influencer rather than, I don't know ...'

'Being a debutante? Of course it is,' said Diana. 'Though I could type. That was the only alternative for my class, at the time.'

Ruth and Marta, both of whom were the beneficiaries of excellent educations, felt a pang of pity, and guilt.

'Of course, the clothes were *lovely*,' said Diana. 'Those dresses with little jackets. And gloves.'

'Ivanov wears gloves all the time, because he's afraid of being poisoned by Putin,' Marta remarked. 'He only takes them off to stroke his cat.'

'Good afternoon, ladies.'

Ruth said, 'Enzo, *ciao*. Did you manage our shopping?'

'Everything but the coriander,' Enzo said. 'In Italy, I regret we do not have this.'

'Please, join us,' said Ruth fondly. He was such a charming man and it cheered them all up to be seated with someone half their age.

'*Macchiato*,' said Enzo. He exchanged some banter with the waiter; Ruth observed that he seemed tired and somewhat low. The same old, same old, she guessed.

Two years ago, in the darkest days of the first lockdown, he had confided in her about his ex-wife, and how keenly he felt the loss of his daughter. She listened with deep sympathy, then told him that once Fede was a teenager, she would have a cell phone of her own, and want to make her own decision about whether or not to make contact.

'But her mother will control everything!' he said. 'You do not know what she was like. Fede left as a child. She will not even have my number.'

'Make sure you are on Instagram,' Ruth said. 'That's what young people look at. Take beautiful pictures of your life here. Whatever your ex-wife says, Fede will be curious about you.'

Accordingly, Enzo had posted a picture of his life every day, as regularly as if he was saying his prayers. He had never owned a camera until he bought an iPhone, and at first made many mistakes. He didn't know how to use natural light, and he didn't even know how to choose the best angles. But before

127

long, he was capturing all kinds of details that he had never appreciated: cats, wisteria, olive trees with split trunks, the food he made for his dinner, anything that made his life look more interesting than it actually was.

'Effectively,' he told Ruth, 'I have become a tourist in my own country.'

'If Fede wants to find you, she will. She's a digital native, unlike us.'

His new hobby allowed him to hope. From the moment he woke up to when he tried to sleep, he was always scrolling through his feed. Each time he saw he had a new follower, he checked in case it might be Fede. She could not have forgotten him – could she? Diana also knew about his suffering. She wondered whether the agonies of a father could match those of a mother, and whether, if Fede did return, she would still love him. But then, she had been taken away – not sent to prep school, like her own son.

Enzo took some snaps of the Piazza della Repubblica while waiting for his coffee. Its main attraction was its Town Hall. Not only did this feature a wide, photogenic flight of stone steps, but it had a number of lavish frescoes inside on the ceiling and walls by Santorno's one modestly distinguished Baroque artist, Buoninsegni. These featured inspiring mythological scenes such as the rape of Europa, the metamorphosis of Daphne and the embraces of Leda and the swan. All were large, and largely indistinguishable from each other, being blonde and clothed chiefly in ropes of fat pearls.

'I suppose no bride can complain that she isn't warned what she's getting herself into,' was how Marta put it.

'Why hasn't Olly used a specialist company for his wedding?' Enzo asked.

'Tania wants it to be #cottagecore.'

'Cottage what?'

'You know, simple and rustic.'

Those adjectives should have warned me, Ruth thought, walking slowly back to Enzo's car, parked outside the city walls. Like Marie Antoinette playing at being a shepherdess, the apparently artless always demands more, not less, time and money. Juicy and Raff had stepped in to help with the catering and the garden, and Enzo, bless him, had sourced twelve round plastic tables that could, with heavy linen tablecloths, pass muster. However, the whole project felt overwhelming.

If it comes to the worst, the wedding feast can serve for my funeral, she thought. It particularly annoyed her that everyone had forgotten to mark her eightieth birthday. She didn't normally ask for or expect anything, but this could be her last decade ... Gloomily, she thought of Beatrix, again. Until Marta arrived, the Dutchwoman had been her closest friend here. She was the same age as Ruth, and lived all alone up in the mountains with her animals – the donkey had come from Beatrix's place – and maybe, Ruth thought, she had been too alone, especially as she needed two sticks or a mobility scooter to get about. She wasn't the sort to ask for company, and luckily had enough money to pay for a cleaner to visit three times a week, but it must have been lonely, especially in winter.

Maybe, she thought, I neglected our friendship. Beatrix was always dear to her, yet having both Marta and Diana so close had made Ruth less inclined to include her as much in everything, so that the twice-weekly meetings in trattorias or at home had fallen away to fortnightly or even monthly ones. Why had that happened? She wasn't a dog person, Ruth knew, and she had no children, so we had less in common than the other two. Beatrix hadn't seemed hurt to be relegated to second, or third, place – but then, at their age, people didn't behave like children in kindergarten.

Ruth herself felt hurt at the indifference with which Tania seemed to behave towards her. She was never rude or ungracious, but neither was there any attempt at the warmth and intimacies Ruth had hoped for. She didn't even seem interested in the family photograph albums left out in the living room, which contained pictures of Olly as a small child.

'Do you think she's attractive?' she asked Marta and Diana, as the three of them walked back together. Marta had met Tania the afternoon before, and Ruth perceived her friend's shrewd old eyes examining the bride with interest.

'She is not, perhaps, *tutta donna*, as the Italians say,' Marta remarked. Her back was causing her to limp, though she tried to conceal this. 'Do you have those stories about children who have been replaced by the fairies?'

'A changeling?'

'Yes, that is the word. She reminds me of those.'

Ruth asked herself whether she was being too critical. After all, though she'd encouraged him to propose, her grandson's choice was ultimately nothing to do with her. She just hoped that Tania and Olly really loved each other. Her own divorce from her son's father had been bad enough, but at least there had been love, before alcoholism took over.

For a true marriage, Ruth thought, is not a swoon into romantic bliss but more like having a companion in arms. What you needed wasn't a lover, but a fighter. Even though she didn't understand what Olly did in his job, she knew that every day he got up and went into battle. She knew this because it was what she herself had done, and to have a partner who was there for you, heart and soul, made it less hard, and lonely.

130

Or am I confusing marriage with friendship? Ruth wondered. These days, she thought that perhaps friendship was even more important than love, especially if you were a woman.

Men were always presented to women as the main event, but it was the supporting cast, your friends, who picked up the pieces when romance had fled. Where were the poems and stories about these? If you were to believe stories, women saw other women only as rivals, and maybe that was so in the brief time in life when men were all that mattered – but heaven help you if you went on thinking this in middle age, and especially once you had children. For if it was true that it took a village to raise a child, what few mentioned was that the village was almost entirely made up of other women.

She wished she could discuss Tania with Beatrix, not least because the two of them had often discussed their different but complementary professions of psychiatry and psychotherapy. It was hideous to know that the Dutchwoman had chosen death in the face of decrepitude; yet it was her choice, and had to be respected, even admired. 'I have had enough and, I am just worn out,' Beatrix had told her. 'My time is up.'

For once, Ruth had not known what to say. Beatrix was the same age as herself, and not ill. She showed no signs of dementia, the disease that Ruth and Marta had agreed between them would be intolerable to put their children through nursing. She was perfectly able to drive, and she loved her animals and her garden. But apparently, even these were insufficient to give satisfaction. Perhaps it was having no children. Beatrix had many old friends in Amsterdam, even though, living up a mountain in Italy, she rarely saw them. She was going to have a party, and then she was going to have a lethal injection.

Ruth had taken in her donkey and her semi-feral cat (much to Dash's disgust), and embraced her gently when they said goodbye for the last time.

'Travel safely,' she'd said, though presumably it would make no difference to Beatrix if she didn't.

It was best not to think of how many names were now crossed out in her address book – another thing that the young no longer had. At least she, Marta and Diana were not going to quit enjoying life for as long as they could.

'You're like the Norns,' her youngest granddaughter Chess teased her, in one of their Zoom chats. She was the only serious reader among Josh's children. 'Or the Furies.'

'Why not Faith, Hope and Charity?' Ruth retorted. 'Or Beauty, Truth and Love?'

'Which of you is what?'

'That's for us to know and you to find out. Just remember we might punish you if you don't behave.'

'Maybe you could teach Olly, then. He's such a dick.'

Olly was not as popular with his siblings and cousins as she would have wished. Some of this was probably envy, because, though perfectly bright, none of them was likely to match his stellar earnings. He was generous to them, and they all enjoyed staying with him in his swanky new flat when in London, but his manner was another matter.

'He's just so bossy,' one complained, and another said, 'Olly doesn't talk to you, just *at* you.'

Ruth had noted that when Olly rang Tania in Italy, she seemed to spend their whole conversation listening. Did her grandson's fiancée have nothing to say? Or did Olly simply not think that he ought to pay attention to what she thought? If so, that wasn't a good foundation for a life partnership. He had a sense of the absurd though, and Tania, as far as she could tell, had almost none. A *changeling*, she thought. What does that remind me of?

Marta left them at the entrance to her flat. The sound of a piano being played began almost at once.

The two remaining friends got into Enzo's car, after the usual debate about which of them should cede the front passenger seat to the other.

'I am sorry this wedding has become so stressful for you,' Diana said, once the dogs had settled.

Ruth said, embarrassed, 'It's not so bad. I'm looking forward to seeing all my family.'

Enzo swerved to avoid a swarm of cyclists in Lycra. '*Ma fate attenzione, cretini!* My apologies, ladies. There are Umbrians everywhere today.'

'How can you tell?' Ruth enquired, with a touch of mischief. 'They look just like everyone else.'

'*Certamente*,' Enzo said. 'No Tuscan would be so stupid.'

'Andrew is joining me soon,' said Diana.

'Wonderful,' Ruth said. 'Perhaps he'd like to come to the wedding as well?'

'Maybe,' said Diana.

She was in a state of painful anticipation. Her daughters' visits were more frequent, but in the seven years she and Perry had lived at La Docciola, Andrew had only visited twice.

'It's sad that you don't see more of each other,' Ruth remarked.

'My husband and son do not see eye to eye. Perry blames Andrew for not producing a son. My daughters think that titles are snobbish and old fashioned.'

'Well, they may have a point,' Ruth said cautiously. 'I mean, it must sound pretty cool, especially if your ancestor did something like saving the king's life in battle, but—'

'Of course, you Americans don't understand,' said Diana

dismissively. 'Actually, my daughters don't, either.' She added, 'That's the trouble with the modern generation. When they aren't pulling down statues, they're rewriting the history books. It used to be entirely respectable to go out and serve Queen and Country.'

'Even if it meant slaughtering the native people,' said Ruth drily. She knew what Diana's views were: that the Empire wasn't all bad: British laws, railways and medicine made it all worthwhile.

True to form, Diana said, 'They live longer lives than Africans who weren't colonised.'

Ruth sighed inwardly. Diana's excuses for this kind of thing made her feel quite ill, and she did her best to keep tartness out of her tone.

'So do Black people in America, but I doubt they are grateful for the slave trade.'

Diana sighed inwardly, too. Ruth's views grated on her as disagreeably tart, if all too familiar these days, and she had diminishing reserves of patience and strength. Last night, she had been woken once again by someone moving around the kitchen. Afraid La Docciola was being burgled, she had staggered downstairs to find no intruder, but Perry, who had got out of the living room and was crashing around in bewilderment. It took an hour to persuade him back to bed.

'I want mercy,' he kept complaining, like a child.

'I *am* being merciful, you silly man,' she replied.

'I don't want you, I never loved you.'

Ruth, seeing Diana drooping, said, 'Would you like to stop off for a little lunch?'

11

More Dead Than Alive

Enzo was convinced that he was damned. Even if he managed to conceal his crime, it was recorded by God's angels, and he would go to hell for all eternity, roasting in a place that he imagined must be very like Naples, or maybe Stansted Airport. Equally of concern was that sooner or later, the body of the man he had shot would turn up. How could it not? This land was full of death, as well as beauty; an entire village near Lake Trasimeno was called Ossaia because it was supposedly the place where Hannibal's army had been slaughtered by the Romans, and even now their fossilised bones kept being discovered. Nothing stayed hidden for ever. Sometimes he believed that he'd dreamt it all, but he'd heard the awful cry of pain and shock. His only hope was to find the corpse before anyone else did.

Each day, as soon as it was light enough to see, he was up and out of doors, hunting, not for the living but for the dead. He took the shell from his pistol at once, pocketing it guiltily in front of his home, but there was no body, and no clue where it could have gone. At times he wondered whether he might be going mad – only his gun was missing a bullet, and on the trunk of an olive in his yard, a silvery, lichen-splashed tree so old that it looked like a human figure twisting in the effort to keep living, there was a smear of dull reddish brown just where someone wounded would put out a hand. Enzo licked his finger and then examined what came off. Definitely blood.

Somehow, the intruder had got away. It was easy enough to disappear in this landscape, with so much vegetation growing up in tangles and clumps. Hunger had once made men carve up the hillside like a cheese, building terraced walls to retain the thin topsoil, on which crops could be grown. How they had managed it without tractors, Enzo could not begin to think, but those ancestors had been ingenious as well as hardy. The olive trees were said to be over a thousand years old, pruned and pollarded by hand each year into continuing productivity, at least until the *contadini* deserted them. Now, most were more dead than alive. Nobody wanted to work like that now, especially not the young. Ruth had dragged her hectares back into order and productivity, but below Enzo's home the trees were suffocating as they sank beneath the brambles. He could not see them without a pang.

Everything was falling into ruin. Enzo did his best to be cheerful, but it was a daily struggle. He was so lonely, that was the thing, and had begun to ache in his joints. All his family was gone, and there was nobody left who remembered the old life out here. The stony road that had connected his home to the village in the valley was barely navigable, even on foot. The intruder must have come up it, however, one or two broken thorns and twigs indicated as much. Could he have fled back in the same direction?

If only he still had Violetta! Not only had she been the best deterrent against thieves, she was the best tracker a hunter could ask for. When he looked at the pedigree dogs of the three old women, or the spoilt pooches of the townspeople in Santorno, Enzo mentally curled his lip. A mongrel like Violetta had ten times the intelligence and personality of any of them. She would have found his victim in minutes, he knew.

Ruth had shown him a bloodied T-shirt with two holes, and asked him if he knew its owner.

'No!' Enzo replied, an easy lie because he certainly didn't know who he'd shot. 'Probably a migrant,' he added.

'Enzo, a migrant is still a human being,' Ruth said.

He knew she had been a doctor before becoming a shrink, but this kind of attitude always made him gloomy. It was nice to only believe the best about others, but hopeless in the case of *those people* whom nobody wanted.

What he would do when he found his victim, he didn't dare think. All the words with his buddies about burying bodies in the woods were nonsense, the rantings of an angry heart, he knew that, and yet he had shot an intruder, and it was real and horrible and he was living with the consequences. When he shaved every morning, he could see his eyes bulging with fear and insomnia, but he still had to continue to work as normal. He was a man, this was what men did, they swallowed their hurt and misery and went on with their duties, and nobody noticed or cared, not even Ruth.

His respect for and gratitude to his neighbour had grown over many years. People had thought her a little bit crazy for buying the Guardi place, but what she'd done with it was exceptional. Unlike so many foreigners, Ruth really loved and respected the Tuscan people, and she'd learned such fluent Italian that he could talk to her in his own language, not hers. She'd listened to him when he had been paralysed by despair, she had given him counsel and hope, and work. He even forgave her for being an American, like his ex-wife.

'Nobody can be blamed for the crimes of their country, dear Enzo,' she said. 'My own people are half the worst and stupidest people in the world, and half the best and noblest, and even I can't always tell the difference in many cases. Your wife will have her own account of matters between you. Every marriage is a story with two narratives, both of which may be true.'

'I swear, I did nothing wrong to her. I was a good and faithful husband,' he said.

Ruth gave him an old-fashioned look. 'I'm sure you were, but maybe she believed otherwise? You do like to remark on pretty women.'

'Well, of course. I am a man. What woman doesn't enjoy being admired?'

'All the same, American girls are not so used to compliments.'

'Maybe that is why so many come here to find boyfriends. It's not a sin to tell a woman you appreciate her looks.'

Yet Enzo knew that what he had done to his would-be intruder was a sin, the very worst that a person can commit. Somehow, he must atone for it – but how?

Repeatedly, he trudged up and down the hillside, veering off into groves, just in case one of them held a body. Enzo knew these hills intimately, having been born in the house where he lived, just like his father and grandfather and all the Rossi men before them; each stone and grove for kilometres around was familiar.

However, the grey-blue cat, out hunting, was new.

'*Salute, micio!*' he muttered. The cat gazed at him with its extraordinary emerald eyes. This was no ordinary moggy.

Its smart leather collar, studded with Medusa heads, was by Versace, its soft grey fur was tinged with cobalt shadows and its elegance could only belong to one person. Somehow, Ivanov's Russian Blue had found a way out of Ivanov's estate to hunt here.

Tentatively, Enzo put his hand out for it to sniff, but it was not like a dog. Instead, it wound itself around his calves in an enticing manner, purring. He looked down at it, and said sternly, 'Run away back to the palazzo, *micio*, before someone kidnaps you for ransom.'

The cat gazed at him, apparently considering this, then melted into the long grasses. All around, the small singing birds suddenly fell silent. He had no doubt that it would kill several before it returned home. However pretty cats were, they were deadly predators, far more so than himself.

He returned to his own hunt. If there was a body lying in a ditch or behind a wall, he would find it. What then? Could the police trace him through the antique bullet? How many other people had pistols like his, left over from before the war? Probably quite a few, but who would admit it? At least he hadn't used his proper hunting rifle, which was kept locked up in a secure, hidden cupboard with his shotgun – his wife had insisted on this, mindful of the tragic accidents that happened with children in her homeland. It was only after she left that he'd put the pistol under his bed, more with the thought of blowing out his own brains rather than anyone else's.

I should have kept my grandfather's gun there, too, he thought.

Searching, Enzo felt as if he were on a treadmill of guilt and misery. Up, down, sideways, scrambling over tumbledown walls and through thickets of thorns – nothing.

A new idea came to him. Maybe the victim wasn't dead,

but wounded. Maybe his intruder could still be saved. The nights were warmer, the river had not yet dried up, and the thickets of broom and heather would give shelter to someone in hiding. He stopped, suddenly. Why hadn't this occurred to him before? *Come out, come out, wherever you are*, he wanted to call. *I won't harm you again.* With new energy, he continued to search. Often, he stood perfectly still, straining his ears, so that even the creatures that fled human beings – the lizards, the small deer, the rabbits – emerged. But there were no sounds out of the ordinary.

'*Porca Madonna!* Where are you?' he muttered.

Enzo knew what he ought to do. He should confess his crime to a priest, and also go to the police. Neither of these were sensible courses of action. He had no more faith in the Church than in the Law. Everything was falling apart, and there could be no trust in institutions, only family; but his parents were long gone, and his one sister now lived in London. He had to search as he lived: alone. So he continued, flinching at every noise echoing around the valley. Was that a cock crowing so triumphantly near or far, or the strangulated cries of a dying man? Where was the dog barking? Was the sharp bang one of a motorbike, or a gun? The curving hills amplified noises. The valley was still lived in by local people whose traditional way of life clung on in tiny hamlets, too viewless for foreigners to be interested in.

When Enzo was growing up, there had been many problems, but it now felt like a golden age of peace and prosperity. Italy had not yet joined the euro. All the borders were coming down, even the Berlin Wall, and the ease with which young Italians like himself could hop on a flight from Perugia to London or Barcelona, or even New York, was exhilarating. The long slump after the *anni di piombo* stopped, and the world of opportunity was no longer a dream on a screen. He'd even married a Californian, one of those blonde, corn-fed girls that every Italian male fantasised about. But then, economies all over the world had crashed and with it, his marriage.

The nightingales drilled into his skull and pierced his heart. At night, he lay flat on his back, rolled on to his stomach, snored briefly, woke with a start, got up to check his doors and windows and then began the whole routine again. He could never catch up on sleep, he was one of the walking dead. Ruth and her friends always seemed to need him to help them, and he had to be there, but all he longed for was rest.

He thought of the old ladies (*le signore*) as friends as well as his employers, and sometimes they spoke to him about intimate family matters. But at other times they spoke to him quite sharply, making it clear that he was not one of them, after all. Ruth had rescued him from near penury when his life had fallen apart, recommending his services to the many other expatriates she knew, but she was his chief employer. He had the keys to La Rosa, and looked after all her animals, including Dash, when she made brief trips back to London. But if she were to discover what he'd done, he had no doubt that would all be over.

Imagine if the man he had shot were to be found by Ruth or Diana! They were close enough as neighbours for it to be conceivable. What if those two black guys, Xan and Blessing, were to be involved? They were nothing like the crazy indigent who had come to his door, naturally, but he could see that they didn't trust him. Each time Enzo passed the beggars hawking their rubbish at the town gates, with their funny clothes and little hats and dark skin, he felt a wince of fear. Was the intruder one of these? None of the Santornese gave them money, but too many foreigners did – not only tourists, but people who should know better, like Ruth and Diana.

'I always think, there but for the grace of God go I,' Ruth said.

'No, *Dottoressa*, you are too smart,' he replied.

'Yes, and why do you think my family wanted me to become a doctor? Maybe some of these folk have skills Italy could use.'

Enzo snorted. What kind of skills could savages have? He'd seen a TV programme about an African tribe that insisted boys killed a lion with their spear before they were accepted as men – pretty impressive, he had to admit, but try killing a wild boar! In the old days, Italians had to get down on one knee while others drove a boar, squealing with rage, towards him. The only place where a boar could be killed was through the mouth, and to do this a hunter had to keep completely still while two hundred kilos of fierce, hairy hog ran at him. If the hunter succeeded, it would be neatly spitted for a roast. If not, well, those wicked tusks were worse than claws.

I am so tired, Enzo thought, rubbing his eyes.

More and more of Ruth's children and grandchildren were arriving by the day, and he was being kept busy shuttling to and from the airport in Perugia. He managed with three cups of black coffee inside him, and the work was not so bad because he enjoyed driving, and meeting people. Ruth's sons were good people, two of them doctors too, and one a musician. They'd been teenagers when he was a boy, friendly and kind, willing to play ping-pong with him on long summer holidays and teaching him and his sister Patrizia to speak English. Strange to see them now, as greying, middle-aged men. He was astonished by Josh's enormous brood. In Italy even two children were considered a big family, and Josh had *five*, ranging from thirteen to thirty.

'You have enough grandchildren for your own football team,' he teased Ruth.

'Yes, I am blessed.'

'Only Olly is still to come?'

'He and his best man are flying from City Airport,' Ruth answered. 'It means he loses less time.'

'Of course,' Enzo said. 'I am sure he must be eager to be with his bride.'

The day before, he had driven Tania to Florence for a visit to the Uffizi gallery. He had never been there before, actually – that kind of thing was for tourists – and was a little anxious about navigating Florence's torturous one-way system, and parking. But fortunately, Raff accompanied them.

'I've never been to the Uffizi either,' he said, from the back seat. 'I'm looking forward to seeing the Botticellis.'

'I last saw them as a child, on a family holiday,' Tania said. 'I've never forgotten it.'

'Is that why you grew your hair so long?'

'No. But it is why I'm being sponsored by a leading brand of shampoo to vlog about it.'

Everything she did in Florence had been planned and staged. People stopped and stared. It was like being with a celebrity, Enzo thought, then realised that, to some, that was what she was.

'*Che bella!*'

'*Bellissima!*'

'*Madonna grazia!*'

Enzo kept by her protectively, and so, he noticed, did Raff, but Tania was completely composed. She talked brightly to her mobile, videoing herself and posing for selfies. In one interlude, Enzo asked, interestedly, 'How do you know how to do that? To position yourself in the best light, and angles?'

143

'I just do,' she said. 'I'm a visual person. Would you mind holding my mobile and videoing me *here?*'

As soon as she removed her sunglasses and pulled off her baseball cap at the entrance to the Uffizi, allowing the torrent of hair to ripple down to her thighs, she caused a sensation. There were audible gasps, even from those who could not, normally, lift their eyes from their own mobile phones.

Within moments, the crowds had fallen silent. Some recognised her from social media, but many others thought she must be a famous model or an actress. A hundred cameras were lofted into a salute as she walked into the museum.

'Venus! Smile at me!' one of the bolder men called. She gazed past them, blankly, just as if she really were the Goddess of Love. Tania never made the weird pouting face that most other women thought necessary; she just looked ravishing and completely unattainable. Enzo and Raff followed in her wake.

It had all been so that she could pose in front of Botticelli's *Venus*, wearing a brand that would be duly advertised in tiny print – an act that was supposedly forbidden, but the Director of the Museum himself came out to meet her. He was a German, and so a Romantic. Not only did he kiss Tania's hand, he clicked his heels together. Enzo regarded this with extreme distaste, Raff laughed aloud, and Tania almost smiled.

'Welcome,' he said. 'For this extraordinary resemblance to la bella Simonetta, we are enchanted.'

Tania inclined her head. Enzo, designated once again to hold her mobile to video the scene, tried not to let his hand shake. He had only ever seen the image, or details of *The Birth of Venus*, reproduced on a thousand postcards, fridge magnets and ashtrays. The real thing, being almost life-size, stunned him.

Of course, it was ridiculous – a woman standing on a giant scallop shell, like a pink prawn in an antipasto, covered only in her own hair. The entwined flying gods, wolf-whistling at her, the rather stern older goddess attempting to throw an embroidered cloak over Venus's serene nudity, the distinctly suggestive bulrushes standing upright in one corner – what was it if not a divine comedy?

'I love my shampoo,' Tania said, in her soft, confiding voice. 'It takes such a lot of product to have the best hair, and I had ever so many problems until I discovered . . . '

When she finished her little video, Raff remarked, 'Do you realise that the exact centre of *The Birth of Venus* is her groin?'

'What?'

'Precisely where her right hand is holding that handful of hair. I've got an app that finds the centre of any image, and X marks the spot. That's what she's trying to hide with one hand.'

Tania said, in an icy tone, 'Really?'

'Unless she's pleasuring herself with her middle finger,' Raff said cheerfully. 'That's a possibility.'

'It's not porn,' Tania said. 'She's born out of sea-foam.'

'The severed genitals of her father, according to myth. Her body is weird, isn't it? One arm is thin, and the other gigantic.'

'She is quite fat, actually,' Tania said.

'And here she is again, in the *Primavera*, dancing with herself in triplicate. Poor Botticelli, he really was obsessed.'

'Why is that girl in the torn dress running away?' Enzo asked.

Raff consulted his cell phone.

'She's a nymph, Chloris, escaping the cold wind of March. That's why flowers are coming out of her mouth. He wants to rape her, only she turns into Flora.'

Tania looked distressed.

'So, she's the same person?' Enzo asked.

'Think of it as a strip cartoon going from right to left.

145

Chloris changes into the goddess of spring with a basket of flowers, which is why she's smiling, and Venus – wearing clothes this time – blesses them all. It's supposed to have been painted to celebrate a wedding,' Raff said.

'Whose?'

'One of the Medicis, probably. Some people think that the man reaching up, who might be Mercury, is Lorenzo de' Medici.'

'I thought he was the gardener,' said Tania. Her eyes met Raff's, and they each looked away immediately.

'I like it,' said Enzo dubiously, 'but why is the Cupid shooting with a blindfold? No hunter would shoot that way.'

'Isn't Cupid often painted like that? It means that love can strike the most unlikely people. Though personally, I think that, when you truly love someone, you see them as nobody else can,' said Raff.

'Look how his arrow is pointing to the nymph who looks most like the Venus in the other painting. Who are they, anyway?'

'The Three Graces. Beauty, Truth and Love.'

'No, that's in the Bible, Tania. Nobody seems quite sure who they are in Greek myth. Beauty, fertility, charm, elegance, mirth . . . '

'In Italian,' Enzo said, 'it's not a compliment to call three women the three graces. It means they are too much together, and are quite annoying.'

'Because they should be paying attention to men instead?'

'Let's keep going,' Tania said, as Enzo shrugged and more visitors crowded in. She bundled her hair back into the hat, put her sunglasses on and walked away.

Raff said, 'I hope the Uffizi gets some money from your vlogging, Tania.'

'It will get even more visitors, so yes,' Tania answered. 'Museums always need visitors, don't they?'

'You have a lot of fans,' Enzo remarked.

'They're called followers,' Tania said.

'So, you are the leader of a religion?'

'No. I'm just selling them something. Though so, I suppose, is religion.'

The thing Enzo had found most moving at the Uffizi was not the paintings of naked women or praying Madonnas, but a marble sculpture of a dog. Its attitude and expression were just like those of Violetta, though it also reminded him of arguments he'd had with Diana about his treatment of her.

'Why do you always keep your dog chained up? She gets no exercise.'

'She exercises herself.'

'Running up and down the yard like a prisoner? A dog is a creature who gives you its whole heart,' Lady Evenlode said, with awful sternness. 'That is why they are carved into tombs as a symbol of fidelity. Don't you understand: Violetta would die for you? Your duty, as her master, is to give her food, and shelter, and *walks*.'

'I do not have the time.'

'Why not? Dogs deserve love. Sometimes,' Diana said, 'they are the only living things that do love us.'

Repeatedly since he shot his intruder, Enzo had been woken by howls, or cries. It was hard to tell whether these were animal or human, whether he was awake or dreaming. Was it a dog? Was it wolves? The worst calls were almost indistinguishable from those of a woman screaming.

Down again into the welcome oblivion of sleep, but then another terrible, high-pitched shriek woke him, and echoed round his head. He sat up, so very tired, and the next moment the dawn branded his face with blinding stripes.

Once again, Enzo walked blearily down the track for what felt like the twentieth time in a week. He felt ill with insomnia, but he *had* to find out what was going on in the valley. Whether it was torture or sex, the sounds were unendurable, and if it led him to the man he had shot, then it was time he faced him.

He took his gun with him, not his pistol this time but his rifle. The hunting season was long over, but if he did find a trapped animal was making those sounds, it would be better to dispatch it quickly. At any rate, he wasn't going into the valley without a weapon.

The most likely source of the cries was the mill-house. A long time ago, it had been the focus of activity every year when the olive harvest came. Now, it was abandoned, a place where couples came to make out away from prying eyes, because its roof was still intact. Who owned it these days, nobody was quite sure. Successive foreigners had tried and failed to turn it into something habitable. There had been attempts a decade ago by some sort of German commune to convert it into an art school, and another as a kind of *agriturismo*, but these had failed and it was soon boarded up then broken into again. The villagers further down the road avoided it.

'It's a *casino*,' they told each other, and indeed, like a number of other abandoned dwellings, it had operated briefly as a brothel.

If the noises were caused by a dog, then Enzo intended to do something to help it. Diana had been right. Poor Violetta, he hadn't even given her a blanket to lie on, just bits of cardboard and newspapers, because she was an animal. He knew that he probably hadn't fed her enough, either, because hunting dogs

148

were supposed to be kept hungry, or taken her to the vet to make sure she didn't get worms.

What a terrible owner I was, he thought. If he saw her now, he would catch her in his arms as she bounded towards him, her sharp little face grinning, and give her the best meat and the warmest place in his comfortless home to sleep. Only it was all too late. She'd died in his arms, and his grief over this was so mixed up with his grief over his daughter that sometimes he thought he was going mad.

So many regrets! It was the worst thing about middle age, far more so than his increasing stiffness and decreasing eyesight. If only I could put things right, he thought. If only I could hear Fede's voice, and know that we would meet again. He once had no doubt at all that one day, he would meet his mother again in heaven, but it is the absence of those still living that hurts those who love them more, adding an edge to loss.

Enzo approached the mill very cautiously from the back. Nobody came this way. Its walls were densely overgrown with corded ivy like bristling serpents, and being next to the river, it was always damp. The exhaustion that dogged his every step made the earth seem to tilt beneath him, and yet his instinct as a hunter made him tread softly. What if someone was actually being harmed in there? What if he found a scene of torture? All kinds of dreadful things happened when you had migrants living among you. He could be attacked and killed himself, he lived all alone. Nobody from the village would investigate, least of all Stefano, who spent his life driving his lorry, and who was probably as unfaithful to his wife as Enzo had been faithful to his own. He had always hated going down this way, even with his sister and the Guardi boys when they were all at elementary school together. It was where you were most likely to encounter a viper, its thick, dark, diamond-patterned coils pouring slowly across your path, because unlike ordinary snakes the poisonous kind weren't afraid of humans. Enzo kept a vial of anti-venom in his fridge, just in case, and had urged Diana to do the same (Ruth didn't need telling.) She'd retorted, 'If I get bitten, it'd be a quick exit at least.'

He could no longer tell whether the greyness all around was his own mental mists or those that rose up from the valley after dawn. The river's clattering, as it poured into the mill-pond, was the sound of fear itself.

What he was looking for, Enzo could not have said. The high, curving walls of the millpond, trembling with tiny ferns, seemed stained by perpetual gloom. The waters that had once turned the mill wheel (now long gone) were as black as ink.

Yet something was floating in its depths: three or four pale objects that looked like misshapen plastic bags, were suspended just below the surface. They kept in formation together, moving very slowly. Puzzled, he stared at these for what felt like a long time, his heart beating strongly in his ears. Then his eyes understood what they were seeing.

The largest bulge was that of bare buttocks. The smaller bulges were those of hands. The body lay face-down, as if someone were trying to look, sightlessly, into the depths of the pool.

'Porca Madonna!' Enzo whispered.

He had no doubt that whoever this was, they were very definitely dead. The corpse had a waterlogged look to it, and its only motion came from the water itself. Enzo stared, his heart in his mouth.

What to do? Nobody swam in the millpond even on the very hottest day of midsummer. It was too deep, too dark, too cold and too sinister. Its waters came down from where the mountains were tipped with snow, and travelled through deep valleys and dense woods where little light reached it. Further down by the ford, the river relaxed and spread, changing character as it became shallow and warm so that village children could bathe there; but not here. Not ever here.

He shivered, watching the blobs of flesh in the misty morning light. It was as if the evil everyone sensed in the millpond had reached out and caught this person, whoever it was.

A man, he was sure.

No sounds came from the mill-house, but that didn't mean it was empty. He waited, listening for any noise that might indicate another human presence, but eventually put down his gun and reached over with a long stick to pull the body closer. It was an awkward business but when he finally hooked the stick into a garment, the corpse drifted heavily towards the wall of the pool.

Death was something he was used to, as a hunter, but the idea of touching the body filled him with nausea. He could see the discoloured skin of the hands had begun to wrinkle and peel away, a revolting version of washerwoman's fingers. He could not turn it over, not that he wished to. Yes, definitely a man. Even without seeing the face, Enzo judged him to be somewhere between thirty and forty. His hair was close-cropped, slightly greying, and his body was muscular though fatty. To judge by the trainer on one foot and the absence of a jacket, he was not a hunter.

He'd watched TV thrillers in which violence didn't matter because it was all make-believe. Yet these days, it seemed as if the seventy years of peace had been the dream. War and murder were no longer events that happened on other continents, across the seas, but right under people's noses, everywhere, just as it had been when Enzo's grandfather was young.

One thing gave Enzo a little hope. This corpse was white. His intruder had been a black man, he was quite sure, and his hair was not short.

'*Chi sei?*' Enzo whispered. Whoever the man was, he was not likely to be local. All the same, a body should not be left here, floating in the dark pool like a soul in limbo. Had it just popped up from the depths of the pond? Or was no one even leaving the mill-house to look for him?

At the thought of what he had come to find his ears once again caught a faint cry. Was it a creaking timber, a human being, or an animal? He sniffed the air, and at last caught the whiff of woodsmoke.

His instincts had been right. There must be squatters, or migrants, or gypsies living here. Perhaps this dead man was one of them, as yet undiscovered. Or perhaps something else was going on here, in this abandoned place at the end of the track.

Very slowly, Enzo began to inch forwards.

12

Tania's Bad Hair Day

Tania's tresses always had to be in perfect condition, which meant that every fourth day was fully booked. People laughed when she said that it took her at least five hours to deal with it, but they had no idea what dealing with over a metre of human hair involved.

At night, she slept with it loosely braided and propped above her head on a silk pillowcase. (Tania was, in fact, a brand ambassador for Bliss Silk.) When she got up, the plait had to be unbraided and combed, gradually uncoiling itself as its weight dragged it straighter. Olly had always been fascinated by this, though her locks had a habit of becoming entangled with him.

'Ow, ow, be careful!' she would cry, in pain.

'Sometimes I feel like there are three of us in this relationship – me, you and your hair,' he said. If she was in a good mood, she would allow him to brush it, reverently, until her body was covered in a long golden veil. If she was not, she would refuse to let him touch her.

'You don't understand how sensitive it is,' she said.

'I know you're very sensitive.'

'No, not me. *It*.'

Her hair did seem to have a life of its own. As soon as she was tense or unhappy, the million snakes that lived in her scalp began to writhe and burn. She could almost hear them hissing all the things she couldn't say aloud.

Nobody who had ever seen her expression would have guessed this, but then it was none of their business, was it?

Hey, spoilt bitch-face, was how some followers replied to her Insta posts. She always blocked them, but they still got to her, and the thing about being a social media celebrity was that although she had an agent, she had no publicist or other support. She was a one-woman show, everything had to be generated by her, and although it was less bad for her #mentalhealth than going into an office, it was not an easy way to earn a living.

Tania had panic attacks so often that she actually set an alarm on her mobile so she could lock herself in a loo at a certain time and scream silently. She never, ever cried, any more than she laughed. Her work was all about projecting an air of serene confidence, because everything on social media was about #lookingperfect and #beingkind.

Maybe this was why she wanted to help Blessing. He looked calm, but Tania, despite being perennially told off for her self-ishness and insensitivity, knew that he was as bewildered and fearful as she felt about pretending to be normal.

'Don't worry,' she said to him. He got so many small things wrong! Tania had always taken it for granted that men would open doors for her to walk through, but it never occurred to him to do so for her until she stopped and told him, quietly, that it was what was expected. Obviously, it must be different

154

in Zimbabwe, but Blessing only had to be shown something once. Nor had he been told that it was rude to burp after a meal.

'In my country, it is a compliment to do this,' he'd said, on seeing the general surprise.

He was a gentle person, though, and she never once felt anxious or uncomfortable when alone with him. How odd that Olly should be his friend! All his usual mates were large, confident, rich and white.

'What do you see yourself doing in the future?' he asked her, as they lay at either ends of the double hammock strung between two olive trees above the house. 'Do you want many children, or just one?'

'I haven't thought much about it.'

'What kind of future do you wish for?'

Tania's mother had once asked her something like this, and she'd replied, 'I want to find a nice man and get married.'

Polly had been appalled.

'That's such a very old-fashioned thing to aspire to.' Then she'd said, 'I suppose feminism is about having choices. But wouldn't it be better to have a career?'

As far as Tania could see, finding a man to marry was far, far harder than having a career. Anyone could have a job now, if they were a graduate, but marriage was something her generation of girls fantasised about because it was impossible in a world of online dating, where people treated each other as disposable. Most of all, she longed for someone she could trust. Falling in love was a hopeless dream, but she hoped she could trust Olly.

Not enjoying sex was Tania's deepest, dreariest secret. If she could cry, it was what she would cry about, because she was so mortified, and everyone was supposed to have a wonderful time unless something was wrong with them. The only thing girls were supposed to be ashamed of was if they had a single pubic hair.

Olly was clever, clean, rich and good-looking. He was also not into the gross stuff that most guys wanted because they watched porn all the time.

'Are you OK?' he would ask anxiously.

'Yes,' Tania said. 'Absolutely.'

Sometimes, she could feel something begin to build inside her, like a sneeze, but it never amounted to anything. She copied the expressions and sounds actresses made in movies, and that seemed to convince him. He'd had loads of girl-friends, but he'd only been in love once before.

'My first girlfriend was so different from you, you know,' he told her. The snakes in Tania's scalp tensed immediately.

'Really?'

'Yes.'

'Different how?'

'Less beautiful, but, you know, lovely. I really cared for her.'

Oh God, Tania thought.

'Why didn't you stay together?'

'We were too young,' Olly said. 'And Granny didn't approve.'

'What's Ruth got to do with it?'

'She thought that I could do better, I guess.'

Tania *was* better. Hadn't she had a perfectly curated child-hood? Hadn't she gone to two of the best private girls' schools in Britain? Even university had been OK, because she hadn't been in one of those awful, shared student houses but a nice flat in Clifton that her father had rented for her. Working in London had been less OK but she was saved by the pandemic, and once she had begun influencing it was all fine. She was perfectly comfortable returning to her mother's house in

Camden Town, and could live in a bubble inside a bubble inside a bubble.

But this had palled once she walked into Olly's place on their first date.

Olly's flat was at the top of a former Victorian warehouse on the South Bank, and it consisted of one enormous room with views across, up and down the Thames. The ceiling was double height, going up into a geometrical forest of blackened beams. Otherwise, it was no more than a shell, with a basic kitchen at one end and a basic bathroom at the other, both left by the developer. Olly had no idea what to do with his acquisition, other than put in a big bed, and a Peloton bike in front of one of the tiny balconies suspended above the river. He was too busy making his millions to spend them.

'I suppose I ought to hire a decorator,' he said, seeing her reaction.

Tania walked around in a kind of dream. What a space! The flat was only accessible by a lift that brought you straight up into the lobby. Nobody could arrive uninvited. The wide waters of the Thames glittered and surged below.

'You like it?' he asked, a little shyly.

'More than anything,' she answered. 'Only, I think there's a lot more that could be done with it.'

'Why don't you?' he said, and that was how they really began dating. He adored her, and she fell in love with his flat.

She decamped from her mother's, and they stayed together all through that strange, peaceful time when nobody was allowed out except to exercise for an hour a day. They could both work from home. A glorious spring segued smoothly into a brilliant summer, and while poor old people died in their thousands, Olly and Tania ran together along the banks to the river, fleet with youth, money and optimism. The

Vispring acquired a tall, upholstered headboard and Irish linen sheets, and Tania added gorgeous velvet sofas in ochre and umber, Afghan rugs, cashmere throws and porcelain bathroom fittings with chrome taps. She had already become a beauty vlogger, but now it became more about #lifestyle, and her followers doubled then redoubled because everyone had become obsessed by home decoration. He gave her a credit card to buy what she needed online, and she videoed herself painting, decorating, and dancing with spanners. She was at ease on camera as she could never be in person. By the time the first lockdown ended, she had one million followers. Four months later, she had two. An agent got in touch, and then the sponsorship and free stuff arrived.

'I can't believe it. It's like magic,' she said. 'Just me and an iPhone, and I've suddenly earned, well, I know it's nothing compared to you, but it's six figures.'

Olly was delighted.

'You could be doing this professionally,' he said.

'I think I *am*,' said Tania.

Why not get married? Her followers loved the news of her engagement, too. At a time when weddings had been indefinitely postponed, Tania's caught the public imagination. All over the world, people were now emotionally and materially invested in her, and as the big day approached, she was gaining thousands more followers by the hour. Her vlogging was no longer about #stylegram, it was about #romance and a #Tuscan wedding.

Both the Noble and the Viner families were largely unaware of this. Olly himself was far too serious to be on any platform other than LinkedIn. He regarded Tania's influencing as a feminine hobby, akin to baking.

'You do whatever makes you happy, darling.'

He was very clever, the sort of cleverness that she couldn't understand but which was all to do with being able to predict the next big thing. She didn't know how rich he was, but he had moved beyond ordinary greed. People didn't understand what he did or why he was paid so much, because they thought it must be like high-street banking when really, he would say, it was more like being a Premier League footballer. His job fascinated him, but he also kept saying, ruefully, that he was going to get out of hedge funding soon and do something more real. When he said this his boss, Angus, would laugh and remark, 'That's what everyone says, you know, and they never do. The money is just too good.'

Tania sat in the sunshine, dreamily pulling her fingers through her damp hair to dry it, and thinking of nothing at all.

'How long does it take you?' Raff asked. 'Your hair, I mean.'

'An hour to wash, and three to dry.'

'It must be a pain for you.'

Tania stopped, surprised. 'It's my USP.'

'Your what?'

'My unique selling point.'

'Are you selling yourself?' Raff asked.

She couldn't tell whether he was serious or not. She watched him weeding for a while, then replied, 'Everyone sells something of themselves, don't they? I mean, you're selling your labour.'

Raff said, 'My labour is something that I *do*. You're selling something that you *are*.'

'Useless but decorative' was how her father had described her. She'd hoped that he might respect her, just a little, for getting married to a banker, but Theo had already sent his apologies for not being able to fly over from New York to walk her down the aisle.

'Cupcake, I have a really big deal going through and I just can't move the date. I'll send you some money.'

'OK, Daddy,' said Tania drearily. He'd been doing stuff like this all through her life, having basically checked out of fatherhood when she was ten. 'I can give myself away. I guess.'

It was all fine. The studio cottage was going down very well on her vlog. Even finding a black insect like a miniature lobster on the walls, which Raff said was a scorpion, hadn't freaked her out, too much. She was looking forward to her big day. Her agent said that it was looking like she might have an audience of four million by then. Every time she added another hundred thousand to her site, the money cascaded in.

'There are so many brands who want in on Tanyaa, you wouldn't believe! Everything from lingerie to luxury safaris.'

She watched two peacock butterflies dance round a rosemary bush, but her tranquillity had been ruffled. Selling herself indeed! It was so judgemental and old-fashioned. Her father's indifference and her mother's dismay both hurt, but somehow it was Raff's view that really got under her skin.

'What do you really want to do with your life?' Raff asked. Tania paused in her hair-drying.

'Blessing asked me that, too. I'd like to be ordinary; I think.'

'Well, why can't you?'

'Because that sort of life isn't ordinary any more. And I'm a brand.'

'I thought only cattle were branded,' Raff said. 'Not people.'

She wondered whether he was flirting with her. She couldn't make him out, but then she couldn't make anyone out. He was terribly annoying, in his happy-clappy way.

Sitting round the fire pit after supper had become a thing at the houseparty. It was now warm enough to eat out, watching the wheeling swallows turn into bats halfway across the violet sky. Every evening, Raff would bring out his guitar. He played well, and had a melodious, slightly hoarse voice.

> *A fine young man it was indeed,*
> *Mounted on his milk-white steed.*
> *He rode, he rode, and he rode all alone*
> *Until he came to lovely Joan.*
> *'Good morning to you, my pretty maid.'*
> *And 'Twice good morning to you, sir,' she said.*
> *He tipped her the wink, and she rolled her dark eye.*
> *Says he to himself, 'I'll be there by and by.'*
> *'Oh, don't you think those pooks of hay*
> *A pretty place for us to play?*
> *So come with me, my sweet young thing*
> *And I'll give you my golden ring.'*

Tania, hearing this, thought of Olly's boss Angus, whom she feared and loathed. He had propositioned her twice, and been incredulous when she'd turned him down.

'Are you really intending to be faithful?'

'Yes, actually.'

'I give it five weeks,' he said.

She could never tell Olly this, because he thought of Angus as his friend as well as his mentor. He had other mates, but Angus was the one who had brought him on as a junior partner, and made him a star in his own right. He was flying out with Olly as his best man.

> *He took off his ring, his ring of gold*
> *Says, 'My pretty miss, do this behold*
> *I'll give it to you for your maidenhead.'*
> *And her cheeks they blushed like the roses red.*

> 'Come give me that ring into my hand
> And I will neither stay nor stand
> For your ring is worth much more to me
> Than twenty maidenheads,' said she.

People were giggling, and Tania turned away, angrily. Did *all* rich men think all women were for sale? Was that what Olly had thought as well? When he'd given her a credit card to spend on his flat, had that been a bribe rather than a mark of respect? Raff looked up, caught her eye, and grinned.

> But as he made for the pooks of hay,
> She leapt on his horse and rode away.
> He called, he called, but he called in vain,
> For Joan she ne'er looked back again.
> Nor did she think herself quite safe
> Until she came to her true love's gate.
> She'd robbed him of his horse and ring
> And she left him to rage in the meadows green.

Everyone clapped, even Tania.

'Go, Joan!' said Ruth.

'An early feminist,' Polly remarked.

Tania did not need anyone else's gold, thank you. All the same, what would Olly do if she ran to *his* gate and told him about Angus? That was the question which, even now, she couldn't be sure of. Perhaps the question was, what would she *wish* him to do?

Raff's just another idiot, she said to herself, watching while he watered the pots in the courtyard. She knew, though, that he would have punched Angus on the nose. He was old fashioned, right down to his unbranded trainers.

Her mobile rang.

'How are the preparations going, sweet pea?' Olly asked in her ear.

'Fine. Everyone is very busy.'

'That's what I like to hear! How is La Rosa looking?'

'Raff's made the garden really nice.'

'Oh, yes. Poor old Riff-Raff,' said Olly. 'Where Granny finds her waifs and strays, I don't know.'

'Isn't there a website?'

'Oh yes. Wafters or something. They're useful idiots, slaving on people's farms out of pure ethics, unlike those of us who have to toil for a living.'

Looking at Raff as he moved about, it struck Tania that he was very fit, not in a gym-toned way but as someone used to hard physical labour. Not tall and slim, like Olly, though not short or fat either. He had excellent manners, never brash or unkind, even to poor Lord Evenlode, and always—At this point, Tania saw Raff had noticed her staring at him, and looked away. Olly chatted on into her ear-bud, and she made the appropriate noises. She sometimes wondered whether he ever listened to what she said. Eventually, her call ended.

'I need to tie up that vine over your head, if you don't mind?'

Tania shifted into a different seat. 'You never seem to stop working.'

'There's a lot to do.'

'When we first came, last autumn, you looked different.'

'I'd been ill.'

'Are you better now?'

'Yes.'

Tania said graciously, 'You've made it very pretty. Tell me what these are called.'

'Rosa Banksiae Lutea.'

163

Tania repeated this, dreamily. 'Did you plant it for me?'

'No. I just gave it a bit of TLC. Plants are like people. They like being looked after.'

Even when he was chatting, he was continually training, pruning, planting, tweaking, weeding and watering them. She watched, fascinated.

'I'm hopeless at gardening. I have grey fingers, not green ones.'

Tania had filled Olly's minute balcony with pots of pansies and miniature roses from Borough Market. It was all about the moment you posted them on Instagram, and then they died. She thought it must be because she was cursed.

'What should you do after they've finished flowering?'

'Roses need deadheading and feeding. Annuals flower their hearts out, and then it's over when they make seeds. So once they finish, take them out and compost them. Perennials, you feed up, cut back and they come back next year better than ever.'

'What a pity you can't do that with people. It's so sad thinking of everyone getting as old as Olly's grandmother and her friends.'

It was hard to believe that Ruth, with her dyed hair and bulgy body, had been the pretty, petite woman in her photographs, or that Diana Evenlode was formerly as beautiful as a model. How was it possible that these ancient, wrinkled people had ever been remotely young? Did they still feel young, inside, or were they as worn out as they looked? Tania, at the zenith of her loveliness, regarded them with a mixture of pity and horror.

'You can't stop ageing, Tania,' Raff said. 'The only alternative is death, which is worse.'

'Doesn't Lord Evenlode disgust you?'

'No.'

Tania made a face. 'Surely he'd be better in a home?'

'No home is better than your own home. Diana needs more help, but what she's doing is admirable, don't you think?'

'It looks grim.'

Raff said, 'Life isn't just what you look like. Dying and being born are both pretty brutal. In-between is supposed to be better, I hear.'

Tania said, 'I've asked my mother about giving birth. She says she can't remember.'

'Mine said it was the best day of her life.'

He sounded so pleased when he said this that she asked, 'Are you close to her?'

'Yes. My mum divorced my father soon after I was born, so it was just the two of us.'

'Was that lonely?'

'Not really. We get on really well.'

Tania said, 'My parents are divorced, too. I suppose almost everyone's are.'

'Not necessarily,' Raff said. 'I don't think any of Ruth's sons are, for instance.'

A large yellow and black hornet droned past, and settled on the table.

Tania yelped, and made to bat it away, but Raff caught her hand in a hard grip and said, 'It'll sting you if it gets frightened. Just keep still.'

She hated being touched, but obeyed. Even the snakes in her scalp froze.

'I'm terrified of those things,' Tania said. 'Can you kill it?'

'It's not the Asian kind that eats bees, so no. They're important to the eco-system.'

The hornet cleaned its face meditatively, then flew off.

'Thank God. I hate nature,' Tania said.

'Why?'

'She hates women. It's like the Venus painting we saw. All she wants is to cover us up, quick, because we're going to die as soon as we fulfil our biological destiny.'

Raff looked at her consideringly.

'Women don't have to have children these days, unless they want to, do they? But most women seem to like them.'

'Well, I'm *not most women*,' said Tania, with hauteur. She drew her fingers again through her drying locks, careful not to snag the sapphire ring on her left hand, soothing her scalp. 'Why isn't it enough to live *my* life?'

'You are perfectly entitled to live it whichever way you please,' Raff said. 'Nevertheless, life calls to life.'

Tania was silent. People, men especially, never talked to her in this way.

'What do you mean?'

'Just that children are the only immortality any of us can claim.'

Tania lost her temper. 'Oh, fuck off!' she said. 'I've never met anyone so – so – so – *presumptuous*.'

The endless entitlement of men! Every day she would get some semi-literate message on one of her social media accounts asking her for 'intimate' photographs, or sending her a dick-pic. As if anyone could love their hideous genitals more than they did. As if the one thing that they could think of doing with a piece of technology more advanced than that which had put people on the Moon was to take pictures of their penis.

Tania had only a few more days to wait, and then she would be removed from this. She longed for a nice house with a big garden and a family-sized car. She longed for bucket-and-spade

166

holidays, and book clubs and a dog, perhaps a golden retriever. She longed, above all, for the snakes in her scalp to slither away and leave her in peace. If the price for this was having a child, she could maybe just about bear it, because all those things that her mother's generation had rejected, she wanted.

Besides Ruth, the only other guest who was nice to her here was Blessing. He was the first friend of Olly's she'd ever taken to, being gentle, quiet and sensitive. The Zimbabwean was looking much better now he was rested. He clapped his hands twice when she gave him gifts, and made her a little bow.

'You are very kind to me, Miss Tania.'

'Just Tania, please. It's all about moisturising,' she said seriously, and she even let him comb her hair, because she understood he was not and never would be predatory to her sex. She didn't flinch once, but noticed that he winced with pain when he lifted his arm.

'What's wrong?'

'I have a small wound.'

'May I see?'

Blessing nodded, and turning his back, shyly slipped off his T-shirt.

'You poor thing! I can put on a better dressing, if you like?'

'OK,' Blessing said.

She found Ruth's first-aid box, and peeled off the clumsy bandage he had put on himself.

'It looks angry. I think I need to disinfect it again?'

She wondered how he had come by a wound in such an awkward place.

'There are bits of grit or something around it that need to come out, too. I can probably get them with tweezers, though I can ask Ruth. She used to be a doctor, I think?'

'I would prefer you to do this,' Blessing said, at once.

167

'I suppose my eyesight is better.'

Tania picked out the grit, very carefully, disinfected the wounds and put on a big square of new dressing. She felt pleased by the result.

'*Maita basa.*'

'What does that mean?'

'It means thank you, in Shona.'

'I could mention your lost luggage on my vlog, if you like,' she offered. 'Did you really fly to Rome? It's the worst airport in Europe. Olly should have told you to go to Perugia, or Milan. Milan is a wonderful city. It's got all the best things about Italy, but it's twenty-first century.'

'I don't care about my luggage,' he said. 'What I need, I have in my heart, and the Cloud. I am sorry I have no bridal gift for you.'

Tania said, 'I really, truly, don't need any more *things*.'

She was upset that he, too, should believe this of her.

He asked, 'What were you like as a child? Were you happy?'

'Very. I had quite a conventional childhood, because Mum didn't work. I can't tell you how nice it was, how safe and peaceful. Just, you know, playing with my little brother and me, and talking and keeping house. But then my parents divorced and she went back to lawyering, and she was never around, just au pairs. And the thing is that you don't seem to stop needing your mother, even when you're a teenager. Do you?'

He said, 'My mother died last year, after a long sickness.'

'I'm so sorry. That must be awful.'

'It's why I was able to leave Zimbabwe,' he said. 'She left me enough money for my flight, and a visa to Europe.'

'Are you living in Italy, now?'

'For the present time. But what I wish is to go to England.

168

My father went there, before I was born, and I should like to find him.'

'There are lots of Zimbabweans in London,' Tania said, and she thought of Job, who had driven her and Polly to the airport. He'd had difficulties, too, though her mother helped him with those. And he was now a teacher in a local school. Maybe if Blessing came to London, they could meet up. Job was a good man, and she liked him.

She quite liked Enzo, too, when he wasn't being too attentive. He seemed so full of himself, until he mentioned that he had a daughter, now thirteen.

'She lives with her mother in the States. I miss her very much.'

'What is she called?'

'Fede. Federica, really. I post every day on Instagram for her, but I am not sure she even knows this, because unlike you, I only have thirty followers.'

Tania said, impulsively, 'Do you? What's your tag? If you follow me on Insta, I can follow you back, and then a lot more people would see your posts because I don't follow many other bloggers. That's how social media works, you know. It isn't just about your own life. It's like that Chinese parable of the long chopsticks.'

'I do not know this story,' Enzo said.

'Don't you? Well, there's this man who asks to see what heaven and hell are like. So, an angel takes him to each one, and in both the places, people are sitting at a table piled high with delicious food, but it can only be eaten with very long chopsticks. Only in heaven, everyone is happy and well fed, whereas in hell, everyone is starving. He asks why this is so, and the angel says, "Because in heaven, everyone feeds each other across the table. In hell, everyone just wants to feed themselves." Social media is like that, you see. If you only post about yourself, nobody is that interested. If you help other people, however, they help you back. Your daughter might not follow me, but other people she knows might, and eventually, she'll find you. Especially if I post a picture of you. It's worth a try.'

Enzo had been quite overcome, though all it had taken her was a couple of seconds.

He kept bringing various Viner siblings and cousins as they arrived, one after another, at Perugia airport. She could hear their voices calling.

'Let's play ping-pong!'

'Anyone for five-aside in the pool?'

'How about a run into town and back?'

On and on they went, and it made her feel super-tired just listening to them. Why couldn't they just be peaceful?

'You're always away with the fairies,' Olly liked to say. It had been far worse at school, where she was always being told things like, 'Take that look off your face', or, 'Don't look like that'.

'Like what?'

'Like *that*,' teachers would reply, as if she was doing it on purpose. It was bewildering, and all she wanted to do was hide.

Olly was arriving in a couple of days, and he always helped her seem more normal, though he often felt he had to explain jokes to her because she didn't laugh at any. She couldn't believe the long hours he put in: he woke at 4 a.m. to watch trading going on in Hong Kong and was in his office by 6 a.m. Even on holiday he spent six or seven hours researching and talking. He spent most of his waking life working, and although he earned a staggering amount, even taking two weeks off for a honeymoon had taken months to organise.

'Don't worry, it won't always be like this.'

'Why don't you leave now? Isn't the City full of horrible people shouting at each other?' she asked.

'You're thinking of films. Banking is about collective effort, and trust. Most of us have at least two or three degrees,' Olly said, adding, 'We're cerebral people, even when we do quite aggressive things.'

'Do you ever worry about the gulf between what you earn and what most people do?'

'Does a Premier League footballer? Banking is actually incredibly complex, but if there weren't thousands of people like me then – to take just one example – aeroplanes wouldn't have the fuel to take off from airports.'

'Is that necessarily a bad thing?' Tania knew she knew very little about the financial world, but she was always urging her followers to be Green.

'Yes, in the modern world,' Olly said patiently. 'Everything you eat, wear and use comes about through a series of trans-actions that most people never think about or see.'

'Do you need to be paid so much, though? I mean, even if I'm an influencer, I know that you can still only sleep in one bed, wear one pair of shoes, drive one car.'

Olly frowned. 'I pay a huge amount in taxes, and give a lot to charity. It's all legal, unlike what that Russian in the palazzo above La Rosa probably did to make his billions.'

'Is he a criminal, do you think?'

'Almost undoubtedly.'

'I'm glad you're not,' she said.

Tania was perfectly happy to drift along in Olly's wake. The richer someone is, the less friction they have to put up with, and any kind of disturbance upset her: she was like a nervous flier to whom the tiniest bump on an aeroplane journey feels like the start of catastrophe. She liked nice things, while also being nauseated by the sheer number of them being sent to her. Being with rich people was another matter, however. Angus had not only supported Brexit, he'd been one of the people who had backed it, making another fortune betting against sterling before it fell. Olly had voted Leave, too. She'd been horrified, but he told her that they'd voted 'heart over head', which made it sound slightly more romantic.

'It's not that I don't like Olly's crowd,' she'd said to her mother, once. 'It's just that I wish ideals were as important to them as the Dow Jones Index.'

'Are you *sure* you want to get married?' Polly asked. 'There are so many things you could do, darling.'

Yes, Tania insisted, she did. She really couldn't see any other future for herself.

13

Marta in the Dark

Out of the night that covers me
Black as the pit from pole to pole,
I thank whatever gods may be
For my unconquerable soul.

Marta was having a bad night, or a bad week, or perhaps a bad year. She'd given up pretending that she wasn't, though when her daughter Lottie called to ask how she was feeling she answered, briefly, 'Not so good today,' and moved the conversation on.

She sat very upright when playing the piano or at a table, and what it cost her to do this was something only the deepening lines on her face revealed. Marta was not vain, like Ruth, and indeed regarded her friend's attempts to hold on to her looks with dry amusement, though she did enjoy manicures, and having her hair cut once every six weeks: these things were a form of good manners to others, like plucking out facial hair. Diana's dentistry filled them both with horror.

'Maybe she likes looking like a horse? English people do love horses, I know.'

'The aristocracy all have teeth like that. It's like not wearing make-up. They think they're above it, somehow.'

'The Queen doesn't!'

'I think some of them look down on the royal family as German arrivistes.'

Ruth was a great believer in HRT, and had enthused about it to both Marta and Diana.

'Whenever my doctor tells me I am too old for it, I tell her that I will kill myself if I stop,' she declared at one of their kaffeeklatsch mornings. 'Hot flushes, insomnia, osteoporosis, brain fog, depression, no thank you.'

'Oh for heaven's sake,' Diana exclaimed. 'The menopause isn't all that bad. I barely noticed mine.'

But Ruth would not be dissuaded. 'Why should women have this misery? I flew in the face of nature every time I had sex and didn't get pregnant. The moment we're no longer fertile we're supposed to crawl away into a hole and die. Well, phooey to that!'

Diana never discussed sex, but they surmised that, having married at seventeen, she had only ever slept with one man and didn't care what he or anyone thought of her appearance.

Strange to think that the appalling Perry was elder brother of my own dear one, Marta mused, but then her husband had been a sport of nature, and he and Perry always held each other in mutual contempt. Before Diana came to live in Tuscany, the relations between her and Marta had been anything but sisterly. Edward had been deeply ashamed of what his father and grandfather had done in Zimbabwe, whereas Perry thought his family history something to be proud of.

One of the worst aspects of Diana's husband was the way he behaved towards her, even before his dementia.

'When I had my sixtieth birthday party, I invited all my mistresses to it,' he'd say to anyone who would listen. 'Diana put them all on the same table, but otherwise, she put up and shut up.'

Marta loathed him from that moment on, and after she'd told this story, so did Ruth.

'Isn't it odd how often women one likes have such appalling husbands?' she remarked to Ruth.

'Yes. There's that Robert Graves poem, isn't there: "Why have such scores of lovely, gifted girls/Married impossible men?" I can't remember how it goes on, but it's funny because it's true,' Ruth said. 'I suppose poor Diana didn't have much choice, did she? I'm glad my own family were just peasants.'

Marta would always repress a smile at this, because though it was true that Ruth's grandparents had come from a Polish shtetl, her parents had been successful Hollywood scriptwriters.

'You married Perry's brother, didn't you? Was he like that?'

'No,' Marta said. 'My Edward was never handsome. Though I thought him so, personally.'

'Ah, but when you love a person, your brain does something that makes them beautiful,' said Ruth. 'That's why people who are beautiful have such terrible love lives. People who see them believe they are in love, and they aren't.'

How nature makes fools of us all, Marta thought. Or perhaps, in Diana's case, what she gave her husband was not love but duty. It was hard to tell the difference. Diana sometimes dropped in on Marta for tea before collecting Perry, and Marta

175

always kept a supply of fruit and cheese especially for her sister-in-law because she looked, frankly, half-starved.

'Why do you let her scrounge off you?' Xan asked, not best pleased to find his great-aunt there during his visit. 'She's such a pain.'

'There is a certain satisfaction in being generous to someone who has been ungenerous to you,' Marta said. 'Besides, I like her. She has many faults, but so do we all.'

'She still thinks that being English is something to be frightfully proud of,' Xan said. 'I mean, why? Everyone who can possibly get an EU passport, does.'

'Well, so it was,' Marta answered. 'I was very glad to have a British passport myself, you know, when being English was associated with fairness and justice, and my own country with . . . its opposite. But countries do not stay the same, dear Xan. They change, just as people do.'

'Do you miss England, Oma?'

'Yes, my darling, and I miss your mother and sisters. But I am perfectly happy in Italy.'

The nights were bad, however. Recently, Marta found herself having a different nightmare: not the one about the Fall of Berlin, but that someone was standing in her bedroom.

She could not tell when this began, but knew only that the intruder was a black figure standing at the end of her bed. Marta wondered whether it was her death. Wasn't Death supposed to be blacker than the blackest shadow? Sometimes, she woke with a start, as if sensing some change in the air; but Otto snored loudly on, and if there were an intruder he would wake and bark. She wondered whether it was the painkillers she now took in increasing quantities playing tricks on her mind. She thought so often about the past – choices she had made and the people she had known, the things she had seen and felt – and she was increasingly certain that she did not have much time left. Death filled her with fear. If she could believe in heaven, and being with Edward again, it would not, but she was convinced of total oblivion. The only time she was less sure was when she played Bach, whose absolute certainty in the existence and goodness of God was somehow infectious, but even she could not do so all the time.

Coming to terms with the end of life looked like a quiet, contemplative affair from the outside, but it took up a great deal of private mental energy and resolve; for although there is nothing anyone can do about the inevitability of leaving life, it is the manner in which it is done that matters. She was in so much pain that she now began to envy Beatrix, but she was not living in Amsterdam, and she was determined to give her annual recital, even if it might be her last.

Marta had achieved many things – escape from the trag-edies of Berlin, a happy (if too short) marriage, motherhood and having three grandchildren. She had enjoyed many lovers before she met Edward (though none since), travelled widely and had a few good friends. But the central preoccupation of her life was always music, and this, she felt increasingly, was a curse not a blessing.

All creative lives end in failure, but especially that of an interpretative artist. Almost nothing remains but the memory of what they have done, and so they are the mayflies of art. There are few, if any, recordings of their achievements, and even where these exist, they can never capture the unique moment of a performance. Marta's two recordings had been excellent of their kind – but now, with a lifetime of experi-ence and craft, how much better she could have made them! She listened to them very occasionally and understood that although they had quality, they were mostly about her youth and promise, both of which, like energy and flexibility, she had taken for granted. Now that she was old and withered and knew so much more about what it was to be human, nobody wanted what she could give. No: not even those rare beings who loved music and should not care that the person who played it was no longer fresh and dewy but haggard and wrinkled and battered by living. That person could tell the young so much that they needed to know! But the world wanted an eternal spring, in all its hope, not the realism of winter.

But no, she reminded herself fiercely. It had *not* been just that she had once been young that her performances were worth hearing. Her recordings of Chopin, Debussy, Mozart and Bach had been heard and treasured by Ivanov and his mother. Somehow, miraculously, they had reached them in terrible circumstances, to be played again and again, feeding their souls with beauty and hope – exactly as art is supposed to do. What other reward could she ask? Everything else – money, fame, prizes – was trivial, compared to this. And now she was going to give her last recital, funded by a Russian of all people. As long as her body did not fail her, she might yet achieve something close to that of Dinu Lipatti at Besançon in 1950, who had transcended mortal agony to leave some of the greatest recordings of Chopin and Bach.

He had been thirty-three, however. She remembered an elderly neighbour many years ago, exclaiming, 'Oh to be seventy again!' who then laughed at Marta's horror, because to a younger person, seventy is unimaginably ancient. Only her seventies had turned out to be very interesting, just like her sixties, and here she was in her eighties, and though she was pained and weakened, she had her brain, and her hearing, and her hands, which was all she asked for besides a good night's rest. With this thought, Marta finally fell asleep and woke, refreshed.

She was still upset by her falling-out with Ivanov, how-ever. Even if their relationship was not exactly intimate, she had come to consider him as a kind of ally. But his rudeness towards her because of the way Otto behaved was unaccept-able. Allowing her dog to be thrown into her car like a bag of rubbish, and telling her to leave!

How dare he treat me so? Marta thought. I am an artist, and he is just a crook.

The time came when she was supposed to hear from the palazzo about her weekly private recital, and she did not. An hour went by, and then another, and she waited for her mobile to buzz. But no call came, and her fury grew. Had she been, as the young called it, cancelled? She wanted to tell him that it was *she* who had decided to cancel *him*, not the other way about. Her pride, which was what she used instead of a stick, stiffened and swelled by the hour until she was quite resolved to never play for him again.

Eventually, Xan came to her with a puzzled expression.

'Oma, is your mobile not working?'

'Why?'

He handed his to her.

'Marta? This is Vasily.'

'Mr Ivanov.' Marta's voice was glacial. 'Why are you calling me on my grandson's mobile?'

'Maestra, please do not be angry with me.' Ivanov himself, for all his measured, glottal tones, sounded distraught. 'My cat—'

Marta was even more incensed. How dare he bring up the business again!

'Why are you calling?'

'I am telling you that it is not safe to visit me today.'

'Why not?'

Ivanov said, 'My cat has been poisoned.'

179

Marta was silent. This was not what she expected.

'How? Did he eat a small dog?'

'No,' said Ivanov. 'We think Novichok was put on his collar. Someone did it who knew that I would stroke him with my bare hands. Maybe they got to him while he was hunting outside the grounds – he was such a brave creature – and too trusting.'

Ivanov's voice had become almost tearful.

'I am sorry,' said Marta, for although she was not, herself, a cat-lover she understood the pain. If you loved an animal, losing it was almost as bad as losing a family member. 'How did you find out?'

'My cook noticed some discolouration on his collar. A kind of powder. We are awaiting analysis of samples from a laboratory, but I am certain it was Novichok. He cleaned himself, his paw touched it, and so he died.' His voice became tight. 'He was such a beautiful creature. My home is being deep cleaned, but my staff are upset.'

Marta remembered the smiling cook and the housekeeper.

'Are they all right? Did anyone else touch it?'

'No,' Ivanov said. 'They are safe, but I fear that my enemy is escalating his attempts.'

Marta was sceptical. 'Isn't he a busy man right now?'

Ivanov gave a short laugh. 'He is like death, always busy. Especially in the present special military operation, which I do not support.'

'Why don't you say so more openly?'

'I don't need to. I live outside Russia. If we are not for him, we are against him. So all my kind are under sentence of death.'

Marta did not know what to think. Ivanov's fears could be justified – but it could also be a manifestation of paranoia. Cats died from all kinds of things. Enzo's dog had been poisoned a few months ago, and surely that wasn't Novichok, was it?

Though, of course, Enzo himself lived barely a kilometre from the palazzo.

'I am sorry,' she said. 'I hope to see you at my recital.'

'I will be listening.'

He rang off, and she handed Xan back his mobile.

'Ivanov thinks his mobile is being monitored. We must stay away from the palazzo.'

Her grandson raised his eyebrows. 'So, no macarons for tea? Peak.'

Marta, irritated by his slang said, 'I cannot understand why, with a first-class degree in English, you can't get a better job than tutoring.'

Xan was distracted, as she knew he would be.

'I can't transform into a banker like Olly. There are no jobs for Arts and Humanities graduates now.'

'Try being a young Italian,' Marta said, moving to her piano. 'No jobs at all here, unless your family owns a business that you can go into. Even being a waiter means you must be related to someone. That's why its economy is stagnating, despite their wonderful free universities, and they all go to Britain.'

Xan shrugged. 'Enzo thinks Italy should leave the EU too. I'm sure he's a fascist.'

'He's a good man. Good people can still have bad politics.'

'You think that because you like flirting with him,' said Xan.

'My dear,' Marta said, 'he is an Italian, and an attractive man. Just because I'm in my eighties does not mean I have forgotten what it's like to be a woman.'

'Oma!' said Xan, aghast, and despite her discomfort, she laughed.

Marta was old enough to remember a time when Italians

themselves had been treated almost as badly by other Europeans as Muslims or Jews or Africans. Young, Nordic women like herself had been warned against Mediterranean men as primitive, superstitious and semi-literate children of nature whose physical charms were equalled by moral torpor. It was quite absurd, and she only had to think of Juicy for this prejudice – pure racism – to be self-evident.

As if summoned by the thought, Juicy let herself in. 'Ciao, Marta, sono qui,' she announced. Juicy was one of the few people Marta trusted with a spare key: an important precaution against the possibility that one day she might keel over and die.

Many who used Juicy as an informal chef didn't know that she was a biology graduate of Bologna University; they assumed that because her parents were *contadini*, they must all be simple-minded. (English people *adored* saying the word 'peasant', Marta noted.) She had obtained the highest mark in her subject in her year, and could have had a great career in Milan, but, after a couple of years working for a big company, she returned home to look after her mother, Maria, who was dying of cancer. It was she who expanded the Guardi family interests into an export business.

'Do you ever feel nostalgia for your old house?' Xan asked Juicy, as she unpacked the meal she had cooked for them. (Marta wanted to feed her grandson well, but had neither the time not the energy.)

'No, I was a tiny child. My brothers shared a bed, and I slept in my parents' room. There was no bathroom at La Rosa, or central heating. When we moved, we left the fifteenth century and joined the new millennium.'

'My family lives in the country, too, but I prefer London. Have you been there?'

'Yes, of course. That's where I learned my excellent English.'
Marta resumed her practice, smiling.

'There should also be some food in the fridge for lunch, if you need extra,' she called to Xan.

'I've looked, Oma, and there isn't.'

'Really? How strange. I only went to the shops two days ago.'

Marta was sure that she had bought more food. She remembered Enzo carrying it back – or was that last month? She was so preoccupied with the recital that she kept forgetting other things.

Xan interrupted again.

'Oma, would it be OK if Blessing stays for a few days?'

'Who?'

'You know, one of the wedding guests. My friend from Zimbabwe.'

'What's a Zimbabwean doing in Italy?' Marta enquired.

'Everyone is from everywhere, aren't they? Ruth says they are running short of space at La Rosa, and there's a spare bed here. He's very quiet, and nice.'

Marta's fingers had wandered into one of Schubert's last sonatas for piano, written when he, too, was in declining health.

'Are you going to play that for your recital?' Xan asked.

'No. Too dark,' Marta said. 'But I will play one of Chopin's sonatas.'

It was like announcing that she was going to be climbing Mount Everest, and he knew it.

'Are you *sure* you are well enough to do this?'

Marta looked up at her grandson's face. 'I am determined.'

The people who came to her annual recitals were a mixture of young and old, rich and poor, residents and tourists. Some were similar to those who would have listened to her in the

Wigmore Hall, though most had probably never heard live classical music in their life before except when a fragment was the soundtrack to an advertisement or a movie. But this was her gift to the people, whether they appreciated it or not.

Otto was sniffing at the floor by the bookcase in her bedroom next door in a most distracting manner. His white paws scrabbled at its base, and he huffed.

'Bad boy! Stop that!' she said to him sharply. 'There's nothing there.'

Xan repeated his question about having his friend to stay.

'Of course,' she said vaguely. She didn't care who he hung out with, as long as they didn't disturb her playing.

'We're all coming to your recital,' Xan said. 'Apart from Olly, maybe.'

'Why not him?' Juicy asked.

'I don't know. He keeps being delayed in London,' Xan said.

'Perhaps he is thinking again about his influenza?'

'Sorry?'

Juicy said, with a touch of contempt, 'Tanyaa.'

'Oh, her. She's an influencer, not a virus. Though come to think of it ... Otto, stop scrabbling. I'll take you for a walk soon.'

The little white dog was clearly desperate.

'Maybe it's a rat,' Marta said. But in her mind, she believed it was Death, waiting for her.

14

The Madness of Despair

What did I do wrong? she often asked herself, driving up to Santorno as carefully as possible. Little boys did grow away from their mothers, they had to. But Andrew had gone from being a loving, lively, beautiful little boy to one whose cleverness was all too often used to shut her out.

'There's no point explaining, Mummy, you wouldn't understand,' he would say, if she asked what was going on in his life

When she inherited Lode, Diana had felt profound relief. At last, she could give her son something worth having. The grace of its architecture and setting was what mattered, not its shabbiness, and his aesthetic sense would at least be satisfied. But because of the Lloyd's crash (actually, Perry's gambling), Lode had to be sold.

'Bad luck, but the money has to come from somewhere,' Perry said. For the first time ever, she stood up to him.

'Why can't you sell *your* family home? Why must it be mine, which is much smaller, lovelier and closer to London?'

'That's exactly why. Some rich banker will want it.'

What a fool I was, she thought. I should at least have kept my inheritance separate from his accounts. That was what wise wives always did, just in case. But she had been ignorant, and trusting, and so the other thing she loved was taken from her.

She had once loved Perry, but he had killed that.

'You used to be so beautiful,' he would lament. 'What happened to you?'

'It's called age. Have you looked in the mirror recently? You're old, too.'

'You only married me for my money.'

'No, I married you because I wanted to go out to live on a failing tobacco farm in Rhodesia with a man who kept fucking other women.'

People who only saw her in public would have been surprised had they heard the sharpness of her retorts. Diana often surprised herself.

Infidelities were common in their class, but nobody ever complained, because to do that was to lose caste. What was expected was that she should be not just a mother, a lover, a hostess and a secretary, but remain as delicately robust as the best bone china: when dropped, she must bounce rather than shatter.

'My dear, why don't you at least allow yourself some *fun*?' said a girl who'd come out the same year, met by chance in Peter Jones as they were both shopping for school uniforms.

Diana told herself she was too fastidious to stoop to such measures. Whatever Perry wanted to do to her, or with her was one thing, but affairs of her own were out of the question. The truth was that she had never been in love with any man but her husband. He'd been handsome, glamorous, and exactly the sort of man she was expected to marry. His sexual appetites had actually flattered her, at first.

'I need sex several times a day,' he told her. It made her feel like the heroine of a Georgette Heyer novel, until she discovered that his attentions were not confined to herself.

Secretaries, shop girls, dancers, nurses, servants, actresses, friends' wives or daughters and nannies were all fair game. People in their world only disapproved of talking about it, and Perry never understood that doing so marked him as a bounder, especially as he did so in front of her, and in company. When they were living out on the farm in Africa, she could stand it, especially because she was so busy with her children, but when they returned to England and Perry became an MP, it was mortifying.

'There's a lady I know, well, not just a friend you understand,' he would say loudly at dinner parties before launching into an anecdote, as if his audience should admire him for this.

By the time she was twenty-nine, however, no son had arrived. She lived in fear of being divorced, for by now it had become very clear that his elder brother would never settle down, and that Perry was de facto the heir. He needed a boy, or the title would go to some distant cousin (there was always a cousin, but that wasn't the point). When at last she presented him with the longed-for male, at the advanced age of thirty, Perry gave her the second ring that never left her finger.

'Your medal for long service,' was what he called it, and the deep red stone was like a single drop of all the blood she had shed. He doted on Andrew as he had never done Etta, Mary and Lettice (always referred to, vaguely and interchangeably, as 'darling'). They were the ones who still flew out to see them both twice a year, bringing garlic-free sausages, Pears soap and Marmite.

'Oh dear,' Diana said, weeping a little, 'I do miss home so very much.'

'Mummy, you could always come and live with us, you know,' Etta said, but somehow the invitation was only for their mother. They knew that their father did not love them. Andrew, however, brought her nothing. His visits were always sparse. He seemed to push her away when she hugged him, as if he could not bear her touch.

Diana fought for all her children to get an education, the education that she had not had. Her daughters could have gone to one of the duller boarding schools, but instead won places at the local grammar, where they thrived, and went on to top universities, and actually even had jobs. Of course, they married young too; they couldn't wait to leave home, she thought. What was it that Tania was running away from? Watching the girl from under her hooded eyes, Diana wondered. As an ex-beauty herself, she could not help being interested in the bride. She saw how Tania shrank like a salted snail from most people, and remembered how shy she had been herself.

Was she the only one who noticed that Raff was in love with Tania? Diana thought that, had she been Ruth, she might have warned Olly to get out sooner. Raff seemed a nice young man, but then anyone who helped her with her husband had to be.

Diana glanced at the immobile figure beside her. Her swollen ankle had gone down in a couple of days, and she was back to the twice-daily routine of getting Perry into the passenger seat of the Fiat 500, folding up his wheelchair and lifting it into the boot, then doing the whole thing in reverse at the other end. It took a lot of effort to do this, though once at the *ospedale*, the nuns helped. He could still stand up for a few seconds if supported under the armpits, but as soon as she couldn't support him, it was all over. The hoist was crucial to getting him out of bed, she wasn't strong enough to lift him when horizontal, but sometimes he seemed to get a kick out of resisting. She knew that somewhere, inside the dementia, Perry was still mocking her.

I can't bear it, she thought, as the little white Fiat waddled torturously up the track, making them both sway. He was denying her the last few years of freedom, the decade that women like herself never admitted was often the happiest in their lives.

'I've never had so many friends as I do now,' one widow had told her, with a kind of wonder. Of course not, Diana thought: your husband had been a drunk and a bore, whereas everyone likes you and only tolerated him. But here she was, with no hope of release. At least her husband could no longer gamble his pension away from their joint account.

'An old man's nurse,' she muttered.

Apart from the State Pension she got a carer's allowance, but it was instantly swallowed up by incontinence pads, and it was becoming harder to pay for the essentials. The endless stratagems just to preserve some modicum of dignity exhausted her; even her walks were partly to collect kindling and branches that could be used in the wood-burner as free fuel. She passed a chap flying a drone below the walls of the Felice estate, a bigger version of those toys that boys had. What was the *point* of such things? It wasn't as if you yourself could fly away.

It was important to distract herself with the landscape she was crawling through, even if her one functioning eye was already burning with strain. Yet as she coaxed the car uphill, the frustration and anger mounted with it, like an invisible passenger. La Docciola's only bathroom was impossible for a confused, disabled person to access without help. She cursed herself for not thinking of this when they had first bought the cottage, and could have put in a wet room, but initially they thought of La Docciola more in terms of a holiday home. She was then still in her seventies, and Perry, in his eighties, was convinced he was going to live for ever. Even getting him to hand over Fol to Andrew to avoid inheritance tax had been a struggle. (Though whenever she begged him to spend some money on essential repairs to the castle, he would answer cheerily, 'It can be a problem for my heirs.')

Had she known then what she did now, she would at least have spent money on a disabled toilet. At the beginning of life, and near its end, every human being is at the mercy of their own excrement. But that was the thing about age and disability: you could never foresee how inexorable and irreversible were the stages of decline. As Marta once put it, 'One day you wake up, and suddenly your knees don't bend properly. Or your shoulder is stiff. Or you have a haemorrhoid. Or you are deaf in one ear. You think it will go away, because that's what always happened in the past. Only now, it never will.'

The figure beside her said, 'Cunt.'

'Please don't talk to me in that nasty way.'

'Stinking bitch,' said Perry.

Diana felt tears start into her eyes.

'Should be put down.'

'Is this about Bella?'

'Just eats and craps.'

'I could say the same of you,' she said.

'Useless.'

The car wrenched round another steep hairpin bend, and

suddenly, Diana lost control – either of the car or of herself. The wheel slipped in her hands, and the tyres spun on the road, and she and Perry tumbled over and over, flopping this way and that with a gritty grind of machinery and a cascade of rocks on metal and the taste of blood.

'I love you, I love you!' she heard herself crying as they fell off the road into the air.

There was a great jolt, and another, the whipping of branches and shrieking of steel. Diana was so confused that she could not tell what was real and what was a nightmare.

When the world stopped tumbling, the car came to a halt, rocking on its small wheels. It was almost upright, but at an odd angle, having careened off the road and into a patch of brambles with an olive at the centre. Perry made no response. He just sat there, as usual, strapped into his chair, looking terribly old and yet, because of his profile and white hair, noble.

Diana had the presence of mind to turn off the engine, then she sat for a long while. She did not know whether she was more shocked by the accident or by the words she'd just said to her husband while falling through the air. Was that really what she felt? *Did* she still love rather than hate him? Was it possible? Or had she said it just because she'd believed they were both about to die, and wanted to comfort him? She heard a clicking noise. She wondered whether it was her heart or cooling machinery.

Eventually, her bladder began to ache as it almost always did every hour, and here the difficulty began. She couldn't get out. Something was jammed, or obstructing the door, and no matter how she struggled, it would not open. The window (luckily the kind that wound down, rather than needing an electric button) descended, then stuck as well. Not even she could get out through a four-inch gap.

Her hands found her bag, and rootled about for the mobile that she kept for emergencies. It was heavier and chunkier than the kind used by her friends – but it was out of battery.

What to do? Despair welled up in her. This road was hardly used by anyone, unless they were going to Ruth's house. Only Enzo remained. But how could she summon him? Would he even look down from the road above?

Of course! She could beep her horn. Diana pushed at the round disk in the centre of the wheel. Her hand was more than usually feeble, but it did emit a brief squawk, like that of a startled hen.

Nothing happened. She waited, and tried again. Nothing. A lively spring breeze rustled the olive leaves all around, birds sang, and otherwise there was silence. Her body was seized with violent trembling. Stiff upper lip, she told herself. She thought of the little dog that she and her friends had released from the hot car, but even if she could cut the glass of her own window, it would be little use without something hard to break it. Some people always kept a special hammer in their car for this purpose. Wasn't there something you could do with the metal prongs of a seat headrest? But she was too weak and stiff to twist around and yank hers out. Of course this was effectively an abandoned hillside, like so many in this depopulated country. Why had she ever thought it would be better here?

Visions of the bluebell woods at Lode floated across her mind. That luminous violet-blue, unique to Britain, which grew in great pools beneath the glassy green of young beech; how could she ever have left it? How could she have left the daily joys of the BBC, Cornish milk or weather that people complained about but secretly loved? Her bladder begged to be released.

O dear, what can the matter be?
Three old ladies locked in the lavatory,
They were there from Monday to Saturday –
Nobody knew they were there.

She had never found the song funny, even as a child. All older women had weak pelvic floors. It was one of the many mortifications of her sex, and perhaps the single worst aspect of old age.

Would anybody even notice that Lord Evenlode was missing? At the *ospedale*, nobody rang to check and the nuns would probably assume that he was too unwell to come into the centre. Unless Ruth and Marta realised; but they were both preoccupied with their own events. She was utterly unimportant. Except to my daughters, she thought, my dear, kind daughters; but they are a thousand miles away.

Families should live as close together as possible, especially in old age. People used to know this, Italians still knew it, but in richer countries the generations avoided each other. It was taken for granted that they had nothing in common, and then everyone found themselves desperate for company and help when it was too late.

It struck her that they might die here in the car. Perry still hadn't moved, though he was breathing, his head sunk low on his thin neck. The anger and loathing that kept her hard cracked, and pity seeped up in her heart. When she looked at him, she remembered the many iterations of the man she had known for over sixty years, from the handsome young war hero, to the amorous husband, to the proud father, to the shrewd farmer, to the victorious politician, to the reckless fox-hunter, to the cheerful adulterer, to the bold expatriate – there were so many different men who had inhabited this body, no wonder it, and she, were worn out. However she felt about the bad things he'd done, they were in this mess together, just as they had always been.

'It's all right, darling,' she said, stroking his hand. 'We'll get out of this fix.'

She undid her seatbelt, and tried to twist in her seat. She could remember exactly what it felt like to be supple as a leaping salmon, but no matter how she tried, the message to her muscles remained fitful. Had she damaged herself? Diana felt each limb, gingerly. No, all in working order but still not able to shift. Please God, not a stroke? She looked at herself in the driver's mirror, afraid that half her face might have frozen, but that, too, was the same. She was just being feeble. Encouraged, she attacked the side window again, pushing and pulling at the plastic handle with her painful hands to crank it down.

Again, she was frustrated. Tears of rage stung her eyes. I have killed us both, she thought.

When she looked up, she saw the wavering shapes of two figures walking along the road just above the car.

She pressed the horn once more, leaning on the button.

'Aiuto! Help!'

Her voice came out more strongly in English, and suddenly the figures were scrambling down the trail of smashed grasses and branches, and they were people she recognised. What were they called? Yes, Xan and his friend.

'Oh my God. Hold on, Diana,' Xan said.

He tugged at the driver's door.

'Jammed,' she told him.

But the other one walked to the passenger side, and lifted it open without any trouble. Fresh air flooded in, and with it, hope. Blessing leant over.

'Grandmother, may I lift him out?'

194

'Yes, yes, of course. Hurry.'

Blessing unbuckled the belt, put his arms around Perry's torso and legs, and picked him up without effort, before depositing him to lie on the long, lush grass where she could see him. Perry seemed barely conscious. Again, Diana felt a pang of guilt and horror at what she had done in the madness of despair. Blessing knelt, feeling for his pulse. There was a strange moment when she could have sworn that he gave Perry a look of absolute loathing, but it passed.

Diana said, reasserting herself, 'Now, would you kindly get me out!'

In no time, Blessing and Xan together were able to push the little Fiat back on to four wheels and pull her free too.

'Are you able to stand?'

'Yes. Yes, I think so.'

She braced herself against Xan's arm, and it came to her suddenly that Xan was not a stranger, was in fact her great-nephew, looking at her with his intelligent, friendly eyes. He is a *person*, Diana thought, surprised; and suddenly all kinds of things began to shift in her heart and mind, creaking and groaning because it wasn't easy to change not just your mind but your feelings, and yet it somehow felt good, and right, and natural.

It was hard to admit that she had not really liked Xan before. She suspected that he hadn't liked her either because such feelings are almost always reciprocal. How could she have been so stupid? She did not understand the person she had been, only a few seconds ago, just as that person would not have understood who she was now.

'My saviours!' she said, and meant it. 'Thank you.'

For a moment they were still in the silvery shadows of the olive grove, with the birds singing all around them.

'You are welcome, Grandmother,' Blessing said.

'I've called Raff,' Xan said. 'He's on his way right now.'

Moments later, Raff came charging up the hill in Ruth's Jeep. He leapt out, took one look at Perry and said, 'I think we should get him to hospital, unless you prefer an ambulance?'

Clearly, he hadn't forgotten her rudeness to him when she had sprained her ankle.

'I expect you will be quicker. The wheelchair folds up.'

'Right. Let's get him on to a blanket, and lift him on to the back seat, it goes flat.'

The three young men lifted Perry into the Jeep, and Diana took the opportunity to nip discreetly behind a bush. The relief was almost agonising, but she also relaxed because she recognised that tone of authority. Her brother and grandfather had had it, too. Army, she thought, probably Sandhurst.

The Jeep shot round the back entrance of the city walls, Raff beeping his horn continually to show it was an emergency, and he got them both into the Accident and Emergency entrance in what seemed like a very short time, even if Diana found herself clutching her seatbelt as he hurtled through the narrow, cobbled streets. They arrived in less than five minutes, but her main thought as they drove into the courtyard of the hospital was that her husband was dying, and she had probably killed him.

15

Xan And Blessing

Xan and Blessing spent much of every day together, talking. Some of this was their fantasies about Wakanda. They had both been enthralled by *Black Panther*, and longed for the film to be true.

'Maybe it exists, somewhere in Africa,' Xan said, uttering the secret longing that had existed in many hearts since its release.

'Maybe it is paradise.'

'Maybe it's like Narnia.'

But Blessing had not read those books, and Xan, though he had adored them unquestioningly as a child, thought sadly that it might be just as well.

In Santorno, he introduced Blessing as 'my cousin', and in the back of his mind, Xan was aware that by doing this he was protecting Blessing from being ignored or even abused when he walked around the town. His feelings towards his new friend only seemed to grow, seeing how vulnerable he was here, and how bravely he dealt with that. It wasn't just the way the Santornese looked at him. He told Xan that, on first arrival, he had been jostled and spat at by a group of young men in the Via Nazionale. Nobody had intervened, everyone pretended it wasn't happening. Xan, who was used to being greeted in the friendliest manner because he went shopping with his grandmother or with Otto, found it hard to believe until he saw a shopkeeper's face change.

'It's upsetting,' Xan told Marta when they were alone. 'Italians are so friendly to everyone else. Why do they hate Black people?'

'Do you know why lifeboats have an axe in them?'

'To chop down trees on a desert island?'

'No. To cut off the hands of swimmers who can't be saved, because otherwise the boat and everyone in it will sink.'

Xan shuddered, and Marta said in her dry voice, 'Over three hundred thousand illegal migrants come to this country every year. At least Italy, unlike Britain, isn't planning to send them to Rwanda.'

'Do you feel sorry for them, Oma?'

'Yes, I do. After the war, many German people lost their homes. We know what it is like to be displaced, homeless, starving civilians. I feel sorry for everyone forced to suffer.'

Xan said, 'But why can't everyone be happy, and live in peace? It ought to be so simple.'

'Oh, my darling. You long for D major, for joy and courage and triumph, but our lives are composed in D flat minor, the key of doom and despair.'

'What, always?'

'No,' she said, smiling at him. 'Maybe not all the time. There are many different keys. But we are not born to be happy, you know. Happiness is a lucky accident, not a right. If it comes, it will be when you least expect it.'

Xan treasured these conversations with his grandmother, because he feared that he might not have many more of them. He knew that she was anxious and depressed about everything, from her sore back to the war in Ukraine, yet she was spirited and brave. She was glad of his arm when walking to the Piazza Garibaldi, but mostly stayed at home, playing. Her will and resilience were formidable, but he knew how much it was taking out of her, and did his best to cheer her up each day.

'Look, Oma!'

He brought back a roll of toilet paper from the market. It had Putin's face on it, with the words 'Putin: *puzza di merda*' on every sheet. They both laughed.

'Trust the Italians to go straight to the fundamentals,' he said.

'Unfortunately, they also sell rolls with the same message and President Zelensky's face on, too,' Marta answered. 'I am wondering if Ivanov would appreciate one, or whether it's too vulgar for him. Would you mind driving again to the palazzo?'

'Have you made it up with him? Or has he discovered his cat wasn't Novichoked?'

She shrugged. Nothing, he knew, was more important to her than music. She was not an activist or a dissident, and when Xan told her about having been on protest marches she was angry with him. Maybe she felt her family had suffered enough for politics, given her own father's internment as a Communist in the camp that had killed him. Xan tried to explain the disaffection and alienation that his own generation had for the government, but she was having none of it.

'All this complaining and waving banners impresses nobody. You live in Britain, in London, the heart of the civilised world. If you want to change things, do it like a grown-up.'

'But how, Oma?' Xan cried, in despair. 'I have no money, no prospects, *nothing*.'

'How do you think? Use that good brain of yours!'

The Russian was just as courteous to them as before, and the tea (this time on the terrace) after Marta's recital, just as lavish. His cat's death had clearly shocked him.

'Such a beautiful creature. I do not doubt my Ilya was killed on Putin's orders.'

It was like a dream, sitting here in the lap of luxury with assassins creeping up on them while they drank tea and ate finger sandwiches and looked at his enchanting view. Xan swallowed his disbelief.

Ivanov seemed to read his mind. His eyes were such a dark brown that there seemed no line between pupil and iris. It was like looking into two deep holes.

'You think me crazy?'

'Everything in Italy feels a bit crazy to me. Especially your palazzo.'

'When I was imprisoned, I said to myself that if ever I got out, I would live like this.'

'Was it very bad?'

'Worse than anyone can imagine. I became so thin that when I left, nobody recognised me.'

Xan was ashamed.

'How did you get out?'

'How does anyone? I had a good lawyer. Now I am a prisoner here.'

Xan said, 'As prisons go, this seems pretty nice.'

'Yes. But I cannot go anywhere, even to a restaurant. I cannot see my wife and children. There is always the risk of kidnap and murder. Putin will try again. He wants to eliminate all opponents. Did you have any more trouble?'

Xan had forgotten about the strange man on his first walk. 'No,' he said. 'It was just a passing incident, I think.'

Ivanov looked at him thoughtfully. 'Let us hope. They certainly could not have mistaken you for me.'

'Are your bodyguards Russian?' Marta asked.

Ivanov laughed. 'No. They are Ukrainian, like my mother's family, from Chernobyl. They have every reason to hate Russia, starting with the way our parents were told to sow potatoes in land poisoned by radiation, to maintain the lie that nothing had gone wrong there.'

'How horrible.'

'Yes. They died of thyroid cancer. Russians are bad people. As soon as they get any money, they spend it on weapons. They are obsessed with their empire.'

Marta said, 'No one people are all bad. I do not believe that.'

'Well,' said Ivanov consideringly, 'maybe just ninety per cent bad. Every country is bad when it has power. The British were bad too, when they had an Empire, and now they live on a small island and believe in liberal democracy. Germany was bad when it wanted the Third Reich, and now it has even paid money to the victims of the Holocaust. That is what needs to happen in Russia, too.'

'I think Britain should apologise for the slave trade,' Xan said. 'If six million Jews were murdered, so were ten million Black people.'

'And where would it end? Should France apologise for the Norman Conquest? Should Italy apologise for the Roman Empire?'

'Just saying sorry, instead of telling ourselves that Britain stopped the slave trade, would help.'

Marta turned to Ivanov. 'What is Putin afraid you will do?'

The oligarch shrugged. 'In Russia, people are arrested and

imprisoned just for holding up a blank sheet of paper. I am opposed to the invasion of Ukraine.'

'Can't you, I don't know, pay him off?'

'No. He claims to have no money, and no car apart from a beaten-up Lada. In reality, he is the richest man in Russia. He owns vast palaces we are not supposed to know about, though Navalny has done his best to make it known, and Putin tried to poison him, too. Meanwhile, all of us Russians who live abroad have had our properties taken, and our bank accounts frozen, just for being Russian. Guilty until proved innocent.'

'Yes, um, sorry about that,' Xan said.

'Of course, there are ways round it. My family has a golden visa in Britain. But it is irritating, very irritating,' said Ivanov. 'Putin does not need Novichok, truth to tell. He just needs to wait until I can no longer pay my security. When I am down to my last two million, they will leave.'

'Is that what it costs?'

Ivanov said, 'What is your life worth? Let me tell you what happens if they don't kill you immediately, but you are arrested.

'You are taken away without trial, and interrogated. It doesn't matter whether you have committed crimes or not, they will find something. They hand you a plate with a hole in, and if you accept it, you must be gay, and then they can rape you as well as torture you, because to be gay is a crime in Russia.'

'My God,' Xan said.

Ivanov sighed. 'We are barbarians. Once, when Russia was great, we aspired to become part of Europe. The aristocracy spoke French, not Russian. You know, St Petersburg was designed by an Italian, Rastrelli? The Baroque style feels natural to us. But the other half of us is from Attila the Hun, so torture, rape and despotism are natural too.'

'Are you a criminal?' He knew it was rude to ask a direct question, but Xan loved nothing more than arguing.

Ivanov said, 'To some people. When the Soviet Union collapsed, I could see that most Russians were facing a change they didn't understand. But I, and a handful of others, did. It was a game, an amazing game, in which a group of us divided up everything that was no longer controlled by the government. There was oil, gas, TV channels, banking, real estate, so many valuable assets. We learned in seven years what it took America and the West centuries to work out. But it was also hard work, getting people who had never had to worry about efficiency to modernise.

'Did we do bad things? It was like the Wild West. We were the ones arriving with bags of cash to pay the nurses and teachers and workers. We were the ones making deals, and getting the economy to function. That is why Putin fears us. We understood how to run a country, when he was just a minor spy in the KGB. We thought that once the people became richer, Russia would be pushed towards democracy. As if democracy could be served up like fries with a Big Mac. But we did not understand that the Russian people always want a strong leader. They loved the Tsar, they loved Stalin, and now they love Putin. That is what money is, Xan: power. Do you understand?'

'What about doctors? Don't they have power?'

'Without money to buy drugs, equipment, training, no.'

'And lawyers?'

'It was my lawyer who got me out of prison. In Russia, as in America, the law is the only system that can challenge the state. But even law is powerless before force. Putin wants my money for himself.'

'Couldn't you, I don't know, give it away to charity? Like Bill Gates?'

Ivanov roared with laughter, then said, 'If I did this, it would make my murder even more likely. So excuse me, I am my own charity.'

When Xan drove Marta back from the palazzo, he said, 'I almost feel sorry for him, don't you?'

'My darling, just because Ivanov values music does not mean he is good, or sane. I am sorry about his cat, but did you ever hear of such a mad idea?'

'It seems a clever way of assassinating someone.' Xan looked out of the window. 'I wonder how the FSB knew that he took his gloves off to stroke it.'

Marta said, 'I wondered about that too. Maybe his servants are not quite as loyal as he hopes.'

What was Blessing's role in all this? Xan wondered. Was it a coincidence that he turned up just when Ivanov's life came under threat? Everyone accepted him at La Rosa, but Xan noticed that he never talked about Harvard, or about Olly.

Xan thought about this, as he walked Otto. Blessing's lost luggage had still not turned up, though he claimed to have filled in a complaint form to the airline. He had no money, and nothing but an iPhone, his passport and a paperback copy of NoViolet Bulawayo's *We Need New Names*. Apart from Ruth's donations, Xan had given him a few of the spare clothes he kept in a wardrobe at his grandmother's, as well as socks and boxer shorts. He agonised about seeming patronising, but Blessing was delighted.

'We even have the same sized feet, I think?' Xan said, and showed him a pair of red Converses. 'I won't wear these any more, because a Tory prime minister ruined the look.'

'But to me they're just shoes,' Blessing said. The Converses, which were almost new, made all the difference. Suddenly, the Zimbabwean looked like a Londoner. Even his hair shone, just like Xan's. 'Tania is very kind to me as well.'

'She is? I mean,' Xan corrected himself hastily, 'is she? For as long as I've known her, Tania has only ever been interested in *stuff*. The one thing that she ever asked me about myself was whether my watch was a Rolex. When I said no, it was from Amazon, I was like a non-person. She's a walking cliché, a spoilt, white, air-head.'

'I think she is unhappy,' said Blessing.

'So would I be, if I were marrying Olly. Oh, sorry, he's your friend, isn't he? But every conversation I've ever had with him, I can time it to within three minutes before he mentions how successful he is. He's a figjam.'

'What does that mean? Figjam?'

'It stands for Fuck I'm Great, Just Ask Me. Ask him any-thing about himself, and an hour later, he's still talking about his great career. Maybe he was different at Harvard.'

Blessing just smiled, and said, 'People change.'

Xan did worry, though. For one thing, Blessing looked too young to have been at Harvard with Olly; he seemed no older that Xan himself, not thirty. He wondered about the small black backpack that Blessing carried with him everywhere, and which was his only luggage. What was in it? He couldn't bring himself to ask, but when Blessing was in the shower, he lifted it up, briefly. He wouldn't look inside, but weighed it in his hands. It was heavier than he expected, and whatever the long tubular shape was inside, it wasn't a bottle of water.

16

The Shadow of Death

'Are you sure you're OK to pick up Olly?' Ruth asked.

'Of course,' Enzo answered.

'My grandson sent me a text to say that Diana's son is on the same flight to Florence as himself and his best man. Could you possibly give him a lift too?'

'Do not worry. I will be there.'

The news that Andrew Evenlode was flying out to see his parents was an indication of how quickly his father must be declining.

Ruth felt a pang of pity for her friend. How would she cope, alone?

'Juicy?'

'Yes, Root?'

'Have you made enough food for me to take to the hospital?'

'I think so, yes.'

Ruth was accustomed to visiting sick expatriate friends in Santorno's hospital, which had a major drawback: it expected the relatives of patients to feed them. She had discovered this when recovering from a minor operation herself.

'But what if you have no family nearby?' she asked Juicy, horrified. 'You could starve to death.'

'In Italy, there is always family,' she answered, leaving Ruth to wonder what she would do when her own time came. It would not be one of her three busy, successful sons who would nurse her here: it would be, at best, a daughter-in-law. Or even a grandchild, probably female. What would the world come to, without women? With these thoughts, she drove herself to the hospital.

In a plain, lofty, whitewashed room, Perry was lying on a high iron bed beneath stiff starched sheets. Diana sat beside him. He had a cannula taped to one arm, a saline drip emptying into his veins, and a catheter snaking discreetly underneath the bedsheet. Apart from this, and an oxygen monitor on one finger, he was clearly receiving little treatment. Was that because he might survive? It would be a merciful release if he didn't, Ruth thought. However, people didn't die just because they ought to. The more she saw of life, the more convinced she became that the good did indeed die young, exhausted by virtue, whereas those pickled in selfishness were the ones who kept going.

Diana looked up when Ruth came in, and for an instant her face was so transfigured by joy that she looked like a young woman. Then she saw who it was, and became an old person ground down by grief and exhaustion again.

'How are you?'

'Bit bruised, but still here.'

'I'm so sorry,' Ruth said.

'All I want is for my son to arrive.'

Ruth said, 'I've brought you some lunch, my dear.'

207

She took off her backpack, and fished out a Tupperware box with a chicken salad that Juicy had made, and a fresh panino, a half-bottle of wine and some fruit.

'So kind,' Diana said, swallowing. 'I am a little famished, I confess.'

'Don't worry about Bella, by the way. Raff has brought her to La Rosa.'

'Poor old girl.' Diana said. 'Thank goodness for those two – Xan and Blessing. If they hadn't found us after the accident, I don't know where we'd be. Surprising how alike they look.'

Ruth said, 'Diana, my dear, we don't make remarks like that.'

'Why not? They *do* look alike.'

'I expect we do to them, as two elderly white women.'

When I die, Ruth thought, I hope it'll be from a stroke, rather than this dreadful *dwindling*. But this is the thing about our generation: we want choice in everything, including death. She pushed the thought of Beatrix away.

'Marta sends her apologies,' she said. 'She'll come and visit you after her recital.'

'I fear she's in a good deal of pain,' Diana said. 'Have you noticed how she winces when she does anything?'

'No,' Ruth said guiltily. 'The last time I visited her, Otto kept trying to hump Dash, and though he tolerated it like a saint, he suddenly lost it and *bit* him.'

'Oh dear.'

'It was no more than a nip, really, but Marta was very upset, and blamed me.'

'I can't *stand* Otto,' Diana said, and Ruth confessed, 'Me neither'.

Again the door opened, and again Diana looked up, radiant, but it was only a nurse coming to check on Perry.

'What do the hospital say?'

'They're not expecting him to live. It's all my fault. I lost control of the Fiat, and my temper.'

Diana looked away, blinking. Ruth couldn't believe her friend really loved the old monster, but there was no end to the peculiarities of many marriages.

'Don't think that, or say that. Nobody could have cared for him better than you have.'

'You don't know the half of it.'

Outside, the church bells began to toll midday.

'What will you do?' Ruth asked, meaning, *afterwards*.

'I don't know.' Diana sipped a little wine, and the red sank into her cracked lips. 'We only moved out here because of the day care, as you know. I wouldn't leave a dog in an English care home, frankly. Well, definitely not a dog.'

'Do you think you will go back to Britain?'

'There is no going back,' Diana answered. 'Even if I threw myself on to the mercy of the State, I doubt they'd find anything for me, especially not in Cornwall.' She gave a wry smile. 'It's funny, you know. You think that you need money when you're young and poor. But actually, when you need it the most is when you're old, and nobody will look after you unless you pay them. Did Juicy make this salad?'

'She sure did.'

Diana said, 'A most enterprising and capable young woman. Who would have thought they'd make such a success of that frightful business?'

When the Guardis had moved off the hillside on to the plain, they had set up not just as farmers but as people who pumped out the cesspits of rural dwellings. In the beginning, they had dug filth out by hand, to transport on carts, and Ruth, stuck behind one of these in her car, had been so nauseated by the stench of sewage that for the first and

209

only time in her life she understood the existence of the Untouchable caste.

Other people had been just as repulsed. The Guardis had been, for a while, a family that it was not altogether respectable to know. Ruth had been quite shocked by the way many locals had spoken about them. One of the very few who did not was Enzo, somewhat to her surprise.

'Whatever people say, they are friends of my family,' he said. 'People pretend they do not need this service, but everyone does.'

Things had moved on, however. These days, it was simply a matter of opening a manhole and attaching a giant nozzle which sucked up the noxious contents into a sealed tank. It was simple, hygienic, and amazingly profitable.

'*Dove c'e la merda, c'e la moneta,*' old Guardi liked to say: where there's muck there's money.

For Juicy's father did much more than empty cesspits. He had discovered that human excrement, if drained, filtered, mixed with sawdust and composted became a fertiliser that, when spread on to the earth, caused olive trees to flourish as never before. It was only what farmers had been doing for centuries before fertilisers were imported, but the soil responded, and his trees became so thickly fruited with olives that nobody could believe it. The Guardi olive oil became the best in the region; he bought more land, with more trees, diversified into vineyards, honey and other foods. Before the decade was out, they became rich.

It was an astonishing story, and what was curious was how, several years later, the Guardis were now regarded as deeply respectable. Each of the Guardis' three children had gone to university, and Juicy's eldest brother now lived in Rome and worked for the Bank of Italy. Juicy, who in her teenage years once worked for Ruth as her cleaner, now had her own highly successful food business that employed a dozen local people.

Who would have thought it? Many years ago, Juicy had been Olly's first serious girlfriend, so much so that he'd actually talked about giving up his place at Oxford to stay with her. They were crazy about each other. Very much alarmed, Ruth had spoken, not to her grandson but to Juicy.

She explained, with some delicacy, that Olly should not trash his future. She did not say that he could do better than to throw in his lot with her, but she did not need to.

'I know I am only a *contadina*,' Juicy said humbly.

'The British educational system is not like the Italian one, where anyone can go to any university. It is a competition to win this place, and it is awarded on merit. My grandson is really smart, and to deprive him of this opportunity would be a tragedy. He *has* to go back to England to study. He can't stay here. You understand?'

Juicy did understand, and what happened next was inevitable. Once at Oxford, Olly embarked on a series of relationships, and they did not meet again for many years. Juicy had applied herself to her own studies, and gone to Bologna University a couple of years later. She had done astoundingly well, gaining the equivalent to a First, and it was she who eventually took charge of the farm to build up the export business.

'Yes, Juicy is quite an heiress these days,' said Ruth.

Had I not intervened, she thought, Olly would now be a washed-up tour guide, like too many young expats here, or even another Ben Gorgle. On her way to see Diana and Perry, she had encountered her fellow American walking through the Piazza Garibaldi. He greeted her with his usual bonhomie.

'I hear the Evenlodes had a crash below the palazzo,' he said. 'Driving with only one eye is a *casino*.'

'So is writing gossip,' said Ruth.

He laughed, and she walked on, furious. If he writes about Diana's accident, she vowed, I will do my best to get him run out of town. There had to be a way, because everyone here broke regulations at least once a year.

The two friends sat in the hospital room while machines made their soft sounds. It was like listening to the ocean going out. Ruth felt her heartbeat slow, at least until she remembered the wedding. Olly's friends were terrible at RSVPing.

'Can we just firm up on final numbers?' she asked him, several times. 'Just, you know, to have some idea about catering?'

'I'm trying, but it isn't quite as easy as I thought,' Olly said, in a harassed tone. 'Some people who said they couldn't come now can, and some who said they could come can't. There are lots of problems to do with flights, which keep getting cancelled at the last minute. Get Tania to chase them.'

'OK,' Ruth said dubiously.

She tried reaching out to Olly's bride, but it was quite hopeless. The girl was totally impractical. Tania's latest fantasy was to say on her vlog that she thought the release of butterflies instead of confetti would be 'cool', and now butterfly farms all over Europe were vying to supply these. Hundreds of dead or dying butterflies were arriving by FedEx. Ruth discovered this in horror.

'Tania, this is an organic farm. We are about helping butterflies, not killing them,' she said, quite sharply.

'They're just insects, aren't they? Let's release them into the countryside where they can live happily ever after.'

'But they won't have the right food to eat.'

'I'm sure they'll find some.'

Ruth felt privileged to even get this much out of her grandson's intended bride. Tania seemed always to be scrolling through her Instagram feed, and had very little to say, or at any rate said very little.

'Do you think millennials really are so very different from us?' Ruth had asked Marta.

'Are they millennials? I thought they were X-Men,' Marta responded vaguely.

'I think you mean Generation Z.'

The world has gone mad, Ruth thought, not for the first time, when her drive was once again churned up by DPD deliveries. A truck-load of Baci chocolates (which even Enzo had to admit were a good thing to come out of Umbria, 'although I am convinced, personally, they were invented by a Tuscan') had been joined by free clothes, crockery, cutlery, bed linen and pasta. Anything that Tania mentioned on her vlog was like a wish that would instantly be granted by a hyper-active fairy godmother.

Ruth was becoming nervous of being actually invaded because some was quite valuable stuff – and she had always been at pains to have nothing in her home that was covetable or new. She'd never put up a gate, let alone fenced her land, and now Enzo had told her that there were some strange goings-on down in the valley, at the old mill.

'I don't know what, exactly,' he said, 'but there is definitely a gang there – I am sure Albanians or Africans — so maybe if you were to make a denunciation, Root, the *carabinieri* could come.'

Ruth raised an eyebrow.

'A denunciation? We don't live in a police state, my dear Enzo!'

He looked unhappy, and muttered about 'bad people', which probably meant that some wretched migrants had taken up squatting there. Nevertheless, she remembered the torn and bloodied T-shirt, and so, on the way to the *ospedale* she dropped in on the police station. It still had a marble slot in its wall marked DENUNCI – left over from Mussolini's time, apparently – but she wasn't having any of that.

'I wonder,' she said courteously to the handsome young policeman at the desk, after she had given him her name and address, 'whether you could very kindly send someone round to the abandoned mill-house at the bottom of the valley? Several items appear to have been stolen from my farm recently, and there seem to be some strange people there.'

'What kind of strange people, *Dottoressa?*'

'Possibly Albanians,' said Ruth, though she hated herself for saying this. She brought out the bullet-holed, bloodstained T-shirt from a plastic bag and added, 'I found this on my property. I believe there may have been an incident.'

The policeman nodded and drew out a form. It took far too long to fill in, but when she left, minus the T-shirt, Ruth felt somewhat relieved. At least that is ticked off my list, she thought.

Diana was now talking about Raff.

'Such a charming chap,' she said. 'He's fixed so many things for me.'

'Raff is wonderful,' Ruth agreed. 'We'll miss him terribly.'

Diana said, 'Is he really leaving?'

'Yes, any day now.'

'Is it money? I tried to give him some.'

'No. I think he's ready to move on.'

Diana said, 'That gel Tania. Does she do anything besides logging?'

'Vlogging,' said Ruth. 'Who knows? We mustn't be prejudiced.'

'Mustn't one?' Diana enquired. 'Why not?'

It was the kind of remark that, back in London, would

have lain between Ruth and Diana like a chasm. Diana had snubbed Ruth's initial attempts to be friendly, which hurt and surprised her. Marta told Ruth that the Evenlodes were snobs, and it was true, they were; yet someone can be everything you most dislike, and yet sympathetic when you came to be better acquainted, Ruth thought. The young seemed unable to see that tolerance was needed in every relationship: they wanted everyone to be as virtuous and pure as they were themselves, forgetting that every human being is a mixture of frailties.

She remembered how, a year after the Evenlodes moved in, she had received a call from Diana.

'Might you drop by? I'm afraid we are in a slight fix.'

This turned out to be Diana's way of saying she was in crisis. Ruth went down to La Docciola immediately, and discovered that Perry was not on but in the toilet. His thin thighs had slipped beneath the rim of the seat so that his buttocks were wedged in the porcelain bowl beneath.

'He's absolutely stuck,' she said.

'Like a cork in a bottle,' Perry added. He did not appear remotely embarrassed, either because he was a stranger to this emotion or because he was in the early stages of dementia.

'You could have called Enzo,' Ruth said, panting as she tried to haul him up. 'He's stronger than a pair of old ladies.'

'No, absolutely not!' Diana exclaimed. 'You're a doctor, he's, well . . .'

A native, Ruth thought. That's what you want to say, isn't it?

But Diana said, 'A civilian.'

How long they had heaved at his arms, she couldn't tell, but with Ruth's strength, and some baby oil, Perry was extracted.

'I thought I was going to Australia,' was his comment, as they hosed him down in the bathtub.

After this, it was impossible for the Evenlodes to be haughty, and Ruth and Diana actually burst out laughing together. For the first time, Ruth was invited into the small living room next to the kitchen, where she found an unexpected delight. All along one wall were bookshelves filled with row upon row of familiar titles.

'Oh!' Ruth exclaimed when she saw these. 'You like *Anthony*!'

'Anthony?'

'Trollope,' Ruth said.

There were those who swore by Dickens, Austen and Shakespeare, and Ruth adored these too, but the unhappy truth was that plenty of perfectly appalling people loved them, perhaps because the very greatest literature is universal and each person finds their own thoughts and feelings reflected in it. Yet Trollope, she was convinced, would never appeal to anyone who was vain or spiteful or self-centred: that was why he was so comforting, and unfashionable.

Ruth said (and she knew that she was being horribly American), 'I sometimes feel as though he's the husband I never had.'

'What a charming thought. I didn't know that Americans liked Trollope,' said Diana. 'Especially not Jews.'

'*Like* him! He's my favourite author. And his greatest creation is a Jewish woman, Madame Max.'

When she had arrived in Britain, it had been Trollope's warm and inspiring presence that enabled her to work out some of the subtleties of an alien culture in which she kept making mistakes. It was thanks to Trollope that she understood that the English did not value doctors, lawyers and other professionals as highly as her own countrymen did, and believed that inherited wealth was superior to that earned by energy and enterprise. He explained so much! Was it because

216

he, like herself, had been an outsider? Was it because he understood the practicalities as well as the romance of court-ship? Or was it because his characters found it hard to take decisions, and almost always regretted them?

At any rate, Trollope became the bond that united them. From then on, whenever conversation threatened to run out, Ruth and Diana could spend a happy half-hour chatting about Alice Vavasor, Madame Max, Dr Thorne, Plantagenet and Glencora Palliser or a hundred others. It was not a passion that Marta could share, any more than Diana could share Ruth and Marta's love for classical music. But it was real enough, and just one enthusiasm in common is sufficient for affection to grow.

'I never had any friends of my own age,' Diana told her. Their relationship, blossoming so late in life and fostered by the events of the past two years, surprised her far more than it did Ruth, who had always been rich in friends.

'What, none?'

'Family is more important to my class,' she said.

'Yes, family is important for Jews, too. In fact, it's really our religion,' said Ruth; and this was how she discovered Diana's immense sorrow at her son producing no male heir.

'But you have daughters?'

'Yes, and grandchildren. Only my son not having a son means the title will pass from Perry's line.'

It was not a sorrow that Ruth could really sympathise with, though, once again, Trollope helped her understand it. Titles were a strange obsession. She wondered whether her guess about Andrew's sexuality was correct, or if he simply exuded the kind of slightly camp charm that was not infre-quently characteristic of certain Englishmen who have spent their adolescence solely in the company of other boys. Ruth

217

understood without being told that Diana adored her son, and was devastated because he apparently cared little or nothing for her in return. Though very different from his father, he was, in this respect, just the same.

Ruth glanced at the figure on the hospital bed. Inside every marriage is a mystery. Why *this* person with *that* one? Did their partner see something about them that was hidden from the rest of the world? Was it desperation, self-sacrifice, pity or lust that brought a couple together and kept them there? Money came into it, Trollope was right about that. She'd read somewhere that extravagant weddings indicated that a marriage was twice as likely to fail. But then her own one to Sam had been a civil ceremony and drinks in a Soho pub, and that had failed too. Poor Sam ... he was one of those drinkers who was the most charming, amusing man on earth with just one drink in him, but it never stopped at just one drink, and then he changed into an aggressive, obnoxious fool. But I could get out of my marriage because I had *agency*, Ruth thought. I had a profession, and an income. Diana has been trapped almost her whole life.

There was a knock, the door opened again, and to her great surprise, Raff and Blessing entered. The two young men stood, hesitating, and Ruth thought, once again, how alike all young people now looked to her.

'May we come in?'

Diana said graciously, 'Do.'

Raff stood by her, but Blessing knelt down by the bed.

'May the Lord Jesus give you mercy, Grandfather,' he said.

Diana bowed her head. 'Amen.'

Ruth's mobile pinged. 'Olly says they've turned off the motorway. Not long, now.'

The sound of Perry's breathing was almost inaudible.

'I wish,' Diana said distressfully, 'he would get here. He'll be too late. And no vicar to give him the Last Rites.'

Blessing said, *'The Lord is my shepherd; I shall not want.*

He maketh me to lie down in green pastures: he leadeth me beside the still waters.'

Diana's voice, and Raff's, joined in; and then Ruth, too, for despite her fierce atheism, she knew the psalm as well as anyone.

'He restoreth my soul: he leadeth me in the paths of righteousness for his name's sake.

Yea, though I walk through the valley of the shadow of death, I will fear no evil: for thou art with me; thy rod and thy staff they comfort me . . .'

The door opened, and there, at last, was Diana's son.

17

The Camper Van

Everything changed when Olly arrived, and yet nothing did. Space was tight by now, but Olly himself was staying in a guest bedroom in the old farmhouse. Tania was still living solo in the little studio cottage, and had been glad of the privacy it afforded.

'A bit old fashioned to have separate rooms, given that we've been living together,' Olly complained to his grandmother, but Ruth insisted.

'It's not right for a groom and bride to sleep together before the ceremony, and you can move into the studio cottage on your wedding night.'

'We're booked into a five-star hotel in Rome for that, Granny,' he said, laughing.

'Oh. You didn't let me know.'

It didn't stop him insisting on sex.

'Just relax,' he kept saying, as if anyone in the world ever did on being told this.

Tania never said 'No', or 'Stop', and he followed a kind of playbook of moves that he believed must be erotic. It will be different after we are married, she told herself, because then I'll be able to trust him, and he'll be more patient. Men thought it was all about their own strength and stamina, not gentleness and dexterity ... It felt as though he was suffocating her, crushing her with his powerful thighs and arms and mouth, she had to make little hollows in her pillow just to be able to breathe. No matter how carefully he began, it would always turn into an act that was focused on his own satisfaction, until, thank God, it was over. Her anxiety was becoming unbearable, and the more she posted about how happy she was, the more she disappeared down the rabbit hole of wanting more and more followers in order not to feel like a total waste of space.

'I can't wait for all this wedding stuff to go away,' Olly said. He, too, had a vague feeling that things weren't perfect, but he ascribed it to what he described as 'the faff'. Every day, Tania would spend hours assembling then disassembling the various arrangements of plates, platters, candles and floral arrangements for her tablescapes on Insta. People loved these; it was a way of sharing ideas, which she enjoyed doing.

'I wonder – which one will I choose?' Tania mused aloud, hovering over some of the expensive porcelain that had been delivered to La Rosa. 'Maybe the Wedgwood? Maybe the Fornasetti? Or maybe ... the paper plates? There's nothing wrong with paper, as long as it's recycled.'

She saw her mother observing all this with a slight crease in her brow.

'Darling, now that Olly is here, maybe you would like more time alone?'

'No, we're good,' said Tania.

She had no idea how a happily married couple should behave. Throughout her childhood, she had never seen her parents kiss, or even touch each other affectionately. Polly was a warm woman; Theo was someone who gave money instead of emotion. Was it the difference between an English mother and an American father? Or was it because (as they all discovered when she was eleven) her father was actually gay? They had probably never been suited. Ever since her parents divorced, her mother had become markedly more confident and dynamic, just as her father had become less uptight and controlling. He'd been miserable hiding his true nature, and she did feel sorry for him on one level while also angry because he must have known, and lied to them all.

When Olly talked about marriage, she felt that in many ways she was older and wiser than he, because she had no illusions. The children of Josh and Anne Viner had flourished in the walled garden of their parents' contentment, and Olly himself expected to repeat their happiness, only with a much larger disposable income.

'You're the one. I knew it as soon as I saw you,' he'd say.

'Really? You've never been in love before?'

'Well, only as a teenager. You know how it is.'

'No,' said Tania truthfully.

Optimistic and upbeat, he was exactly what she needed to make her, in his words, 'more human'. Those she'd grown up with were almost always gloomy about everything because so much didn't live up to their ideals, whereas Olly just laughed. He was never on social media himself, so he never saw the comments about how trolls bet that she 'liked it doggy-style' or said she was 'a spoilt little cow'. Some of them attacked her for being white or middle-class or thin, some called her fat, trashy and ugly, and some claimed that they found her boring.

Tania never responded, but each time it felt like a little piece of her soul had been chipped away.

'Why do you do this influencing?' Blessing asked. 'Does it make you happy?'

'It's what I can do.'

The nightingales were driving her crackers. Sing, sing, sing, night and day. How could such little birds make so much noise? She remarked on this as she walked through the olive groves with Raff, picking wildflowers for her new tablescape.

'They're singing because they must,' Raff said. 'It's one of the greatest forces in nature.'

'It's unbearable.'

'Why?'

'Well, half is like a wheel squeaking, and then, it keeps changing into something lovely. I wish they'd leave me in peace.'

'I expect the females feel the same way.'

'How long do they keep it up?' She blushed as he laughed. 'I mean, how long do they sing for?'

'About six weeks. You've just hit peak nightingale time.'

Tania watched as he chopped out twigs from within the tree branches. She liked him making things tidy. People had mocked her for liking things to be neat and orderly, but what was wrong with that? She could see the trees needed to feel the air moving through their branches.

'When I was little, I used to have a plastic bird-shaped whistle for the bath that made those sounds.'

'Actually, that particular one is a blackbird.'

'How do you know?'

'Different song. It's richer, and shorter. A nightingale is unique,' Raff said. 'It's like being in love. You can't mistake it for anything else.'

223

Last night, he'd sung a Cornish folk song about a couple listening to a nightingale together.

My sweetheart, come along!
Don't you hear the fond song,
The sweet notes of the nightingale flow?
Don't you hear the fond tale
Of the sweet nightingale,
As she sings in those valleys below?

Despite herself, Tania had been charmed. She understood that it was a song about finding sexual happiness, that the valley was in the girl's body. The melody, with its descent through the scale, was at once comical and touching, and the real nightingales clearly enjoyed it, too, given that at least five joined in.

So be not afraid
To walk in the shade,
Nor yet in those valleys below,
Nor yet in those valleys below.

Olly had been scornful about it afterwards, calling him 'Granny's all-singing, all-dancing pet', but Tania sighed deeply when Raff ended, and applauded with the rest. He had made her feel happy and dreadfully sad, but at least he'd made her feel *something* other than fear.

'So what else do you do, when not cultivating the earth and singing folk songs?'

'I had a job. A good one, that I loved. But I left it last year.'

'What happened?'

Raff said, 'I needed a change.'

224

'You told me you'd been ill, didn't you?' she said. 'What was wrong with you?'

'Oh, a few things. PTSD, mostly.'

'Loads of people had that, with the virus. I hope you're better.'

'I am. It helps being in nature.'

Tania said, 'I wonder why?'

'We are part of the natural world. I've never felt that more than when living here.'

'It's a special place, isn't it? And Ruth is special, too.'

'She certainly is,' he said. 'I love the way Italians call her Root. Whereas her name in English means "regret".'

'I thought it meant "friend",' Tania said. 'I like her, though I don't think she likes me.'

'Why do you think that?'

'Most people don't,' Tania said. 'I'm used to it. I annoy them, even though I don't mean to be annoying.'

'My mother had that problem too, when she was young. But she was very opinionated – still is, actually – whereas you don't seem like that.'

'Oh, I have opinions. Only somehow, it seems as bad if you don't express any as if you do, at least if you're a woman.'

Raff clipped some more dead twigs. 'Why shouldn't you have views? I mean, as long as they aren't bonkers or spectacularly unpleasant. A friendship or a marriage should be one long conversation.'

Tania paused to consider this, then said, 'That sounds exhausting.'

'I think when people really trust each other, conversation can be silent, too. Those are some of the best.'

They were walking slowly along a mown path through olive groves.

225

Raff said, 'Keep an eye out for snakes. Most are quite harmless, but there are vipers.'

Tania saw several slim shapes with bigger heads rising up in the long grasses, and gasped.

'Are those snakes? Over there?'

'No. Wild gladioli. The leaves look like swords but they have bright pink flowers when they open.'

'It's like walking inside that painting we saw at the Uffizi. The *Primavera*.'

Raff bent over, and chopped off several more twigs. 'It's a wonderful painting. You can almost hear the music, the bare feet on that black grass.'

Tania considered this. 'That girl trying to run away, with half her clothes torn off, vomiting flowers. So sinister.'

'It's an allegory.'

'I don't think anyone turns into a goddess after being raped, though.'

'No. But people do start off as one thing and become another.'

'Yes,' Tania said. 'Like Blessing.'

Soon after Olly arrived, Tania had brought the Zimbabwean over.

'Look, here's an old friend,' she said. Olly smiled politely.

'Great!' he said. 'Nice of you to come. I hope you've been well looked after?'

'Yes,' said Blessing, almost inaudibly, and even she knew from Olly's expression that this was a meeting between total strangers. Olly moved off a moment later. Tania heard him say, 'So how do you know Tania?', which meant he assumed that Blessing was her guest, not his. But if he wasn't a friend of Olly's, what on earth was he doing here?

Blessing was a mystery – a charming one, but not what she had thought. Everyone accepted him as a wedding guest because he'd arrived with Xan, wearing that old Harvard sweatshirt and he'd slotted right in . . . Tania began to use her own secateurs to snip olive twigs.

'Who cuts your hair, Raff?'

'I do, with an electric razor.'

It was very short, and thick, and stood out all around his head like a bright aura. Maybe that was why animals liked him. Only yesterday, a swallow had flown into the living room, and smashed itself repeatedly on the windows trying to escape. Everyone panicked, including Tania, who screamed and put her arms over her face and hair.

Instantly, Raff had plucked the frantic bird out of the air, clasping it in his cupped hands. He said in a low, soft voice, 'It's all right. Quiet, now. I'm not going to harm you. Look.'

He opened his fingers a chink, and the swallow's red-cheeked face poked out at once, looking almost inquisitive and not upset at all. Tania asked, 'Is it hurt?'

'I hope not.'

'What does it feel like?'

'I can feel its heart beating very fast,' Raff answered. He walked steadily towards the garden, and she followed, still trembling with shock but fascinated. 'It's frightened, but I think it knows I'm going to help it, not eat it. You wouldn't think something this tiny could fly thousands and thousands of miles, would you? They sleep in the air. Imagine that.'

He opened his hands once they were outside. For a moment, the swallow clung to his fingers with spindly claws, then it swooped off.

She could have sworn that it looped back moments later, as if in thanks.

Every creature seemed drawn to him. Dash was begging for attention, and when Raff bent to scratch the white patch on the spaniel's head it rolled over, spreading in shameless ecstasy.

Ruth's feral cat glided across with its tail upright, mewing for its share of caresses, and then the old white horse and the donkey came trotting up to greet him and have their noses scratched. He brought out a handful of bran, whistled, and held it up; a cluster of sparrows descended to peck at it.

'You're like someone in a Disney cartoon,' she complained. 'Why do they like you?'

'I suppose I like them.'

'But I like them too,' said Tania. 'They don't come to me.'

A faint, warm breeze blew, scattering a sudden shower of petals.

'I'm not nervous. Maybe that helps.'

Tania felt wretched again. 'Were you there when Olly met Blessing?'

'Yes. Olly didn't seem to know who he was.'

So it hadn't been her imagination. She said, softly, 'I can't decide whether Blessing is someone Olly has forgotten he invited, which is bad, or an interloper, which is worse.'

'The latter, I'd say.'

'Do you think he's a paparazzo?'

'I think it's possible that he's a refugee.'

Tania said, 'But he brought those fancy macarons for Ruth!'

'Xan could have given those to him. Marta mentioned that Ivanov always gives her a box of fancy cakes left over after each recital. He'd come on from the palazzo.'

'Why would Xan do that?'

'To help a brother? Xan has a kind heart, and Blessing may be in some kind of trouble. Juicy and Ruth found a T-shirt just before you arrived with blood on it.'

Tania thought of the wound she had dressed. She shivered. 'You think he was attacked? Why?'

'I don't know, but Italy is on the front line of a migrant

228

crisis. Do you know how many people are trying to move from Africa and the Middle East to Europe, because of climate change and famine, and war? Millions and millions.'

'I can't imagine it.'

'Nobody can, but Blessing is obviously not a crook. I can't think why else he'd be on this hillside.'

'My mother is always rescuing refugees claiming political asylum. It's really hard.' Tania tried to sound cheerful because the truth was she had sometimes felt like saying to Polly that she needed rescuing, too. 'She spends her life helping Afghans, I think, or maybe Syrians. And now, of course, Ukrainians.'

'Yes, political oppression is taken more seriously by our leaders than merely dying of hunger and thirst,' Raff said drily. 'In any case, this is speculation. It may just be that Olly forgot. He has a lot of friends, doesn't he?'

'Loads. But thinking back, didn't everyone assume that he was one of us?' said Tania.

Raff said, 'I don't make assumptions about anyone, I hope.'

'People make assumptions about me,' Tania said, and a note of anger crept into her voice. 'How I walk, how I dress, how I have meltdowns. How I have permanent resting bitch-face.'

'I expect it's because you don't simper.'

'I don't know how to.'

'Why should you?' he asked.

'Because it's *normal*,' Tania said.

'You don't have to do what everyone else does.'

'Everything has always felt too intense to me,' Tania said. 'Sounds, tastes, smells, feelings. People think I'm weird.' She stopped. 'I expect you do, too.'

'Can I ask you something?'

'You can ask,' she said drearily. She had hoped he was different.

229

'Would you like a cup of tea? I'm thirsty. My camper van is nearby. We could sit in the shade of the pine tree.'

'Oh. OK.'

Tania could see the blue-and-white vehicle up ahead.

'Is that where you live?'

'Yes. I have what every English person in Tuscany wants: a room with a view.'

She asked cautiously, 'May I see inside?'

'Be my guest. I'll be outside.'

The tiny fridge, the little cooker and sink hidden by a counter-top, the lockers beneath the bench seats, the shelves crammed with paperbacks built even into the door of the van, the blue and yellow checked curtains over every window and the seats upholstered in matching fabric all charmed her.

When she stepped out again, she said, 'It's like a mobile doll's house.'

'Except, I'm not a doll,' he said. 'Any more than you are.'

'No ...' Tania glanced at him, then away again. 'May I photograph it for my vlog?'

'No.'

'Why not?'

'Because I'm a private person.'

Tania shrugged. 'OK. I just like the interior.'

'My mother did it. She used it as a mobile studio.'

'Is she an artist?'

'Yes, a painter. She spent a few months living near here, before I was born. It's where she met my father. I always wanted to visit Santorno because of that.'

She kept thinking of the van's interior, fascinated by the cleverness of its design.

'Do you sleep on a bench? It looks very narrow.'

'The table slots down in the middle to make a double bed

across the width of the van. There's a cushion that goes on top of it. It's perfectly comfortable.'

'You could go *anywhere* in something like this,' Tania said. 'Wake up in a different place every day ... Did you travel around before you came here?'

'Not really. I was too knackered. But I'm going on a road trip next week.'

'You're leaving?'

'Yes. In three days.'

'You mean, the day of the wedding.'

'Yes.'

Tania stared at him. 'Why?'

'I have another life to go back to.'

'A girlfriend? Or a boyfriend?'

'Neither.'

'Why not?'

He said, 'Because ... Oh, what's the point? Because I don't want to see you throwing your life away.'

Tania looked at him blankly.

'Why does my marrying Olly matter to you?'

'Because I *like* you,' Raff said. 'And that has nothing to do with your being ridiculously pretty.'

She said, 'I'm not pretty on the inside, you know.'

'Nobody is pretty on the inside.'

Tania said, in a tone of suppressed fury, 'I've made up my mind, and that's *that*!'

As she went down the hill, she could feel her mobile buzzing like a trapped hornet in her pocket. It was Olly, of course. He was waiting for her in the cottage.

'Where have you been?'

'Just out for a walk. I thought you needed a rest.'

'What I need isn't a rest,' Olly said. His mouth tasted acrid.

231

'Ow, ow, be careful! Don't touch my hair!'

'God, you might as well be wearing a chastity belt,' he muttered.

The snakes in her scalp writhed. Tania sighed and raised her arms for him to slide off her dress.

18

Enzo's Visitor

Every day, Enzo expected to be visited by the police. The body he had seen in the millpond couldn't go unnoticed for ever. Sooner or later, someone would find the corpse, and then they might find the other one of the man he'd shot. Already, he'd started from his bed because he thought he'd heard something buzzing round his home, like a small helicopter or a very large insect. Was he under surveillance of some kind? But when he flung open his window, there was only the empty air.

He found himself drawn back to the mill, and a vantage point where he could watch the squatters through his binoculars. There was a people carrier, and initially he could see the Africans climbing into it, presumably to go off to beg. It was all organised, just as he and his hunting buddies had believed. Maybe I should tell them, and see what they suggest, he thought.

On reflection, however, both the corpse and the existence of a second victim were best kept to himself. He'd told Ruth about the migrants in the mill-house, and there was no knowing what his buddies might think was an appropriate response. They all hated and feared the invaders, and yet Enzo was finding it harder and harder to feel the loathing of before. Hatred is a habit, like so much else; and the awful feeling that had come over him when he'd pulled the trigger had shocked him. Killing another person wasn't just a matter of an instant's impulse. It was something you had to live with, for as long as you lived yourself.

There was another thing that haunted him. What if the figure had not been a thief and a murderer, but an Italian just asking for help? What if it were someone lost, like his own daughter? He had no idea what she looked like, now. His own hair was inclined to be bushy when uncut. Hadn't Fede had quite curly hair too? What if – and this was his worst nightmare – the intruder had actually *been* Fede?

He'd forgotten so much about her, apart from her soft voice saying, 'Papà?' His name always had a question in it, as if she wasn't quite sure whether he was there. Which, thanks to her mother, he wasn't. He didn't even have a photograph of her. His wife, or ex-wife, had taken them all.

Enzo trudged down the hill. He knew this path so well that he could probably walk it in his sleep; indeed, he wasn't sure now whether he was entirely awake.

When he'd been a boy, his father had been given a wall calendar by the Banca di Firenze, a present sent out to all its clients (which perhaps helped explain why it later got into financial trouble). It was a lavish affair, beautifully printed on thick parchment-like paper, and each month showed a different image from a Florentine fresco depicting the journey of the Magi. Each king, richly robed, was mounted on a prancing white horse, but what Enzo had particularly loved was the way they were in a long procession that wound its way up and down an entirely familiar landscape of mountainous, wooded hills dotted with cypress trees. Naturally, the Nativity was happening in Tuscany – where else? There were castellated towers, just like that of the Palazzo Felice, and hawks catching doves, and hunters on horseback spearing deer in groves like the ones he himself walked through. It looked lively, colourful and fun – the way this landscape must have done, long ago, before the balance between the wild and the cultivated tipped over into encroaching chaos.

'What a pretty picture,' Stefano had said when he saw it.

Stefano and he had gone to elementary school together. Nobody liked Stefano because his father was an Umbro, even though Stefano's father had died when he was a boy. They were poor, and so Enzo's mother was always having them round for a meal. She had a soft heart.

'You're the same age, you should be friends,' she told Enzo.

'Imagine if I said to you, here's another thirty-year-old woman, be friends?' Enzo told her. 'I hate him, I hate them both. They aren't like us. They're *Umbri*.'

'They are good people.'

At fourteen, their paths had divided because Enzo (naturally) was smarter than Stefano and went to the *liceo classico*, whereas Stefano had gone to the technical school for stupid people, and at sixteen left school altogether to begin lorry driving. He had done pretty well out of this, transporting local goods all over Europe, whereas Enzo had stayed at university as long as possible to avoid military service, gone abroad, and then, when it was thankfully abolished in 2005, returned, drifting from one job to the next because his family, like so many others, lacked the right connections. Enzo's wife had never been able to understand this; she thought he was a loser. But Stefano's wife and child were still living with him in the village, he had bought his own home, and whenever they drove past each other, his old schoolfellow gave him a long, derisive blast of his horn. Each time, Enzo hated him so much that he wished he would die.

Truth to tell, when Enzo and his buddies gathered, it wasn't really a migrant he was thinking of when he pulled the trigger. It was Stefano. Stefano, with his luck and his cockiness and his lorry that had made him a well-travelled, well-paid, well-respected citizen. When Enzo had just a little more sleep, he realised that he was poisoned, just as his dog had been, but by disappointment. It was all mixed up with missing his daughter. Sometimes he thought that if he could talk to her, it would be enough – not holding her, not seeing her, but just hearing her voice and knowing she was thinking of him as he thought of her, every day. Occasionally, he would receive a call on his cell phone from a number that he didn't recognise, and he always hoped it was Fede, not the Fede he would never recover but some new incarnation, a teenager with long skinny legs and big new teeth perhaps but still his beloved child.

It never was.

Everyone had a reason for banging off guns, and mostly they were not happy. One of his buddies had lost his business after being denounced for the under-payment of taxes, something absolutely everyone who wasn't stupid did, but for which he was punished as an example to the rest. Another had a wife who refused to have intimate relations with him for over twenty years. A third had a son who was born disabled, and would never be able to walk or talk. They were kind to each other, in the gruff way of men. Men didn't talk, they grunted, but their grunts communicated all kinds of things, in a digni-fied, masculine way. Their conviction that they were the secret guardians of their community had given them a common purpose, and self-respect.

'If we don't do this, who will?' said the man with the disabled son; and the one whose wife denied him said, 'We must protect our neighbourhood.'

After their target practice they would drink beers and watch American videos together, the sort in which regular guys like themselves, only with more muscles, took on gangs of crooks and emerged victorious to live happy and rich in the company of pretty women. Enzo, the only one among them to have been to the States, knew that it wasn't quite like that – he'd been privately horrified by the obesity and above all the travesties of Italian food – but enjoyed the companionship.

However, being a criminal had changed what he felt about himself. These days, when he went into town, he almost cringed. What would people say if they knew? He didn't want to look too carefully at the African beggars, but was reassured when he saw that most of them seemed to have very closely cropped locks, rather than the wild frizz he had glimpsed before he pulled the trigger.

How could anyone make a living out of begging? Enzo worked six days a week, but the price of food and fuel kept climbing, and everyone said worse was to come when the gas was cut off. It was all the fault of the Russians, though Italy's own prime minister had told Italians that it was a choice between air conditioning and freedom, so he was being blamed too. There was also no fertiliser for the crops, and no carbon dioxide to keep fruit fresh, and many countries in North Africa were predicted to starve for lack of wheat. Who would have thought that such a large, dull country as Ukraine could turn out to be so crucial to the world? People were talking about nuclear bombs and freezing to death, and even though the next winter seemed a long way off in springtime, it made everyone gloomy and angry.

Though even Ivanov, it seemed, was being given a bad time by Putin. Why else were all those men with shaved heads and guns guarding him? The deliveries that came by van had to leave goods at the guardhouse where (it was said) they were checked for bombs, radioactivity, infections and heaven knew what else. They had been proud of the restoration of the palazzo, and all the famous people who had visited Santorno because of Ivanov's hospitality, and now they worried what would happen to them if the oligarch left, or was killed.

'*Chi monta più alto ch'e' non deve, cade più basso ch'e' non crede,*' Enzo muttered, looking at the tall poppies in the grasses. It was satisfying to think that those who climbed higher than they should would face a fall, but at the same time, if a big man like Ivanov fell, he'd bring several people here with him. He couldn't help wondering whether the dead man he'd seen in the millpond might not in some way be connected to the oligarch, rather than the wretched migrants. Was it a coincidence that within weeks of the war, this quiet part of Tuscany should have a murder happen? On the other hand, Italy was in the grip of so many crooks that the dead man was probably just one of many.

These thoughts and feelings churned through his mind, as he was walking up and down between Ruth's house and his own. Nature, which had once existed purely for his own amusement, now touched his heart painfully. What was it about the nightingales' song that made his soul tender? They seemed to be encouraging him on that fateful night, but these days, they were reproaching him. When had he become like this? Was it when he held his dying dog in his arms, and she had given him the faintest of licks? Or perhaps it had begun when he started to take photographs of his life, because paying attention to anything, no matter how small and ordinary, is to discover that nothing observed is unremarkable.

Repeatedly, the words that all Italian schoolchildren get drummed into them from Dante's *Inferno* circled in his mind. He knew every path through every tangled wood, but he was lost.

> *Nel mezzo del cammin di nostra vita*
> *mi ritrovai per una selva oscura*
> *ché la diritta via era smarrita.*

His wife had found it cute at first, living in the Tuscan countryside; then (once Fede was born) crazily unhygienic and dangerous. She wanted to go back to California, or even to Rome; anywhere but what she called 'the fucking badlands'.

She had been lonely, and now he was lonely too. He went everywhere, into people's homes and gardens, but nobody visited him. The road was too rough, his home was too humble, and he never invited anyone. Yet a few days after he discovered the body in the millpond, he returned from his labours to find a sleek black car parked in his yard, and a man about his own age sitting on the wooden bench outside.

Enzo tensed, instantly watchful. He thought he recognised his visitor, but could not be sure.

'Good evening. May I help you?'

To his surprise, the man answered in Italian.

'Good afternoon, Mr Rossi.'

Enzo asked, distrustfully, 'Are you police?'

'No. I am Vasily Ivanov. Your landlord.'

He put out a gloved hand, and Enzo shook it, tentatively. This was most unexpected. He had often met the old Contessa

239

Felice, up at the palazzo, many years ago. In those days, tenants had always been invited with their families to a harvest festival once the grapes were picked. It was a traditional event, with as much food and wine as everyone could eat. It was one of the things that his American wife had deplored.

'Don't you think it's disgusting, the way that you were expected to grovel?' she'd exclaimed.

Maybe so; but now the contessa was dead, he missed it. Was it so bad, for everyone to get together over a free meal?

'*Prego*,' he said, politely opening the door. He looked down into the yard. Through the darkened windows of the car, he glimpsed two other men. They were big types, with a look of such toughness that it made him quake just looking at them.

'My bodyguards,' said Ivanov, following his gaze. He made a gesture to them, and they nodded. One was clearly watching something on a screen in the car. 'Satellite images,' Ivanov said. 'Of the surrounding countryside.'

Enzo swallowed.

'Is there some kind of trouble?'

'I hope not. At least, not for you.'

'May I offer you a coffee?'

Ivanov said, after a pause, 'Black.'

Enzo lit the stove, tamped some coffee grains into the little percolator, and filled the base with tap water from the stone sink. He hoped that, when his landlord noticed how very unmodernised his home was, he would not demand more rent. His gas came from a tank under the cooker. There was no central heating, no hot water, and the windows shook when the wind blew. The terracotta-tiled floor wobbled in places where a beam was giving way. It had three interconnecting rooms, no proper bathroom, and the ground floor still had empty pens for animals as well as his tools. Yet he was the only person left who knew how to look after the land in the old way.

When Enzo saw how Ruth farmed, he wanted to laugh. Those rich hippies had no idea. In his father's youth, the terraces had been tilled by white oxen, and the food they got out of the earth was the difference between survival and destitution, so the arrival of chemical fertilisers and rotovators had been miraculous. He still had to pump water for the cistern up by hand from the yard for his vegetable patch, and his electricity, which cost a fortune, cut out every time there was a thunderstorm. Yet if his rental were converted and modernised, it would make some foreigner a large and pleasant second home: that was his fear. Even though his ancestors had lived in this farm for hundreds of years, and had probably even built it in the first place, as a tenant he had no security. His dream, when he married, was to buy it from the contessa, perhaps with some money from his wife's family. She would have sold it to him, too, being so desperate for money that, rumour had it, she paid her cleaner in antique furniture; but there was no hope the Russian would.

Ivanov nodded his head when his coffee was poured, into Enzo's best cup (which meant the only one without a chip). He waited until Enzo himself had drunk his own before taking a sip, and Enzo wondered whether this was out of courtesy or fear.

'Perhaps you are asking yourself the reason for my visit,' he said, at last. 'I have come to ask you to do two things for me.' Again, Ivanov paused. 'One is to kill as many wild boar as you can. I know you are a hunter. Frankly, they are a pestilence.'

'*Si, signore*. Certainly. But I am only allowed to kill them in season,' Enzo said. 'From September to March.'

'If you were to happen to see one out of season . . . '

'I could be denounced,' Enzo said.

'By whom? The only other people living on this hillside are foreigners. They are as plagued by wild boar as I am.'

'That's true enough.'

'Besides,' Ivanov said, 'I think perhaps you did shoot something last week. Did you not?'

Enzo went very still.

'How did you know?'

'A man in my situation always hears a gunshot. I also know the difference between the sound of a rifle and a pistol, just as I know the difference between a dog and a wolf. I must take precautions, you see.'

Ivanov opened the front of his elegantly cut jacket, and Enzo glimpsed the gun strapped to his side. He felt his face become cold and stiff.

'*Signore* . . .'

'So tell me, were you shooting at an animal?'

Ivanov's dark eyes were more frightening than any weapon.

'No,' Enzo said. 'I was shooting at a man. An intruder.'

'What did he look like?'

Enzo said, in a rush, 'Nothing like another Russian, I assure you. Or even a European. I think he was an African.'

Ivanov raised an eyebrow.

'Africa is a continent, not a country.'

'One of the migrants. You know.'

Enzo made a gesture, rotating his hands to indicate curly hair, or possibly lunacy. Ivanov regarded this with distaste.

'Was that enough to get him killed?'

Enzo said sullenly, 'I thought he was a thief. I didn't kill him. He got away.'

'And yet,' Ivanov said, 'I hear that a dead body has been found in the millpond at the bottom of the valley.'

The police must have told him, Enzo thought. Information like that would have been conveyed immediately to Santorno's richest resident; they would be paid to do this. But the news had not reached Enzo, which meant that it was being kept quiet.

'Had he been shot?'

'No,' Ivanov said.

'Well, then. Nothing to do with me. Besides,' Enzo said, 'he wasn't African, was he?'

As soon as he said this, he realised his mistake.

'So you *do* know something about it,' Ivanov said.

Enzo sighed. 'Yes. But only what I discovered by going to the mill in search of the man I shot. The other man – was he Albanian?'

'Why do you ask?'

'Most criminals in Italy are Albanian,' Enzo said, with assurance.

Ivanov looked at him again with those dark eyes that could change in an instant from warmth to coldest stone, and Enzo said, embarrassed, 'Of course, not Russians.'

The Russian suddenly laughed. 'There is no end to your prejudices, is there? Signor Rossi, the men who try to kill me are almost certainly Russian. Who else would Putin send? But in this instance, you are probably right. He was Albanian, and so was his partner.'

'People traffickers?'

'Yes, it seems so. One has disappeared, so perhaps it was he who killed the other, but the other people they were transporting have also vanished. Has that house been used for traffickers before?'

Enzo thought it possible, just because Santorno was not far from the *superstrada* that led, eventually, to the north, to

Germany and France. Not that he had ever spoken to any of those people, but it was what everyone knew, just as they knew that the charities who picked up sinking inflatable boats could be summoned by mobile calls and were part of a criminal network plaguing Italy.

'This is what I would like you to do,' Ivanov said, interrupting. 'I am interested in anyone living in these hills who is not a tourist or a migrant. I do not think the FSB will make the mistake again of staying anywhere where there is CCTV, but there are plenty of houses here that are not lived in most of the year. I wish you to be my eyes and ears. The police here are not – how can I say it . . . ?'

'I understand,' Enzo said, his chest inflating. He was happy to be able to render this service to a rich and important man. 'We all say that the only test a *carabiniere* has to pass is having a brick broken over his head. I have my contacts, and will let you know of any news.'

'Good,' said Ivanov. He paused. 'I have had information that there will be another attempt on my life soon. I will reward you well if you help me.'

Enzo swallowed.

'If I have any information, who do I call?'

'What is the number of your cell phone?'

Ivanov sent him a WhatsApp. 'This number reaches my head of security. Remember, anything you think strange, I am interested.'

Enzo was relieved to hear his car pull away and go carefully back up the uneven, potholed road. I should have asked him to mend it, he thought, listening to the sound of displaced stones. Or put in a bathroom.

He did not expect any more disturbances, but that evening, when he came home after a day of picking Ruth's guests up from the airport, he went to check on his pistol. He had not touched it since shooting his intruder.

But when Enzo went upstairs to his bedroom, and felt under his bed, his hand met nothing. The pistol was gone, vanished into the dust that lay thick as wool beneath the frame, and he had no idea who had taken it.

19

Marta's Recital

At some point, Marta understood that mortality does not creep up on us stealthily, but in sudden bursts, like puberty. The difference is that while the metamorphoses of youth bring independence, those of age bring the opposite.

To Marta, this was a dreadful prospect, almost worse than the physical pain. Even if she had always known it might be a possibility, she'd avoided confronting it in the hope that it might never happen. She did not want to have a carer, or to live with her daughter, and she wanted above all to keep playing. It was not just what she did, it was what she *was*. Her professional career, modest though it was, had given her life purpose and meaning. But whatever it was that had enabled her to ignore everything but the music had deserted her, until she passed through the menopause.

What a miracle that had been! Where other women complained about brain fog, fevers, exhaustion and the rest, Marta had felt the drag of the female condition fall away. *This* was what she was born to do, and she was going to do it. All those years of existing to one side of her own life – looking after first her husband, then her daughter, then her grandson – were done, and she was free to step back into its centre.

Some people had been very surprised by her renaissance.

'Can't you do it as a hobby?' asked one. No: a vocation is not a hobby. Sometimes she thought it was more like a disease, or a curse. It gave her no rest unless she attended to it, but when she did so, she was herself.

I should never have given up performing, she thought. Had she continued, she might have gone on building an international audience, like those other women pianists she admired – Argerich, Larrocha, Uchida, Hewitt. Almost all of them childless, but wasn't that usually the case? You had to choose, as a woman, between the life of the body and that of the art.

In the last fifteen years, when she was retired, elderly and living alone, her career enjoyed a minor revival. She'd performed in churches, and she gave private recitals; never at grander places like the Wigmore, or St Martin-in-the-Fields. So things continued, until Ivanov got in touch.

It was like being given a new lease of life. To play in public once more, to have an audience again, could not give her back her youth, but Marta was happy – or if not happy, at peace. Performing still demanded everything, mentally and emotionally, and she was ready to give that, only now, it seemed, her body could no longer cope.

She went to the doctor, wasting precious time in his waiting room to have her lungs and heart listened to, her blood and urine sampled, her eyes and ears examined. He was mystified by her intense pain.

'Maybe your liver?'

'There is nothing wrong with my liver,' said Marta irritably. 'It's my back.'

'*Dottoressa*, it is probably age,' he said.

When Marta relayed this to Ruth, the latter snorted.

'Why do men always say this to women? Don't listen to him, my dear. Go back to London and see a specialist. It's probably osteoporosis, but even that can be helped.'

'I'm not sure I'm even registered still with my old GP.'

'Then see a private doctor. You have the money, don't you? Though you might also consider how much of this might be psychological.'

'I am not imagining it.'

'I know. But there is some research indicating that back pain can be the result of an inflamed nerve, rather than a skeletal problem.'

Ruth had so much energy and determination, Marta thought, she would never grow old. Long ago, she watched her friend at work in the bowels of the Royal Free Hospital, unseen. Marta was there because Lottie, then aged twelve, had broken her arm, and needed it set in plaster. At the far end of the A&E treatment room was a large, well-lit Perspex cubicle. Inside this were four uniformed policemen, restraining a very muscular man who was half naked, streaming with sweat and clearly crazy.

'What's the matter with him?' Marta asked the nurse in an undertone. Even twenty metres away, she felt nervous. 'Drugs?'

'Psychotic. Thinks he's Jesus Christ.'

Then in walked Ruth. Marta had never seen her at work, but the hair was unmistakable. She spoke, briefly, to the four policemen who left, reluctantly and her friend's small, white-coated figure then sat opposite the giant lunatic, talking to him. It was one of the bravest things that Marta had ever seen, but after a while, the man was no longer sweating, shouting and showing the whites of his eyes, but just very tired and quiet and bewildered.

Marta never told Ruth that she had seen her do this, and she suspected her friend would not even remember the incident now. It was simply what she did. Many years later she told Marta that, as she'd become increasingly disillusioned with medicating human suffering, she had become convinced that listening and talking could help some more than drugs. Marta understood that she'd poured something invisible out of herself for this madman that was not altogether different from what she herself gave when she played.

Unlike herself, however, Ruth was just as buoyant as she'd been forty years ago. She had told her friend, with the appalling frankness of her nation, that she'd gone on enjoying the best sex of her life until well into her seventies.

'Who with?' Marta asked.

'Oh, you know that Canadian photographer who visited every autumn?'

'But he's *twenty years younger than you*,' Marta said, shocked but slightly envious.

'So? I'm not going around showing guys my passport, am I?'

'What happened to him?'

Ruth shrugged. 'Died. I'm looking for a replacement.'

There were women who could not live without a man, even at their age, and those who (like Ruth) still enjoyed the physical side. It was an affliction that Marta was glad to be free from. She had adored her husband, body and soul, but never wanted anyone else after his death. Yet she met women, old as well as young, who begged her to introduce them to any available bachelors, because even knowing that you would have him snoring all night beside you was still somehow better than being peaceful, alone. It was astonishing how women couldn't see this, because they had been trained to see having a man, any man, as some sort of prize.

'Maybe Beatrix is right,' Marta said to Ruth. 'Maybe it's better to choose death while we still have all our faculties.'

'Never! If I weren't tied up with this fricking wedding, I'd visit Beatrix in Amsterdam and try to talk her out of it,' Ruth said. 'I am convinced she is doing this out of loneliness.'

There is a difference between loneliness and solitude, however, Marta thought. Had Edward lived, she knew they would have gone on being happy together into old age. If it had to be a choice between love and music, she would still have chosen love.

Being old was very different from what it was in her youth. Then, old women were still supposed to creep around, wearing beige, but no woman Marta knew did so now. Even the black-clad widows she once saw in Santorno a couple of decades ago had somehow vanished. If she felt like smoking, she would, and if she was angry, she could swear, and if she still wanted to dance to the Rolling Stones then the sky wouldn't fall down.

But each week, it became more of an effort. Anything she ate seemed to ricochet around her large intestine like a pinball in a machine. Her sense of balance had deserted her. She found it necessary to grab hold of supports to steady herself.

'Why don't you try one of those cool folding sticks, like sub-machine guns?' Xan asked when they walked slowly up the main street to the piazza for coffee. She clung to his arm as the Via Nazionale tilted like the deck of a ship. Each step was painful, but she told herself that if she persisted, it would do her good.

'The Queen doesn't use one.'

'I think, Oma, she does these days.'

Marta made a dismissive face. 'She is twelve years older than I am.'

She had to stop, mid-step. Her grandson looked at her, concerned.

'Wait, it will pass,' she growled. Yet a dreadful certainty was growing. 'It *will* pass.'

Only by clenching her will like a fist could she keep practising, though the daily application of morphine patches (donated by a friend whose partner had died of cancer) had some efficacy. J. S. Bach was always her balm, but Couperin and Chopin were torture, and as for Scarlatti! But she had to play something Italian for this audience, even if few of them would know or care about the nationality of composers.

Xan loved classical music, because she had taught him, and she had wondered at one point whether he might even follow her in becoming a professional. But he'd lacked the obsessive need to practise that makes a born musician fixated on playing from the age of four. She was not altogether sorry to see this.

It annoyed her, privately, that Xan's new friend was still staying with them. She thought she wouldn't mind, but any other presence now felt intrusive.

Blessing was very polite, if nervous. Marta sent him out to do a small daily shop for her, and he cleaned her flat which (she had to admit) she could not keep on top of without help. He could cook, too. Grudgingly, she had to admit he was useful, but she wanted her grandson.

'It's nice to have you to myself for a bit,' she said to Xan as they sat together in her tiny garden. Above its high walls she could hear the bells tolling. 'I haven't seen you in such a time.'

'I'd come more often if I could afford it.'

She heard the unspoken reproach in his voice, and it annoyed her.

'What about your savings? You must have something put aside for a rainy day?'

Xan said, 'It rained.'

'But I gave you sixty thousand pounds when I sold my house!'

To her, it sounded like a huge sum of money, but it was just 1 per cent of what she had made on the sale of her house in Hampstead. Even if she had then spent £3 million buying herself a two-bedroom flat in London, and her (much cheaper) flat in Santorno, and even if there had been taxes and lawyers and estate agents and certain disbursements to her daughter and grandchildren, she was still sitting on £3 million. He knew it, and she knew it, but she refused to feel guilty.

'Yes, and thank you very much for that, Oma, because I have no student debt, which is more than most people my age. Only there is nothing left. I'm barely making a living wage, with rent and everything. If it weren't for Zoom, I couldn't even be here now, because I can at least teach online.'

Marta knew that Xan was not exactly having an agreeable time in his twenties. But that was what youth had, instead of, well, money.

'Why do you find it so hard to take control of your life?' she asked. 'Nothing will happen to you unless you *make* it do so.'

Marta knew that he didn't have a proper job, and he didn't have a girlfriend, and the two were probably connected. Young women might believe they were very different from her generation, but few would look at a young man without prospects – or whatever they called it now. To be desired, you must make yourself desirable, and Xan, though as handsome as he was clever and kind, would not be considered such by any woman worth having until he had a career.

'Things will get better,' she said, seeing his miserable expression. 'Have faith.'

'In what? I don't believe in God.'

He was so lucky, but seemed not to realise it. When she, Ruth and Diana met they often marvelled at what their grandchildren seemed to take for granted.

'I cannot believe how many gadgets the young own,' said Marta. 'Even Blessing has a mobile!'

'When we got married, we barely had the money for a refrigerator, let alone a television,' said Diana. 'Yet they still can't seem to commit to an appointment. In our day, we had to write *letters*, and we were still punctual.'

'A lot of things have become cheap, thanks to the Chinese,' Ruth remarked diplomatically.

'Yes, and if we had any sense we'd stop trading with them, too.'

Marta sighed, sitting at the keyboard again. Her dog kept scratching and snuffling at the bookcase in her bedroom. 'Otto, stop that!' she said sharply.

'He's just bored, poor dog,' Xan said. 'I'll walk him in a moment.'

Marta wondered who was walking Diana's Labrador, now she was effectively living in the hospital. Raff, no doubt. He had confided in her, and although she was not a singing teacher but an accompanist, she'd been able to give him some advice about breathing, and even suggest some of the songs he might sing.

'Whether they will be effective, who knows? *Lieder* worked for me.'

'What I really need is *L'Elisir d'Amore*,' he said.

'It's all in the mind, you know.' She looked at him with a slight smile. 'My husband seemed a very ordinary young man, until I heard him.'

'But he was a gifted professional singer.'

'You must believe in the power of music.'

She had to believe this, and in herself. It was the day of her recital, and pain and nausea had shrunk her stomach.

'Oma, you *must* eat lunch, or you will have no strength tonight,' Xan told her.

'When my mother was passing, she was the same,' Blessing said.

'I'm not dead yet,' Marta said, with asperity. 'Will you be going back to Zimbabwe?'

Blessing said, after a pause, 'In my country, it is not safe for me.'

'Why not?'

'Men who . . . love other men are not supposed to exist.'

Had her grandson known his friend was gay? She guessed not, though Xan said immediately, 'I can't imagine how hard that must be for you.'

'I cannot change what I am,' Blessing said. 'I do not believe God made me to live my life in a country where a man like myself is beaten, arrested and even killed. I hope . . .' He looked at them both. 'I hope this does not offend you?'

'No, *of course* not,' they said together, shocked.

'Will you stay here?'

'It's possible. I have family in Italy, too.'

'Zimbabweans?'

'No,' said Blessing. 'I have some white relations. But . . . it's a long story.'

'Let's talk about this after my recital,' Marta said.

All her thoughts and energies had to go into her performance, and only that.

It was a warm evening. The piazza swarmed with people – some tourists, satisfying casual curiosity, but most of them

254

local, including many expatriates. The swifts looping shrilly overhead, the clangour of the church bells and the slap of feet on stone were all sounds that had probably not changed for centuries. A natural amphitheatre, the square had wonderful acoustics, and younger people sat in rows on the stone steps of the Town Hall, looking down at the stage. All around, the bars and restaurants were full, for everybody liked free entertainment. There was a general buzz of interest. The only thing that would have made them happier would have been an appearance by Ivanov himself. It was rumoured that he had bought the one property with a balcony overlooking the piazza, formerly the home of the Communist Party, to listen without being seen, but nobody could be certain.

The festival was called the Maggio Musicale, or Musical May. Though less well-attended than the annual Sagra del Cinghiale the following week (in which townspeople paid a small sum for as much roast wild boar as they could eat), it had greatly added to Santorno's popularity. This year's programme had included a Venetian string quartet that had given a rendition of Vivaldi's *Four Seasons* the day before ('I wanted to die', Xan reported back), a selection of arias from Verdi and Puccini sung by a Danish tenor and a Romanian soprano, and a Florentine flautist playing Enrico Morricone's theme tunes from spaghetti Westerns (which everyone loved). But Marta was the star turn.

Vaguely aware of a number of familiar faces in the crowd – Ruth's houseparty, Ben Gorgle, Enzo, Juicy and a number of fellow Germans who strode up and down the hills with Alpine sticks – she sat down at the Steinway. Diana, of course, could not be present.

There was a fulsome introduction by the mayor, and then Marta began.

The notes, the notes, only the notes, she told herself. The music was on her iPad, timed to click forward, but more importantly in her muscle memory. Her hands, her wrists, her arms, her stomach and her back were in the grip of that imperative. Precision, speed and daring matter as much as any musical ability or emotion. Like an athlete, she had been in training all her life for this.

Her body was singing with fire, and yet her playing had to make familiar pieces appear as if plucked fresh out of the air. She must convey deep emotion yet not succumb to it herself, for the instant she did so, she would be lost.

To Marta, who could read music as easily as a reader can read words printed on a page, there were no barriers between what she saw and what she played. At any moment her fingers might slip, and the life-force that she was pouring into them might fail, but *they must not fail*. Her back shrieked, her heart throbbed, her head rang, but the dead spoke through her.

'Great music feels to me as if it had already been written,' she said to Xan. 'Even if every note is stamped with the composer's mind, it comes from outside the mortal sphere.'

She began, of course, with Bach. He was the one she had adored from the start, and although she could fill an entire programme just with his keyboard pieces, she had chosen the first and second of the *Goldberg Variations*. She could feel the audience relaxing, as he worked his enchantment. It had been written to help an insomniac aristocrat, but what it did was bring peace, rather than somnolence, she believed: the peace in which music should be attended to.

Marta's programme was of composers from all over Europe, a deliberate choice. There was Couperin, Bach's spiritual sibling, exquisitely beautiful and restrained in 'Les Barricades Mystérieuses', those pulsing fractals of sound approaching and retreating. Then the long trills of Granados's 'La Maja y el Ruiseñor'. She had first played this long before she had ever heard a nightingale, all those gentle, anguished minor notes. Now her audience was prepared to be rallied by Chopin's famous 'Sonata in B Minor', with its call to arms, a summons to war and heroism to remind those who could hear of the desperate battles being waged yet again in Eastern Europe. Her left hand was making huge leaps up and down the keyboard even as the right was performing impossible feats of dexterity. Pain was running down her arms and back in electric flashes. It wouldn't show, it must never show, she was wearing an ancient black beaded crêpe dress from Yves Saint Laurent that both braced and scratched her flesh, though she felt her neck become clammy. She put that dress on as a warrior put on armour. How many of those who listened and watched could understand what it was costing her? Few, if any. That was the point. Her business was to transport them to a different state of being, not to falter or complain.

If once she left the stage, she would not return. She longed, with all her soul, for it to be over and yet also for it never to be over. Satie's 'Gymnopédies', his acrobats swinging gracefully, defiantly, over the void of oblivion. She was burning through the life she had left, summoning the energy and fire of her youth. A Scarlatti jewel, the K32, every quaver another red-hot needle through her joints, but one of his best. Rameau's 'La Poule' with its lively, comical rendition of an insistent, beady-eyed hen pecking in the dirt. She could hear one or two people laughing at the wit of it, because the hen was also all mothers, constantly anxious and preoccupied. Then Debussy's 'L'Isle Joyeuse', its triplets rolling up the keyboard and swimming chromatic energy, calm one moment and then black as ink the next, the incarnation of erotic bliss ... Watteau's lovers embarking for the enchanted island of Venus, laughing, chatting, half turning back, but all moving towards the barge where a half-naked god waited in the golden mists, light and grace and joys ephemeral.

The notes vanished into silence as soon as they left her fingers, would be remembered (if at all) as a vague feeling of happiness by at most two or three people present. She had never been more alive in these last few minutes, or more abstracted into music. Lastly, Mozart's 'Ave Verum Corpus', transcribed by Liszt, heart-piercing in its perfection and seeming simplicity. The extremity of agony it described, its acceptance of suffering and death as a state of grace, demanded as much delicacy in its pauses as in each precise note. Just over three minutes, but they wrung the last drops out of her.

Then, it was done. A sea of hands pulsed applause. She tried to rise, to bow, to acknowledge them, but the piazza and everything in it was becoming like an old black-and-white photograph, turning upside down and inside out. She felt herself falling, staggering, and yet agony continued, skewering her spine. Marta knew she was going to faint, she could hear gasps of concern, or maybe it was her own labouring breath, as she fluttered in and out of consciousness. Was this death? She would not have minded so much, if it stopped the pain.

How she got back to her flat, she never knew. Perhaps she levitated. Perhaps Xan and Blessing carried her. She had a dim impression of faces saying something, but all she wanted was her bed, and Otto, who comforted her just by his presence, and Edward, whom she would never see again.

She swallowed more painkillers, Xan put on another morphine patch and she tried to sleep, whimpering. The doctor was called, and wanted to move her to the local hospital, but what was the point? What could they do for her except wait for her to die?

'Not here,' she whispered.

'Oma, they have really good hospitals in Milan, you know,' said Xan. His face was drawn in anxiety, and so was Ruth's – her dear, kind friend who would do anything to help, she knew.

'No,' Marta said. 'I need England. I wish to see Lottie, and my home.'

20

The Truth of the Matter

Diana had been at a number of deathbeds in the course of her life – her mother's, her grandfather's, her brother's and her nanny's – but she always forgot what a long, slow, boring and horrible process it was. The grief, the compassion, the anxiety, the guilt, the memories all gave way to the simple longing for this to be over. Surely, a body must know when its time is up? Yet what a fight even the most worn-out one puts up against extinction!

Perry's exceptional health, which had been his insulation against sensitivity to others, now prolonged his life, torment- ing them both. He had two more strokes, but his heart carried on, as did his other organs. She was too tired even to grieve, although she knew that, when he went, a huge portion of her own past would go with him. Even if he had repeatedly hurt and humiliated her, her whole life since she was seventeen had been intertwined with and interpenetrated by his. Even her hatred had been an aspect of love, and when he died, she would be frantic, seeking a support that was no longer there. For he had supported her, even as he had undermined her, that was the paradox. They had not been twin souls like Marta and Ed, but it had been a marriage, and when it ended she had no idea how she would cope.

What will I do? she thought. How shall I bear it? Who will I be, without him? He had insulted, irritated, betrayed, oppressed and depressed her and yet, he was all she had had.

Diana had to get up and move about, she had to eat and drink and do all the usual animal things that her own body demanded, although she could not sleep any more than she could weep. It was agonising to see the plastic tubes going into her husband's flesh, but agonising, too, to feel the loneliness and loss of purpose approaching. I have failed in everything, she thought, even killing us both.

Was it her fault that the car had gone off the hillside? She had told Ruth it was, but when she tried to recall whether it had been an involuntary spasm or a deliberate one, she couldn't decide. She remembered that he'd demanded Bella be put down. The dog was his, always watching him with her sweet, stupid worshipful brown eyes – dogs, in her experience, always loved men, even though it was Diana who fed and walked them and took them to the vet. All Perry could see was that she was useless, now he no longer needed a gun dog and had a ruined back.

Would Ruth or Marta have managed such a husband? Debutantes had been taught how to get out of a car gracefully, arrange flowers and do ballroom dancing, but were ignorant of even the simplest way of pleasing a man. Yet even had she known, it would not have been enough. He would always have behaved as he did, and neither of her friends would have managed him any better. Claudia Felice had seen what he was.

'He is a Don Giovanni, my dear. Not a type to take seriously.'

Her daughters wanted to fly out to support her but Diana begged them, in short irritable texts, not to. (She was proud of being able to do this, very slowly, on the mobile they had bought her.)

Hv no room, hotels full bcs of wedding, she told them.

The deeper truth was that she wanted some time alone with her son. The last time he'd come to La Docciola was almost two years ago, between lockdowns. She had been deeply touched by this, though he'd actually used his trip to see Ivanov about a painting, the Artemisia Gentileschi that had once hung in the palazzo, but which had been sold by Claudia in the 1990s and retrieved by Andrew. Restored and rehung, it was the palazzo's crowning glory. Perhaps I should have accepted Ivanov's invitation to tea, she thought, but I couldn't bear seeing what he'd done to it. Andrew had assured her that the Russian had not put in gold lavatories, but she still wanted it to be as it remained in her memories.

'At least La Docciola has absolutely nothing worth stealing,' she remarked to Ruth.

'When people have nothing, anything is worth having,' Ruth said. 'Even Enzo's been burgled, remember.'

'I suppose so,' said Diana, worrying again. When Perry died, his pension and her minute allowance as his carer would vanish, too. She ought not to be thinking about money when her husband was dying, and yet ... how could she not? There is never a time in your life when money does not matter, except, perhaps, in childhood.

Diana had actually found herself jealous of her old friend, the only one (until Ruth and Marta) she'd ever had, because it was clear that Claudia talked to her son as she could not. She was an intellectual, an aesthete who had grown up in Milan, and Diana was just a countrywoman, whose education, such as it was, came entirely through listening to the BBC and reading. She couldn't hope to keep up with the tastes and information of an Oxford don, but she hoped that, despite this, he still loved her.

What went wrong between us? Diana often asked herself this, crying silently as the old do. That beautiful little boy, who had loved her so much, whom she still loved even now he was middle aged, was lost. She tried to count her blessings. All her children were healthy. She had four grandchildren from her daughters, who were excellent women. Andrew was a Fellow of All Souls and had a serious reputation. His personal life was a mystery, however. A brief marriage in his mid-thirties had been a mistake and she'd never met any girlfriend before or after. Was he incapable of intimacy? Was he homosexual? She didn't care, if only he'd talk to her again.

She did not put it like that to herself. If she expressed sorrow, it was only that Andrew was now approaching sixty, and it was clear that an heir would never arrive. Even Ruth couldn't understand why she was obsessed.

'Does anyone still care about that stuff? You have other grandchildren, don't you?'

'Yes, but only from my daughters. A title has to go from father to son, down the male line.'

'If the Evenlode name dies out, is it a tragedy?'

'Some would say it'd be a good thing.'

'Why?'

This was the kind of question only an American could ask.

'Let's just say that if a statue had been erected to Perry's grandfather, it would have been torn down.'

'Oh *dear*,' said Ruth.

'It was different in those days,' Diana said. She knew attitudes had changed, and perhaps she had changed too, even if the name Zimbabwe seemed to twist in her mouth. Yet she had meant no evil, had been excited and thrilled by the idea of going to Africa to help her new husband there. Her father, whom she had never known, had been a vicar: she envisaged a project in which she could do good to the native people, perhaps setting up a little school for the children on his estate.

How to explain the convictions with which people had lived in the colonies? It had never crossed her generation's minds that they were not entitled to rule the races to whom (so they believed) they brought so much civilisation. The Evenlodes had, for a while, been national heroes. Perry's grandfather, who fought alongside Cecil Rhodes, had been made a viscount, an honour perhaps not unconnected to the fact that his diamond mines had yielded a particularly large jewel to Queen Victoria.

But by the 1960s, all that was starting to change. The diamond mines were long gone, but the farm remained, and so did Perry's vehement views. He'd opposed Independence, of course.

'Would it be so bad to have more of a partnership?' Diana suggested timidly. She had read a novel called *The Grass is Singing*, and found herself made quite uncomfortable by it. 'There might be some advantage in bringing the brighter ones on board.'

'The only thing standing between us and a terrorist revolution is if we stand firm,' Perry had told his wife. 'The idea the kaffirs can ever govern themselves is ludicrous. They're the laziest people on earth. The only thing they're interested in is fucking and beer.'

White people were vastly outnumbered by those they had

conquered, and believed they must hold the whip-hand – literally in Perry's case given that he would flog any workers who displeased him. She steeled herself against the screams, and would come out later to try to treat the wounds, but knew it was pointless to say anything even if she could see the resentment against Home Rule growing. Her fears had been justified and more and more terrs, as they were called, increased their attacks. When the Evenlodes left Rhodesia, soon to become independent Zimbabwe, they felt that they had achieved a narrow escape from a doomed continent.

'They will regret it,' Perry said. 'Chaos and starvation will follow. That chap Mugabe is a disgrace to Sandhurst.'

He was not wrong. At every atrocity, Perry became more and more gloomily triumphant, as if Zimbabwe had been conquered seventy years before by British moral superiority rather than violence and theft. Diana had accepted everything her husband told her until Andrew was sent away to prep school.

'It'll make a man of him,' Perry said.

The absurdity of this for a little boy, let alone a sensitive, affectionate, clever one of six years old, was never questioned. Had someone broken in to threaten their children with a gun or an axe, she and her husband would both have fought like tigers to save them – but a school was the machine that made their class conform.

She was not even allowed to show her agony before, during or after Andrew was deposited at his, crying in private and deeply ashamed of her weakness. Her small, pretty, blond son had waved bravely as they drove away, his figure shrinking as if swallowed up by the red brick walls, which in turn vanished into the muddy grass of vast playing fields.

Are you all right, darling? Tell me, Diana would write. In return, he would send home letters in his round, wobbly handwriting, not about things they had discussed like dragons or magic but about lessons and sport and tuck. They were censored, of course. When he returned for Christmas, she tried to hug him. It was like holding a dummy.

Outwardly, it was a great success. The establishment drilled its pupils so well that even less bright ones passed the Common Entrance. Andrew had won a scholarship to a great public school. He'd succeeded superbly, and once he grew tall had even been an athlete, something that ensured popularity.

'Running gives me the chance to be alone,' he'd said to her. When he emerged, he was a greyhound – lean, driven, nervy, eternally chasing the rabbit he could never catch.

Maybe that was just his nature, Diana thought. Of course he couldn't remain a mummy's boy – that would be shameful and wrong. All she could do was to hope that some spark of the child he had been remained, however deeply it was buried.

'How are you?' Andrew asked. No kiss, no hug, just a brief touch on her upper arm.

'Not too mouldy,' she replied. 'How was your flight?'

'The usual *sic transit*,' he answered. 'Small child kicking me in the back.'

'And otherwise?'

'Busy,' Andrew said. 'I've bought a house.'

She looked up hopefully. Could there be someone new? 'In Oxford?'

'Gloucestershire.'

'Ah. My favourite county.'

'I can show you a picture of it.'

He took out his mobile, but just then, the monitor started to go into spasms.

Was it her imagination, or had Perry's pulse picked up

266

briefly on hearing that his son had arrived? Diana's eyes stung as she looked at him.

Six pregnancies (two of them miscarriages) between eighteen and thirty, all to produce this man who was still the apple of her eye. Only I might as well not have tried, she thought, looking at the rings on her finger.

Various people came and went, a couple of other expats (though not Marta) with whom she had been on moderately cordial terms, one of the nuns Perry had liked, who prayed for him right there in the hospital room, and eventually her daughter Etta. Dear Etta, always gentle, stubbornly affectionate and wanting only to help. She had her own sorrows too: her son Jake, recently divorced, seemed to have inherited a good deal of Perry's worst characteristics. (Did children and grandchildren inherit temperament as well as looks and brains? Increasingly, Diana believed this.). Despite what she had said, she was glad of her daughter's presence. She was a comfort, and took over arranging practicalities from Andrew.

'I think it's as well to be prepared, Mummy,' Etta said.

Slightly to her surprise, another regular visitor was Raff. He would come in and sit down quietly on the other side of the bed, not saying much but often bringing her small comforts, like a cushion to sit on and a cup of Earl Grey tea with homemade biscuits. She supposed that somehow, he'd become fond of the old man. Men were different to other men, revealing sides to each other that were different to those they showed women.

Diana did not object when Raff took her husband's hand and held it. After all, he'd been one of their rescuers, alongside Xan and Blessing. She felt comfortable in his presence, as she rarely did with strangers.

'Would you like me to read to you?' he asked.

'I don't know. Maybe. I'm so deaf now, and I hate talking books,' she said.

'It might take your mind off, though?'

She nodded, and he began to read a copy of *Doctor Thorne* aloud. It was one of her perennial comforters, with its tale of young love and great inheritances that, against all odds, came to exactly the right people. Her good ear, always attuned to minute differences of caste, noted that he had a nice, clear voice, not top-drawer but he pronounced words properly ... Diana felt herself relaxing, listening to her favourite author. Andrew disdained him, of course.

'There's more genius in a single line of Dickens than in the whole of Trollope,' he'd said; Diana longed to point out that readers did not always need the fulminations of genius, actually. Sometimes what they needed was, instead, consolation, wisdom and kindliness.

When she woke, she was not even conscious that she had been asleep. Someone was saying her name, softly and insistently.

Andrew was in the room again, and so was Raff. Her daughter Etta was crying quietly.

'Daddy's going,' she said; and then, in the next breath, he was gone.

They all sighed. Diana felt utterly numb, whether with exhaustion or indifference she couldn't tell. Etta got up and opened the window, so that fresh air and the sounds of life could come in. What was left was so clearly just a body, an empty shell. How strange, Diana thought, that after such a life of making so many people miserable, he should have had a peaceful death, surrounded by family and friends. Unless, perhaps, his death had actually come when she sent the car over the edge of the hillside, because after those terrifying moments of falling and impact, he'd never recovered consciousness. Maybe those had been his last moments, and she had after all been revenged on him. There were papers to sign, and Andrew – who spoke much better Italian than she did – took over this dismal duty. Then, at last, they could pack up and go back to La Docciola. The Awful Shower, she thought, and for the first time felt her eyes sting, remembering Perry's acerbic jokes. Tuscany had been horrible for him, too, poor chap.

Would she, too, eke out her life there? It looked ravishing in spring, but the thought of spending another broiling summer in Italy, let alone another freezing winter, was unbearable, for so many reasons, not least that she knew that without him, she would not have the incentive to try to keep it all going.

'You must be shattered,' Etta was saying. 'I've made up your bed with clean sheets, and tidied up a bit, I hope that's all right.'

'We didn't realise you were getting Daddy out of bed with a hoist,' Andrew remarked. 'You should have asked us for help.'

'I managed,' she said shortly. Asking for help was not in her nature, it never was. They should have known this.

When they drove back down the hillside, Diana looked out of the car window and saw the strangest thing. In the skies above the valley there was a shape catching the sun in the evening light. It was not a bird, she was sure, and it seemed to be following the car in its bumpy passage down the track below the Palazzo Felice. Nobody else saw it, and with her declining eyesight she could not make it out clearly, but just for a moment she wondered whether it might be Perry, looking at her one last time.

21

All Families, Happy or Unhappy, Are Mad

Xan was desperately worried about Marta. Even before her collapse she had been in agony from her back, and it was not getting any better. Once he had brought her breakfast, and helped her on and off the toilet – not something he ever expected to do for his grandmother, to be honest – she collapsed back on to the bed.

'Go on, go out! Walk Otto. He needs the exercise, and so do you,' she croaked. 'Go to Ruth's! You need to do more than look after a cranky old lady.'

Even as an invalid, she was formidable, and Xan *was* desperately bored. There was only so much he could do on his laptop, and although he just about managed to do a couple of Zoom tutorials with pupils in London, his screen kept freezing because her connectivity was predictably bad. Staying here was costing him money and despite his attempts to explain how dire matters were, financially, his grandmother didn't seem to realise just how little he had to spend. Marta gave him her bank card in order to buy food, which was something, but he couldn't help his resentment rising in tandem with his anxiety. They seemed to be getting through surprising amounts of supplies, but although she hardly ate anything Xan and Blessing both had healthy appetites.

'I'm sure there were more tins in here,' Xan muttered. 'Have we really got through all the rice already?'

'If Italians sold sweet potatoes and corn, I could make you a Zimbabwean meal,' Blessing said.

'I don't think they do. They don't even have stuff like chickpeas or okra. Besides, Marta needs to eat plain food. Juicy says she should 'eat white', which I think means no red meat or tomatoes.'

Ivanov rang Xan on his mobile to congratulate Marta – having watched the recital remotely, it transpired – and to send his best wishes.

'It was excellent, really excellent,' he said. 'I recorded it. If she wishes, it could be released on YouTube. But I think, Alexander, that she needs to go to a proper hospital.'

'I agree,' Xan said. 'The trouble is, she won't leave. One moment she says she wants to go back to London and the next that she can't move. My mother and I are trying to persuade her.'

Marta was infuriatingly stubborn. In a way, it was admirable: Xan remembered how even when she'd broken her leg seven years ago she'd insisted on lifting weights in hospital every day even when in bed so as not to lose the strength in her arms, and her pianism. Now, she just lay there.

'It will pass, it will pass. Go out, my darling; just don't let him in.'

'Who?'

'*Die schwarze*,' Marta muttered. 'I see the black man every night.'

271

Xan said gently, 'Oma, the only Black people here are me and Blessing.'

'I think – I think he is my death.'

Xan looked at her with concern. Was this the start of dementia? The doctor made another visit. Luckily, he spoke good English.

'It could be sciatica,' he said. 'Or a spinal disc? Without a scan, it's impossible to know.'

'She won't be moved.'

Xan called Lottie twice a day. His mother was in the middle of a crisis, both with one of his sisters, who was having a troubled adolescence, and also with her housing project in Devon. She was always busy, but this time seemed more so than ever.

'I can fly out, but not unless it's life or death,' she said. 'Is it?'

'I hope not. She's in a lot of pain, but not running a temperature.'

The big fear was cancer. Marta's mastectomy had been over twenty years ago, but it could have come back, and metastasised. Xan could not imagine how terrifying it must be, to feel your body devouring itself, unstoppably. If she were really sick, she would have to be brought to England, there was no way she could be nursed in another country.

I've got to get out of this mess, Xan thought. Marta is right, I've got to get a grip. I can't go on drifting. His mother's voice churned in his ear.

'Could you take her to a hospital in a big city?'

'She can't even sit up. An ambulance, maybe. What she really wants is to go to a London specialist.'

'Could she fly from Florence, First Class? I'm looking at that online, it's perfectly doable.'

'I don't know. I'm trying, Mum.'

'If you can help sort this, darling, it would be such a relief.'

Otto was being walked so much that the little dog was quite unlike his normal, irritating self. They went into town together, past the smart boutiques and antique shops that occupied spaces where there had once been a butcher, a hardware store, a greengrocer, a bank ... The march of the trivial and superficial was everywhere, but at least the piazza remained the same, with benches for the locals to sit and watch the foreigners, and café tables for the foreigners to watch the locals.

Both camps asked Xan how his grandmother was, the Italians adding, 'La poverina!', and some complimented him on her recital. She had made friends here, but the Italians seemed far more enthusiastic about classical music even when they were ordinary people who probably lacked the university education that he and his mates had to have even to get a basic job. He wondered whether this was because Tuscans really did have some special appreciation of art. While walking into town with Blessing, Xan was hailed by Enzo, and could not refuse a few minutes of conversation.

'You've met my cousin, Blessing?' Xan said pointedly.

'Yes, yes, ciao,' Enzo said, uncomfortably, then launched into fulminations about a house conversion on the opposite side of the hill.

'What foreigners do to our old houses is disgusting!' he said. 'They buy simple cottages and farmhouses, and want to make them into villas, with more rooms and swimming pools and big windows until they look like something from California. They are meant to look as they do. A Tuscan builder, even if he's completely uneducated, just knows how a wall is supposed to be built, and what looks good. But in America, everything that is made by nature is beautiful, and everything made by man is horrible; whereas here,

273

everything made by man is beautiful, and everything by nature is not.'

'I don't think that is true, at least not of nature in Italy,' Xan said. 'The flowers here are amazing.'

'But they grow in places where human beings have changed the landscape. You should go up into the woods, where I hunt,' Enzo answered. 'Nothing there but thorns and chaos, and wolves.'

'Wolves?'

'Yes, you can hear them howling at night. I would shoot them, but it is not allowed.'

Enzo sighed, and Xan said, 'Do you always want to shoot animals?'

'Personally, I would rather shoot criminals,' Enzo said. 'The police are investigating the mill at the bottom of my hill. They found a dead body there, have you heard?'

'No. Who was it?'

'Some Albanian guy. Or maybe another Eastern European. Nobody cares about those, but it ought to be stopped. It's a magnet for whores and drug dealers, that place. And Africans.'

Xan could feel his friend vibrating with fury when Enzo left.

'Sorry. I know he's a bit much, but my grandmother is fond of him.'

'Men like that,' Blessing said, 'they are why I had to leave my country.'

'I'm sure he wouldn't *actually* shoot anyone,' Xan said.

Blessing shook his head. 'You do not know what people can do to each other, my friend,' he said.

He peeled off to do some food shopping so Xan turned around and walked back to the edge of where the town parterre met the countryside. This was where he had been with Otto when that weird man had stopped and harassed

274

him. It was a recollection that still made him uneasy. He must have mistaken me for Blessing, he thought. There was no other logical supposition, but if so, what was his friend involved in?

It was another warm day, the sky a luminous majolica blue that he never saw in England. Every step into the countryside revealed more and different flowers, some like white stars close to the ground, some rising in spires of pink or violet or deep blue out of tall, feathery grasses of exquisite elegance, the kind of beauty that would make anyone glad to be alive.

Xan walked along the steeply curving road, then took the turning off it. Marta was insistent that he should visit Diana to offer condolences on the death of Lord Evenlode.

'I don't see why. He was a revolting knob.'

'He was a blood relation of my husband's – and there-fore, yours.'

'I have relations on my father's side who would probably spit on his grave.'

Marta said, exhaustedly, 'Xan, my darling, think of it as the only way to shame them.'

'If they're capable of shame.'

'Of course they are! And Diana is a good woman. Try not to judge everyone so harshly.'

'Why not? I know what they think of us. If we say anything to challenge their politics, we're woke, and if we don't want to be challenged, we're snowflakes.'

His grandparents' generation all believed his own were spoilt and petulant, but they had no idea what it was like to be young in Brexit Britain . . . Even getting Marta to apply for a German passport so that Xan and his sisters could get one in turn had been resisted.

'Why should I want to revisit the country I rejected?'

275

'Because I might want to live and work there myself, given that Germany still seems to value culture.'

'Only because it has the money to do so. As soon as the consequences of the embargo on Russia begins to bite, that will vanish. Art needs a superfluity of money and energy, Xan. Do you think that people value books as anything other than fuel once winter bites?'

'Yes. They must. Books are what we are, as human beings, just like music and art and theatre. We're not pages of code, or chemistry, or money.'

Thoughts like these had him striding along the stony track down to La Docciola, whacking nettles with a stick. The small stone cottage stood at the end of a long, grassy track, and had, inevitably, a fine view of the valley and hills opposite. (When people here visited each other's homes, the view was all they complimented each other on, as if each one had somehow been responsible for creating it.) The Fiat 500 was parked nearby, somewhat resembling a dented meringue after its accident, and Diana was seated on an old cane chair outside, reading a dog-eared copy of the *Spectator*. Her elderly Labrador began barking when it saw them, and heaved itself up to thrust her grey muzzle into Xan's hand.

'Oh, hello,' said Diana.

Approaching, Xan was astonished to see how much better his great-aunt looked. Ten, even twenty years had fallen off her face. She must have been so tired, he thought; or perhaps it's relief at being a widow. It was a slightly shocking thought.

'Marta sends you her condolences.'

'How nice of you to visit.' She accepted the basket of fruit he had brought, on his grandmother's instructions, because Marta was stern about the discourtesy of ever arriving anywhere empty-handed. 'Come and meet my son, Andrew. I don't think you have done so before, have you?'

The new Lord Evenlode was washing up in the cramped, chaotic, whitewashed kitchen, side by side with Raff. He wore faded red corduroys and a check shirt, having probably been born that way, like one of the animals in Edwardian children's literature.

'You won't remember, but I met you years ago at Fol when you were a child,' he said. They shook hands, then Xan said,

'Hi, Raff.'

'Hi,' said Raff. 'Andrew, Xan helped get Diana and Perry out of the car when it crashed.'

'Ah,' said Andrew. 'Well done.'

'It was nothing,' Xan said, embarrassed.

'I'm sorry not to have known your grandfather. I have so few respectable relations.'

'I never knew him either,' Xan answered. He always felt hesitant about his kinship to the Evenlodes, even before he'd discovered their appalling history.

Xan looked from the younger man to the elder, and Andrew Evenlode said, 'Raff is my son.'

They were very different – one tall and lean, the other stocky and fit – and yet he could see the similarity. Marta had mentioned how Xan himself resembled her husband, and now Xan saw that they all shared the same forehead, and cheekbones, and fingers. Diana gave a short laugh.

'Oh,' said Xan, after a pause. He felt bewildered, and yet oddly pleased. 'Why didn't you say, Raff? Is it some big secret?'

Raff and his father exchanged glances.

'It's . . . complicated,' Raff said. 'Ruth didn't know. Nobody here did.'

Xan said sympathetically, 'I didn't meet my own father until I was about to go to university.'

'My son has always known me,' Andrew answered, with a touch of haughtiness. 'He just hadn't met my side of the family.'

'Why not?'

'I wanted him to make his own way in life, not forced into a straitjacket. I didn't want all that, and neither did his mother.'

'Why not?' Xan asked.

'Emma is . . . how can I say? An iconoclast.'

'What Andrew means is that she has a mind of her own,' said Raff, and grinned. 'You know, against the patriarchy, the class system, capitalism, the lot.'

'So does nobody else know?' Xan asked.

'No,' Raff replied.

'It was our right,' Andrew muttered.

Xan nodded. 'OK.'

He was full of questions. Was Raff some sort of Trustafarian? Why had he spent nine months working on Ruth's farm without telling anyone of his connection to Diana and Perry? How weird that they should be cousins! Or was it second cousins? Of course, Xan had loads of those on his Nigerian side. But it was peculiar to live and work so close to your grandparents for so long, and not let them know.

Maybe he's ashamed, as I am, of the colonialism, Xan thought. Or maybe Perry was so awful that he didn't want any contact, apart from when Diana hurt her ankle. He could see the attraction.

Raff carried a tea tray through to the living room. Xan, following, recognised the remains of a much grander style huddled beneath the cottage's low, beamed ceiling and whitewashed stone walls. The sagging chintz sofa, threadbare Turkish rug, faded button-back armchairs, bad oil paintings and lumpen pieces of brown furniture were all familiar

278

hallmarks of his mother's people. The only thing that made it slightly unusual were the quantities of books shelved all along one wall, presumably acting as insulation.

'The way we live now,' said Diana, following his gaze. 'I brought a few odds and ends from Lode. You read English at university, didn't you?'

'Yes, I did,' Xan said politely.

'I would have loved to do that, in another life,' she said.

'You never told me that,' Andrew said.

'Apparently, you are the only one who is allowed to have secrets,' she answered.

She was clearly very angry, and if she had only just discovered her relationship to Raff, he wasn't altogether surprised.

'I loved looking after my children,' she said. 'It would have meant so much to know yours.'

'You have other grandchildren,' Andrew said calmly.

'But not this one. Not my son's son, the one I most wished to have.'

Embarrassed, Xan examined a framed photograph of the Evenlodes, flanked by what were presumably their servants in front of a long farmhouse, its deep veranda punctuated by white columns. His great-aunt was wearing a full-skirted 1950s dress, his great-uncle a kind of safari suit. There were three very blonde little girls there, two in Diana's arms, and one in those of a Zimbabwean woman, presumably a maid.

'So, there you have it,' said Andrew Evenlode, behind him. 'The black man's burden.'

'You're not in this photograph, I think?'

'I wasn't born then,' Andrew said. They went out through narrow French windows on to a little stone-paved terrace, and sat down at a wrought-iron table. 'Isn't that so, Mummy?'

'You were the last throw of the dice. Almost killed me, but

luckily I was in England by then,' Diana said. 'Now tell me: Who is Raff's mother?'

Andrew said, 'She's a painter called Kenward.'

'Oh!' Xan exclaimed. 'My grandmother has some of her work. I thought she was a he. She's quite famous, isn't she?'

'Yes,' Raff said.

He smiled at his grandmother, who frowned.

'Why did you keep her a secret? Is something wrong with her?'

Andrew said, in an exasperated tone, 'Not at all. She was a student of mine at Oxford ... which is one reason why we didn't want it known. She became pregnant with Raff before she graduated.'

'But why not? Why on earth *not*? I simply don't understand it.'

Diana looked really upset, and Xan, though he had little sympathy with the whole malarkey, did feel sorry for her.

'The short answer is that Emma and I are chalk and cheese. She's a free spirit, and according to her, I'm a dried-up stick. We were barely together before we parted.'

Xan, looking at the flush on his face thought, Not as dried up as all that.

'I still think it abominably selfish,' said Diana. She, too, had colour in her cheeks. 'Doesn't family mean anything?'

It was clear that she was working herself up into having a tremendous row with her son. Otto began to bark.

'Sorry,' Raff said to Xan in an undertone. 'Why don't we go back to La Rosa and leave them to thrash it out?'

'Good idea.'

The two of them slipped away. Raff began to laugh, and after a moment, Xan joined in.

'Are *your* family as bad as that?'

Xan thought for a moment. 'Yes. All families, happy or

280

unhappy, are mad. I suppose it's to do with seeing people too close up, instead of at a distance. My side is bonkers, too. Not that anyone has a title, or anything.'

'Believe me, I don't want that.'

Xan thought to himself that, were he Black, Raff might not be quite so cavalier.

'Does it mean you are rich?'

'No, not at all. I grew up in a cottage hardly bigger than Diana's. My mother wouldn't ever take a penny from my dad. At least you can feel proud of *your* side of the family.'

'But we're both descended from an ogre.'

'To some, I'm afraid, he's still a national hero. Anyway, family isn't destiny, is it?'

Raff was an easy person to talk to, and Xan found himself confiding his various troubles with Marta, and her conviction that she was being visited by her death.

'I hate the idea that she's going mad, as well as being in agony.'

'It could be the painkillers.'

'What do you think we should do? She won't leave without Otto. I can't see him flying on a plane, and she can't return by car.'

'There must be someone who could drive him to England. I could drive Otto back myself, if all else fails. I'm leaving on the day of the wedding.'

'That bloody wedding. I can't see what they see in each other, can you?'

'I don't really know him,' said Raff, after a pause. Xan understood. It was what polite English people always said when they absolutely loathed someone.

They watched Otto exploring the base of a tree, stumpy tail wagging.

'Do you think he knows that nobody likes him? The dog, I mean, not Olly.'

'I hope not,' said Raff.

Xan said, 'You like her too, don't you? Tania, I mean.'

'Who wouldn't?'

'Because she's so pretty?'

'It's not just that. I think she's amazing. But she's marrying someone else.'

'I'm sorry,' Xan said. 'I don't like either of them. Tania used to go out with my best friend, you see.'

'But different people bring out different qualities in each other,' said Raff. 'Don't you think?'

'I'm not sure. Are people just chemical reactions?'

'Maybe. If she marries Olly, it'll be terrible for her. Like my poor grandmother and grandfather.'

'That bad, do you think?'

'Olly needs someone strong and spirited to stand up to him, then he'll be fine. But Tania isn't like that. He'll become a bully, and she'll become a broken flower.'

Poor Raff, Xan thought. He liked him instinctively, and there was some perceptiveness in what he said. Tania and Bron hadn't been right for each other, either. What bad luck to have fallen for someone who was about to marry some-one else ... but he knew enough about Tania to know how stubborn she was once she decided on a course of action. She had one of those train-track minds that meant she wouldn't deviate.

'Don't tell her about me, please,' said Raff suddenly. 'My family, I mean.'

'I wouldn't anyway, but why not?'

'Because I want to be liked, or disliked, for myself. Not any other reason.'

At the fork in the road, Raff turned to La Rosa and Xan returned to the town, and to his main worries.

By now, he was certain that Blessing was not really a wedding guest, but some kind of chancer. Yet Xan could not help liking him. In the beginning, he'd been so delighted to find another Black man in Hampstead-by-Tuscany that he'd rushed into all kinds of assumptions. He'd been the one who had enabled Blessing to pass, quite deliberately. But whether he could get Blessing into Britain was another matter.

If only he were a nurse, Xan thought. Then he'd be given a visa, because Britain was desperate for nurses, and doctors, and all the other jobs from fruit picking to meat-packing that remained unfilled. But Blessing wanted to start a business. He'd revealed this to Xan the evening before.

'You know who is Britain's first Black billionaire? A Zimbabwean. He founded Econet Global, to build my country's first mobile phone network. He was born in my city, and it's because of him that almost all Africans now have a mobile phone.'

'Why can't you set up a business there?'

'Too much corruption,' said Blessing. 'And I want to live in the mother country. To study, and work there is my dream.'

But what was going to happen to him when it was time for Xan to return to England? Marta couldn't continue to put Blessing up on her own, especially not if she was really ill.

When Xan returned to the flat, he found his grandmother was much worse. She almost screamed when he touched her.

Xan rang his mother from his bedroom. Lottie sounded both anxious and exasperated.

'Oh, why did she have to go and live abroad? Silly woman! We've got to get her back. Start packing for her, and yourself.'

Blessing was out. His little pile of new belongings was by

the twin bed opposite Xan's, with the black nylon rucksack. On impulse, Xan lifted it, and despite his reservations about what he was doing, unzipped it, and put his hand in. His fingers encountered a hard metal shape. Even though he'd never touched such a thing before in his life, he knew what it was; and suddenly, Xan felt very afraid.

22

A Labour of Love

If Marta returned to England, or died, Ruth thought, she would lose the companionship of one of her dearest friends. It was selfish to mourn this, but still, an old friend is like a leather shoe that fits your foot perfectly. New ones could look smarter, but an old one has moulded itself to your body or perhaps moulded your body to it. Patched, resoled, cared for, it will go on and on shielding and supporting the naked foot within for a lifetime ... Maybe that might seem an insulting simile, but feet are, after all, crucial to independence and mobility.

If Diana left too, then she would once more be alone. Bad enough to have lost Beatrix, but if the other two left as well she would feel lonely as she had not for many years. There were other people around whom she liked, but not *enough*. Marta was special; they had known each other for over fifty years, growing into intimacy together as people, especially women, do, through chance as well as choice. They had been mothers and neighbours together, and shared many chores, meals, advice, woes. Ruth had given Marta unstinting kindness and support when she was widowed, and Marta had helped her in turn when Ruth was divorcing Sam. They were temperamentally and politically compatible, laughing at the same kind of joke and even going on holiday together. At one point, they had both hoped that Ruth's youngest son Daniel might marry Marta's Lottie, for their children were almost of an age.

'Marriage is far too dangerous a business to be left to the young, really,' Ruth said, but their hopes had never come to fruition.

Although she had no time, Ruth made time to visit Marta. She rang the bell, and was buzzed in.

Marta's bedroom was cool; its wooden shutters half-closed against the sun. It was a most glorious May morning, and yet not glorious at all for her friend, who was lying almost flat on the bed, with Otto on the duvet beside her. Even in the dim light, Ruth could see that Marta was looking as grey and gaunt as a leafless tree. Her thick white hair stood up in clumps, and her spectacles were bleary.

'Is it very bad?'

'I am not so good today.'

Ruth had never had back ache, which she ascribed to arch supports, a good mattress, sex and Pilates. In her heart, though, she knew it was all just luck, and perhaps being a few years younger than Marta. People often said that you could be fine until your mid-eighties, but then everything began, inexorably, to collapse. Yet I feel just the same, Ruth thought – a little stiffer in the morning, and needing stronger reading lights and more frequent trips to the bathroom, but that was normal. Her skin was more lined, and she needed hair dye but her looks were hardly changed at all. Maybe it was the compensation for not having been pretty when young. She stayed the same, while women like Marta and Diana changed.

'What painkillers are you taking?'

'Fentanyl.'

'My dear, we must get you to London if you won't go to an Italian hospital.'

'I will *not* leave Otto.'

'He's got a pet passport, yes? He's had rabies shots?'

Marta's eyes were half closed. 'My daughter insisted.' Then she said, 'I am thinking that Switzerland would be better for me. Dignitas.'

'That is the pain speaking, not you,' said Ruth, horrified.

'All I am now is pain,' Marta answered. 'My life is all D minor, now. I will never hear the major key.'

At least Marta did have family. Ruth knew people who decided not to have children at all, out of a sense of responsibility to the planet; and she always wanted to say, 'But what about your responsibility to yourself?' The idea that friends would always be there to step in ignored the dour facts of mortality, and selfishness. Very few people will care for another without a blood tie, or deep love.

This was another reason why she had been so glad that Olly was getting married. He was over thirty; it was time he started a family while he was young enough to enjoy being with small children. But it was also because, despite her own unhappy experiences, Ruth continued to believe in family.

'My dear, we all want to help you.'

Marta said, clutching her hand suddenly, 'Just stop the black man coming in.'

'What man?'

'The one who comes out at night.'

Ruth, disquieted, patted her friend's hand. 'Drugs can do strange things to your brain.'

Marta muttered, 'They come through the wall.'

Xan was watering Marta's tiny garden. Ruth went out to chat to him, shaken by her old friend's outburst. Dementia or a stroke could bring all kinds of horrors out of the closet.

'Xan, are you aware that Marta is hallucinating about black men coming into her bedroom?'

'Yes. I don't know if it's the drugs.' Xan looked down at his ankle. 'Stop that, Otto!'

'Poor dog. He's just doing it because he's bored.'

As she trudged back to her car to return home, Ruth felt despondent. No more kaffeeklatsch, and no more cosy suppers together. Looking up at the dark leaves of the little park just before the parterre, she smiled wryly. All for one, and one for all, like the Three Musketeers, except what adventures did old ladies have?

'If only I'd taken advantage when I was young,' she muttered to herself. 'If only I had taken more pleasure in having unlined skin, and a *neck*.'

It was not as though she didn't see her friends' faults. We are all clear-sighted about other people's failings, while our own hover, like the ghostly nose in the middle of our face, just out of focus. It would never have occurred to her that she was doing anything wrong in trying to meddle with her grandson's life, because she loved him.

She had tried very hard to love Tania. Ruth had taken one look, last autumn, and decided that here, at last, was the fountainhead of the next generation which she hoped to set on the path of happiness. For this was not something that was bestowed like manna from heaven. Happiness, as every American knew, had to be pursued as a moral duty, it had to be hunted down, trussed up and dragged home by the victorious. It pleased her to think that, had she been a matchmaker, Tania was exactly the kind of girl she might have chosen.

'Such a lovely young woman,' she said to Polly. 'They make a perfect couple.'

'I hope so,' said Tania's mother. 'We are very fond of Olly, too.'

Many years ago, Ruth had not approved of Josh's choice – Anne was only a nurse, and her handsome, clever, eligible sons could, frankly, have married almost anyone. She hoped he would be a hospital consultant, like his elder brother. Instead, he had become a GP in Devon and Anne produced five children. They were very nice children, but only Olly had inherited the talent and good looks that Ruth anticipated from her progeny. She hoped he would be the star that his father, frankly, was not. Tania was beautiful, she was from a highly respectable family of lawyers, she was successful – what was there not to like? So why, now that she knew her better, did Ruth find herself sighing about the whole thing?

'I want to celebrate life, love and spring,' she heard her grandson's future wife say, in dulcet tones. Ruth turned, expecting that she was talking to Olly; but she was, as so often, doing a vlog. She speaks more to her iPhone than to her fiancé, Ruth thought, and she remembered telling her friends that the guests who arrived and immediately asked for the key to the wi-fi, as Tania had done, were always a disaster.

Tania had 'decided to go the full Botticelli'. The courtyard was now twined with blossoming white jasmine, in addition to the roses that Raff had trained up it, and the influencer had helped herself to much of this without even asking her hostess whether it was all right. Even Ruth, who had grown up in Hollywood, was shocked.

La Rosa was her home, a place she loved and had laboured over for more than thirty years, but to Tania it was merely a backdrop. The tablecloths were scattered with pink roses just like those in *The Birth of Venus*, and Ginori's marketing department had sent over a porcelain dinner service for 120 guests, decorated with scallop shells. There had already been numerous videos about which designer wedding dress she should choose. The two that Tania seemed to be favouring, vaguely modelled on the long, flowing robes worn by the nymphs in the *Primavera*, tended towards a tiered look last seen on the new wife of Britain's prime minister. It was, frankly, the most absurdly themed party that Ruth could think of since her schooldays, when seven actors were hired from the Little People Agency because her classmate was obsessed by Snow White.

'I'd almost prefer if she were into pole-dancing,' she muttered.

Ruth retreated to the kitchen, where a mountain of rabbit pieces and Enzo's wild boar sausage was browning in the oven. What to make for Tania tonight, though? She could handle vegetarians, but it was monumentally boring, not to mention depressing, having a vegan to stay. Fifty things to do with tofu, but none of them really appetising, she thought. It was all Ruth could manage not to sneak in some meat stock to the dreary little snack she prepared for the pre-wedding meal.

Could Olly really live on vegetables for the rest of his life? Surely not! He was an enthusiastic meat-eater, of course he was, with all the energy and ebullience of one. Ruth sighed, remembering Juicy's story about asking for red wine to drink with her breakfast when she was working as an au pair in Britain.

'It is a most wonderful invention, the Full English Breakfast, but coffee with such a dish would be an abomination to an

Italian,' she told her hosts. 'We have *wine* with red meat, not coffee or tea! They refused, in case it set a bad example. However, I found a way round it.'

'How so?'

Juicy smiled, mischievously.

'I had a little glass of red wine with my Full English, and told everyone it was Ribena.'

What a smart girl she was! Strong, funny, independent and brave. Ruth could not suppress the wish – but that was all in the past, and she'd had a hand in it. Ruth could hear the happy couple talking, or rather bickering.

'You shouldn't have drunk so much at your stag night,' Tania said.

'It's all very well for you, you never touch alcohol.'

'No, I don't,' she answered sharply.

'Because it's too much fun staying on your high horse?'

'I don't ride, either,' Tania said blankly.

She really was an odd young woman. Thank goodness for food, Ruth thought. Juicy began bringing enormous platters to the long line of tables in the courtyard, where most of the Viners were knocking back Ruth's wine. Xan had joined them, she was pleased to see. Everyone exclaimed in pleasure at the delicious smells rising from the platters, apart from Tania, who grimaced.

'I don't eat anything with a face,' she said.

'God,' Olly's brother Kit remarked. He knew about the long-ago affair with Juicy. 'You've passed up a lifetime of sex and pasta for *this*?'

'Shut up,' Olly said savagely. 'Shut up, shut up, shut up.'

Tania, at the other end of the table, was deep in a monologue with her own brother and mother. Ruth hoped she hadn't heard Kit.

'I think it might rain,' Juicy said brightly, bringing in some dirty plates.

'The weather app says it should be fine by midday.'

'Yes, but it's never reliable up here in the hills.'

By now, most people were flushed with wine, so Ruth thought it was time to make a short speech. Almost everyone here, apart from Xan, Enzo, Juicy and Angus, was either family or about to be, and having missed out on marking her own eightieth birthday she wanted to say a few words before tomorrow's main event.

She tapped her glass with a fork several times for silence. Nobody took any notice, so she did it again. There was a slight diminution in noise.

'SHUT UP, EVERYONE!'

Instant silence.

'Thank you, Olly. I just wanted to say what a pleasure it is to have you all here at last,' said Ruth. 'Here, in this beautiful place, surrounded by those we love, we can celebrate our health and happiness.'

'Not to mention wealth,' said Xan, rather too loudly. 'Remember that?'

Ruth was thrown off her stride. She flushed uncomfortably.

'Yes, that as well. I never thought that I'd be living the dream—'

'Why not?' interrupted Xan. 'After all, you were able to buy an enormous great house in London before you were thirty.'

'Yes, it just so happens I did—'

'It just so happens? Come off it,' said Xan. She could see he was drunk. 'Your generation had free tuition, no student debt, cheap council mortgages, proper jobs, the lot. You didn't know you were *born*. Of course you could buy a second home in Tuscany. We can't even buy *one*. No matter how hard we

292

work, most of us will never have anything but crap jobs, for ever.'

'Oh, fuck off, you whingeing snowflake,' said Angus. He, too, was red faced. 'I'm so bored of all the millennials whining. You lost, we won, because you couldn't even be arsed to get out of bed to vote.'

Despite her distaste for Olly's best man, Ruth couldn't help feel glad of his support.

'For your information, Xan, there aren't student loans for an American medical degree. I paid my dues, and I bought my home, long before your mother was even born. But yes, I'm aware how fortunate I am.'

'You're just living in Hampstead-on-Tuscany,' Xan said. 'All virgin olive oil and white people.'

'What do you suggest, then?' Ruth asked, stung. 'Giving all we have to the poor, like St Francis?'

Xan stood up, his chair falling backwards on to the terracotta tiles with a loud bang that made several people jump.

'Just check your fucking privilege,' he said.

He walked off, furious. There was a shocked silence, then people started chatting again.

'Well, that was awks, wasn't it?' said someone.

Raff said, 'I know he's very worried about his grandmother. I'm sorry, Ruth. You've worked so hard at giving us a lovely time.'

'Well, thank you,' Ruth said. 'I know how hard you and Juicy have worked, too.'

She was hurt, nonetheless. *Of course* she was living in a bubble, that was scarcely news, but was she smug about it? She did the best she could, but one person's good intentions couldn't alter or atone for the mistakes of the system could they?

Angus was asserting that people of colour now had advantages that poor white boys could only dream of. Enzo, unfortunately, was nodding his head in agreement, and talking about the Five Star Movement. Ruth could see her elder sons attempting to debate this, politely and reasonably, but then Angus placed a meaty paw on Juicy as she went by.

'I can see why you're called Juicy,' he said. 'Come and sit on my lap.'

The next moment, Olly sprang up, and shouted, 'Hands off!'

Angus goggled at him.

'Just having a laugh, mate.'

Juicy said, almost in tears, 'Olly, no. Please.'

'Do that again, and I'll deck you.'

Ruth had never seen Olly so angry. All the smooth City manners were stripped away.

'Don't tell me you're going to be an arsehole too,' said Angus, burping.

Ruth saw what looked like tears on the young woman's cheeks, but her self-control and tact were absolute.

'Leave him, Olly. Do not make *brutta figura*.'

Watching Juicy walk away, Ruth thought how she had been transformed. The little *contadina* who had been her cleaner was now a woman of charm, elegance and poise, and she had to get over her own prejudices. Moreover, she had seen her grandson hug Juicy when she first arrived, and ask, '*Come stai? Mi vuoi bene?*'

Juicy answered, '*Ti amo come sempre, Olly.*'

I still love you. It was the kind of thing that English and American girls exclaimed, flippantly, to friends. Juicy said it lightly, and yet . . . Italians only said those words to someone they really did love. It was one of those differences between two cultures. She had never known Juicy to have a boyfriend after Olly, though she'd assumed she must have done so. Was it possible that Juicy's feelings remained the same?

What if she had been wrong to encourage them to break up? What if she had, effectively, told Giuseppina Guardi that she wasn't good enough for Olly, not because they were both too young but because she herself was a bit of a snob? Ruth had always detested the Republican Party, she recycled, she was a feminist, and yet in her heart of hearts, she knew she had fallen prey to the oldest and most poisonous vice of all. And I myself am so proud of being the descendant of peasants, she thought.

Watching her grandson follow Juicy with his eyes, she saw an expression that she had never seen when he looked at his intended bride. It was clear that Olly had feelings for the Italian, too. Tania was sitting there like the Queen of the May, perfectly lovely and totally oblivious, like all self-centred people. Or am I being unjust to her, too? Ruth thought.

Ruth wished she could have Marta or Diana beside her to discuss the predicament, but she had to face matters on her own. All her unease came into focus. If this marriage went ahead, it would be a disaster. It was no good thinking that Olly and Tania could always divorce. What mattered was that they should not marry in the first place.

'Mate, lighten up,' Angus was saying to Olly. 'She's only the help.'

Olly gave him a look of despair.

My grandson must shake free of him, too, Ruth thought. If he stayed in Angus's orbit he would become just as rigid and venal as his boss.

There were good and bad bankers and capitalists, surely, and she had no doubt that a strong wife, someone who was sensible, principled and warm, could counteract Angus's influence, but Tania was not that person. She was too rigid, too controlling. Their life together would be one of miserable irritability and mutual exasperation, especially once they had children.

So, how to stop this wedding? Olly wouldn't listen to reason, she knew, but maybe there was another way . . .

Ruth reminded herself that she, who had never been con-ventional, had passed into the realm of I Don't Give a Shit. Hadn't she, Marta and Diana agreed about this? What was the point of old age, if not to see more clearly than the young?

'Hell, why not try it?' she muttered to herself. She rose, and pottered off to her kitchen.

She brewed some coffee and found a jar of honey, left behind by her dear old photographer. What fun they had both had! She did miss him, but she would not think of that. The secret of happiness is to look forwards, not back, as Marta said.

Do I dare do this? Ruth thought. It was probably a criminal act. No responsible therapist could do such a thing, and she would be struck off if it were ever to come out, not that she had practised for over twenty years. I don't give a shit, she reminded herself, and looked at Tania again. Tonight, she was wearing a dress of pleated silver, with a halter neck and a full skirt. She looked as lovely as a goddess, and, in the setting of her farmhouse courtyard, ridiculous.

'Shall I take out coffee, Root?' Juicy asked.

'Would you, dear? Thanks. I think most people are having mint tea'

'Olly and I will have coffee.'

Everyone got up and gathered round the fire pit. Sparks from burning logs flew upwards. The tea was poured out, and circulated with some of the Baci chocolates that Tania (or rather Tanyaa) had been sent for wedding favours. She gave two Deruta mugs of coffee to Juicy on a small round tray.

'Here, Juicy. This is for you and Olly.'

'I prefer black, with sugar.'

'I know,' she said. 'It has honey in it.'

She watched Juicy bring out the two mugs she had filled, decorated with a hand-painted design of two blue-birds facing each other, to the table and sit down with Olly. They began to sip, and chat quietly, heads almost touching. She tried to watch them without seeming to. Tania didn't even notice.

As before, Raff brought out his guitar, and strummed for a while.

'A song, a song!' called the younger Viners.

Raff said, 'Well, as it's my last evening . . . '

He tuned the instrument briefly, then began.

So early, early in the spring
I shipped on board to serve my king
I left my dearest dear behind
She ofttimes swore her heart was mine.
My love, she takes me by the hand
'If ever I marry, you'll be the man!'
A thousand vows, so long and sweet
Saying, 'We'll be married when next we meet.'
And all the time I sailed the seas
I could not find one moment's ease
In thinking of my dearest dear
But never a word from her could I hear.

He sounded angry and hurt. Had he left a girl behind in England? Did people still wait for each other, in an age of Tinder and hook-ups?

At last we sailed to Portsmouth town
I strode the streets both up and down
Inquiring for my dearest dear
And never a word of her could I hear.
I went straightway to her father's hall
And loudly for my love did call
'My daughter's married, she's a rich man's wife
She's wed to another, much better for life'
If the girl is married that I adore
I'm sure I'll stay on land no more
I'll sail the seas till the day I die
I'll break the waves rolling mountain high.

'What a sad song,' said Ruth, after the applause. He had sung particularly well, she thought. 'It touches the heart.'

Angus made a snoring sound, either because he was bored or because he'd fallen asleep.

Raff said, 'I like it because it's about an abandoned man, rather than the usual abandoned woman.'

'Do women get left more often than men, or do they just complain about it more?' Olly asked.

Juicy said, 'That depends whether you ask a man or a woman!'

'I think no sex has the monopoly on sorrow and regret.' Raff yawned. 'I'm going to turn in for the night. I'm setting off tomorrow morning.'

There was a general outcry at this.

'Why aren't you staying for the wedding? You'll miss all the fun.'

He smiled, and sketched a wave. 'You won't even notice I'm gone. Goodbye, Juicy; goodbye, Tania.'

Tania looked up, but said nothing.

He left the circle of firelight and began to walk up the hill, guitar slung over one shoulder. Ruth walked a little way with him on the mown path in the long grasses of the groves.

'My dear Raff, I'm sorry you're leaving us. You've been by far and away my best helper, and I can't thank you enough.'

Raff said, 'It's been a pleasure. Thank you for all your hospitality. It's a wonderful place. I'm sure you have my replacement all lined up.'

'Yes, in fact. A nice Ukrainian family.'

She could see him smiling at this. 'Of course. Isn't that the latest fashionable thing?'

'It's the least I can do for some of those poor people. Though I'm starting to wonder whether the farming isn't becoming too much for me. Maybe I should let nature have her way.'

'That would be a pity. After all, why did you do it in the first place?'

'At first, I just wanted somewhere where my sons and I could spend the holidays. But then, it became a labour of love, and ... I suppose I want to leave a tiny bit of the world in better shape than how I found it.'

'There you are, then,' Raff said. 'As for me, well, it's been life-changing, too. A labour of love, in fact.'

'I've always meant to ask, what will you do when you go back?'

'I'm not sure.'

Ruth could not help prodding him a little. 'What did you do before?'

'Something I grew out of.'

Ruth said, 'Those songs you sang weren't just because you liked them, were they?'

'What's too silly to be said can be sung, don't they say?'

299

They walked on, and all kinds of intuitions surfaced in Ruth's mind. Eventually, she said, 'Why don't you tell her?'

'Because she's marrying your grandson. Besides, what could I say?'

'I know. Planet Tania,' Ruth said.

'I don't think it's that, exactly.'

'What else could it be?'

'I thought you were the shrink.'

All around, the nightingales throbbed like wounds. Poor Raff, she thought, and poor Olly, too. If four people were going to make each other unhappy simply by pairing up with the wrong person instead of the right one, it would be a tragedy. Serious people dismissed finding happiness in love as the stuff of comedy, but the whole point was that the choices that led to happiness rather than unhappiness were found on a knife-edge. Ruth had spent decades of her life trying to heal the consequences of terrible decisions. She knew her grandson: she knew that, though very clever at one thing, he was over-confident, impatient and an idiot in matters of emotion. All of these faults would be made worse if he stayed with Tania, but ameliorated if Juicy was in his life. Could her honey possibly work? There was no knowing what magic mushrooms might do. They could put you in touch with your deepest feelings of bliss, or they could render life, temporarily, grotesque.

Guilt and alarm flooded through her. She was not, after all, a believer in medication for the problems of being human. Recreational drugs were one thing, but the enthusiastic adoption of Prozac for depression had filled her with deep alarm. Suffering could not be sedated. It had to be worked through, with support, counselling, practical help and thinking about what you needed to do to change in your life – but Big Pharma was making far too much money for this. It took longer, it was riskier (because it was undeniable that in acute cases, some drugs did work, even if nobody really understood why) but its outcomes were better. Yet here she was, administering a very tiny dose of a drug, without consent, to two people she cared deeply about in the hopes that it would bring them to their senses.

'Oh, what have I done?' Ruth murmured to herself, when she left Raff to continue on his way. She had tried to be so wise and kind, but when it came down to it she was a silly, interfering fool who was old enough to know better.

The olive groves looked more and more like human figures, enchanted into stasis as they wrestled and strained beneath the thickening night sky. Even those hollowed to mere shells of bark still produced both leaves and fruit in heroic quantities, and she loved them for this, for their lively defiance in the teeth of pestilence, global warming and age. Yet they were doomed. When I go, she thought, they will sink once again beneath brambles, and there will be no help for them.

Tired and miserable, she trudged home, and almost bumped into the double hammock strung between two trees. It was quivering, like the cocoon of a gigantic butterfly about to split open. Ruth was moving quietly, but even so, she could see in the dim moonlight the bodies of her grandson and Juicy, kissing as though they could never stop.

23

Tania Among the Nightingales

Tania, too, had slipped away from the circle of firelight.

However unresponsive she might seem, and however bad at interpreting other people's expressions, she was not blind, or stupid. Obviously, Juicy was the girl whom Olly had been in love with as a teenager. Clearly, it wasn't all over, not a bit of it, and when she passed them making out in the hammock it was all she could do not to video them on her mobile and shame them online to her millions of followers . . . but vindictiveness wasn't her style.

Am I angry, or relieved? Tania thought. Her scalp itched and writhed. She thought of her brother once saying she had the Medusa stare. Maybe, Tania thought, I *am* Medusa. Except that the person turned to stone is myself.

Ruth's little spaniel scampered ahead of her, tail whirling.

'Dash!' she whispered. 'Dashy! Come back!'

His plumy tail caught the moonlight, and the white patches on his body and head appeared then disappeared as he plunged into shadows. Dash knew where he wanted to go, and was soon bounding up the hill. *Free! Free!* his high-pitched bark seemed to say. *Follow me!*

She enjoyed dogs, perhaps because, like herself, they didn't like looking human beings in the eye. Why did people insist on that kind of intimacy? What was the point of it? Yet if you didn't, they thought you were snubbing them, just as they thought she was rude for not smiling all the time. She always felt that people were grabbing at her, if not with their hands then their eyes ... At the thought that she was not going to have to be with Olly again, she was filled with a kind of lightness, as if a weight pressing down on her head was miraculously lifted. All those weeks and weeks of feeling more and more trapped, unable to move or speak, all the pretending on her vlog ... Yes, what to do about her vlog? And what to do about the wedding?

Tania, though she had never met any of her followers in person, felt a kind of responsibility for them. Although people said that social media relationships were completely fake, she didn't feel they *were*, necessarily. There were trolls and other sad, sad people but most had actually been really kind to her, maybe because unlike some influencers, she wasn't only posting about herself. Whatever else her vlog had done, Tania had raised millions for charity. She'd persuaded people to get vaccinated, she'd donated to Médecins Sans Frontières and The Trussell Trust and Sightsavers, all just by talking on her little iPhone. She'd posted about the environment, and veganism, and mental health. Nobody over forty understood what an influencer was. They thought she must be vulgar, but there were really smart, stylish, even satirical influencers too, from Kitty Spencer to Tinx, all of whom she admired very much. People still confused the medium with the message, and just

303

because the message was confined to three minutes, did that make it meaningless? When Tania had first done her little dance in the pink unicorn costume just two years ago, she'd never dreamt that it would change her life, but wasn't there something wonderful about that?

Plus, her own earnings were real enough. She didn't need Olly's money to buy a flat in London or a cottage in the country, because she already had her own. She'd worked really hard every day to gain her four million followers, and she'd done it by herself, without any bots or fake accounts.

It was all because she had caught a fraction of the world's attention at a particular moment, she knew, just as she knew it was a wave that, like all waves, was doomed to die beneath her. She needed to move on, somehow. But when she thought of Olly and Juicy so completely wrapped around each other they might as well have been one person, she didn't know what to do, because giving up the dream of safety that he offered might take more courage than she was capable of.

The long, silvery grasses with their feathery tips tickled her as she walked up the hillside, following Dash's white tail. The ground was already cracking from the dry spring heat, and the path was pitted with holes made by some rootling creature. Everywhere, the wild gladioli poked stiffly out of the ground, their swollen tips gleaming in the moonlight. Tania shuddered, because even though snakes must all be asleep she couldn't help worrying about treading on one of them. And what about the giant porcupines, whose long, sharp, bony quills Ruth collected in vases? Or the wild boar? She heard a pattering sound and turned, alarmed, but it was drops of water falling out of the sky.

No sooner had Tania noticed this, than the rain began in earnest. It fell in such heaviness and force that she was almost blinded, and from down below, she heard distant cries as Ruth's guests ran indoors for shelter. Overhead, the sky had become almost completely black apart from a thin edge of moonlight where the clouds shredded like moth-eaten silks. Yet the nightingales continued to sing, competing with the noise of running water. Piercing, fierce, insistent, their songs were on the very edge of what she could bear.

The whole hillside rang with wild music. She ran towards the camper van, and banged on the door.

'Raff! Raff! Let me in!'

A rectangle of dim yellow light opened in the air. He was wearing shorts, and glasses, and clearly about to go to bed.

'Oh. Hello.'

She was shivering, and her hair hung down in heavy coils, dripping into her calves.

'I'm soaked.'

His shadowy face did not seem particularly friendly.

'I'll get you a towel.'

Inside the van, the rain was hardly more muffled. She wrapped the towel around herself, looking everywhere but at him.

'I'm still wet.'

He brought out another folded towel. 'I haven't got another.'

It was cramped in the van. The bed was made up just as he'd described, the table slotting neatly between the benches, and covered by a thick foam mattress that matched the pads on the benches. Hesitantly, she sat down on it and squeezed the rainwater out of her hair until the towel became damp and heavy. Dash had already jumped on to the bed, and was snoring loudly.

'My hair,' she said, dismayed. 'I'd washed it yesterday for the wedding. And now the snakes have come back.'

'Snakes?'

'That's what it feels like in my scalp. I've had my mother check me so many times in case I've caught nits.' She saw his mouth twitch. 'You probably think that's funny.'

'I expect the feeling is because you're tense. You have more nerves in your scalp than almost anywhere else, and they are all coiled about. And you do have an awful lot of hair,' he said. 'Maybe you'd feel more comfortable if there was less of it?'

Nobody had ever suggested this to Tania. She stared at him, shocked.

'You mean, cut it off?'

'Yes.'

'But my hair *is* me,' she said.

'No it isn't. It's part of you, and it is remarkable. But … I wonder whether having quite such a lot of it isn't a burden?'

Tania muttered, 'I couldn't cut it.'

'I've sometimes thought that all those paintings of maidens being offered up as a sacrifice for monsters might be kept there by their hair, rather than their chains,' said Raff.

Tania sniffed. 'I forgot, you are a painter's son. Is that why you're called Raphael?'

He nodded. 'Yes. My mum loves him. I've no talent for it myself. But I'm quite good at making and mending, and growing things. All those dull, practical jobs.'

The rain drummed on the roof, and yet through it all, she could hear the birds.

'Those nightingales are *still* singing,' she said plaintively.

'It's a matter of life or death. He must find his mate in the night, as she flies past, or die without issue.'

'Is it only the male who sings?'

'The females do too, in the day. But mostly yes, it is the males, and once they've found each other, they fall silent.'

'I've never seen one.'

'Most people haven't, even if they look. They are small, brown birds, the size of a robin, and they mostly stay on the ground, in brambles and scrubby bits of land that people don't value. There's nothing remarkable about them, apart from their song, and the immense journey they take every spring from Africa. They aren't built for speed, like swallows and swifts, and yet somehow, they come.'

Tania looked around.

'You're very tidy.'

'It's how I was trained.'

'By your mother?'

'The Army.' He smiled at her surprise. 'They make you do lots of ironing. Even your socks.'

Tania said, 'Why did you choose that?'

'It seemed like a good move. I wanted adventure. I even wanted to go to Afghanistan.'

'I saw stuff on the news about that. It looked awful. Though not as awful as what's happening now.' Tania made a face. 'Was that why you sang about breaking waves mountains high?'

'It's a dry land, not the sea. All rocks and mountains. The people are wonderful, though. But in the end, we could only save a handful, not even people whom we owed help to.' Raff's voice sounded strained. 'It's all such a mess.'

Tania nodded. 'I *hate* mess. I feel that if I can't keep everything tidy, I'll collapse.'

'What made you feel that so strongly?'

She looked at the black windows, where rain was running down in a continual stream.

'I just do.'

'In the Army,' Raff said, 'they teach extreme tidiness because it's easier to find what you need in a conflict situation.

307

But order is also a psychological refuge. It helps you cope. There's nothing messier than someone with their guts hanging out after an IED blows up.'

Tania said suddenly, 'So this is why. Since you ask. I went to a party when I was thirteen, at the house of a girl at school. I didn't have any friends, and she was popular. It was full of people I didn't know, guys as well as girls. Her parents were out. I had no idea what to do. Mum had dropped me and rushed off, as always. I was given a drink. It made me woozy. And then some boys, they took me upstairs to a bedroom and . . . they . . . each, they each went on top of me and—'

She burst into tears, rocking backwards and forwards where she sat. It felt like vomiting. When she stopped, her head ached, and she felt quite empty.

Raff said, 'I never wanted to murder anyone until now.'

'What good would that do?' Tania smeared her nose with the back of her hand. 'I don't even know to this day who they were. Only it was horrible and I felt so awful, so dirty and stupid. My mother thought the party would just be, like, balloons and a birthday cake. She thought we were all still children. And I was a child, I hadn't even started to have periods. Parents have no idea what boys expect, the stuff from mobile phones. So you see,' Tania said, 'I'm the mess, I'm the mess, and . . . I don't know if I'll ever be ironed out.'

Raff said, 'You are very brave to tell me. Put this round you.'

He handed her a blanket, again without touching her. He'd left the camper-van door open, too. All this she noticed, because she always did.

'You didn't go to the police?'

'No. That would have destroyed me, and Mum, and everything.'

308

'Is that why you want to be married?'

Tania nodded, drearily.

'I want to be normal. I want to be with someone who can protect me. Only, Olly doesn't love me. And I don't love him. So the mess goes on.'

She blew her nose on the toilet paper he handed her. He had sat down on the bed beside her, but far enough away for her not to feel frightened. 'Sorry. I *never* cry.'

'Men never cry either. Though I did, when we left those poor bloody Afghans.'

His eyes looked tired, behind his glasses, and his short hair was sticking up. She looked away, and buried her fingers in the spaniel's warm fur. It crossed her mind, briefly, that she had never talked to anyone like this, or for so long. When her mother had taken her to see a therapist, she'd lied. Of course she'd lied. She'd been lying her whole life.

'Is that why you came to Italy?'

'Pretty much. I couldn't cope with being back,' Raff said. 'The stuff that normal people think interesting. *Love Island*, what's for dinner, how annoying politicians are. When you've spent years sewing up children, and seeing your mates die, it seems so stupid, and too full of people, and noise.'

'I have that almost all the time,' Tania said. 'My idea of hell is a nightclub. Or *Love Island*.'

He snorted.

'I think, when I go back to England, I'll live in the country,' he said. 'Somewhere quiet. I'd like to try farming. Ruth has inspired me. Though I'd also like to help refugees.'

She hugged a pillow. 'Did you lose a lot of friends out there?'

'Yes. That's why you fight, you see. Not for Queen and Country, but for each other. Twelve of my men died out there. One minute, they're the fittest people you ever know, and the

309

next they're missing a leg or an arm. Or dead. No matter how lucky you are, the penny drops that next time it could be you.'

'Why did you join?'

'Boredom, mostly, and growing up with a single mother who loved me but who has her own life. The Army put me through university, and it gave me training and structure. I thought that marching, ironing and shouting were normal. But I loved it, for a while.'

'Were you hurt? I mean, physically?'

He shook his head. 'A few scars. But I did some bad things.'

'I'm sorry about your friends,' Tania said. After a pause, she added, 'I've never had a friend, apart from my brother.'

'Why not?'

'I'm too boring.'

Raff said, 'What about your four million followers who find every detail of your life completely fascinating?'

'Well, firstly, they aren't my friends, are they? Just people online. I'm bad at real people, as you've probably noticed.'

'No, I hadn't. I think real people are pretty bad at you, actually.'

Tania was silent. It was tempting to believe that the world was out of step, rather than herself, but also unlikely. Yet somehow, she had to find a way. She thought of the trapped swallow, fluttering frantically and dashing itself against the windows of La Rosa, and of how Raff had caught it out of the air to carry it to safety in the living cage of his fingers.

'Are you violent?'

'No. Being trained to fight is different. I have killed people, at a distance. For a long time, it was like being in a real-life video game, it doesn't feel real. Now, I'm useless.'

'But Ruth is always singing your praises.'

'Well, I'm good at digging latrines,' he said, with his faint smile. 'And I like growing stuff. I have to hope that I'm good for something, as a civilian.'

They listened to the drumming rain, the nightingales, the snoring spaniel.

Tania said, 'Olly still cares for Juicy, you know?'

Raff lay back and put his arms behind his head. He had taken off his glasses, and she could see the oddly naked look of someone whose eyes do not function without help. There were deep lines on his forehead. He was not, like Olly, someone who exuded confidence and invulnerability, quite the opposite. Yet she knew that he had done things and understood things that the other never would.

'She's still in love with him.'

'Did she tell you that?'

'Yes. She's a good person.'

Tania said, 'I saw them together, just now, making out.'

'And you're upset.'

She put her head, which felt very heavy, on her knees. 'I don't know what to do, and I'm so, so tired.'

'Sleep, if you want,' Raff said. 'I won't hurt you.'

'I know,' she said.

When she opened her eyes again, the rain had stopped and it was light outside. The birds were chirping noisily, and the ditches were swollen with water, but something was missing. She listened, and for the first time, there was no nightingale singing.

Raff was asleep. Very carefully, she got up and went out of the camper van. Dash had already left, and she was glad because Ruth would worry about him otherwise.

Every plume of grass was hung with drops that fell, flashing, to the ground, and soon she was soaked again. The gladioli stems had opened into flowers, a delicate, brilliant pink, butterflies not snakes. Everything was the same, and everything was changed.

At La Rosa, she paused for a moment, then walked on down. It was a fine morning, and she wanted to enjoy her freedom.

The rough track widened and levelled off. She came to a stone cottage, and outside it, to her surprise, was Diana Evenlode, kneeling down on the grass, her white head bowed as if in grief.

'Hello?' Tania said hesitantly.

'Good morning,' Diana replied, looking up. 'You're an early riser.'

'I heard . . . I'm sorry about . . . your husband.'

Diana straightened up, and Tania saw to her relief that she'd been deadheading with a pair of scissors. 'Don't be. Tea?'

'Yes, please.'

Tania followed her into the kitchen, and looked around at its whitewashed walls, and a high window through which a shaft of dust slid down from the deep blue air beyond.

'This is like a Vermeer.'

'You enjoy art?'

'Yes,' Tania said. She added, because she wanted to say his name, 'Raff's mother is a painter.'

'You know her?'

'No. But she has a website. There are lots of paintings of him as a child on it.'

Admitting that she had looked at these made her hot with embarrassment.

Diana, busy lighting the gas stove, paused a moment. 'You like Raff?'

Tania gave no answer, but her blush deepened. She could see Diana smiling.

'No milk, sorry.'

'I don't drink dairy.'

'Why not? Are you allergic?'

'No, but, you know, the planet . . . '

'Nonsense!' Diana said. 'Nothing is more natural than cows' milk. As long as they're raised properly and not treated cruelly, that is. You mustn't waste away, and as a woman you must look after your bones. That's what has kept me going, you know – strong bones. Though Italians think we're babies for wanting milk in our tea and coffee.'

'I keep wondering,' Tania said, 'when I'm going to feel grown up.'

'In my day, you were thought to be middle aged by thirty. These days, it's forty, or is it sixty? I'm not sure one ever grows up, really. I think you just get old, which is a different thing entirely.'

'How depressing.'

'Not really. Life must be lived in prose,' Diana said, but added for the first time, 'just not without a sense of wonder.'

'Wonder,' Tania repeated. 'Raff has that. And kindness.'

'He seems a very nice young chap,' said Diana. 'Such a pity his parents never married.'

'I don't think things like that matter any more, do they?' Tania said. 'Besides, they did. Marry, I mean.'

'Are you sure?'

'Well, yes. They must have done, because he told me they divorced after he was born.'

Diana turned, her face flooded with animation.

'My dear, tell me more.'

24

The Old Mill-House

Enzo looked everywhere for his gun, but it was gone. He knew this, even though he went on looking, unable to believe both that he had been so foolish as to keep it under his bed – what a childish place for it – or that he had failed to lock up before leaving, as he normally did. That was the problem with being at the beck and call of three old ladies, he thought. He was always running around for them, and even when he was invited to a family supper, as he was before the wedding, he was never sure whether he was a friend or a kind of servant.

Now some person, known or unknown, was walking about with his pistol, and apart from the danger it posed to other people, Enzo was furious at the loss of an heirloom. He'd revered his grandfather, though he remembered him only dimly, and the gun, which had kept the family safe in these very hills during the Occupation, had come to him as a sacred gift (even though it had been his mother who had actually raised the rabbits and hens and vegetables that kept them fed).

It had to be one of the migrants who had stolen his gun. After all, nothing else was missing this time, no food or knives or clothes, as far as he could judge, only this one thing. Could it be the migrant he had shot? How else would anyone know that his gun was in his bedroom? Was he waiting to take revenge? That would be natural, but if he went to the police, all kinds of awkward questions might be asked. Besides, maybe the thief wasn't intending to shoot *him*. He could be after anyone, including Ivanov.

But again, anyone trying to assassinate the oligarch would have much more sophisticated weapons. They'd all heard about the attempt in England, those two goons with the Novichok who'd managed to kill a poor woman but not their intended victim had been an international laughing stock, so stupid that they'd even been caught on CCTV. Out here in the countryside, though, there were hardly any security cameras, and any number of empty houses, hardly inhabited except for one or two months a year ... No wonder Ivanov wanted more local eyes and ears looking out for strangers. He'd probably be safer in a city than sitting up on a hilltop for everyone to see.

The mill-house was a pretty good foxhole. It probably didn't have electricity, but most cookers ran on gas cylinders, and it had a fireplace. The nights were increasingly warm, and in any case those Albanians were used to the cold, surely. But the presence of people traffickers would make it less safe, and now that the body in the millpond had been found, it was the last place an FSB agent would still hide.

An assassin would probably not go to a *pensione* or an abandoned house. They'd stay in another town, and come as a day tourist, much like the Salisbury killers. They'd still need somewhere to camp out, however. If I could find them,

Enzo thought, Ivanov would reward me – he is still a very rich man. Maybe I could get him to put in hot water, or even mend the roof.

'You're very quiet these days,' Ruth said to him. 'Have the preparations given you too much trouble?'

'No, not at all,' Enzo said.

He wondered whether he should tell Ivanov about the theft of his pistol, but it might just irritate him.

Personally, Enzo would not have chosen to hide away in a Medici fortress. As a gilded cage it was no doubt luxurious, but also too isolated, and there was more and more crime in Tuscany. Thieves even tried it on with locals. Juicy had told him that once it was known that he was becoming one of the richest farmers in the region, her own father had been approached by a gang of men who demanded bribes to leave him alone.

'But he pointed to the ceiling, and showed them the camera that was recording everything for the police, and they left in a hurry,' she added. 'You know, the Mafia is moving north.'

'Everything bad comes to us from the south,' Enzo said automatically. 'Well, apart from Hannibal.'

Juicy gave him a long look. 'Do you think that is how it is? All bad things come from outside, rather than our own hearts?'

Enzo thought about this. 'Well . . . not always.'

It occurred to Enzo that perhaps he should pay the old mill-house another visit. Ivanov said the traffickers had vanished, along with their passengers, but maybe they could have left some clue.

Accordingly, he walked down the rutted road from his own house to the mill quite openly the afternoon before the wedding. His path was not easy; even in the days since he had last spied on it, more brambles had grown up, and they snagged his trousers like kittens that would soon become tigers. Once, it had been a good little road, one of the stony *strade bianche* that turned to white dust in summer, but perfectly accessible to a vaporetto or a Fiat. It connected the hamlet where he, Ruth and Diana lived to the village below, to the life of a working community with a school and a shop and a tiny church.

The valley was a steep one, especially towards the bottom where the river ran, rippling and gurgling to itself until dried by the fierce summers. Any noise Enzo made would be covered by this, though further along there was the village where Stefano still lived, and where they had both once gone to school, to fight and tumble in the playground . . .

Overhead, he could hear an annoying mechanical buzzing, a strimmer perhaps, or the daily flights from Perugia passing overhead to go to London or Frankfurt or Barcelona, filling him with envy and regret. All those people flying off, but he was never among them. So many people went abroad, even Stefano with his lorry, and here he was still, despite having gone to the *liceo classico*. There were animals, usually sheep, who did not need penning in with fences because they were hefted to an area of land and unable to leave it. He felt like that. He'd tried leaving, but he was always drawn back, by the lack of money, the lack of confidence, by, essentially, fear of the unknown.

He walked up to the mill-house and tapped on the door of the first floor. Nobody answered, so he turned the handle. It opened, and he knew at once that the mill was abandoned again. There is an echo to uninhabited placed that is unlike any other. In the good times many years ago, Enzo himself had earned a respectable living finding houses like these and selling them to the Americans, British, German and Dutch people whose fantasy project it was to own a piece of Tuscan real estate. He'd been good at persuading them to part with unimaginable sums, not just the tens of thousands of euros they were actually worth but hundreds of thousands, even millions. But then they realised that the Belle Arti would not allow extensions and swimming pools, or the felling of ancient olives and cypress because these were part of the historic fabric of Tuscany, and they became very upset, especially when fined and made to put things back as they ought to be. They did not understand that, due to hot summers, a house that faced north-east rather than, as in colder ones, south-west, was desirable. And then, when they did convert their former farmhouses, cottages or stables, they found that the damp rose up and the heat beat down, and no matter how ravishing it was to look at, their fantasy would always be profoundly foolish.

The mill had not been intended as a place to live in, but it had been an essential part of the village. For six weeks, people from many other villages would bring sack-loads of fruit, stripped by hand and looking like so many green and violet beads. These would be crushed by the two giant granite wheels, once pushed by the waterwheel but then by electricity, whirling round and round in an equally gigantic vat. The crushed olives were squeezed on to coir mats with a hole in the middle, stacked one on top of the other, and pressed beneath a round metal plate operated by a monumental wooden screw. It was the simplest possible kind of machine, and there was so much juice in the tarry paste that even stacking the rope mats caused oil to pour out. It might have been the heart of the land, it was so thick and green and gold; and that first pressing was never sold but kept by those who owned the trees to be used for constipation, high blood pressure, diabetes, eczema, cancer and arthritis, as well as the dressing of both wounds and salads. But hardly any olive oil now was Tuscan. It came from Greece, Spain, Turkey, and perhaps Sicily and Puglia, all of which were naturally inferior. Apart from hobbyists like Ruth, only the Guardis kept it going locally, and their produce was mostly exported to Italian delicatessens like the one that Giusi's brother and Enzo's sister ran in London.

I should have married a local girl, like Giusi, Enzo thought, and raised a family here, but instead I have lost my only child, and Giusi will probably have none. It made him sad, for his neighbour was a lovely woman who could still have children, but we both lost our hearts to foreigners.

He sighed, and looked through the rooms to see if he could find anything. There was grey dust on many of the surfaces, perhaps left by the police in trying to obtain fingerprints, and a tattered sheet from a pornographic magazine in one corner. Otherwise, not a stick of furniture or even a candle. Had people really been living here? Yes, because there was evidence that a fire had been made. He went down to the ground floor, which was more like a cellar. He saw iron bars on the windows and only a dim greenish light coming through from high up. It looked like a dungeon, though probably, when converted by a fancy architect, it would be a fine living room. If the traffickers really had kept migrants in here, then they expected them to sleep on the cold concrete floor without even a sheet of plastic.

Enzo could not help shivering. He had a bad feeling about this place. Just one thing remained, in a corner: a tiny pink sock, so small that it looked like a bit of dirty rag.

Seeing this, Enzo felt a strange emotion. He remembered when his own daughter had had feet this size.

The migrants that he saw on television news reports seemed ant-like in their uniformity, but when some of them carried children in their arms, he felt especially furious. How dare they! The inflatable dinghies they crowded into to cross the Mediterranean were bad enough, but seeing their children was the last straw. When Italian women could not even afford *one* child, why should his country take in those from Africa? Let them sort out their own problems, their wars and bad governments! Enzo's grandfather had been in Eritrea in the war. It had been the only time he had ever left Santorno, and he'd described it as a hellish place, all dust and savages, the dregs of a continent that Italy – being last in the queue – had chosen to colonise.

'We should have left them alone. The blacks have nothing to do with us,' he would say, before spitting on the floor.

'*Porca Madonna!*' Enzo said angrily.

The pink sock upset him deeply. Whatever he'd expected to find was not this. It took time for him to collect himself. So they have a child with them, he thought. Maybe it had been born on their journey, in some camp or ditch, probably not in a hospital as his own had been. What a terrible time his wife had had! It was no wonder women wanted fewer children, if any, given what they went through, and yet while Italy's population fell catastrophically, that of the poorest countries continued. He put the tiny sock in his pocket, and trudged back up the hill. At least there was no evidence of the man he had shot. Maybe he had left, with the rest. Whoever they were, the police had not found them, just the drowned Albanian.

The higher he rose, the better he felt. He could see Ruth's groves, immaculately tended.

It was Ruth who had brought back farming on this hill. The painstaking labour of clearing and pruning olive trees, observed by Enzo over many years, alongside the replanting of vines, commanded respect. He was especially interested in what she did to the vines.

'Why are you planting so few, and not feeding them with fertiliser?' he once asked her.

'Ah.' Ruth looked at him over her half-moon glasses. 'Well, I've done a lot of research and although my wine will never be of the quality of Montalcino or Montepulciano, apparently what vines respond to best is suffering.'

'Suffering?'

'A vine that is fed and watered makes hundreds of leaves but very few grapes, all of them hopeless for wine. If, however, you cut off all but one stem, and even most of the roots, you force a vine's roots to go deep down, searching for water. And then its one stem spreads out above the ground in the hot sun, all along the wires, and the grapes it produces have thicker skins, and it is the *skins* that make good wine, not the juice.'

Enzo was not altogether sure what she was intending to say, but he took photographs for Instagram of the best olives and vines.

Look at this! he wrote in English on the keyboard of his mobile. *My family live here for over two thousand years.* Thanks to Tania, his followers on Instagram had gone up to 150, some of them, he could see, in America. Was one of them Fede? Every time he saw a new name on his feed, it felt like a chance. He had put his mobile number and email on his entry, just in case she looked. He felt sure that his ex would never give it, if asked. She would have told their daughter that America was the only place she belonged, because this was what she believed. It was what, above all, they had quarrelled about.

Of all the countries in the world to take a child to, America was surely the worst. The terror that Fede might have died in one of the school massacres, fires and earthquakes that seemed to happen more and more often there was always with him – even though fires and earthquakes were not unknown in Italy, either. However, Enzo hated the country now as much as he'd once loved and admired it. As far as he was concerned, it was the place that had stolen his daughter.

The little pink sock stayed in his pocket, and it felt like a maggot eating into his thigh. He got up, he worked and he collapsed into another night of insomnia, and then it began over again. The nightingales sang, even when he kept his windows shut.

'*Basta! Imbecili!*' he shouted at them. 'Give me peace, I beg you.'

One evening a few days before the wedding, trudging back down the hill from La Rosa, Enzo rounded on his home to see a young black man sitting on the flight of steps. He froze, stomach roiling.

'What are you doing?'

Blessing smiled. 'I think this is yours.'

Enzo reached out a hand for his gun, then stopped. It might be a trick.

As if reading his mind, Blessing brought out a single new bullet. It lay in his palm.

'I think this is yours as well,' he said.

All at once, Enzo was very frightened. He had wondered about the appearance of a second black boy on the hillside, but because Blessing had come with Xan and was welcomed at Ruth's home, he'd accepted that he wasn't one of *those people*. The unease that he felt with Xan always subsided after a few minutes in his company, and his cautious sense of ease had spread to include Blessing, too. They looked alike, with their high cheekbones and curling hair, and he'd believed Xan when he claimed the other was his cousin. Was that a lie, too? Enzo's confusion was compounded by mortification. He'd tried to kill this man, after all.

'I didn't know it was you,' he said. 'The other night, I mean.'

Blessing looked at him thoughtfully.

'Do you shoot at every person who comes to your door? Or only those whose skin colour you dislike?'

Enzo muttered, 'I thought you were someone who meant me harm.'

'Instead, I was trying to escape it.'

'So you *were* with those ... those bad people in the mill house?'

Blessing said, 'I was being kept there against my will.'

'Why? Had you done something wrong?'

Blessing said, with barely restrained anger, 'They kidnapped me. I was escaping them.'

Enzo said, 'Tell me you didn't shoot anyone with my pistol?'

'It was necessary to have a weapon,' said Blessing, 'but no. They gave up my companions immediately when they saw the gun, and left.'

'But what about the dead one? I saw him, in the millpond.'

'He was their leader. He tried to stop me leaving, having already taken my money and passport. We struggled, he slipped and ... I didn't wait to see what became of him. I wanted to get away. That was all I wanted, to escape them. I did not know he had drowned, then. He is on my conscience, but not too much because of what he was doing.'

Enzo did not know whether to believe this. 'So why go back?'

'I couldn't leave the others. This is why – excuse me – I borrowed your gun, for a while. I had to go back to help them, and also to retrieve my passport and wallet. They are very cruel people. Once they get hold of you, they ask for more and more money from your relations back home, and if you do not get it, they hurt you.'

'Did they do this to you?'

323

'No, but they had only just caught me. They could not understand that I was in Italy legally, as a tourist. Well,' Blessing grimaced, 'not *quite* as a tourist.'

'Where are your friends now?'

'In a safe place. They will not stay for long.'

'Where are they trying to get to?'

'Somewhere else.'

It was clear that Blessing did not trust him, and why should he? Was his story about the trafficker falling into the millpond true? It was possible, especially at night, when a poor swimmer might well sink and drown in its cold, deep water.

'I would like my gun back,' said Enzo sulkily.

'I will leave it here, at the top of the stairs,' Blessing said. 'I have removed the bullets, and you will find them in another place, because I am not a thief. If you don't tell Ruth and the others about me, I won't tell them about you. I am still wounded where you shot me, so I do not think they will have any difficulty believing what I say.'

'Promise me you will do them no harm,' said Enzo

'Why should I? They have been only good and kind to me.' The accusation was unspoken. Enzo knew he had not been good, or kind. He thought of the bloodstained T-shirt Ruth had shown him, with its two bullet holes. Somehow, Blessing must have bandaged his wound. To have gone back for his companions was, he had to admit, a brave thing to do.

'Goodbye, Enzo,' said Blessing. 'Remember what I have said. It's your choice, as it is mine.'

Enzo was ashamed, and also angry. He waited until Blessing had walked away, and then he searched for the bullets, found them, and put them away with his pistol. Then he went up the hill. This time, he carried his shotgun.

At the crossroads, he hesitated. One way led to La Rosa,

where he could march in and denounce Blessing as an impostor to the wedding party. Ruth would be alarmed and upset, though with Americans, you could never tell. One moment, they were buying duct tape and expecting the world to end, the next, they were smoking pot, voting for Obama and decrying capitalism. Enzo debated with himself, then turned in the opposite path and walked until he came to the walls of the Palazzo Felice. The annoying buzzing noise returned, like the whine of a giant mosquito. He looked up.

There, skimming above the olive groves, was a strange little machine. It had twin propellers, like a miniature helicopter, and as he watched, the machine swooped and hovered, just like an insect about to sting.

Enzo, in a fury of frustration, lifted his gun and fired. The machine fell instantly. He began to walk over, and then, quite suddenly, the ground shook, and the air darkened with rocks, earth, shrubs, flying out from where the machine had been a split second before.

He wondered why he couldn't hear anything. There was a small cut on his arm, and an immense bewilderment as he found himself looking up into the sky from a patch of thick, prickly gorse.

When his hearing returned, he took out his mobile, and called the number that Ivanov had given him.

'I think I've just destroyed a bomb,' he said.

25

Marta Sees Death

Marta was not herself.

'I can't believe I have to go through so much *fucking* pain in order to die,' she snarled at Xan.

She never swore, normally, but the agony in her back and down one leg was now unremitting.

Xan and Blessing were nursing her, in relays, and as they helped her to drink, wash and change, she found she neither knew nor cared which was which. Without them, she would be dying of thirst, or bedsores, or despair.

'*Danke, liebchen,*' she gasped.

Her English was fading, as if she were a child again. She longed for her mother, her poor brave mother who had survived the unspeakable things that the Russian soldiers had done, and who had managed to hide her child so that it would not happen to Marta, too. Brutes, all of them! She had grown up and become a woman in turn, fierce and tough and wilful, only now all those hardened layers were sliced away, and beneath them was the small, defenceless grub of herself, shrinking from the cruel beak that jabbed and jabbed again.

In addition, there was the terror that she was losing her mind. There would be a slight breeze on her face, and then a shadow would cross her eyelids, and she knew that her intruder was back; though when she woke there was nobody there.

Beside her, Otto slumbered on, oblivious, and this more than anything convinced Marta she was hallucinating. Surely, her dog would wake if there really were a stranger in her bedroom? The little white terrier was going deaf, but there was nothing wrong with his sense of smell.

Sometimes, she dreamt of Edward.

'I am yours, and you are mine,' he told her, and in her dream she stepped out of the ring of flames and was happy again.

Did people still fall in love this way? Modern couples seemed to be far more cynical and equivocal, though she had seen it in that young man whom she had taught as best she could to sing properly. He had a tuneful voice, but she had made it better; after all, what was the point of being an accompanist to a tenor if you did not learn some technique? If she could believe that she would be reunited with her husband after death, it would be worth going through all this . . . only she could not. She was a rational being, and both ghosts and miracles were impossible.

Marta shifted, and moaned. She longed for oblivion, but the figure that haunted her promised no comfort.

Was it Death? He had no scythe, but why would he be there if not to cut her life's thread?

'He was here again,' she told Xan.

'Who, Oma?'

'The black man.'

Xan said, as before, 'The only Black men here are myself and Blessing.'

'No, the *other* one.'

With an effort, she tried to calm herself. All is well, she told her heart. She was at home, in bed, and her body would mend itself. If she was hallucinating, it must be the morphine patches. They made her feel nauseous, but if she stopped putting them on it would be worse. Otto jumped off the bed, and walked, claws clicking against the terracotta tiles, to sniff at the base of the bookcase.

'He is obsessed,' she murmured.

'I'll take him out,' Xan said. 'Come on! Walkies!'

Stumpy tail wagging, Otto whined and scratched. It was maddening.

'Leave it,' Xan said. 'I'm going to get some mousetraps.'

He clipped the lead onto Otto and led him to the world outside. How Marta longed to see it again! To be ill at this time of year was the worst punishment, especially to an elderly person, for whom seeing the world renew itself is always hopeful.

Is this my last spring? Marta thought. Even the fresh verdant tops of the lime trees she could see out of her window were enchanting. She was so dreadfully bored, too. Even music had deserted her.

She thought she had accepted discomfort and diminution. Goodbye, she had said silently to her breast, her womb, her hips, her appetites: goodbye and good riddance. I myself am still here. But she had not reckoned with her spine collapsing.

As a distraction, she tried flicking through magazines and TV channels, only to be enraged by all the advertisements aimed at the elderly or disabled. These were always represented by slim, fit women who did not look a day over forty, stepping nimbly into special baths without a stick or wheelchair in

328

sight. Nobody wanted to be reminded of what old age actually looked like, did they? Just you wait, Marta thought, because soon, almost everyone is going to be like me.

Even so, she was a little surprised when Diana dropped by.

'It's good of you to visit me,' Marta said, suddenly aware that her hair was unbrushed, and that Diana, despite ever more eccentric clothes (Indian shawl, padded gilet, leather boots), remained elegant.

Her sister-in-law sat at a distance, back to the window where the light would not show the worst of her wrinkles. She brought a posy from her garden, swiftly put into a jug 'because the chaps will no doubt forget to do this'. Blessing was busy making one of his puréed vegetable messes next door in the kitchen. These were almost all that Marta could now eat.

'How are you doing?' Diana enquired.

'Not so good today.'

Marta found herself wondering whether this was a visit from friendship or charity. It hardly mattered, really. How strange that sisters-in-law who had cordially disliked each other for decades should have become close! Yet not so strange, because they shared many memories, and there was now probably nobody else left who had these particular ones, not even their children. She remembered how beautiful Diana had been, the perfect hostess and mother with her four blonde children.

She never disliked the English so much as when she was with her husband's family.

'Still tinkling away?' Perry had asked her; and to his brother, 'Still yodelling, Ed?'

What gave people like the Evenlodes the right to be so contemptuously dismissive of the art to which she and Edward had dedicated their lives? But Perry was incapable of seeing the value in anything, unless it brought wealth or power. Poor

Diana, Marta thought. Nobody deserved a man like that. She was looking a good deal brighter, at any rate.

They chatted a little, about Perry – he was being cremated, and his ashes taken back to Cornwall.

'Will you stay at La Docciola?'

'I hope not. My daughter, Etta, is offering me a home with her. I do want to go back. I've never been in love with Italy, like Ruth.'

'Ah. And of course, next month, the heat begins.'

In England, people look eagerly for news of a dry, sunny day. In Italy, from May to September, the prayer is for rain.

Diana gave her a concerned look.

'Do you really not think it would be better to be in hospital?'

Marta said, 'I have collected a store of painkillers. If what I have is cancer, I intend to take them all.'

'But my dear, what if you don't need to? What if you could be cured?'

'At our age,' said Marta, 'we aren't living longer, but dying longer. Beatrix has the right idea.'

'You say that, but only a few days ago you were able to perform a virtuoso recital. Or so people tell me,' Diana said. 'Unfortunately, my hearing is now so bad that it would probably have been wasted on me.'

'You're able to hear what I say, I hope?'

'Mostly I'm lip-reading.'

So this was why Diana chose to sit where she did. I thought it was vanity about wrinkles, Marta thought, slightly ashamed.

'We'll end up like those three old women in Greek myth, passing round an eye and a tooth.'

'I have nothing left but La Docciola.'

'And – your jewel,' said Marta.

'My ring?' Diana lifted it up, and the red stone on her finger scattered flecks of rainbow. 'I don't even know what it would sell for. It's Rhodesian, you know. One of our servants' children found it, grubbing about in the mud. She just thought it a pretty piece of glass. But Perry knew. You don't grow up in that country without knowing what an uncut diamond looks like.'

'Why is it red?'

'Because it's a blood red diamond,' Diana said. 'Perry got it made into a ring in England, when I finally gave him a son. He called it my medal for long service.'

'If it's a diamond, it must be worth quite a lot.'

Diana said, 'I have no pension. And it was just as well he did give it to me, because it's the one thing besides Fol that he couldn't gamble away. He couldn't get it off my finger, you see.'

'If it's valuable, why do you wear it all the time?'

'I like it. The colour makes people think it must be semi-precious.'

'I know it's not, because you used it to make the circle in the window of the hot car. Only diamond cuts glass.'

They both giggled.

'It was a naughty thing to do, but it saved that poor dog,' said Diana. 'I still don't give a damn, do you?'

'No,' Marta said.

Marta's next visitor was even more unexpected. The doorbell rang, and the next thing she knew, Ivanov had entered her bedroom.

'Excuse me, Maestra. Your grandson said you were receiving, and it is better to say what I have to say in private,' he said.

Marta opened her mouth to say that it was Blessing not Xan who had let him in, but thought better of it. She gestured feebly.

'I have come to say that I am returning to London very soon. My private plane is at Perugia airport.'

'I thought they had confiscated things like that for Russians.'

'My dear Marta, *qui siamo in Italia*. It is not registered to me, but to a medical charity. They may try to seize my palazzo, but if so, that will be tied up in legal battles for years. Besides, I am known to be an opponent of Putin – who has just tried to blow up my home. Thanks to Enzo, this did not happen.'

'What did he do?'

'He shot down a drone with a bomb.'

Marta gasped. 'Is he all right?'

'Yes. A little deaf in one ear, but that should pass. I think I must go back to England. I think you should fly with me.'

Marta was astonished, and touched.

'You are offering me a seat?'

'Yes. To tell the truth ...' Ivanov looked faintly embarrassed. 'I need your help to get into Britain. If I come with you on a medical evacuation, we can whistle through the airport and my passport is less likely to be examined. All you need is a letter from your doctor here.'

'That's very kind. I'm still not able to sit up, however.'

Ivanov made a gesture of dismissal. 'My plane is small, but more comfortable than a commercial flight. If you wish, you can be lying down the whole way, drinking champagne.'

Marta's head was in a whirl.

'But what about Otto?'

'Otto?' said Ivanov blankly. 'Ah. The dog. Well, he will have to be left behind. I do not like dogs. They are not permitted on medivac flights, in any case. But your grandson may accompany you.'

Marta grimaced. Of course it was unthinkable that she should leave her dog behind.

'If you decide you wish to come, then call and say you are thanking me for the fruit. An ambulance will come for you.'

He saw her face, and added, 'Your dog can always be couriered, you know.'

Marta said, 'Thank you, Vasily. I will think this over. I would – if it is possible – like to return.'

Ivanov took her hand in his gloved one, and bent over it with exquisite courtesy.

'I am happy to help you, Maestra, in any way I can.'

When Ivanov left and Xan returned, she called both young men into her bedroom to tell them of his offer.

'Will you accept, Oma?'

'I am not wedded to Italy, like Ruth. I should go back. But Otto must go first. I am not leaving until he does.'

She had no energy, but the thought of seeing her dear Lottie and her granddaughters gave her a little hope. If the doctors could cure her, she would walk Otto on the green hills of Hampstead Heath once again. Marta fell into a doze, smiling.

When she woke, it was night, and a strange man was standing at the end of her bed.

26

Blood Red

It had taken no time, and a lifetime, for what Tania had told Diana to sink in, and then, when she asked Andrew, he confirmed it. Her grandson was a legitimate heir.

'Once again, you've chosen not to tell me something that is *hugely* important.'

'It really isn't worth making a fuss about,' he said, coldly.

'Yes, it is. Don't you understand what this means? If it doesn't matter to you, then it does to me and your late father. We deserved to know.'

'I could not care less about the viscountcy,' he said.

'I would not have put you down as a Communist.'

'I'm not. But what I care about is the life of the mind, not social class, which as far as I can see is responsible for most of the worst aspects of British life.'

'Oh, Andrew! We are what we are.'

She resented the way that she belonged to the only group of people to whom every bad thing could now be ascribed.

From having been admired and feted a hundred years ago, anyone upper class was now supposed to be a brute, a scoundrel and a thief.

If working-class people were presented in the way we are, there would be outrage, Diana thought. Not that anyone would be sorry for aristocrats, ever. People still thought that if you were posh, you must be privileged and powerful and rolling in money, but there always had been people like herself, who were none of those things. She was the poorest person she knew, at least among the expats.

Enzo once told her that because there was no primogeniture in Italy, families had to share all inheritance, which was why they lived in multigenerational households – not because (as foreigners fondly presumed) they loved each other but because there was no alternative. Nobody could afford to set up on their own.

'If we are forced to sell, then often you see the men working as labourers on the family home, and their wives as cleaners, just to keep an eye on things. It's a very, very sad situation.'

'I often felt I was doing that anyway, at my husband's place,' she told him, but of course he didn't believe her. Why would an aristocrat clean her own home?

But the news that there was an heir was like a life-giving elixir; her existence had not, after all, been in vain. Other people set their hearts on certain achievements, whether this was winning a race or producing a perfect soufflé, and these were just as pointless as a viscountcy. Diana knew all this, and she brooded over it.

'I could have died out here, not knowing,' she said to her son.

She thought of how Raff had found and picked her up on the hillside after her fall, and how he had also rescued herself and Perry from the car crash. Such a dear, good boy! No wonder I felt I could trust him immediately, she thought (forgetting how, in fact, she had not). He must have been around all winter, when she visited Ruth, and she regretted not having got to know him then.

When Raff visited her again, she asked why he hadn't made himself known to her.

He looked awkward.

'You had enough on your plate.'

'Oh, but it would have made us both so happy,' she exclaimed. 'Your grandfather would have welcomed you with open arms.'

Then she remembered what Perry had been really like. Yet the strange thing was that now he was dead, most of the memories of his behaviour were becoming softened and blurred. She loved him, despite everything, and they had remained together to the very end. Wasn't that more important than the affairs, the gambling and the abuse? Only the last few years had been *really* bad, and much of that was surely his dementia. It was with a sense of profound relief that she packed up the hoist to return it to the day-care centre, along with the waterproof sheets and all the other accoutrements of age and disability.

Her anger towards Andrew subsided, but not her hurt. She asked, 'Was I really such a bad mother that you couldn't confide Raff's existence to me?'

He gave her his look.

'I didn't think I could trust you not to tell my father. And then the whole shades of the prison house thing would have begun again. Prep school, public school, bullying and browbeating.'

It was true, she thought.

'I would still have liked to know Raff as he was growing up.'

'You can get to know him now. His mother and I are proud of him.'

'He's leaving Italy, isn't he?'

'Yes. But you could always see him in England.'

Diana sighed.

'How am I going to do that?'

'I was thinking that you might like to come back. You know, to live.'

'There's only one place I'd like to live, and that was sold twenty-five years ago,' Diana said bitterly.

'Yes,' Andrew answered. 'But now it's been sold again.'

'To another Russian billionaire, I expect.'

'To me.'

She could feel the blood leaving her face, the shock was so great.

'You mean Lode? You've actually bought *Lode*?'

'Yes. I sold Fol. Did nobody tell you? I thought they would. It's going to be turned into flats. Best thing for it, really. Who wants a castle with fifty rooms?'

'Fifty-two,' Diana said automatically. She knew because she'd cleaned them, all by herself.

'Exactly. Ridiculous. So a developer wanted it, and for the first time ever, I have some money. I saw your old home was for sale in *The Times*. It was in a bad way, so billionaires weren't interested.'

Diana was silent for a few moments, as vivid images rushed through her head. She thought of the mile-long avenue of five-hundred-year-old oak trees, the undulating hills dotted with sheep and the pale gold Cotswold stone of her childhood home.

'I seem to remember Lode was frightfully cold,' she said, trying not to smile.

337

'I've had it properly insulated,' said her son. 'Ground-source heat pump, loft insulation, the lot. Of course, it'll be Raff's too one day, not that he knows any of this either.'

'What a lot,' Diana said, 'you have been keeping from me.'

Through the deep lines in his skin, the face of the small boy he had been shone through, like a lamp switched on inside a shade.

'Yes, I suppose so. But don't you have a few secrets of your own?'

'Probably,' said Diana.

Alone again, she pottered around the garden with Bella. Her poor old Labrador dog who was now in the last quarter of her short life, half-blind too, limping, too, and very deaf.

'You're such a good dog, Bella. You've been good all your life,' she said aloud, partly because it was what Diana felt she had been herself, and nobody had ever said that to her. The Lab groaned when summoned for a walk, but Diana still did it even though she suspected they were hardly necessary. She could remember Bella's youth just ten years ago, when every squeaky toy and excursion was greeted with bounding joy; now, she lived in the daily expectation that she would come downstairs and find her dead. Mostly, the dog slept. Poor Bella was too elderly to stand being put into quarantine for six months, and Ruth had offered to take her in, as soon as Diana told her about leaving Italy. She felt bad about doing this, but this hillside was her dog's home now. Oh, to be free, at last! She would put La Docciola on the market, not that anyone was interested in a second home here with the coming economic storm.

She sorted through Perry's old clothes, wondering whether there were any that Andrew or for that matter her daughters might like. Maybe the raincoat, and the tweed jacket? She could still smell Perry's familiar smell, although his body was already cremated.

There were some cotton shirts of a make that lasted for ever, and an old pair of thick striped red and blue wool school socks that were worth keeping. Half the clothes she wore had been Perry's anyway. Cufflinks, yes, and mother-of-pearl studs for a dress shirt; Andrew might like those, perhaps. The stalactites of a life lived, accumulated drip by drip in some unseen cavern of existence.

There was a faint tapping sound at the French window. Downstairs, Bella gave a series of deep, menacing barks.

'Hello?'

Diana went carefully down the wooden stairs to the kitchen, and saw Blessing being greeted enthusiastically by her dog.

'Do come in,' she said politely. 'Tea?'

'No, thank you.'

'Water?'

'Lady Evenlode . . . ' he began.

'Diana, please.'

'Lady Diana . . . '

She gave a half-snort. 'No, not her, either.'

Blessing sighed. 'Perhaps it would be easier if I showed you something.'

He took out his mobile in its battered leather wallet, and showed her its screensaver.

'This is my mother, Munisha,' he said. 'She passed last year.'

'I'm sorry,' Diana responded automatically. 'You look like her.'

'And this,' said Blessing, clicking another photograph, 'is *her* mother.'

Diana looked at the photograph more attentively. 'She seems . . . '

'Familiar? Yes. She is in the framed photograph you have from your life in Zimbabwe.' Blessing enlarged it. 'That is my grandmother, Mercy, and here she is again. It was online, in a magazine.'

That accursed article! Diana stared at the photograph. She could not deny that the two women were very similar.

'What an extraordinary coincidence, that you should wind up here.'

'No,' said Blessing. 'I came here to find you. My mother was the daughter of your husband. Lord Evenlode was my grandfather.'

There was a long silence. The Labrador gave a sudden gruff huff that made them both jump.

'Well,' said Diana, 'I don't expect she was the first, or the last. As you know,' she laughed shortly, 'my husband has recently died, so he can't confirm it.'

Blessing looked at her, his eyes at once innocent and shrewd.

'I am a part of your family,' he said.

'My late husband was what is politely called a philanderer. But you are not part of *my* family.'

Diana summoned all her hauteur, and Bella growled, but Blessing did not quail.

'He loved my grandmother, Mercy, and she . . . she gave him the diamond you wear on your finger,' he said. 'It was found by my mother, as a child.'

Diana felt herself go cold. So this was what his visit was about.

'I'm afraid that this stone was given to me by my husband,' she said. 'It is mine, not his. I am sorry if you don't believe me, but it's true.'

'I do believe you,' Blessing said. 'As I hope you believe me.'

'Even if I did,' said Diana, 'I can't give you my ring. It's the only thing of value I have left.'

'A blood red diamond,' said Blessing. 'It is worth a great deal. Maybe as much as half a million pounds.'

'I hope so. I intend to sell it when I return to England, because I have no pension.'

Then the horrifying idea came to her that this young man might be ruthless enough to take it by force, perhaps with a knife. She knew it would not come off unless the ring, or her finger, were cut. God knows, Perry had tried often enough, thwarted only by the swelling of her knuckles.

She closed her eyes. When she opened them again, Blessing had not moved.

'I am not going to harm you, Grandmother,' he said. 'I promise.'

Diana put her hand up to her throat.

'How do I know that?'

'I am a Christian,' he said. 'And I would never hurt another human being, least of all my grandfather's wife. I know what it is to be hurt.'

'So what do you want?'

'I need to get to England.'

Diana said at once, 'They won't let you in. I'm sorry, but there's nothing I can do.'

'Even though my grandfather was English?'

'It makes no difference, I'm afraid. If you had an offer from an employer ... It's all about money now.'

Her diamond ring was burning on her finger. How much *was* it worth? She thought of her three daughters and her son, all of whom had safe, comfortable lives thanks to having been legitimately born to white parents with British passports. And now her son had handed her the greatest gift of all, which was not a jewel, but Raff.

She looked at Blessing (that name! She supposed it must

341

be traditional) and saw the intelligence in his face. What an absurd situation this was! She looked at Bella, who was now lying on the floor, apparently fast asleep. She could bring a dog back to Britain, but not a grandchild.

'I don't want to offer you false hope,' she said. 'My country has become a hostile environment to all immigrants, including refugees. If you get there, you would have a long struggle, and maybe face deportation. I really can't advise it.'

'But if I do get there,' Blessing said, 'I was wondering whether I might, for a time, find shelter with my grandfather's family?'

Diana said nothing. Inside herself, the struggle that had begun when Xan and Blessing dragged her and Perry out of the car was continuing. Not strangers, but people. Not people, but family. Not they: us.

He continued, in his soft voice, 'I would greatly prefer, you see, to live in a home rather than a prison. Or a camp.'

Diana considered this. She thought about Lode, which had plenty of rooms, and how very lonely she had been living alone, and how lonely she would probably be for the remainder of her life.

'If you can get to England,' she said, 'you would be welcome to live with me.'

27

The Door into the Dark

Xan was woken by a scream from Marta, and frantic yapping
from Otto. He ran into her bedroom, and was astonished to
see a complete stranger standing there, his hands raised.

'Who the hell are you?'

The man broke into a stream of broken English.

'Sorry ... so sorry ... please ...'

'Oma, are you OK? Has he hurt you in any way?'

Marta said, 'You can *see* him? I am not mad?'

'Yes, he's real. How did he get in?'

'I told you, through the wall.'

It was difficult to hear anything over Otto's snarls and barks.
The little terrier was dancing about, displaying surprisingly
sharp teeth and a temper. Reluctantly, Xan was impressed.
The intruder was actually cowering back, despite being ten
times Otto's size.

'My brave doggie,' Marta said, almost in tears. 'He defends
his mistress, see?'

'But how did he get in?'

'There is the entrance,' said Blessing, behind him. Then Xan remembered that the bookcase by his grandmother's bed concealed a door. It was kept in place by an iron hook, and presumably the slight crack between the wood and the wall had been enough to lift this up.

'What are you doing here?' Xan asked, advancing on the intruder. Like Otto, he was filled with an almost blind anger and protectiveness. Unconsciously, he raised his fists, preparing to strike.

The man spread his hands out in a placatory gesture. 'Food. We came only for food.'

'We? There are more of you?'

He nodded, and pointed at the floor. It took a moment for Xan to understand.

'You are living in the cellar?'

Marta's cracked voice said, 'You always said that I could hide an entire family of Jews down there.'

'They are not Jews,' Blessing said.

Xan turned on him.

'You know this man? Are you responsible for this?'

Blessing nodded.

Xan's sense of betrayal almost choked him. 'But I trusted you. I *covered up for you.*'

'I brought them here to hide. He means no harm.'

'Why should I believe you?'

'They do not need much,' Blessing said. 'But they have a baby. The mother cannot feed her. They have suffered so much to get to Europe and need to recover their strength. I could not let them . . . You understand, Grandmother.'

'Yes,' Marta said. 'Get them food, Blessing, and Ivanov's basket of fruit. I don't need it, they do.'

Xan was silent while his friend went with the stranger into the kitchen next door.

'How many are there?' Xan asked Blessing, who had reappeared with two carrier bags.

'Seven, counting Eden.'

'Where are they from?'

'Eritrea.' Blessing grinned. 'Would you prefer it if they were Nigerian? There are many refugees from your father's country, too, Xan. Half the world wants to move to the other half. Only this time, it is not the white people stealing from Black ones, but the other way about. There will be more, many more, because of the famines, the droughts, the wars. People are starving.'

Xan knew this, and yet his anger at the intrusion into his frail grandmother's bedroom still burned, as did his feeling of betrayal by someone he had helped and trusted.

The intruder gave an anxious smile. 'I am sure you are very nice. As long as you are nice to people, they will be nice to you.'

Xan did not know whether to be shocked or touched by such naivety. Yet if this man had survived goodness knows what to get here with this belief intact, then perhaps, he thought, it might not be so silly. He was still feeling bad about how rude he'd been to Ruth. It was the wine, partly, but also his roiling resentment about the inequality between his generation and his grandmother's, and between white people and Black ones. Each time it died down, the memory of being strip-searched returned to him – the feeling of rage that the only thing that mattered about him was his skin.

'You should have demanded a lawyer,' his father told him, afterwards. 'Did nobody tell you that you are allowed one?'

I think, Xan thought, I will not just demand a lawyer. I

shall *become* one. The idea had not occurred to him before, but now it was obvious. Why else did he love arguing? Why did he care so much about inequality and prejudice? What else was he going to do with his First? What finer thing could he do with his life than use his brains to fight for his fellow men and women, and for justice? It would mean another two years at least of being a poor student, and yet more tuition fees unless Marta helped him; but it would be worth doing.

'Nobody wants Eritreans, least of all here,' Blessing said. 'Yet their country was invaded by Italy over a hundred years ago, just as mine was by Britain. Now it's torn apart by civil war, and its people are little better than slaves. What can they do but leave? Where else should they come, but here?'

'Oh for God's sake,' Xan said.

Eden put his hand over his heart and bowed.

'Sorry to frighten. Thank you, sorry,' he said.

He handed the bags to another shadowy person who stayed at the top of the cellar steps. From below, he heard the mewing sound of a baby, quickly hushed. Xan had heard it before, and not realised where it came from. There were so few babies in Santorno; so few children. Juicy had lamented this, and yet the idea of Italy becoming multicultural like Britain was seemingly inconceivable – despite Italy itself having been just such a place two thousand years ago. Would it change? Could it? It was not impossible, even though it, like Hungary, was lurching towards electing a Fascist government that intended to stop migration.

'What did you do, in Eritrea?'

The man said, 'In my country, I am software engineer. My wife, nurse. My friends are journalist, musician, teacher, dentist and doctor.'

Xan made the same patronising assumptions that his own white family had made about his astrophysicist father and felt ashamed. What did professions matter? They were still people, in fear and need.

When the man vanished back into the cellar, and the door into the dark was again latched shut, Xan said, 'But how did they get here, to Santorno? Come to that,' he said to Blessing, 'how did you? What were you doing on the hillside when I found you?'

'Yes, tell us that.'

Marta was so pale that she looked like old cheese.

'I was looking for Lord and Lady Evenlode. I had read about them in an article online. That is why I came to Italy first, and how I knew I would find them here.'

'My God!' Marta snorted. 'Not that man Goggle?'

'Gorgle,' Xan said. 'I read it, too.'

'Before she died, my mother told me that her father had been Lord Evenlode. Her own mother had been like a wife to him in Zimbabwe, even before he married Diana.'

Xan began to laugh. 'We are actually cousins, then? My lie turned out to be true.'

'Second cousins,' said Marta. 'Diana saw this. I did not. You do look very alike.'

'We both hoped, my mother and I, that he might help me get to England.'

'Not him!' said Xan. 'And besides, even if Perry had wished to, he couldn't.'

'Diana explained that to me. But she said that she will give me a home if I can get to England.' He saw the scepticism on Xan's face. 'I know it is impossible,' said Blessing, 'but I will *make* it possible.'

Xan said, 'Go back a bit. How did you get here in the first place? I take it that you did not cross in a boat?'

'No,' Blessing said. 'I came on a plane, like anyone. My

mother was not rich, but I sold everything for this, and a Schengen visa. Italy is not so difficult from Zimbabwe. Not like England.'

'How did you get *here*, though?'

Blessing said, 'I caught the train from Rome. But after that, things became more . . . complicated.

'I had no idea where in the countryside my grandfather was living, and no Italians would speak to me. So when I walked up to the old town, I asked the only other Black people I could see – the men by the town walls. They told me there was an old lady, very English, who gave some of them a little money each week on Saturday.'

'They must have been thinking of Diana. She always gives money to beggars at the kaffeeklatsch.' Marta smiled. 'One of them said he would give her a blessing in return.'

Blessing nodded. 'I knew that if I could find somewhere for the night, I could return the next day, and ask her. They told me that they were driven up every morning by some white men to beg. I asked if I could go back to the place where they were living.'

'Selling trinkets must bring in more than I thought if it's worth driving them to the city and back every day.'

'I don't think it's only trinkets that they sell,' said Xan, 'is it?'

'I don't know. But the white men were traffickers, I thought that if I failed to get help here, they might be able to smuggle me into England, but they had other ideas.

'My companions were trapped because they had nowhere else to go. Everyone was against them, and everyone could see what they were. I was not like them – yet – and I *did* have somewhere to go. They took my passport, and my money, and my mobile. I was cut off from everyone, just like my companions, a prisoner.

348

'I knew that if I could get out, I could find my grandfather. So that night, I escaped.'

Blessing fell silent, and Xan prompted, 'And then you met me, on the hillside.'

'Yes!' Blessing's face changed. 'Yes. It was a true miracle. I was lost, hungry and hurt, and I met you. You thought I was a wedding guest. I did not lie, but you made it easy.'

Xan shrugged. 'I wanted so much to believe that I wasn't the only Black person there. And also, you had that sweatshirt, didn't you?'

'I found it on Ruth's washing line. I was cold, and I hoped an old top would not be missed,' said Blessing. 'I needed a clean shirt. Somebody had shot me, you see—'

'*Shot* you?' Marta exclaimed.

'Let me guess. Enzo.'

Blessing nodded. Xan said in great anger, 'Oma, I told you not to trust him!'

'It was still night-time. He was half-asleep, and afraid I was a thief.'

'Are you OK now?'

Blessing pulled off the T-shirt he had been sleeping in. Xan saw a long, ragged scab on the side of his torso. 'The bullet did not go into me,' he said. 'It hurt for a while, but Tania put a dressing on.'

'*She* knew?'

'Tania's a good person, you know.'

'I'm sorry.'

'Of all people, you are the one with least to be sorry about,' Blessing said.

'What will you do now? And what about your companions?'

'I need to find them transportation out of Italy.'

'To France? But it's awful there – people camping under plastic in the freezing cold and rain, then drowning in dinghies trying to get across the Channel.'

'Everywhere is bad, and yet we cannot give up hope. Hope is what keeps us alive.'

Marta said, 'Ask Enzo.'

'Enzo won't help! And even if he could, he can't drive seven people over the border.'

'No, but he'll know someone who can.'

'But Enzo *hates* migrants.'

'Enzo likes helping. People.'

Marta was exhausted. Blessing brought a glass of water to her lips, and she swallowed two more painkillers, grimacing.

'Oma, we must think what to do with you, first. That takes priority.'

Marta said, 'I am not leaving without my dog. Please do not nag.'

Xan felt like groaning. It was the middle of the night, he was very tired and, having just recovered from the fright of finding that half a dozen strangers were regularly intruding in his grandmother's bedroom, she was putting bloody Otto before her own needs. He wished very much that his mother was there, but she wasn't.

'Couldn't Otto stay with Ruth for a while?'

'No, my darling. Otto and Dash do not get along.'

Xan sighed. 'Oma, I can drive your car, with Otto, from Italy to London, while you fly back with Ivanov. He has a pet passport, doesn't he? Well, then, all you need do is give me a letter saying that I'm your grandson and bringing him home for you, and it should be OK.'

The relief on Marta's face was very clear. Although Xan could think of few things that he would like less than being cooped up with the little white terrier for the better part of another week, it was the least he could do.

'But where will you stay?'

'I would need some money to cover that, and the ferry, but I think it might be an adventure.'

'I will pay you, my darling.'

'Thanks.' She would pay for his legal training, he thought. It was not cheap, but she definitely would.

'And the wedding?'

'I don't mind missing that.'

Privately, Xan thought that he was best out of it. He'd enjoyed La Rosa in the spring; but the whole thing was farcical. Of course, Olly was a massive knob, but all the Viners seemed to have taken against Tania, which wasn't like them at all because the rest of the family were nice, sensible Devonians.

Outside, he heard rain begin to pour, pattering on the stones and tiles of Santorno.

'It looks like the big day will be a washout in any case,' he told Marta.

'I am not entirely sure why Ivanov is being quite so kind, with this private flight of his,' she said. 'I do not think that I should travel all by myself with him.'

Xan groaned.

'I don't know what to do,' he said to Blessing. 'Here she is, with this wonderful offer of a free flight home on a private plane, and she won't take it. Here you are, longing to get to England, and here I am, wanting to help my grandmother while also bringing Otto back. I wish I could duplicate myself.'

Blessing said, 'Maybe you can.'

351

28

The Wedding Day

When Ruth flung open the shutters of her bedroom and saw the landscape that she had devoted almost half of her life to, she almost groaned. At the very least, there should be thunderclouds and lightning flashes to warn of imminent disaster, but those had all gone. She ran her hands through her thick, springy curls, and got dressed, relieved to see that Dash had returned in the night. He seemed fast asleep, but as soon as she made to leave her bedroom his eyes opened and he sprang off her bed to follow, as usual, and demand his breakfast.

'You bad boy!', she told him. 'What were you up to last night, I wonder?'

Dash gazed back, his rich brown eyes inscrutable, and seemed to smile into his whiskers.

Olly was sitting under the pergola, pale and staring into the middle distance.

'Here, honey,' said Ruth, bringing him a piece of toast, English breakfast tea and a couple of paracetamols. She looked at him anxiously, guiltily. When she had taken magic mushrooms with her lover, it had all been very pleasant and mind expanding, but her grandson did not look happy at all.

'I think I'll be sick if I eat or drink anything,' he muttered, but he swallowed the pills.

Poor boy, she thought.

'You looked as if you were having a ball last night.'

Olly said, 'It was the most amazing, transcendental experience ever.' Ruth sighed with relief, but then he said, 'Only a terrible, terrible mistake I must never repeat. I've made a mess of everything. I've betrayed Giusi and I've betrayed Tania.'

'Is that all?'

Olly looked at her for a moment, wincing, and said, 'No.'

'If you are having second thoughts, there's still time to back out.' This was what Ruth longed to say, but dared not. Hadn't she interfered enough already?

All this time, she told herself, I thought I was Madame Max, and it turns out I am my least favourite Trollope heroine. Lady Lufton in *Framley Parsonage* had got everything wrong; she was a bossy old snob who had very nearly ruined her son the hero's chance of happiness. And oh heavens, wasn't Tania *just* like Griselda Grantly? Unhappy reflections such as these, which would have meant no sense to anyone else, preoccupied her.

'I love Giusi but she would never fit in with my life in London. She can't leave her family, or her business.'

Ruth said nothing. The idea that Olly himself might leave and work remotely from Italy was one he would have to discover for himself, if at all.

'It's not too late,' she said, but her heart sank. Sooner than break his word to Tania, he'd make everyone bitterly unhappy.

The rest of the family were all having a lie-in, and so, for the first time since he'd arrived, she was alone with her grandson. They sat under the pergola, looking at the view and drinking their tea in silence, broken only by Dash sniffing at the base of plants and pots.

'What a nice life he must have,' said Olly. 'Just, you know, pootling about.'

'I hope so,' said Ruth. 'Peaceful, at least. Castrated.'

'Would it be worth it? I mean, not to have a libido?'

'When I became post-sex,' said Ruth, 'I found vast areas of my brain were suddenly free to do things like read Italian.'

'I already speak Italian,' said Olly. 'Giuseppina taught me.'

'You never call her Juicy, like the rest of us.'

'No, I don't,' he said. 'It makes her sound like, I don't know, a fruit.'

'I see,' said Ruth.

'What? What do you see?' he asked aggressively.

'That we'd better start calling her Giusi.'

Olly said nothing. Then he threw his coffee mug at a wall, where it smashed.

'Fuck. Fuck. Fuck.'

'What are you going to do?'

'Nothing. There are all these people here, the most important people in my life, and I can't just let them down.'

'A wedding is not a public performance.'

'Really? That's exactly what it seems like to me. I can't do that to Tania, with her four million followers. But I can't go through with it all, either. It's killing me.'

'What's this, mate? Wedding nerves?'

Angus loomed over them. Olly's professional charm slid over his features like oil.

'I need a stiff drink.'

'Ah. Good preparation for married life,' said Angus. 'I should know. Been married three times. Even pre-nups don't help.'

Maybe if just one of your marriages had worked out, you could be a nice person, Ruth thought, though plenty of nice people still have bad marriages, as she knew.

Angus left to nurse his own hangover, not bothering to say hello to her.

Ruth said, 'Whatever you decide now, just remember that it's serious. Marriage is a turning point in any life, for good or bad.'

She went indoors, laying out breakfast ingredients and utensils as she went because somehow, even though her sons and their wives were middle aged, everyone reverts to childhood in their parents' home. Upstairs, she changed into a smarter version of the denim blues she always wore, with her best dangly earrings and a long necklace of Mexican turquoises intertwined with her spectacles. There was no point in altering her normal style for one of those outfits that English women were supposed to put on, all hats and skirts, though it was predictable that Tania's mother would do this. Ruth liked Polly, but she had thought, even before all this, that there was something off about Tania's father not coming to her wedding. She was still out of pocket for the wedding feast, too, which was galling. Was she really going to have to pay for this whole event herself?

All kinds of things were going wrong. Enzo had texted her to say that he might not be available to ferry the guests into town. Neither Xan nor Blessing were able to come, due to Marta's illness.

Three down, Ruth thought, though such a rush of texts and emails from wedding guests were arriving at the last moment, she barely had time to acknowledge them. Some were inextricably delayed at the airports, because everyone had suddenly decided it was safe to travel again, and others had arrived without telling her they intended to do so. People under forty were extraordinarily rude to hosts, and still expected loaves and fishes, not to mention water being turned into wine. It made her very cross.

The rain of the previous night had refreshed the land, and spring was so abundant it was hard to believe that the planet was endangered. Each year, heatwaves began earlier and lasted longer. What can we do, apart from what I'm doing already, Ruth thought, not flying, reusing, recycling, only eating meat once a week, having solar panels. Three of Josh's five children were saying they didn't want to have children because they were so gloomy about World War Three, world hunger and the destruction of the environment.

But what was a wedding, if not an expression of optimism about the future? Tania's cake, its upwardly mobile tiers of confected aspiration, dominated the fridge. Soon Tania herself would emerge, watched by millions online. No wonder Olly, for all his misery and guilt, couldn't bring himself to put a stop to it all.

'No champagne?' Ruth queried, looking at the downstairs bathtub filled with ice and bottles, but Giusi said, 'No. In Italy, we have our own sparkling wine, Franciacorta. In my opinion, it is *much* better.'

Her chestnut hair drawn back into a tight ponytail, the Italian was wearing a lot of make-up. She looked at Olly, and he looked at her, and Ruth saw identical expressions cross their faces. This wedding must be *excruciating* for them both, Ruth thought, and I've made it all so much worse. The problem with life is that people do not just have to understand their feelings for things to be put right. They do not need to be told what they should do by someone wiser. They have to become who they truly are; and for that, it takes courage.

She looked out at the lawn, with its soft, lush grass, remembering the vision that had made her sink her life savings into the house. It had changed her future by suggesting what she needed to do to find happiness, not all of the time but most of it.

When I die, I will be alone, because of this, Ruth thought. The bitter winters, the broiling summers, the snakes, the scorpions, the bad plumbing and worse internet, the hunters and thieves and prejudices of provincial society were all in one scale, and paradise in the other.

'Good morning! Is Tania up yet?'

'I don't know.'

Contrary to surmises, Polly was wearing a tailored grey silk dress, knee-length and gathered under the bust with a wide tie, but no hat. Her hair was washed and styled. For once, she did not resemble someone who had woken up and been dragged backwards through a bush. Ruth had always wondered where Tania's looks came from, and now she saw what Tania might look like in middle age: attractive, but not with the radiant beauty she had now. Of course not, that would pass like spring itself. The round tables were all being laid out by Giusi's many helpers in the courtyard, who had arrived to get the wedding breakfast set up. The scents of roasting meats and bubbling sauces reached Ruth's nostrils. Swags of white and cream flowers were festooned along the pergola.

Ruth thought, What I wanted was my own eightieth birthday party, not this farce. Even Beatrix's deathday party seemed more appealing. There had been no response to her WhatsApp message, so presumably her friend was already dead. And now Marta, too, seemed to be on the point of dying, and Diana was going to leave; she'd asked if Ruth would take her Labrador in because she was going back to England to live with her son, so Ruth was being dumped with everything, and didn't she, too, deserve support?

More and more guests were emerging from their bedrooms. Some of the family decamped to go to have breakfast in Santorno. A host of Olly's friends were staying in hotels and pensions, and would make their way to the Town Hall. Olly had a drying clot of blood on his chin where his razor had nicked it; he looked good in his suit, and so did Tania's brother Robbie. One by one, Ruth's nine grandchildren assembled, including Tania's bridesmaid, in a charming organza dress embroidered with tiny blue cornflowers. It was probably the prettiest thing Chess had ever worn, and she was almost drunk with delight, touching the fabric reverently one moment, and skipping about the next like the child she still was.

'Look, Mummy! Isn't it the gorgeousest thing you ever saw?'

'You need a wreath of flowers,' Ruth said, affectionately. 'How nicely you've done her hair,' she said to her daughter-in-law. She recalled that she had not entirely approved of her, either, though these days they both chose not to remember this.

I am probably the mother-in-law from hell, she thought, and even worse as a grandmother. It's a miracle that any of them want to see me at all.

It was clear that Olly and Tania's wedding was going to go through. They would have to make the best of it, and if it was a disaster, she could only hope they ended it before they had children.

The smart shiny car that was booked to transport the bride and her mother, herself and Tania's bridesmaid pulled up. The courtyard of La Rosa began to empty.

But as time went by, there was no sign of the bride.

'Shall I go and check she's all right?' said Polly, as the hands of the kitchen clock moved towards eleven. 'She's cutting it a bit fine, isn't she?'

They had not rehearsed the ceremony, though Tania had paced the length of the Via Nazionale to the piazza, and up the steps of the Town Hall a couple of days before. Chess was going to be carrying Tania's long, gauzy veil; she was just the right age to be thrilled by it all. Ruth had watched them walking, one ahead of the other, and though Tania had been ostentatiously disguised beneath dark glasses and a baseball cap, people still knew who she was. The giveaway was carrying a selfie stick.

'I expect it's nerves,' said Ruth.

Tania's agent was also hovering anxiously. She was a pin-thin woman who had flown out the day before, and who was wisely staying in a nearby hotel, but she was the one wearing the mother-of-the-bride hat. Apparently, she was also a professional photographer.

'It's all about getting the right angles,' she said. 'Tania's my best client, everyone loves her story.'

What story? Ruth thought. Pretty, privileged white girl gets married to a rich guy. Was the public really so undemanding? But then, who would be interested in a story about older people? Someone like herself and her two friends was supposed to be invisible, inaudible and negligible, as if they had nothing left to do or say. No wonder old women preferred to be portrayed as witches, or Fates, or Furies, even if in her own case she had failed to do anything helpful or life-changing at all.

Tania remained locked in her cottage, with the shutters closed. Ruth knew that it was rigged up with a special ring light and a camera stand, to capture the bridal preparations.

Maybe she was videoing herself trying on different garters, or something.

'*Dottoressa* Root,' said the driver, 'it is time we leave.'

'Olly?'

He shook his head. 'I'm going now. See you at the Town Hall.'

'Polly?'

'She never listens to me,' said Tania's mother.

'I could always do it,' said Angus, 'but I might not be answerable for the consequences if I find her in her underwear.'

'No, please don't,' said Ruth. 'I guess I could try'. After all, this was her home, and Tania had to come out.

She walked across the courtyard and tapped on the glass of the shuttered French windows.

'Tania, honey? Are you OK in there?'

A muffled noise came from within.

'Hello? May I come in?'

'No! Yes! Oh God!'

Tania's voice sounded very different from usual.

When she opened the door to the studio cottage a crack, Ruth saw an interior of complete chaos. Clothes, shoes, undergarments, make-up, hairbrushes and more were strewn everywhere, as if by an explosion. In the middle of it, lit by bars of light coming through the slatted shutters, crouched Tania.

She was wearing one of the wedding dresses that had been loaned to her, or at least half wearing it. It was white, tight, embroidered, tiered, and to Ruth's untutored eye more suitable for a human sacrifice than a celebration, except that she could not stand up straight.

'The zip has stuck on my hair,' Tania said despairingly.

It was clear that she had been chopping at it with a pair of scissors. Dismayed, Ruth looked at the long coils of copper and gold lying on the floor. More than half her locks had been lopped off. The remainder hung raggedly around her shoulders, still with the movement that made it look almost alive, but no longer the thigh-length weight of before. She was extremely pale, and looked as though she had been crying.

'Oh my dear,' said Ruth. 'Do you need help?'

'Don't *touch* me!' Tania said.

'But I don't see how you can do all this by yourself.'

'That's the point of my vlog,' said Tania. '*Everything* must be done by me. Everything. That's what my followers expect.'

'Well, I don't know anything about fashion, but maybe a cloth with cold water will help your eyes,' said Ruth, moving to the kitchen sink. Even though her heart was sinking, her instinct was to try to make this go smoothly. It's just wedding nerves, she told herself. Even dishevelled, Olly's bride remained the prettiest young woman she had ever seen (outside the movies) but she also wondered whether she was having a nervous breakdown.

Like an automaton, Tania accepted the cold cloth, and Ruth, putting her spectacles more firmly on her nose, grappled with the recalcitrant zip. She felt a strange resignation to this whole affair. Her job was to make things easier for the couple, not to ask questions. The zip resisted, having one of Tania's long, long hairs caught up in its workings, which had caused other hairs to tangle into a great knot. Patiently, Ruth pulled it out, and eventually the mechanism glided smoothly up, sealing Tania inside the dress.

'Oh,' said the bride.

The sparkling crystals on the elaborate white embroidery reminded Ruth of nothing so much as a pillar of salt. Quickly, she pulled away any remaining strands caught on the dress.

361

'Your beautiful hair,' she said sadly. 'Still, it will grow again, I guess.'

Tania turned on the video camera of her mobile and began brushing out what remained with short, fierce strokes. However wild her locks had looked, she was clearly used to managing them, and within a minute they were twisted and pinned up into a chignon, while she went on chatting in her bright, artificial manner about rollers, and jabbing in grips and pins with savage determination to keep it all in place. Lastly, she sprayed it all to make it set in a stiff, shining mass.

'I've put on my Christos Costarellos dress *before* my make-up, not after,' she said. 'Make-up needs to be as delicate as a butterfly's kiss, especially if it looks and feels as natural as Clinique. Though my lipstick is by Mac, for better stay-ing power.'

Tania applied cosmetics with a swift, practised hand, and without a trace of the sensuality or gentleness that most women tended to have when touching their own face. Ruth watched in fascination. It was so long since she had put on the mask of femininity herself that she had almost forgotten its rituals, the dabbing and smudging, and artifice. When Tania finished, no trace of the tearful, unhappy girl remained.

'Something borrowed,' she held up a pair of diamond and pearl-drop earrings, 'from my grandmother Betsy, who sadly can't be with us today, and something blue . . . ' She showed her followers a loop of elasticated pale blue silk that Ruth realised was a garter for the stockings she put on her thin, shapely legs. 'Something old . . . ' She pulled out a lace-edged handkerchief. 'And for something new, my lovely bespoke per-fume, La Primavera, from Gallivant of London, one hundred per cent vegan, and organic.'

She closed her eyes, and squirted it around herself. A

delicate, delicious floral scent filled the room, like that of lilac, jasmine and fresh green grass. Despite her horror, Ruth couldn't help but like it.

'All I need now is my bridal crown,' Tania told the camera brightly. 'Which was made for me today, by R – Ra – by La Rosa's own gardener.'

She lifted a circle of creamy roses and jasmine on to her head, where it promptly slipped to one side, giving her a drunken look.

'I just need to fix this,' she said, and jabbed in another pin. Ruth could see that her whole head was bristling with fine steel spikes. It must feel like being tortured, she thought.

Finally, the long floating veil was attached.

'There, I'm ready.'

'Aren't you going to put some shoes on?' Ruth whispered.

'What? Oh. Yes.' Tania turned to the camera. 'I'm not wearing ordinary shoes. I'm a modern bride, so I've decided on #trainers! By Ellen Von Berg. Aren't they gorgeous? White vegan ones inlaid with pearl studs, and sooo comfortable. I couldn't walk down that cobbled Italian street in stilettos.' She gestured wildly, then said in an aside to Ruth, 'Take my mobile off the stand.'

Ruth hissed, 'I don't know what to do with it.'

'Just hold it up, and point it at me. My agent will take over out of doors.'

Gingerly, Ruth held the selfie stick aloft.

'You go first,' Tania said. 'Backwards.'

Humbly, Ruth did as she was told, though she had to open the door without turning round, one handed. It was like leaving royalty. Perhaps, she thought, I can be like one of the attendant nymphs in paintings, one of those older women trying to throw a cloak over the body of a goddess. Tania was not exactly naked, but her silk dress was almost transparent. Everyone clapped as she appeared in the doorway of the studio cottage.

'Oh!' said Chess. 'You look like a fairy princess!'

Tania's agent relieved Ruth of the mobile.

'The groom is at the Town Hall,' she murmured. 'Let's go.'

29

The Turning Point

Tania had not been so frightened since her first day at school. All these people, staring at her, it was like her #worstnightmare. It *was* her worst nightmare, but it was real.

Her mind did what it usually did, and shut down. She felt as if she was moving very slowly, under ice. The pressure all around made it hard to breathe, or hear, or speak, or smile. Every moment was an ordeal, and what is especially horrible, she thought, is that I have done this to myself. I am selling myself, just as Mum said. I should never have said yes, never have accepted Olly when he proposed, never have gone out with him at all.

I must go through with this, though, because the alternative is years and years of more internet dating, or being alone, and I can't cope with either of those, Tania told herself. I need to live on dry land, like the woman in Raff's song, not on waves mountains high, which would terrify me because I'm a coward and get seasick and will never, ever enjoy sex any more than I can laugh or cry. All that was destroyed. That was what those boys took from me, not just my virginity but the ability to feel anything, including trust.

Better to do this with someone who doesn't love me, because then he can't be hurt. Raff deserves someone better, who isn't damaged and fake and always wearing a mask.

The car had stopped just outside the city walls. Even a wedding party could not be driven all the way up the Via Nazionale to the Piazza della Repubblica, because the whole town was pedestrianised apart from very early in the morning when merchandise was delivered to shops. They would have to get out and walk the length of Santorno's long, narrow, ancient and photogenic main street. But of course they would: this was why so many people chose Santorno for their wedding day. Being normal, they enjoyed parading about in their finery, and being the centre of attention, instead of wanting to shrink into themselves, and hide in a dark place.

Even if those watching her as she arrived at the gate of Santorno were a minute fraction of those who would be watching online, there were still crowds of them. Whether this was because everyone loves a wedding or because the local people knew she was an internet celebrity, or because they had nothing better to do, it was horrible. All those eyes and mouths and hands and bodies. The bars and cafés lining the Via Nazionale were rammed with gawkers, taking videos of their own. She was the day's entertainment, the public spectacle.

But I hate being looked at, Tania thought.

This wasn't like talking to the tiny dark lens of her mobile. All those people, their noise, their unpredictability, were what she could not control. As her mother and agent fussed around her, twitching her veil into more aesthetic shapes of crisp gauze, she stared everywhere but at the crowd, looking down and smoothing her dress.

'Be careful,' she said to Chess.

Olly's little sister looked very sweet. Both outfits were loaned, but Tania knew that the moment her followers saw her own dress, a thousand factories in the Far East would be rushing out cheap versions of it to fill department stores within hours, always assuming they could copy its special features.

'Be careful,' she said again. 'One of the flounces could come loose.'

The small circular parking space outside the town gates had panoramic views of the plains below, and, in its middle, a verdigris bronze War Memorial. Tania gazed up at it, trying not to cry. An angel, wings outstretched, was tenderly catching the body of a dying soldier, naked apart from his helmet. It was a curiously touching sculpture, though most people ignored it, for on a normal day, several bright orange buses would swing cautiously round this as a turning point, stop to disgorge passengers and return to the plains below. Today, the circular space was empty of vehicles, apart from a blue-and-white VW camper van parked under the trees.

Tania stopped dead. She could see Raff sitting in the driver's seat. The expression on his face, shadowed by the evergreen leaves overhead, was invisible, but he was there. She had expected he'd want nothing more to do with her, that he'd be angry or acrimonious or, worst of all, indifferent.

What had happened between them the night before had left her both astonished and confused.

'Ask me anything,' Raff said. They were lying on his small double bed, listening to the rain galloping across the roof of the camper van, and the nightingales were still singing.

'Are you gay?'

'No. Nor am I promised to anyone else. Tell me what you're thinking.'

'I'm dreading this wedding.'

'Does your fiancé know this?'

'Well, he shouldn't be surprised.

'Tell me something else.'

'No, it's your turn. If you could wish for anything, Raff, what would it be?'

'My wish is for someone who loves me, and who wants to be with me, not anyone else.'

'How can you tell?'

'I usually can.'

'But the men I've been with,' said Tania, 'not one has made me want them – not really. Not the ones who made my heart beat faster, because they looked so handsome, or said they'd set me on fire. I'm no good at sex, you know.'

'So why are you getting married?'

'At least if I marry, I don't have to do hook-ups.'

Raff sighed, and in his exhalation, she heard exasperation. He said,

'What would you like to be different about your life?'

'I wish I could be normal,' said Tania.

'Normal in what way?'

'To be peaceful. To know joy. To feel real.'

'Yet you are real, and you are safe, right now,' said Raff.

'Are you sure?' said Tania, and she kissed him in the darkness. He lay still, breathing. 'Yes.'

'Am I safe with you?'

'I am a normal heterosexual man.'

'What is a normal man, though?'

Raff said, 'In my case, one who tries to be decent. Apart from that, I can make no claims.'

'You know I'm getting married tomorrow. I'll be that rich man's wife you sang about, much better for life.'

'If you marry him, that's your choice. If you don't, that's your choice, too. I'm a poor man, Tania, and an ex-soldier. I can't offer an easy life.'

'I'm not marrying Olly for his money. I have my own.'

'Then why are you?'

'Because,' said Tania, 'I'm afraid of big waves.'

The church bells were ringing, not for her wedding but for midday. Clang, clang, clang, their clamour sent the swifts screaming overhead. They were making the exact noise that she longed to make, only her tongue had withered in her throat.

She turned away from the van, and hugged Chess.

'Don't worry,' she whispered. 'You're doing great!'

Everyone took photographs of this.

Just in front of her, her agent was taking pictures too, with the speed and proficiency of a professional. Each one was worth a small fortune to the brands that Tania was endorsing, and to Tania herself. The jewellery she wore, the underwear, the cosmetics, every detail had been negotiated. They all wanted a piece of her, her hair, her skin, her teeth, her youth, her banal romance. Just as all catwalk shows ended with a bridal outfit as their climax, she was coming to the end of her performance.

Tania began to walk up the street to the piazza. It was a long, long walk, and her tiered dress felt as though it were designed to make her able to move only in tiny, mincing steps. Her veil floated behind her in the faint breeze, and she walked steadily so that neither she nor her little bridesmaid would trip on the stones. Many of the onlookers were photographing and videoing her themselves.

The bars and cafés, shops and workshops of the town moved past as if they, not she, were slipping away. It was just a couple of hundred metres, and yet somehow it seemed never-ending. Eventually, she arrived at the square, with its clock tower and its wide stone steps lined with terracotta pots of frilly, bright pink azaleas leading up to the Town Hall. At the top of these stood the wedding party, with Olly in the middle. It was not a church, but the grandeur of the Renaissance building was just as impressive.

Slowly, Tania ascended the steps.

Her head felt lighter, even if the floral wreath Raff had made for her circled it like a crown of thorns. She had felt so wonderful with him, so happy and natural, and now there was not a single part of her body that was not a hot, prickling mess of panic.

She saw Olly standing, pale but determined, at the wide area on top of the stairs. He was miserable too, but he wouldn't hurt her. She could hear music (recorded) coming from inside, not religious, of course, but Ed Sheeran's 'Perfect'. Olly's choice, but she had gone along with it because Sheeran, like Olly, was so obviously a nice guy, and wasn't perfection what she herself had always wanted?

On the last step of all, she felt something tear, and turned. Her young bridesmaid had stumbled, and the bottom tier of the wedding dress came off.

Olly's sister gave a cry of dismay, but Tania said, 'No, don't worry. It's all right, it's part of the design. Look!'

She seized the long folds, and pulled, and as she did this her wedding dress changed. For it was not as it appeared to be. The gathered silk came away from its hidden fastenings, and suddenly, she was wearing a short dress, not a long one.

'You can dance in that!' said the little bridesmaid.

'It looks a great deal better,' said Tania, to the millions of followers watching. 'Don't you think?'

Down below, people were clapping and cheering, as if this were all a performance laid on for them.

'*Brava!*' they called. '*Bravissima!*'

Tania looked at Olly and took the sapphire engagement ring from her finger.

'Give this to Juicy. She's the one you love, and I don't love you.'

Diana said, 'Who do you love?'

'Raff,' said Tania. 'I love Raff.'

Olly looked astounded, then furious.

'The bloody *gardener*? Have you gone mad?'

'Probably,' Tania said, and yanked off her veil before running down the steps.

Without the suffocating swathes, she could move quite easily, springing back along the main street in her white trainers with great energy and determination. People had barely gathered their wits, when she was gone, running for the city wall and the place where the camper van had been.

The bars and the shops and the people dawdling up the Via Nazionale all passed in a flash, and Raff had started the engine, and was just turning round the War Memorial to drive away. She had no breath to call him, but reached out her arms.

He stamped on the brake, jumped out, and stood there.

'What happened?'

Tania said, 'I'll break the waves rolling mountains high.'

371

30

Enzo's Enemy

Ivanov's reaction to the drone was to send four of his men down to inspect it. Enzo had never seen so many guns, all far bigger and more powerful than his own, but it was his that had hit the bomb. He felt an immense relief, not just because he had for once done a good thing (albeit by accident) but because the bomb, had it gone off over the palazzo, would have caused serious damage. They examined it gingerly, took it away, and soon found the would-be assassin, knocked unconscious by the explosion. He, too, was taken away.

The small crater where the bomb blew up remained in the hillside, with a few charred olive trees and rocks to show where it had been. Enzo limped back home to lie down. A few hours later, the oligarch rang.

'Congratulations.'

'What will happen to the assassin?'

Ivanov said, 'He will be kept for questioning, then exchanged for a Ukrainian captive. Eventually.'

Enzo shivered. He did not think the agent's future would be long, or pleasant.

However, Ivanov had more to say.

'I am giving you your house. It is of no value to me, and you have done me a good service.'

Was it a dream? If so, it was the first pleasant one for a long time. To own the house where his family had lived and rented for centuries was beyond anything he could have hoped for ... It would change everything. A sensation filled him that he did not recognise, a sort of lightness and buoyancy, as if he had been ill for a long time and had woken up to find himself cured.

Soon after, Raff dropped in to say goodbye. Enzo was surprised to find how much he regretted the young man's departure.

'*Ciao*, my friend. We'll meet again,' Enzo told him, clapping him on the back and kissing him on both cheeks.

'I hope so, too,' Raff said. He looked sad, more like the young man he'd been on first arriving, Enzo thought. 'Let me know if you come to England. I don't know where I'll be living yet, but you're always welcome.'

'And you here.'

Later, when Enzo heard how Tania had run away from her wedding, he realised why the young man had looked so bad. Raff thought he had lost, but then, at the last moment, he had won the heart of his *inamorata*, and run off with her. Women! In any case, the VW camper van had shot off down the hill and not been seen again, though social media was full of clips of Tania stripping off her bridal dress before she fled Santorno. Apparently, her vlog had reached even more millions of viewers as a result: for however much a public enjoys a fairy-tale wedding, it greatly prefers a runaway bride.

'I bet it was what she planned all along, for publicity,' said Angus. 'Little minx.'

'No, I don't think so,' Ruth said. 'She was genuinely miserable. I don't think she planned anything.'

'But it's so – so *Hollywood*.'

Ruth said. 'Real brides run away too, you know. And real grooms. Big weddings aren't for everyone. If you ask me, they should always be small, and private.'

'All the same, she made me look like a bloody fool in front of millions of her bloody followers.' Olly's anger, mixed with petulance, would have been funny until he added, 'And Giusi, too. She didn't deserve that scene.'

'Isn't she the one you should be thinking about?' his grandmother suggested.

Even more surprising was the news that Raff was Diana Evenlode's grandson, and heir to a title. Ruth was blasé about this, but the others were taken aback, especially Olly.

'She must have known,' he said bitterly. 'I never thought she'd be a social climber.'

'No, of course not. How could she?' Ruth replied. 'None of us knew, including his own grandmother. I'm sorry if it's hurt your pride, dear boy, but I could see them falling for each other every night. He was singing to her, you know, just like the nightingales.'

'Is that all it took? Some soppy love songs?'

'What did it take for you? The heart wants what it wants.'

Enzo, listening to all this as he ferried Ruth's family back to La Rosa, wondered what would become of all the food, but it turned out that none of it was wasted. Some of it, Giusi took back at once to sell, but the rest was going to Ruth's own party, for her own family and friends instead of her grandson's.

'It's going to be my much-delayed birthday party,' she told

374

him, with satisfaction. 'I can even repurpose the cake, I believe. Besides, I don't expect we'll be waiting very long for another wedding, do you, Olly?'

'I haven't asked Giusi yet.'

'Well, hurry up. She's waited almost fifteen years, and I don't think she'll wait much longer.'

'In fact,' Enzo added, 'if you don't ask her, I will.'

'But Enzo, you're over forty!'

'So?' Enzo ran a hand through his hair, which was still thick and lustrous. 'We are good friends. I have known her all my life, and my sister is in business with her brother in London. She's a very pretty girl, smart, and a wonderful cook. What more could anyone want?'

Ruminating on this, Enzo dropped in on Marta. He was shocked by her appearance. In three days, she seemed to have aged a decade or more, shrivelling and withering. Only her eyes still had a fierce, burning determination.

'I have a request to make of you, Enzo,' she said.

'Anything,' he said. 'What may I do to help?'

'I need you to find a way to get some people I know out of Italy.'

'What kind of people?' Enzo asked cautiously.

Xan said, 'People who are escaping bad things in their own countries.'

'Migrants.'

'Refugees.'

'Which country?' Enzo asked; and Xan said, 'Eritrea.'

Enzo was silent.

'It probably means nothing to you,' said Marta.

'It does, in fact,' said Enzo. 'Don't you know, Eritrea was once called Abyssinia? One of my grandfathers was there, in the war. It was the only time he was ever out of Italy. But why do so many of them come here? Why can't they stay in their own country?'

'They are escaping a totalitarian state,' said Blessing. 'Indefinite, forced military service. It is the North Korea of Africa.'

Enzo felt a stirring of sympathy, not least because he had escaped military service too.

'Imagine if that lasted years and years,' Blessing said. 'You could never work or have a business.'

'*Che casino.*'

Xan said, 'Can you think, Enzo, with all your connections, of a lorry driver who might be able to take them out of Italy? Perhaps you have a friend?'

Enzo beamed.

'I do not have a friend with a lorry,' he said. 'I have something better.'

'What's that?'

'I have an enemy with one.'

Since then, he had been busy. He had no idea when and where Stefano was next driving abroad, but Giusi, who was a regular customer, did.

'He's leaving tonight,' she said. 'We're sending our regular supplies to other countries.'

Enzo did not ask where to, but Giusi's brother had a delicatessen in England, so it was probably there. Every month, there would be a delivery of organic olive oil, wine, salami, prosciutto, cheese, pesto, herbs, honey, artisan pasta, panforte, dried porcini and other delicacies that would fall on the people of England like rain on a parched land – or so he liked to imagine, though rain was one of the things that Britain did not lack. Or perhaps it would go off to another European country, crazy for Italian food, which was, after all, the best in the world.

376

At the very least, such a consignment of strong-smelling meats and herbs would conceal migrants smuggling themselves across the borders from detection by dogs. More than this could not be guaranteed.

'Don't ask me why I need to know,' Enzo told her. 'We never had this conversation, OK?'

'Sure,' said Giusi.

After this, however, he took four of the seven passengers to the outskirts of the Guardis' farm, with Xan and Blessing driving the rest in Marta's car. He knew where Stefano lived, but it would be no good putting the Eritreans on to the lorry before it was loaded up: there would be no hiding places for them. Only when it was full could all seven of them be concealed, and for this to be possible, Enzo knew he must find a way of stopping the lorry on the way out, and keeping the driver distracted for a good twenty minutes.

'Stefano will probably want to punch me on the nose,' he told Xan. 'And so will Giusi, if any of her exports are missing. They must not eat her exports! But for you, I will try.'

Each of the migrants had showered in Marta's flat before leaving. This had been Blessing's idea, and it reassured Enzo, just a little, because he had been expecting the stench of sweat and filth. A lifetime of prejudice is not overcome in a day, and although he was much less anxious around Blessing, he was still afraid of these strangers. He had never been in such proximity to so many Africans, and it kept giving him a little shock each time he saw another dark face in his rear-view mirror. But to them, he thought suddenly, *I am the one who is different and frightening, and maybe to them I look like a ghost. It's the same for them, but worse because here, all that is familiar to me is strange to them – this bend in the road, this wall, this cluster of houses, this row of oleander* trees – and just for a moment, he was able to imagine it through their eyes.

'It's only twenty minutes away,' Enzo kept saying aloud as he drove the group to just outside the Guardis' farm in the plain below. He was sweating and trembling the whole journey, but at the same time weirdly elated. All the failures of his life, all the sorrow, bitterness and regret were falling away. Was it becoming a home-owner? Was it doing something bad that might turn out to be good?

At any rate, he was not just a man eking out his life on an abandoned hillside, without honour or purpose. Even his car, crammed with people almost sitting on each other's laps on the back seat, felt as if it was more solid and less flimsy. He pointed out one of Santorno's finest churches.

'San Francesco,' he said. 'You know who he was?'

The man Xan called Eden nodded. 'My country is the oldest Christian country in the world.'

Enzo was abashed. How could he have missed the crosses hung round each neck? Far too large, and made of wood, but all the same . . . He was reluctant to let his suspicion go, because to reject what you are not is always simpler than to accept what you, in fact, are.

When they had all been delivered to the gate of the Guardi farm, the tall thin man who seemed to be the leader made sure they all hid in the bushes by the entrance. He was as shabby as the rest, held together, it seemed to Enzo, as much by will as by the belt round his waist, but he drew himself up, and bowed, his hand on his heart.

The Journey of the Magi fresco in Florence that he had loved as a boy came into Enzo's mind. Two of the kings were white men, riding splendid white horses, but the handsomest of all was Balthazar. Enzo had never forgotten the expression

378

of weary patience on his dark, bearded face, or its nobility; and now it was before him again, minus the magnificent gold crown and the robes. The fresco had been painted in the Renaissance, long before black people, he had assumed, were in Italy. Was it possible he had been mistaken? Enzo realised, uncomfortably, that that he must have been. For the painter must have seen such a man, or men, walking the streets of Florence as if he belonged there. How strange, Enzo thought, that I have never thought this before.

He felt something in his pocket, and held it out.

'I think this belongs to the child.'

The man took the tiny pink sock, and said, '*Sì.*'

Enzo said awkwardly, 'If you eat any of the food in the lorry, don't touch the salami. It's very salty, and will make you sick.'

'We know about salami,' said the man. 'In Asmara, we have it, and pizza and ice cream. You Italians left us with that.'

'We have prepared food and drink for them, in any case,' Blessing said.

They hid behind a clump of laurel, and when the lorry came roaring down the drive, loaded up with merchandise, Enzo's car was waiting in the middle of the road.

He had jacked up the body of it, and was in the process of removing a perfectly good tyre. He expected that Stefano would hoot at him, and be as rude as they usually were to each other. The lorry braked with a nasty grinding sound. Here it comes, thought Enzo, bracing himself. He heard a heavy door open, and footsteps.

'*Salve*, Enzo.'

Enzo looked up. His former schoolmate was standing there, grinning.

'*Salve*,' Enzo said uneasily. 'I'm sorry, I'm having problems with this. It won't take long.'

In the corner of his eye, he saw the migrants flitting on to the back of the lorry, one after another.

'Let me help you.'

Enzo was astonished. 'No – no – I can do it.'

He unscrewed the bolts as slowly as he could, sweating from anxiety rather than effort, making a great show of how tight they were. To keep Stefano's attention on him, he began to chat.

'How is life with you these days? How's your mother?'

'So-so, as always. Poor woman.'

'I remember, is it her liver . . . ?'

Enzo knew that he was opening a rich stream of lamentations as soon as he mentioned this, for inevitably, Stefano's mother did indeed suffer greatly from her liver, like so many in Italy. By the time Enzo, making sympathetic noises, had unscrewed the bolts, rolled the old wheel to one side and extracted the spare tyre from his boot, dropped some bolts on purpose, found them again and fitted the spare, a good fifteen minutes had passed. The migrants were all stowed away, and to confirm this, Xan and Blessing came strolling down the road from the Guardi farm.

'Hi, Enzo,' Xan said in English. 'Are you OK?'

Stefano halted his litany, and eyed them both. In his expression, Enzo could see the automatic dislike and distrust that he had experienced himself. Trust an Umbro to be a racist, he thought.

Enzo said, in Italian, '*Salve*, Xan. Stefano, this is Alessandro, grandson of the distinguished pianist Marta Konig, who lives in Santorno. Also his cousin, Blessing.'

'*Piacere*,' Stefano said reluctantly. 'Excuse me, I not speak English.'

'So, Stefano, where are you driving today?' Enzo asked, in his most genial tone.

'Germany,' Stefano said. 'Next week, Britain.'

'Always a man of the world.'

Stefano shrugged and looked down.

'You describe yourself,' he said. 'You are the man of affairs, Enzo. All I do is drive, turn around, drive back. It's a lonely life on the road. It is good to chat to an old neighbour, instead of just blowing our horns at each other.'

It had never occurred to Enzo that his old adversary was now just another middle-aged man like himself, full of disappointments and regrets.

If he delivers the Eritreans, Enzo thought, that is good; and if he gets caught with his human cargo, then that is also OK. It makes no difference to me. Maybe I will stop by his place, another time though. After all, just because you were once enemies as schoolboys, it doesn't mean you remain so for the rest of your life.

'We all have problems,' he said.

He put out his hand to shake Stefano's, but the other man drew him into an embrace, and kissed him on both cheeks.

'There! Even if I am an Umbro, and you are a Tuscan, we are still neighbours,' Stefano said, clapping him on the back. Enzo found himself smiling, then laughing. 'Come by for a chat, soon, OK?'

'*Arrivederci*, Stefano.'

'Did they all get on safely?' Enzo asked, when they were alone again.

'Yes. They have cat litter,' said Blessing.

'Ah, of course.'

Xan added, wrinkling his nose, 'That was Blessing's idea, because the journey will take at least ten hours.'

Enzo wondered whether it would be better for the migrants in Germany than in Britain, and whether they would be better there than in Italy. He had only the vaguest idea of how other countries treated asylum seekers, but his impression was that Germany was more compassionate. It could afford to be, he thought. So much of what appeared to be morality came down to money ... and yet, Enzo knew, the greatest individual generosity is almost always that shown by the poor, who despite having less to give will share what they have because they know the bite of want.

He felt so tired, driving up the hill to his home (*his* home!) that he could hardly keep his eyes open, but he felt himself smiling. Really, the thing to do would be to cut back all the thorns in the road from his house to the valley and ascend that way instead of driving all the way round, up to Santorno and then down past Ruth and Diana's houses. There were still one or two people living in the village whom he would like to see again. His mother had always said that he and Stefano ought to be friends.

Bumping slowly over the potholes of the road down from Ruth's house, Enzo had to brake. A wild boar, a sow about the size of his dog, was lumbering across his path. She stopped, and at the sight of her solid, hairy grey bulk, long nose and longer tusks he froze. For a moment, they stared at each other, bristling on both sides, then she snorted and veered off, followed by a trotting litter of stripy brown-and-cream piglets.

'Until autumn,' Enzo said, pointing an imaginary gun after them.

He was about to start his car again when his cell phone rang. Again, the unknown number.

'*Si?*'

There was silence, and then a girl's voice said, '*Papà?*'

31

Marta's Flight

The three women who met by Marta's bedside were united by age, the love of grandchildren, and the fact that two of them would no longer be living in Italy.

'I was so happy when you came to live here,' said Ruth to Marta, 'and I'm very sorry to be saying goodbye.'

Marta, paler and frailer than ever, was waiting for the ambulance that was to transport her to Perugia airport. She said, 'If I survive this, I hope you will come and see me in London, both of you.'

'Of course,' said Diana.

'If I can, I will.'

Ruth had not been on an aeroplane for two years, and although the flight was under two hours, the idea of toiling up and down the steps at Stansted made her quail. Few elderly people could face air travel, not with knees cracking like pistols, and vertigo, and all the fuss. Still, she thought, there was always Florence, and British Airways, which arrived right in the heart of London. There was the train to Milan, and then to Paris, and to London. She could drive Dash and herself, or be driven. She was still curious, energetic, and it would be good to visit her family instead of asking them all to come to see her.

'At our time of life, every parting may be for ever,' said Diana; but Marta said, 'Death is just a bend in the road, dear friends. Who knows what lies around that corner?'

'As long as it's not a blue camper van, I don't care,' Ruth retorted.

The wedding was now universally agreed to have been a mismatch. There had been a lot of chat about it on social media, and it had even trended on Twitter for a couple of hours, until the world moved on and found other things to amuse it. Two days later, it was as though it had never been. Angus had flown back to London but Olly, having booked his honeymoon, had disappeared. So, it happened, had Giusi.

'She must have known about the viscountcy,' said Xan. 'I mean, come on, this is Tania. Why else would she have chosen a poor man over a rich one? Just think what it'll mean for her vlog.'

'No, she really didn't know. And had she done so, it would have made no difference,' said Ruth sharply. 'She and Raff are in love. So are Olly and Giusi. I really do think this is for the best.'

'When did you realise?'

'It dawned on me over the past two weeks. I don't think they knew, until the night before the wedding.'

Ruth smiled, for she intended to keep her own role in this secret. People took such appalling risks for love. Their futures, their money, their fertility, their happiness, their sanity, all their eggs in one basket. Yet if it worked, if you chose wisely and well, then it must be worth it all, including the anguish of being bereaved. Who will be left for me? she wondered. All the people I had buzzing around just a few days ago, with their wants and needs, and suddenly I'll be alone on the hillside. If only Beatrix hadn't left. She must be dead. There had been no word from Amsterdam in response to her plea, but then, why would there be?

'Do you think they'll get married?' Marta asked. 'Raff and Tania, I mean.'

'I do hope so,' Ruth said. 'Though marriage has many drawbacks, it's like democracy: appalling until you consider all the alternatives that have been tried and failed.'

'Of course they will,' said Diana. 'At Lode, I expect. But it will be just family, and no vlogging or influencing of any kind.'

'My dear, you may find that Tania has a will of her own. Though from what I saw on her wedding day, I suspect she is going to do something different in future.'

They all held hands, very gently.

'Oh, I forgot to tell you,' Diana said. 'Raff texted his father that they are heading back to England, but slowly. He sent the loveliest picture of them both somewhere in France, laughing.'

'I never saw her laugh, did you?'

'No,' Xan said.

Ruth said, 'I shouldn't be surprised if there isn't a touch of autism there.'

'I think it was more being very unhappy,' Diana retorted. 'That's the trouble with being a beauty. To be loved, or hated, just because of the way you look rather than what you *are* is equally awful.'

'Well, I think it's charming,' whispered Marta. 'You realise, he is my own great-nephew too? He looks very like Edward. Such a handsome boy.'

'At their age, everyone is handsome. Even though they don't know it,' said Ruth. She felt the loneliness creeping up on her, like fog. She had Dash, of course, and her farm, but even her dear friend Enzo might be going away for a while. His daughter had got in touch, just as predicted, and he was planning to go off to see her in the States.

'My dear, I do hope that Xan is travelling back with you on the plane,' said Diana.

'No,' Xan said, 'I will be bringing Otto back, by car. Blessing is going with her.'

'But how? I thought he had no passport valid for Britain.'

'He does,' said Xan. 'He's using mine.'

Xan's plan, quickly outlined, was simple.

'You've always said how similar we look,' he said to Diana. 'I have two passports: an English one and a German one, thanks to my grandmother and Brexit.'

She snorted. 'But that's illegal.'

'The day he decides to become a lawyer, he commits a serious crime,' Marta whispered. 'This will be interesting.'

'But what about the photograph? You have some similarities, but he's darker than you, Xan.'

Xan said, 'My English one has a photograph of me from when I was sixteen. I look almost nothing like I did then, and if people can't tell the difference between us now, then I doubt a machine will.'

'I can tell the difference,' Diana said. 'Even though I have only one eye.'

'Maybe, but facial recognition is designed by white people,' Xan said. 'All they see is a Black person. It's worth a try. If Blessing gets caught, he'll say he stole it from me. It's only got six months left, in any case.'

'You're still breaking the law.'

'I know, but it's a crap law,' said Xan. 'Blessing has just as much right to claim asylum as anyone, plus he had an English grandfather. The only thing Perry didn't do was legitimise the child of Blessing's grandmother.'

'What about Ivanov?' Ruth asked. 'Surely, he'll see that Blessing isn't you?'

'He's already mixed us up once,' Blessing said. 'I don't think he can tell the difference, especially if I wear a mask. Our hair and eyes are close enough. Marta has agreed to help me. She's going straight to hospital in London, and Lottie will be there.'

'Rather a shock for her, I should think,' said Diana disapprovingly. It was beginning to dawn on her that the offer she had made Perry's grandson might, after all, have to be honoured. But I'll be home again, she thought, with my son; and besides that, nothing else mattered.

'What about you?' Ruth asked, though she already knew the answer. Diana's time at La Docciola had been one of almost pure endurance, and once she was packed up she would not be returning.

'I'll miss our talks about Trollope,' said Diana.

'I will miss you both so much,' said Ruth. 'I do hope my Ukrainians are nice. I'm sure they will be, poor things, though they won't be old friends.'

Her mobile, which had been buzzing in her pocket repeatedly, now began to make the irritating bonging noise of a new WhatsApp message that probably meant one of her family was trying to get in touch. She pulled it out of her pocket, and squinted at it. 'Still, I'm glad you are going with Marta on the flight.'

'All I need is for you to call Blessing by my name, and for Blessing to call Marta Oma. I'll report my UK passport lost tomorrow,' said Xan. 'He has my address in London, and I've told my flatmates to expect him. It will all work out, you'll see.'

Marta whispered, 'I'm glad you and Otto are friends, too. He's a good companion.'

Ruth looked down at her mobile, and began to smile.

'Excuse me a moment.' She stood up, and went out into Marta's tiny garden. 'Beatrix? Are you a ghost? Is it really you? Oh my goodness! You didn't? No, stay right there, don't move. I'll be home soon.'

The doorbell rang, and Xan kissed his grandmother. He had tears in his eyes, they all did. A part of him was saying that he should go with her, but the other part, the newer, fiercer one, said that he must help his friend, and that if he passed up this chance it would never come again.

'Don't worry, Oma. Otto and I will see you in two days. I'm going to hide now, and Blessing will put on his mask.'

Marta closed her eyes, and said, 'My darling.'

The ambulance men arrived, and among them they saw one who looked familiar. Wearing the same clothes as the other paramedics, Ivanov blended in perfectly.

'Hello, Xan,' he said to Blessing, his dark eyes crinkling. 'Have no fear. I will be with Marta as well, the whole way.'

Marta wondered whether he, too, had a different passport that would not show up on the manifest. Was it just getting to Britain, or would he enter under a false name? Would Blessing claim asylum, or would he pretend to be her grandson? Her daughter would know at once, but it was really not her problem. Nothing was her problem now.

The paramedics slid her off her bed and on to a stretcher, then carried her up the stone steps and out of her front door into the street for the last time. She had only lived there for a handful of years, yet she loved it, with its buzzing Vespas, its clanging bells, its smells of coffee and cooking, its small splashing fountain and big luminous sunsets. Marta looked up at the lime leaves that were giving way to stone walls with their tufts of pink valerian, their scarlet poppies. Someone was holding her hand in his, and she was comforted by this, the touch of another human being, as they drove, siren blaring, to the airport.

How strange that things are still happening to me at my age, even now, she thought, as she was carried up on to the aeroplane. It trundled into position on the runway, and came to a complete standstill. Its engines rose to D sharp minor, and then, as they changed to a roar, to D major, and she began to move, faster and faster and up and up and up, into the blue air, arrowing north, indomitable.

Afterword

The Three Graces has had a particularly long gestation – perhaps as long as 1990, when my first novel, *Foreign Bodies*, was published. I always wished to revisit Santorno and find out what happened next to some of its protagonists.

I grew up in Italy, and my childhood in Tuscany was very much not the kind featured in glossy magazines. It was one without swimming pools, air conditioning or even (in the beginning) electricity and running water. I've seen how much (and how little) it has changed, especially as Italy found itself on the front line of a growing migration crisis from North Africa and elsewhere. In showing some of the suffering and prejudices that have arisen from this, I mean no disrespect. I detest and despise racism, but I do not think it is best combated by hatred and/or the fear of depicting people who are not white. I have met many Enzos, and they are not all evil, even if their views are deplorable. Italy is a young country, far younger than America, and its problems of unity and its fears of foreigners are founded on centuries of war. Despite this, and endemic corruption, it is the third largest economy in Europe, and a democracy. I have faith in its people, especially now that its young are receiving better education (including, unlike Britain's own, free university tuition).

Like many art lovers, I have always been obsessed by Botticelli's *Primavera*. That mysterious and wonderful painting suggested a good deal of the marriage plot of this story. How does the terrified, half-naked nymph, fleeing her blue-faced pursuer, transform into the smiling, crop-haired Flora? Why is the flower-filled grass black? Who are the Three Graces? And why do women in myth, young or old, always seem to be in triplicate? Almost every main character in my novel corresponds to one in the painting.

It only occurred to me to make Tania mildly autistic quite late in the novel, when I was wondering why Botticelli's women look so inexpressive. Female autism, so often undiagnosed due to girls' and women's ability to 'mask' it, is a fascinating and often excruciating condition that a number of real-life models and influencers suffer from. For readers, I recommend *Letters to My Weird Sisters* by Joanne Limburg, Holly Smale's Geek Girl series, and Elle McNicoll's *A Kind of Spark*.

I began writing this book in 2020, when many writers thought they should be writing about disease and dystopia. Let other pens dwell on guilt and misery, as Jane Austen said. I was confident that a vaccine would save us soon – and that when the pandemic passed, it would give rise to a wave of weddings and the longing to travel abroad again. I also thought it would be fun to set the novel very specifically in 2022, a hundred years after Elizabeth von Arnim's *The Enchanted April*, which, alongside E. M. Forster's *A Room with a View*, is one of my favourite fictions set in Tuscany. (A third, less well known than it should be, is James Hamilton-Paterson's comic novel, *Cooking with Fernet Branca*.)

As my faithful readers know, I carry characters on from one novel to the next, with major characters becoming minor ones, and vice versa. Each of my Three Graces has appeared previously. Ruth Viner first appeared in my second novel, *A Private Place*, as the mother of the three Viner brothers. Marta Koning is Lottie Bredin's mother in *The Lie of the Land*, where the teenaged Xan also first appears. Diana Evenlode is in *The Golden Rule*, as grandmother to the odious Jake, and her son Andrew is the hero of *Foreign Bodies*, the narrator of which is the teenaged Emma Kenward. Blessing's father is in *Hearts and Minds*.

My cast of characters age more or less in real time, and I wanted to write about characters who were a generation above my own. Almost all literary fiction focuses on the young, the fertile and the strong, and yet half our lives is now lived when we are none of those things. Why should that time be less interesting? I know that a lot of over-fifties have adventures, love affairs and new experiences and that they remain intensely interested in books, art, clothes, travel, politics and the news. It is my belief that there is beauty in age, and strength and courage. As my father liked to quote, 'Old age is not for sissies', and the experiences of the elderly should be listened to even if, like Diana, they may hold views that have become outdated and repugnant.

The country of old age merged with that of expatriate life and mass migration. I am the child of migrants myself, and I grew up haunted by my father's reports for the UN of famine, over-population and environmental catastrophe in Africa and Asia. The contrast between these and what I witnessed of *la dolce vita* in 1960s and 1970s Italy are what made me a novelist.

The Russian war with Ukraine dawned after I finished the first draft, but my oligarch, Vasily Ivanov, was there from the start. He is not based on any particular real-life Russian, though those who have watched the BBC documentaries about the imprisonment of Navalny and Khodakovsky, may recognise one or two lines about what opposing Putin feels like.

Many of the houses in my books have been inspired by real places, so I would like to thank Diana Allan for the generous loan of her cottage below Cortona, Carol Gavin for the loan of her house, Franca Capacci and Guido Salvietti, Rupert and Donatella Palmer and many others who extended kindness to us over many years. I hope Sophia Bergqvist does not mind that I took the name of her family winery in Portugal, and transplanted it to Tuscany for Ruth Viner's home.

This is a story above all of friendship as a lasting and important form of love. To all my friends, men as well as women, I give thanks. All novelists are snappers-up of unconsidered trifles, but those (living and dead) who have given me specific help, advice, anecdotes and information about many issues in this book include: Rennie Airth, Michael Arditti, Su and Euan Bowater, Alice Boyd, Celia Brayfield, Marika Cobbold, Benedict Cohen, Jill Cohen, Juliet Cohen, Constance Craig-Smith, Zelda Craig, Giulia Favero, Tanya Gold, Linda Grant, Sebastian Grigg, Rachel Kelly, Josa Keyes, Kathy Lette, Penelope Lively, Antonia Lloyd-Jones, Michelle Lovric, Alison Lurie, Ysenda Maxtone-Graham, Lucasta Miller, Charlotte Mitchell, Harriet Mullan, Rachel Polonsky, Imogen Robertson, Kate Saunders, Francesca Simon, Kate Stuart-Smith, Jane Thynne, Roddy Williams and Louisa Young.

I would like to thank Dino Diaccati for many witty and informative conversations about Tuscan food and wine, and especially for a memorable day at Torrenera, drinking Brunello di Montalcino wine. His website is dino@tuscancontacts.com, and I recommend him to any visitors to the Cortona area.

Many years ago, my mother left South Africa for a year in post-war Italy, where she at last saw the Renaissance art that she had only been able to study at Wits University via a collection of cigarette cards. In Florence, she met a handsome young Italian, Enzo Turchetti, who taught her to speak fluent Italian, sparking off a life-long passion for Italy that she passed on to her family, leading to us moving there to live in 1965. He became a friend of us all, and his charm and *sprezzatura* remained a delight for many years, and if he is still living, I hope he will forgive my using his first name for a character I couldn't help but enjoy.

A number of the stories in here are true – there really is a hugely successful Tuscan family farm business which came about through composting human sewage, for instance. There was a real Dutchwoman who chose to be euthanised, and then changed her mind after her deathday party because she realised that she had been suffering from loneliness. Most important of all, and thanks to my heroic sister Constance, our mother was herself airlifted out of Cortona three years ago, in agony, and was cured in a London hospital: she is now ninety-five, and still beats us all at Scrabble.

Professionally, I would like to thank my agent Cathryn Summerhayes, Jess Molloy, Annabel White and Grace Robinson at Curtis Brown, my editor Richard Beswick, my project editor Nithya Rae, copy editor Alison Tulett and proofreader Antonia Hodgson, my jacket designer Nico Taylor, my publicist Susan de Soissons and all at Little, Brown. I appreciate all the care, tact and expertise given to my manuscripts more than I can say.

My beloved husband Rob Cohen, and our children Leonora and William have been an inspiration as well as a support.

Lastly, this novel is dedicated to three fellow novelists:

Kate Saunders, Kathy Lette and Jane Thynne. We met when our children were babies, and they remain the funniest and loveliest women I know.

Credits

Epigraph
Alison Lurie, *Foreign Affairs* (New York: Random House, 1984)

A More Interesting Existence
'I Wish I Knew How it Would Feel to Be Free', written by Dick Dallas, William Eugene Taylor, lyrics © Universal Music Publishing Group

Qui Siamo in Italia
'Stand By Me', written by Ben King, Jerry Leiber, Mike Stoller, lyrics © Sony/ATV Music Publishing LLC, RALEIGH MUSIC PUBLISHING, Downtown Music Publishing